# DOUBTING RIVER

Melissa C. Alexander

# DOUBTING RIVER



ISBN: 979-8-9912048-0-4

This book and its artwork are 100% AI-free!

*This book is dedicated to the real River
and all the beasties that fill my life with joy.
Including my husband.*

*Really, darling. You're my everything.*

# Table of Contents

*For want of a nail the shoe was lost.*

*For want of a shoe the horse was lost.*

*For want of a horse the rider was lost.*

*For want of a rider the message was lost.*

*For want of a message the battle was lost.*

*For want of a battle the kingdom was lost.*

*And all for the want of a horseshoe nail.*

*—Fourteenth-century proverb*

# PROLOGUE

ccepting money for doing something any good neighbor would do didn't sit right. Jake Gibson had half a mind to drop the fifty dollars Janelle had foisted on him in the collection plate on Sunday. The other half of his mind ran through the alarmingly long list of bills that could benefit from the unexpected cash.

His old truck squeaked and groaned through the turn off Mississippi Highway 61 and bounced hard through one of the winter potholes too big to go around. Jake soothed the truck like a fractious horse. If someone didn't repair this road soon, one of the snooty city people in the new subdivisions would break an axle and raise holy hell.

He swallowed the uncharitable thought. Those city people paid the taxes that would get this road fixed (someday), and they paid six dollars a dozen for eggs from his wife's "free range" chickens. Seemed like price gouging, but Elle swore they paid more at the Kroger in Vicksburg.

"The market drives the prices," she said and stuck by her pricing. Jake smiled at the memory. As the neighborhoods, monochrome and unappealing in any season, gave way to bare trees and fallow fields, the patchwork of muted grays and browns reminded him that it would be several months before the hens started laying again. Maybe he would sneak the fifty dollars into Elle's grocery money.

A honk drew his attention to a newer model F-350 approaching in the oncoming lane. Jake waved as it passed. Oscar must be headed to the training field already.

Jake glanced at the time on his phone and stepped harder on the gas. No need to burn through Oscar's goodwill by being late, even if his friend had made it clear he considered their project — training a curly-coated retriever for a field trial — a fool's mission. *Everyone* considered it a fool's mission.

Jake's jaw tightened stubbornly. This fool's mission was his chance to get back in the black and stay there. Just because the professional trainers in the area failed with River didn't mean he would — and it didn't mean the dog was a washout. Simply meant River needed a different program than their line-bred Labradors. The pros failed because they couldn't work outside their box.

A quiet thought niggled in the back of Jake's mind that it might not be that simple, but he silenced it. If he wanted to get caught up on the mortgage, he needed this. Bless Mr. Forbes for taking a chance and trusting him with his imported retriever. Another quiet thought questioned why Forbes would do such a thing, but Jake silenced that too.

His truck's tires crunched on the gravel driveway as he arrived home, a familiar sound that never failed to settle the stresses of the day. Except maybe today. Despite the chilly weather, Elle and their nine-year-old son, Lucas, were locked in intense conversation near the barn — their faces as stormy as the December sky.

They swiveled toward the sound of his truck, and Lucas ran to meet him, a long-legged retriever close behind. "It's not fair!" Lucas said as Jake emerged from the cab.

"What's not?" Jake knelt and rubbed the dog's ears, the only part not covered in sawdust and — Jake sniffed — horse manure. "What happened to River?" Lucas himself looked like he'd gone exploring in a swamp and fallen prey to a morass of quicksand, but that was pretty much a daily routine for the nine-year-old.

His wife joined them. "Your son took that dog and disappeared this afternoon."

Jake gawked at her. Routine this was not. Water dripped from her nose and her chin. Her auburn curls hung limp in her eyes, and her jacket sported a set of four perfect paw prints walking their way from her left hipbone to her right shoulder. "What happened to *you?*"

"Three days!" Lucas said. "She grounded me for three days."

*Oh, oh.* Jake knew exactly where Lucas had been and why he hadn't told his mother. Jake looked back and forth between them for a long moment. "Lucas," he said finally, "put on some dry clothes. Oscar's waiting for us."

The boy glanced at his mother. Her jaw had tightened, but she didn't speak. He started to turn away, then paused. "River…"

"I'll take care of him," Jake said.

"Yes, sir." Lucas fled to the house.

The boy made it as far as the front porch before Elle's temper exploded. "Why are you making me the bad guy?"

Jake took off his jacket and wrapped it around her shoulders. "I'm not," he said as soothingly as he could. "It just worked out that way."

Indignation blazed. "This isn't funny!"

He chuckled and wrapped an arm around her waist before she could pull away. "I'm kidding, I'm kidding." He used his sleeve to blot the water from her face and hair. He stopped suddenly and frowned. "Why are you wet?"

She glowered. "Kink in the hose." She wrapped her fingers in the warm fabric of his shirt. "You might want to talk to our son about putting it away properly when you talk to him about disappearing this afternoon."

Jake tucked a damp curl behind her ear. She'd progressed from *your son* to *our son*, so it was probably safe to admit his part now. "I knew where he was," he said softly. That was entirely true. "I gave him permission to play in the woods." Also true. Just not the whole truth.

Her eyes widened. "What! Why didn't he tell me that?"

Jake tried to find an excuse but finally just shrugged. "He's nine?”

Elle glared. “And did you give him permission to take that dog with him?”

He glanced at River, who had decided sawdust and cow manure were itchy and was aggressively scratching his back on the prickly winter lawn. *A little decorum would go a long way right now, dude.* “No, I did not,” he said, serious for the first time, “and we’re going to have a talk about that.”

A loud *creak* caught their attention, and they glanced toward the house in time to see Lucas complete his monkey-like swing over the railing on the front steps on his way to the barn. Elle opened her mouth to scold him, but Jake gave a gentle squeeze and shook his head. She sighed and looked aggrieved.

Jake chuckled softly and kissed her forehead. “Go get warm and dry. I’ll clean up River and then be the bad guy.”

She rolled her eyes. “You? The fun parent?” She huffed and tried to glare at him but failed.

He kissed her once more. “Twenty lashes and bread and water.” He looked around for River, who was now relaxing on his back sucking on one of his front paws. “Come on, buddy.” The retriever leapt to his feet and fell in beside him, tail wagging.

Elle gave the dog a quick scratch between his eyes, then poked Jake in the chest. “I’ll be satisfied with extra chores and a sincere apology.”

“From him or me?” he called back as he headed toward the water spigot on the side of house.

“Both!” But amusement lightened her voice.

Jake watched Elle go inside as he gathered the hose to give River a quick rinse, relieved her earlier irritation had vanished. But the tension in his own stomach hadn’t lessened. Lying by omission hurt his heart — and Lucas’s heart too.

Well, nothing to be done about it now, especially when they were due at the training field in a few minutes. He turned his attention to River. Even in the December chill, the retriever enjoyed being sprayed by the hose, play bowing and snapping at the water, then settling when Jake tired of his antics. The dog had already gotten most of the muck off, so it took little time to finish the job. When his shower was done, River shook himself thoroughly, rolled in the grass again, and then trotted off to find Lucas.

Jake followed, assessing the dog's easy strides to be sure he was fit for a training session. River bore only superficial resemblance to the Labradors that dominated field events. Like the Labs, he was a retriever, but his muzzle was a little longer, and the smooth fur of his face morphed into slight waves on his forehead and then into crisp curls, small and delicate on his ears, larger on his neck and body. His curls gave him what would have been an almost lamb-like look had the fur been longer or his body less powerful. His movement was relaxed and balanced; his off-leash adventure with Lucas hadn't stressed him in the slightest.

The relationship between River and the boy amused Jake, though he couldn't help but worry a bit about what would happen when the dog went back to Mr. Forbes. This was a project; River wasn't a gift, and they absolutely couldn't afford to buy the dog — especially once he started winning. He glanced at his phone and pushed his concerns to the side. If they didn't get a move on, they'd be late.

Jake found the two in the barn near River's chain-link kennel run, playing tug with a knobby white retrieving bumper. A plethora of other training equipment lay in a pile on a nearby hay bale.

"You were late," he said in greeting.

Lucas glanced past him to be certain his mother wasn't with him. "Mom wasn't supposed to be home until three."

"And you were supposed to be home at two. What happened?"

"I left River's leash at Grandma's. He was really good, though, until Mr. Halsey shot a duck. Then he took off."

"You shouldn't have crossed Mr. Halsey's field," Jake scolded, imagining the crotchety old man taking a pot shot at the trespassing duo rather than a duck.

"I didn't! We were in the woods. River saw him anyway."

Jake frowned. "He wasn't shooting toward the woods, was he?"

Lucas shook his head. "No. He was at the top of the hill, shooting the other way. River got the duck, though," he added casually.

Jake stared at him. The "hill" was a hill only because the rest of the region was flat Mississippi bottomland. The little rise bisected a long, narrow field with woods at one end and a pond at the other. "River marked a duck from the woods and found it in the pond?" His forehead creased as he thought. "That had to be two hundred yards."

Lucas tilted his head. "How far is that?"

"Two football fields."

Lucas screwed up his face as he tried to reconcile the comparison.

"Incredible," Jake muttered. Then frowned again. "But that doesn't change what happened. How many times do I have to tell you? The kingdom was lost —"

"I know, I know. All for the want of a horseshoe nail." He looked disgusted.

Jake suppressed a grin and managed to sound stern. "Yes, all for the want of a horseshoe nail. You forgot the leash, and now we're late. And if we don't get a move on, Oscar will leave, and we won't get any training done tonight."

Lucas sighed, clearly unimpressed by the logic. "Am I grounded?"

"Your mother's punishment has been lifted, but I'm grounding you for one day for taking River without permission." Lucas's expression grew stormy, but he didn't complain beyond dragging his toe in the dirt. "And you owe your mother an apology" — Jake lifted a finger to stave off an argument — "a real one. Why didn't you tell her that I had given you permission to go play in the woods this afternoon?" It was, after all, the truth. Just not the whole truth.

Lucas shrugged and stuck out his bottom lip. "I don't know."

Jake sighed. When did nine become preteen? He waved at the collection of training equipment. "Come on, let's get ready."

The boy brightened. "Can we train with real birds today?" River tugged at the bumper in his hand, and he tossed it for the dog to fetch. "I bet you can get some pigeons from Oscar."

Jake opened the cabinet next to the dog kennel where all of the training bits and bobs were stored. "We've talked about this. We're not ready for live flyers yet." He dug through the collection until he found a pair of foam dummies weighted and painted to feel and look like dead ducks.

"But River has retrieved lots of real birds. Oscar said so. When he was in New Zealand, he retrieved real birds all the time. I told you what he did today. He didn't have any trouble at all."

"I didn't say River couldn't do it. I said *we're* not ready. We need to test him, bit by bit, to find out what he knows and what he doesn't. There's a huge difference between hunting in New Zealand and American field trials. We've got to figure it out systematically, starting with the basics. And that means we go slow."

The boy kicked at a hay bale. "All right. But I think he's bored."

Jake bent close as if he were sharing a secret. "You know what? I think he is too. Since he did so well with the pond, what do you say we try some water retrieves today?"

Lucas wrinkled his nose. "Isn't it kind of cold?"

"Not to River." Jake suddenly swept the boy up and hung him, upside down and backwards, over his shoulder. For a split second, the boy was silent, then his body began shaking with irrepressible giggles. "We're late. Hurry up, and get the stuff," Jake said, turning so Lucas could reach the training supplies.

It wasn't easy to manage all the bits and pieces while hanging upside down. Of course, the snickers Lucas couldn't control and the dog that kept jumping up and licking his face didn't help, but they managed to hold on to everything all the way to the truck.

Elle approached, shaking her head. "Jake," she admonished. "It's a wonder he doesn't have brain damage. Look how red his face is."

Jake swung him around and set him on his feet. "Just trying to get the blood flowing up there. Want him firing on all cylinders."

"Mm-hmm." She didn't sound quite convinced, but at least she seemed amused and no longer angry.

The bed of Jake's pickup sported a silver "dog box" designed to hold multiple hunting dogs and their equipment. He'd bought it used off Craigslist from some guy near Vicksburg. It wasn't fancy like the pros had, but it worked fine, and Lucas told him he looked like a real dog trainer with River riding in the box.

Lucas shoved the equipment into a compartment on the driver's side, then ran around and opened a second compartment on the passenger side. Jake lifted River in, then carefully fastened the latch. Lucas crawled into the truck's cab.

"Don't forget," Elle said as she and Jake walked around to the driver's side, "your training partner has cows to feed, you have a porch rail to fix" — she shot Lucas a glance that told him she hadn't missed his earlier gymnastics — "and we promised to attend the live Nativity at the church tonight."

Jake slid in behind the steering wheel. "How could I forget? Chasing Ethel McKelvey's ass up and down Main Street is a December twenty-third tradition." He rolled down the window and turned the ignition key. The truck *put-put-putted* to life.

Elle leaned in. "I hope you're talking about her donkey." Lucas giggled, and she winked. "You're going to have to watch Lucas tonight too. I promised to sell ornaments in the church booth."

"Grandma will be there." Lucas clicked his seat belt into place. "I can stay with her."

"No, you can't." Her tone was flat. She met his eyes until he nodded.

Jake suppressed a sigh when the joy evaporated from Lucas's face. Before Jake could say anything, Elle tapped his arm.

"Speaking of the McKelveys," she said, "I heard Tom might be looking to hire somebody to help build some new fence in his back pasture before the early calves come."

"All Tom McKelvey has to do is ask, and the whole county will turn out for free."

"Free won't pay for a new alternator or my textbooks. New quarter starts right after New Year's. I had to charge —"

"Don't worry about that." He silenced her with a quick kiss. "We'll get the money. Have I ever let you down?" He grinned. "Home for dinner!"

She smiled and stepped back so he could turn the truck around. "Be careful."

They started down the drive. "Nahhhhh."

Her laughter followed them onto the road. Jake watched in the rearview until he couldn't see her anymore, then glanced at his son. Lucas gazed out the window, his expression more pensive than sullen. Jake nudged him with his elbow. "Whatcha thinkin' over there?"

Lucas shrugged without looking at him. Jake waited. After a minute, Lucas said, "I wish Mom didn't hate Grandma so much."

Jake considered that. "She doesn't hate her," he said finally. "They're just too alike and too stubborn, and your mom can't let go of some stuff that happened a long time ago."

"A long time ago, like when you got married?"

"Like even before that."

Jake watched Lucas try to reconcile such ancient history. Apparently, it was too much because he switched topics. "So if River wins this contest, will Mom stop worrying about money?"

"Field trial. If — when — River wins a field trial, I will be the man for training around here, and our troubles will be G-O-N-E. Trust me, Lucas, that dog is our golden ticket."

"I don't know why Mom's going to school anyway. I know I wouldn't go to school if I was a grown-up." Lucas watched the scenery pass for a long moment and then blurted the words he'd apparently been holding in. "I think we should tell Mom the truth."

Jake pulled up to the stop sign at the turn onto Highway 61 and stopped. "We've discussed this. I thought you understood."

"I do understand." Lucas kicked the dashboard. "It isn't fair!"

"Maybe not, but don't take it out on my truck." Jake made the left onto the highway. "I don't like this either, Lucas, but I don't see any other way to do it."

The boy crossed his arms and huffed. "It's just...she just...she just ought to be reasonable."

Jake laughed a deep belly laugh. "I agree. I don't recommend you tell her that, though."

Glancing at his son, Jake saw his eyes widen suddenly. "Look out!"

Jake glimpsed a blur of tan and swerved to avoid the buck that leapt in front of them. The truck careened and skidded. The last thing he glimpsed was the deer's eyes, rolling in terror, an instant before the collision flipped the animal onto the hood.

Glass shattered.

A lurch, a sudden halt.

Then silence.

A minute passed before Jake was able to force his eyes to open and focus his muddled mind to process what he was seeing. When it did, he yelped and flinched away from the buck, its face just inches from his own. The deer was beyond reacting. It had come partially through the windshield, its body wrenched and twisted by the impact. The neck was at an odd angle, the antlers wedged between him and Lucas.

Jake exhaled, his aching head finally beginning to make sense of what happened. *That was close!* He could barely even see the boy past the body of the deer. "It's okay, Lucas," he said. "We're fine. Just give me a minute."

He pushed at the buck's head, then shoved hard, but it didn't budge. He tried again. No luck. Maybe he could slide out. He fumbled with the seat belt, but somehow the tip of one antler had jammed in the clasp.

"Lucas, give me a hand here." The boy didn't answer, and Jake suddenly realized his son hadn't made a sound. Jake looked over. "Lucas?"

Lucas was hunched forward, held by his seat belt, eyes closed, as if he were trapped in that moment before impact, praying they wouldn't collide.

"Lucas?" Jake's voice shook. All of him shook. *Lucas.* He tentatively reached out, trying twice before he mustered the courage to tug his son's sleeve, jerking away when Lucas slumped toward him, head lolling back to reveal a small cut and swelling on his right temple. Jake grabbed the boy's shoulder and shook him. "Lucas, wake up. Wake up!"

To his relief, Lucas made a sound low in his throat and blinked his eyes. He lifted his head, wincing as he did. Blinked again and sat up straighter. "Dad?" His voice sounded groggy, but his gaze seemed focused when he looked over.

"We're okay, but I'm stuck," Jake said, trying to sound calm. The coppery scent of the deer's blood coupled with the animal's musky scent turned his stomach. He tugged at his seat belt again.

Lucas tried to wiggle between the antlers to help him, only to find himself restricted by his own seat belt. He jiggled the clasp, pulled on it, then pressed as hard as he could, the effort showing in the tendons on his neck.

A claustrophobic feeling crawled down Jake's back. *What if they were both stuck?* Suddenly, the belt popped loose and retracted with a *whir.* Jake and Lucas stared at each other, and then laughed in relief.

A horn blared and tires squealed. Jake looked past the deer with a gasp and took in their situation all at once. They were on the highway facing oncoming traffic — or what would be oncoming traffic if he could have seen it. The road angled left, limiting his view — and the view of anyone coming toward them. He grabbed his seat belt and jerked at it. "We've got to get out of here."

Lucas pressed the seat belt's release button. "Stop pulling on it!" He finagled it, alternating yanking on the belt and smashing the button.

In the distance, a rumble began and grew louder. Jake looked around them. Beyond them, the car that had almost hit them had stopped, and a man was getting out. He couldn't see beyond the curve, but the rumble vibrated his seat now. "You've got to get out of here."

"No, I've almost got it —"

"Lucas, go!"

The rumble became the blare of a horn, then the squeal of brakes. The seat belt slithered free, and Jake threw his shoulder against the door. But it was already too late. He looked back and, for the briefest moment, caught his son's eye. Before the blackness, his last thought was of a dog's leash and his favorite proverb. *All for the want of a horseshoe nail...*

# Chapter 1

Rivulets of rain ran sideways across the bus window, blurring the scenery beyond. Charm Freeman slumped in his seat and gazed out without focusing on anything in particular. What was there to see? Bare branches, brown grass, gray sky, and the sporadic farmhouse washed out from years of hot, humid summers and wet, humid winters. Even the occasional remaining Christmas decorations had given in to the malaise: inflatable snowmen and plastic Santas sagged under the steady downpour, more besieged than jolly.

A green highway sign pocked with rusted bullet holes declared his destination just seven miles away. His stomach roiled, and he dug two loose Tums out of his jacket, chewed them up, and washed them down with a swallow from the flask he kept in his back pocket. Probably that burrito he'd had for breakfast. Or maybe the sushi before leaving St. Louis.

Sushi. Where the hell was he going to find decent sushi in hillbilly central? *Don't worry about it,* he told himself. *You don't have to stay long.* He rolled his shoulders. *Probably shouldn't have come at all.* Guilt and regret intertwined in his gut.

"No," he said out loud. "I owe them this much."

A teen with short, spiky hair and half a dozen piercings in her ear sat across the aisle. She glanced up from her Kindle, her eyebrows raised.

In a flash, his face transformed from scowl to smile. The implied disapproval melted from her face, replaced by a shy grin. When her gaze dropped back to her e-reader, his smile slid away, and his attention returned to the passing landscape.

It had been dark the last time he was on this road. Too dark to see the houses. And he'd been going the other way.

Nothing outside looked familiar. Just farm after farm. They all looked alike and likely belonged to some big conglomerate now anyway. How was he supposed to remember any specific one? A few properties stood out but not because they were familiar. Whatever farmhouses had stood on those properties when he was a boy were gone, replaced by McMansions with fancy gates. Who on earth would want to build out here in Nowheresville?

Something small flew past the edge of his vision, jerking him out of his musings.

"Like a hottie like him would ever be interested in a freak like you," sneered a voice somewhere behind him.

"Hey, freak, want another donut?"

He swiveled halfway in his seat and spotted a pair of bleached-blonde cheerleader types sitting two rows back. They leaned into each other, snickering, overcome with their own cleverness. The small thing that had caught his attention turned out to be bits of powdered donut they were tossing at the girl across from him, who now sat with shoulders hunched and Kindle held tight to her chest.

Charm went cold, then hot. One of the girls happened to glance his way and caught her breath. She slunk low in her seat.

Her friend, on the other hand, managed to look both affronted and annoyed. "What?"

His glare didn't waver.

She glared back and stuck out her tongue. "Who are you staring at?" When he didn't look away, she made a show of looking around the bus for support. "Hey, this guy is staring at me, and it's making me uncomfortable."

No one responded.

Her friend slid further down and stared at her hands. The girl rolled her eyes, flounced into the seat, and grumbled, "We don't answer to you."

His gaze still didn't waver.

After several more uncomfortable seconds, she muttered a reluctant, "Sorry."

Probably not, but the best he was going to get. He turned his attention away from the blondes to the girl across from him. She glanced sideways and mouthed, "Thank you." He nodded, hesitated a moment, then slid over into the seat next to her.

Her eyes stayed fixed on the space below the seat in front of her. "You don't have to do this."

"No, but it will drive them absolutely nuts." A half chuckle, half sob burst out of her. He stuck out his hand. "I'm Charm."

She sniffled. "Like Prince Charming?"

"Like 'charm the stripe off a polecat.'" At her blank look, he added, "It's a nickname. Since I was four."

"And your real name is so horrible you'd rather be confused with a fairy tale character?"

"Better than being associated with the son of a bitch I'm named for."

She blinked, then smiled. "I get that." She turned off her Kindle and shut the cover. "I'm Riley."

"Whatcha reading?" he asked.

"*Into the Wild*. By Jon Krakauer."

"Awesome. Love Krakauer."

In a move reminiscent of the girls two seats back, she rolled her eyes. "Yeah, right."

He patted his pockets, then failing to find what he wanted, reached across the aisle and grabbed a well-worn paperback from the seat he had vacated. He held it up: *Into Thin Air* by Jon Krakauer.

She laughed. "No shit."

He grinned. "Krakauer's cool. You always know some serious crap's gonna hit the fan, but the adventure getting there is amazing."

"I know, right? I haven't read that one, but this one totally makes me want to sell everything and run off to Alaska. I mean, I know the dude starved to death, but the idea of getting away from everything and everyone — " She stopped, and her cheeks flushed red. "Stupid. I live in Biloxi. Where the fuck am I going to run off to?"

Charm looked out the window and saw himself boarding a bus at sixteen, duffel bag in hand. "Anywhere you want."

The bus slowed, and he looked around to orient himself. A shiny new sign welcomed him to a town no longer familiar: "Collier, Mississippi, population 3,319." Population had almost tripled in the last eighteen years. A new-to-him red light at the north end of town explained the slowdown.

"Jesus. Last time I was here, this corner had an ancient gas station and a crappy restaurant on it."

Riley snorted and peered out at a not-so-shiny-new shopping center with a Walmart and a modern Exxon. "Not in this millennium."

"You aren't old enough to remember the whole millennium."

She flipped him off.

The bus turned east off the highway in front of the Walmart and then turned south at a T intersection. Another half mile rocking and rattling over potholes and layers of repairs and the bus rolled into the town square.

The Collier bus station shared the southern edge of the town square with a '50s-style gas station with a single diesel pump (used by farmers who didn't want to drive their tractors to the highway) and city hall. Charm sighed, reminded of Leon, Collier's mayor since before Charm was born. And high school science teacher. After that incident with the flash paper and the bucket of frogs, Leon had seemed to have it in for Charm.

*And that was Jimmy Lee's doing anyway.* The memory stung even after twenty years. Well, Leon would have to be old as Methuselah now. Charm wouldn't have to worry about him anymore. The building's faded blue-and-white awning, the same one that had been there as long as he could remember, came into view as the bus turned in to the station. And sitting under the awning, reading his paper, was Methuselah himself. Charm groaned and shook his head.

"Christ. It's like I never left."

"Collier!" The bus driver's gaze met Charm's in the rearview mirror.

Charm closed his eyes and didn't move. Vicksburg used to be a pretty nice town. He could just keep riding.

"Hey!" the driver said. "This is your stop. You gettin' off or not?"

Charm blew out a deep breath. "Yeah. Yeah, I'm gettin' off." He unfolded his lanky body and headed toward the door, then turned back and tossed his seatmate the dog-eared paperback. "Read it. And send me a postcard from Everest." He flashed one last grin and walked out.

The rain splattered the bus's bottom step with big, soaking drops. The driver crammed a hat on his head and jumped out to get the luggage. Leon hadn't bothered to look up from his newspaper when the bus pulled in. Probably wasn't expecting anybody to get off. Or maybe the old goat was too deaf to hear the rolling behemoth. He looked up now, though, and pushed himself to his feet.

Charm imagined the long minutes it would take him to hobble the twenty feet to the bus and waved him back. "Stay dry. I can get it." As soon as the bus driver got the compartment open, Charm hopped down, hauled out his duffel bag, then took quick refuge under the awning. The driver secured the compartment and reboarded the bus. The gears ground, the engine revved, and the bus pulled away and headed south. Total time in Collier: less than two minutes. Charm watched his ride to freedom drive off and exhaled loudly.

"You waitin' on somebody? Need directions to the bed-and-breakfast?"

Charm looked over. Leon had closed the gap and was scanning him up and down with a puzzled expression. *He can't place me.* Charm flashed the same smile he'd used to captivate Riley. "Neither. I've got other plans." He glanced out at the town square. A few parked cars, but the sidewalks were empty, and he realized the bus had been the only vehicle he'd seen on the road.

The old man squinted at the deserted square. "Whole town's out at a funeral," he said, answering the question Charm hadn't asked. "A young father. Left a wife and the cutest little boy you ever set eyes on."

Charm blinked at him. *Today? The funeral is today?* He heard himself mumble, "That's too bad."

"Yes, sir, it's tragic. He's gonna be missed around here." He started back to his bench but hesitated and looked around at the empty parking lot. "You sure you don't need directions over to Miss Rose's? She runs the bed and breakfast."

"No thanks." Charm tried to picture the roads beyond the square. Which way was the damn cemetery? Probably near that Walmart. He slung his duffel over his shoulder and tugged his jacket up around his ears. A tap on the shoulder stopped him before he stepped into the rain.

The old man held out the newspaper. "Don't get too wet."

Charm paused, then took the paper. "Thanks." He glanced at the rainy sky, held the paper over his head, and started north across the square.

* * *

It wasn't hard to find the cemetery — Collier's only one — or the funeral. Charm passed cars parked on both sides of the road a good three blocks before the cemetery, and the line continued along the dirt road through the cemetery to the graveside, where a mass of dark-clad bodies stood huddled under umbrellas. Leon hadn't exaggerated — it really did look as though the whole town was here. *She* would appreciate that. Gratitude loosened the knot in his stomach.

The rain just sprinkled now, but he slipped under a wide-branched oak to escape both the mist and the notice of the mourners. The minister's voice drifted over the crowd. "Blessed are the poor in spirit, for theirs is the kingdom of heaven. Blessed are they that mourn, for they shall be comforted. Blessed are the meek, for they shall inherit the earth."

It was almost over. That was all right. He'd been here for part of it, and most of what he needed to say, he would say in private.

"Blessed are the merciful, for they shall obtain mercy. Blessed are the pure in heart, for they shall see God. Blessed are the peacemakers, for they shall be called the children of God."

"Amen," the crowd responded, and the service ended. The crowd stirred with a murmur of soft conversation and began migrating toward the cars. Charm turned his head away as people drifted past, snippets of conversation floating behind them.

"…held on this long."

"…should have waited till the boy could attend."

"…not sure if he'll walk."

The words faded on a gust of wind. Charm pulled his jacket tighter and tried to picture the man these people came to respect. But all he saw was a sixteen-year-old kid with a goofy grin. The last eighteen years vanished, replaced by the two of them in the cab of Jake's Blazer at the bus station on a rainy Friday night.

*Charm wrenched open the door. "I owe you," he said, sliding out.*

*"Cut that shit out," Jake said dismissively. His voice sounded rough, like he'd smoked too many of his mom's Camels.*

*"No." Charm's voice was serious. "I owe you." He shut the door and started toward the bus station. After a few steps, he turned and yelled back, "I'm good for it!"*

Charm snorted. Yet another person let down.

Focus on the living.

A dozen people lingered near the coffin. His eyes scanned the group. There. Someone shifted, and he caught a glimpse of auburn hair. Ellie. She'd been a gawky eleven-year-old when he'd seen her last, and he'd been a teenager with big ears and acne. Would she recognize him? Hell, maybe she'd forgotten he existed. Maybe they'd all forgotten.

Ellie stood in the middle of the group, focusing her attention on each in turn. Everyone seemed to want to touch her. A hug, a squeeze of her hand, she accepted it all but initiated nothing. Her shoulders hunched, seeming close to buckling under the weight of grief and exhaustion. She tried making her way toward a limo at the head of the line of cars but could go only a few steps at a time before someone else would stop and hug her. Those moments seemed to give her some energy, and she would pat their hand and nod and continue on her way again. Once she faltered, her body shaking with a sob. Several people rushed in to bolster and pet her, but she straightened, and they backed away.

The path to the limo lay nowhere near the tree where Charm stood, and he would have remained there unnoticed had she not hugged a friend and looked right at him. She froze. Heads swiveled to see what she was looking at, and they froze too. So much for doing this privately. A deep breath buoyed his courage, and he walked to meet her.

The group opened as he approached. She stared at him so quizzically he wondered if he'd misread her. Maybe she hadn't recognized him. Maybe she wondered who he was. But when he drew close, she whispered, "Charm?" He nodded and reached out to embrace her.

Ellie moaned and launched herself at him. "No!" Her fists pounded against his chest. "Not you, not you!"

He caught hold of her wrists. God, what had he been thinking? Back from the dead at a funeral. *Great timing, Freeman.* He gave her a light shake. "It is me."

Her body sagged, and she sobbed. He pulled her close, and after a moment, she yielded, her fingers clutching his jacket. He tightened his hold.

"Hello, Charm."

It wasn't Ellie who spoke, but it could have been. The woman to her left shared Ellie's frame and rigid posture. Ellie's eyes were a vivid blue like Charm's, but they were shaped like the muddy green ones staring at him. Only the hair was different: Dot Freeman's hair was cropped close and white. Charm nodded a curt greeting without releasing his sister. "Hello, Mother."

Her cheeks flushed with an emotion Charm couldn't read. "I thought maybe you'd come when your father died." Dot motioned vaguely toward a grave near Jake's.

Charm avoided looking at it. *How could Ellie bury her husband near that bastard?* "I bought a round at the pub. Kept the memory pure." Regret knifed through his gut as soon as he said the words, but his apology stuck in his throat.

"Stop." Ellie sighed and straightened. When she looked up, whatever had maintained her before had found its footing again. She lifted her hand to stop her mother's rebuttal and glared at each of them. "Why are you here, Charm?"

A dozen explanations about debts and promises, none of them sufficient, ran through his mind. He started to answer, stopped, and took a breath. "I want to help."

His mother sputtered, but a look from his sister stopped her from speaking. Ellie glanced at the people around her, so wrapped up in the unfolding scene they'd forgotten to be circumspect in their eavesdropping. Some had even forgotten to close their mouths. Charm scowled at old Mrs. McGillivray, who had taken two steps forward and was trying to turn up her hearing aid. Ellie crossed her arms and tilted her chin toward the limo. "This isn't the place to discuss it."

A cough, a mumble, and the people around them scattered in directions so random Charm wondered how many were actually headed toward their cars. Before nightfall, the entire town would know Ellie's brother had returned.

He paused and looked back at the grave, considering, for a moment, going over to pay his respects. What would he say? Words seemed so…inadequate. No. His debt to Jake would have to be repaid another way. Charm filled his lungs with Collier air, tossed his duffel over his shoulder, and joined his family in the limo.

- 22 -

# CHAPTER 2

The ride to the church wouldn't end. In reality it took maybe five minutes, but five minutes alone with people who were studiously ignoring each other felt like an eternity. Ellie and their mother shared the forward-facing seat but perched on opposite ends, each staring out her window. An empty strip of black upholstery formed an uncontested border that even their coats didn't dare cross.

Charm took the rear-facing seat and stared at the strangers across from him. Jesus, they were old. In his mind he'd frozen them at the ages they were when he left. Ellie had to be, what, twenty-nine? Eighteen years older than the last time he'd seen her. Lines had formed at the edges of her eyes and grimly set mouth, making her look older than she was. Similar lines and the same tight jaw and thin lips appeared on his mother's face. Mirror images the two women were, down to the crossed ankles. They even reached up to brush their hair aside at the same moment. Charm started to laugh but swallowed it behind a cough.

They turned in unison to look at him. The unvoiced pain and a sort of pleading in his mother's gaze made his stomach flip-flop, so he focused on Ellie instead. Her eyes brimmed with such a helpless bewilderment that all at once he took in the whole of her — a woman who had lost her husband, who had no dependable family, who had to bear the weight of it all herself. A flush of shame warmed his face, and he studied his jeans, wishing he had at least dressed properly. Respectfully. "I shouldn't have come," he mumbled.

His mother made a noise in her throat, and he looked up. Ellie shook her head. "No, no. I'm glad you did." A tear spilled down one cheek. With a quick glance toward her mother, as if to see if she had noticed, she swiped it away. "It's just…I'm not even sure you're real."

Charm shifted in his seat and looked anywhere but at her. "I'm real. Lousy timing and all."

"Jimmy Lee told you? You flew in from Europe?"

He met her eyes, surprised. "Europe…um, no. No, you caught me between trips. Yeah, uh, Jimmy Lee emailed me a couple of days ago." A pang of bitterness soured his mouth. *Why couldn't he have told me earlier?* "Didn't tell me much. Said there'd been a car accident, and Jake…died."

She nodded. "The accident happened right before Christmas. They hit a deer and went into oncoming traffic. Docs said from the beginning there was no chance, but it was Christmas, you know?" She sounded wishful, as if hoping the Christmas magic might undo everything that had happened. But it didn't, and the hope drained from her voice. "He hung on for two weeks."

An image of Jake — a high school jock who'd left a game-night celebration to drive his best friend to freedom — filled Charm's mind. He tried to imagine Jake as an adult, a husband and father, but that brought a sickening flash of him wrapped in bandages, pale and still in a hospital bed, Ellie beside him, praying for a miracle. *One lousy miracle. Was that too much to ask?* Charm pushed the images away and concentrated on what else she had said. "They?"

"Our son was with him. Lucas." The name came in a trembling breath. "He survived." She fell quiet for a minute, and he could see her struggling to find words. "His leg was shattered. His" — she patted her thigh — "femur. The doctors call it a comminuted fracture. They did surgery and nailed it all back together. I don't really understand it all."

Charm shuddered. "Can he walk?"

She hesitated. "He says it hurts too much. He's…not doing well." The limo slowed, and Ellie looked out. "We're here."

*Here.* The First United Methodist Church of Collier, where the funeral director waited. Charm recognized the dour African American man as Henry Gannaway Sr., the father of his high school friend Bird. Mr. Gannaway gave Charm a long, appraising look when he climbed out of the limo with the family but didn't let an unexpected appearance mar his well-rehearsed spiel. Since their last encounter involved a hearse and a joyride, Charm didn't mind skipping the trip down memory lane.

Gannaway shook their hands, extended his deep sympathies, and urged them to call him if they needed "anything, anything at all." Ellie's assurances seemed equally practiced, but they sufficed, because with a nod, Gannaway joined the chauffeur in the front of the limousine and drove away, leaving the three of them standing alone in the empty driveway.

Ellie wrinkled her nose and groaned. "God, I wish this day were over."

"Isn't it?" Charm scanned the area for activity but saw only an older Chevrolet sedan he guessed belonged to his mother.

"No. Now everyone gathers at my house, tries to stuff me with pasta salad, and tells me how lucky I am to still have my son."

His mother adjusted her hat against the drizzle that had started again. "They only want the best for you. You should give them the benefit of the doubt." She shot Charm a significant look, then tugged on driving gloves and headed toward the old sedan.

He glared after her. "Subtext much?"

Ellie managed a half grin. "No filter." She snorted. "Honestly, it's kind of refreshing."

"Is she helping you with Lucas?" They fell in step to trek across the parking lot.

"Oh God, no. I'm not that desperate yet." She fluttered her fingers and motioned toward the car. "She stayed with him in the hospital, when Jake was…you know."

Charm tried to picture his mother as Florence Nightingale, but the closest he could get was Jack Kevorkian in a nurse's uniform. "Poor kid."

"Lucas adores her." They paused at the car. "How long are you staying?"

Panic tightened his gut. *Staying?* His mind spun with excuses, but before he could choose one, she burst out laughing.

"God, I wish I had a camera to capture that expression. I'm not asking you to move in, Charm. I'm offering a place to sleep tonight."

"I'd planned to crash at Jimmy Lee's…"

She shrugged. "Whatever." She reached for the door handle. "You want the front?"

Shit. Did he insult her? "Back is fine." He grasped at the politest response he could think of. "I'd rather stay with you, but I didn't want to put you out."

She made a face. "Someone has to eat all the casseroles people are dropping off." She slid into the front seat.

He turned the situation over in his mind. It would be all right. One night of family time would fulfil his obligation. Then he could leave and bury the past for another eighteen years. He could survive that. He shoved his duffel bag onto the back seat and climbed in beside it.

One night, and all debts would be repaid.

He hoped.

* * *

Ellie's farm lay northeast of town, just beyond the farthest reaching of the new subdivisions. When asked, she described the house as "the old Christensen place." Charm should have known the way, but the rows of cookie-cutter homes had spread like the omnipresent Mississippi kudzu, obliterating decades-old cropland, swallowing familiar landmarks.

They pulled into a place vaguely familiar and parked next to an ancient white pickup near an even more ancient barn. Charm got out and hefted his bag over his shoulder, taking advantage of the moment to look around. He remembered now. This had been a plot of land sandwiched between corn and soybeans, house and barn set back well away from the road among snarls of weeds, rusty cars, and farm equipment.

Instead of scrap cars, a dozen vehicles — belonging, Charm guessed, to guests and not the occupants — lined the road and drive. The house and barn seemed different, less run-down, transformed by brick pathways, flower beds carefully put to bed for winter, and two solid climbing trees with limbs stretching toward the house. So damn quintessentially Southern. There was even a picnic table. An ache tightened his throat. Pain tangled with longing. He swallowed both.

A pair of ladies who had arrived before them paused to stare, but when he made eye contact, they dropped their heads and hurried to the house. The door swung open before they could knock, and an older woman invited them in.

He squinted at the woman in the doorway. "Who's that?"

Ellie smiled at the woman and nodded when she waved. "Ruth Walton. Minister's wife. Offered to stay with Lucas while we…" Her voice trailed off.

While they buried the kid's dad. Right. Simply mentioning — or almost mentioning — Jake sent a visible tremor through her body. But a deep breath later, her shoulders straightened. *Always the strong one.* Charm caught hold of her fingers and gave them a squeeze. She gave no other outward sign of having noticed, but for an instant her fingers clutched his with a desperation that belied her emotionless exterior. Then she dropped his hand, lifted her chin, and pushed onward.

The house faced the driveway rather than the road. A line of brick pavers made a path to the front porch, and the driveway curved around the end of the house where there was a screened-in porch. Charm vaguely remembered it led to a laundry room off the kitchen. He wasn't sure which door to head for, but their mother led them to the front porch. Apparently, even family used the front for funerals.

Ellie lifted a warning hand when Charm reached for the railing to the right of the stairs. "Other one. That one's the victim of an adolescent monkey." She didn't sound pleased.

Women swarmed them before they'd even gotten through the door.

"Lucas was an absolute angel…."

"We've got the food set up buffet style, so you won't need to do a thing…."

"We're putting extra in the freezer. Where's your Tupperware?"

The flurry of innocuous conversation failed to conceal an irrepressible buzz of curiosity. *He's back! Where has he been? How long will he stay? Why did he leave?* Every eye in the room fixed on Charm.

Before he could speak, his mother's hand pressed against the small of his back. "Y'all remember my son, Will."

He cringed at the use of his given name. "Charm."

A dark-skinned woman with close-cropped hair stepped forward and took his hand. "We remember Charm. Some of us remember him all too well." Her tone sounded gruff, but delight shone in her eyes.

He cocked his head, then smiled his first truly genuine smile since arriving in town. "That's because some of you liked me so much, you wouldn't let me go home at the end of the school day." Sixth grade had been a long year. He kissed her cheek. "It's good to see you, Miz Harris."

She snorted. "I assure you, I was not late with dinner three times a week that year because you were so likable. If you hadn't done that extra credit assignment and passed, I don't think I'd have kept teaching."

His posture stiffened, but he forced himself to chuckle. "It would have been the school's loss, because you were the one that inspired me to write that essay." The piece of the Berlin Wall she had passed around, a chunk of concrete splashed with spray paint from a tagger's can, had hummed with history. He had felt the cold, felt the hope, heard the cheers as each East Berliner crossed the border. The essay had almost written itself. Ms. Harris had urged him to enter it in a national contest.

*Excitement made him bounce from seat to seat on the bus. Europe. Germany. Maybe they could do more than Germany. Maybe Switzerland.*

*Maybe even Italy. Charm burst through the bus door before it fully opened and didn't stop running until he reached the barn. Silence rang in his ears, hay not stacked. No one in the office either. Or the field. He finally found his father in the living room, sitting hunched over in a chair in front of the fireplace.*

*He pushed the essay into his father's hands, making sure the grade was visible. "Look…A+…Ms. Harris…contest," he managed to gasp between breaths.*

*His father looked up, eyes red and unfocused. "Contest? What contest?"*

*Charm took a deep breath and blew it out. "National contest. First prize…trip to Germany. Ms. Harris says" — another deep breath — "Ms. Harris says I have a good shot at winning."*

*"Waste of time!" His father shoved the essay back at him and stood. He grabbed his jacket from the sofa and stuffed his arms into the sleeves with more force than required.*

*Charm stared. "It's our chance."* Why didn't he understand? *"We can go. Just like — like we always talked about."*

*His father snatched the paper and waved it in his face. "Grow up, Charm. You're stuck here, just like I am." He wadded up the report and tossed it in the fire, then stomped toward the back door. "We're never getting out of this goddamn town."*

*Charm watched until the red A+ scorched to black.*

"You really should have entered that contest," Ms. Harris mused, bringing him back to the present. "You might have won."

He forced himself to laugh. "Do you know what that would have done to my rep? Extra credit was bad enough."

Ellie stepped forward and put her hand on his arm. "I know Charm is anxious to catch up with everyone, but I think he'd probably like to freshen up first." Sympathy darkened her eyes. In a low voice, she added, "Guest bedroom upstairs, second door on the left."

"Thanks." He flashed the room the most winsome smile he could manage, then fled the room, guilt weighting his steps. Here to mourn the death of his sister's husband, and she's feeling bad for his childhood disappointments. *You're a real winner, Freeman.*

The room behind the second door on the left smelled like lemon Pledge, and the hardwood floors had a just-mopped shine. Such a

Southern thing to scrub down a room that wasn't even going to be seen. He ran his fingers over a hand-carved finial on a bedpost. Nice work. Familiar. This had been his parents' bed. He looked around. All the pieces in the room had come from their childhood home. His positive appraisal vanished. His mother apparently foisted hand-me-down furniture like she foisted horrible tuna casserole and unwanted opinions.

He fingered the patchwork quilt on the bed. The last time he'd seen it, the quilt had been on his childhood bed. When he'd wanted to replace it with something less girly, his mother had taken it as a personal slight against his grandmother's handiwork. (Because she'd stitched it by hand. Uphill. In the snow.) He traced one of the geometric patterns in the brightly colored quilt and snorted. Guess it was a personal slight only until she didn't want it anymore herself.

A five-minute shower and a quick shave revived him. A nip from his flask, and when he reappeared downstairs fifteen minutes later, the smile he cast to the room was genuine enough only someone who knew him well would know the difference, and no one here did. His mother chatted with three other ladies in an animated fashion so out of character he had to look twice to be sure. When she saw him, her eyes narrowed for an instant. *Yep, that's her.*

He nodded to a couple of familiar faces, accepted a glass of sweet tea from an older woman he didn't recognize, and ignored the people whispering and glancing at him surreptitiously. Not much had changed in eighteen years.

Like the furniture in the guest room, the furniture here felt familiar. He frowned and tried to place it. It wasn't from the house, but he recognized it. He shook his head. Maybe it was the style.

He picked up a framed photo from a table. *Ah, that's what Jake looks — looked — like now.* The smiling man in the photo held a large fish and smoked a pipe. Charm couldn't help but grin himself. They couldn't have been more than twelve the first time Jake stole one of his father's pipes and some tobacco. Jake thought the pipe made him look mature. Charm looked at his friend's familiar goofy grin and shook his head. *Nope. Not a bit.*

"It's your favorite, honey. Just eat a little bit." Ellie's voice drew his attention to the sofa where she was peddling a heaping plate of fried chicken to a young boy.

"I'm not hungry."

The boy's left leg, immobilized by a knee brace and propped up at an awkward angle with pillows, rested on a chair. Ellie sat beside her son and waved a chicken wing. "One piece. You don't want to hurt Miss Debbie's feelings, do you?"

Charm wound his way through the gauntlet of friends and neighbors and perched on the arm of the couch. "Might as well give in, kid. She learned from the Queen of Guilt."

The boy regarded him through hazel eyes half-hidden under a mop of blond curls. He didn't smile, simply blinked and tilted his head to the left, as if considering a puzzling question, but when his mother offered the wing again, he took it with a sigh.

Ellie smiled and pushed his hair off his face. "Lucas, this is who I was telling you about. This is your Uncle Charm."

The boy studied the chicken in his hand. "Hi."

"Hi." Charm searched for something to say. "You look like your dad. Except for the hair."

"Color is Jake's. Curls are mine," Ellie confirmed.

Lucas looked up at his mom. "Can't you just call Mr. Forbes —
"

"Not today!"

Several pairs of eyes swung in her direction. Charm tensed. The sharp tone niggled at memories he didn't want to touch and made his stomach clench. *Don't talk about it, and it won't be real. Ignore it, and everything will be all right.*

A deep breath and Ellie's calm demeanor returned. She lifted Lucas's chin. "You thirsty? Want something to drink?"

The boy shrugged, then nodded.

"I'll get it." Charm stood, glad to have something to do. "What do you want, kid?"

Ellie didn't wait for Lucas to answer. "Juice." The boy rolled his eyes but didn't bother to argue.

Charm winked at his nephew and headed for the kitchen. "Juice it is."

"With a twisty straw!" Ellie called after him.

Food overflowed every flat surface in the kitchen. A team of three repackaged what they could, labeling containers with masking tape and a Sharpie, filling the fridge and freezer. *There is no way*, he thought, eyeing the mounds of food, *all of that is going to fit in Ellie's refrigerator.*

"Don't worry, honey. There's a deep freeze on the back porch." The group's designated labeler waved her pen toward the back door. "I'm adding little notes too. God bless 'em for helping, but" — her voice dropped to a stage whisper — "some of these ladies should stick to the deli counter up at the Super Walmart."

"That's sacrilege, and you know it." His mother breezed past Charm. "Walmart doesn't make their food with love." She drawled out the last word.

"Little comfort when love tastes like shit."

His mother laughed and touched her on the arm. "Angeline, would y'all excuse us? I'd like to talk to my son for a minute."

Charm gritted his teeth and marveled at how the Antichrist had managed to appear so human. She'd actually been funny. Not so funny he was suddenly anxious to chat, at least not in private. But the ladies filed out anyway. On the way past, Angeline offered him a brilliant smile.

"Why are you here?"

His mother's question brought him back to himself. "Lucas wants juice. Excuse me." He moved past her and began opening cabinet doors, searching for a glass.

"I meant, why did you come back to Collier?"

Success. Glass in hand, he turned his attention to the juice. "You might have missed it, but my sister's husband — my best friend — died." The most easily accessible drink in the overstuffed fridge was a carton of Newman's Own lemonade. Behind a rather complex stack of variably sized food containers were bottles of cranberry, apple, and — he snaked his hand through the maze and turned the bottle around — pomegranate juice. *Ew.*

"I know Jake was your best friend, but you haven't seen him or your sister in nearly twenty years. You weren't here when they got married. Or when Lucas was born."

His stomach tensed. Why couldn't she accept that he came back for the funeral? Frankly, his reasons were none of her business. "You're right. I've been an undeniably selfish bastard." *Lemons are a fruit, aren't they?* That made it juice. He grabbed the lemonade.

His mother pulled a tall blue plastic cup from the cabinet. "If you're going to do that, use an opaque cup so Eleanor won't know."

*Eleanor.* Ellie hated her name almost as much as he hated his. Of course, his mother used it. He accepted the offered cup. "Look," he said, pouring the drink, "being here is pretty much my personal definition of hell. I don't want to be here. You don't want me here. I'm not staying." He opened a drawer and searched for the requested straw. "I only came back to make sure she's all right." That was close enough to the truth.

No straw. He checked another drawer. Then another. *Where, where, where. Where is the twisty straw?* He hesitated. *What? What is a twisty straw?*

"I never said I didn't want you here. Why would you think such a thing?"

Anger turned the anxiety in his belly hot. She had the nerve to sound surprised? Before he could respond, his mother opened the dishwasher and retrieved the wayward item. The clear, narrow tube, straight at the bottom, made an intricate combination of curves and loops near the top. A twisty straw. Obviously.

"Just talk to Mr. Forbes." Lucas's impatient voice drifted in from the living room.

"Stop," Ellie said sharply. "I said we'll talk about it later."

Charm and his mother exchanged a glance and returned to the living room.

"You always say that. We have to get River back," the boy persisted.

Charm cleared his throat, but before he could ask what was going on, the woman who'd let them in earlier — minister's wife…Walton…something Walton — waddled past him.

"Elle," she said, "Arthur and Ed set up the computer and that little TV in Lucas's room. Would you come give them your blessing before they decide to knock out a wall and build an entertainment system?"

Ellie's eyebrow arched. "Definitely." She rose to her feet, then turned back to Lucas. "I'll be right back. Your uncle will sit with you."

Charm's mouth dropped open, but he snapped it shut as quickly. "Absolutely."

He edged onto the vacated sofa cushion and pasted a smile on his face. He kept it there until Ellie and his mother disappeared upstairs and the curious faces in the room finally returned to their own conversations. Then he exhaled, let the smile slip away and turned his attention to the kid sitting beside him.

The boy was staring at Charm's shoes. Charm had changed into a more appropriate button-down shirt and khakis, but the dusty white sneakers were the only shoes he'd brought. He flushed. Why hadn't he tossed in some loafers?

"My friend has a pair of Pumas like that," the boy said. "Only his are red. I wanted some, but Mom said I'd outgrow them too fast." For emphasis, he wiggled the foot propped up on the stack of phone books. The overlarge sheepskin moccasin warming his toes flopped off.

Charm rescued it and compared it to the size of his own shoes. Even his own foot looked small in comparison. "I don't think that will be a problem anytime soon." He stuck it back on the boy's very normal-size foot.

Lucas giggled. "My dad's." He wiggled the slipper again, and his smile faded.

*Shit.* Charm's stomach dropped. There it was. The elephant. What should he say? What if the kid started to cry? Jesus, what a nightmare. Where was Ellie?

"Is that for me?"

Charm looked at the cup in his hand. "Shit — oh, sorry. Yeah, here." He thrust the cup in the kid's hands. Topic, topic, topic. "So, um, who's River?"

"A dog." The boy's voice was glum. "Mom hates him."

"That's not true." Okay, Charm didn't really have any idea, but he figured it wasn't likely she'd waste energy hating a dog. "She's been really busy with…everything. You've got to cut her a little bit of slack. Just give her some time."

"She doesn't understand." Lucas's pitch rose. "River's going to be a champion. He's gonna be a champion, and then everything will be all right!"

Charm guessed he had about five seconds to head off the waterworks. He patted the boy's shoulder awkwardly. "Hey, buddy, if the dog is that important to you, I'll get him for you."

"Charm!" Ellie's sharp rebuke rang through the room.

Lucas swiped at his eyes. "Really?"

Charm looked up. His sister glared at him from the bottom of the stairs. What was the big deal? It was only a dog. Her expression warned he was about to make a very big mistake. *Sorry, kid. I spoke too soon. We'll have to ask your mom.* Even as his tongue formed the words, he heard himself say instead, "Sure. I can do that."

Ellie's jaw clenched. "Charm, can I talk to you in the kitchen?"

He gave Lucas a smile he hoped was reassuring, then followed his sister into the kitchen.

"How *dare* you interfere with my son," she snapped before he was through the door.

"All I did was offer to get his dog for him." *I was just trying to help.*

Righteous anger gave Ellie height. "That dog was in the accident. He survived, but I don't have any clue what kind of shape he's in. Hasn't Lucas been through enough?"

Embarrassment heated Charm's cheeks. "I'm sorry. I didn't realize."

"Because you didn't ask. You plunged right ahead, like you always have." She bit her lip and looked away for a moment. Then she crossed her arms and met his eyes. "What are you doing here, Charm?"

His whole face burned as his anger flared again. Jesus Christ, why was everyone asking that? Wasn't it obvious? "I came to help. You're my sister. He was my best friend."

"I don't need help! I can take care of myself."

"What about the farm? And Lucas?"

"I can handle it!"

Charm shook his head and stepped back. "I have no doubt," he said in a normal tone. "I bet old Jake must've felt pretty useless around you." A sharp pang of regret knifed through him when a tear spilled down her cheek.

"You wouldn't know, would you?" She turned away.

Charm stared at her a moment, then stalked to the front door. The gazes of Ellie's neighbors followed him, burning him with accusations and questions. He paused for a moment. *Go back. Just go back and make it right.* But his legs wouldn't turn around. *Run, Freeman. Do what you do best.* He grabbed the truck keys hanging near Ellie's coat and purse and fled.

# Chapter 3

The keys belonged to the ancient white pickup parked near the barn. It took two tries to start it, and the engine sputtered and hesitated a couple of times on the way down the driveway, but once it got on the road, the truck became a serviceable escape vehicle. Escape to where wasn't certain or even important. Anywhere without stares and questions. Coming back here had been a mistake, a serious mistake. Ellie didn't need him — she'd said it herself. Maybe some debts really couldn't be repaid.

When he reached the highway, Charm turned toward town. Where else could he go? Vicksburg, maybe, to catch a bus. No, his stuff was still at Ellie's. He patted his pockets and swore. So was his wallet. Not a lot of money in it, but without it, he couldn't go far. He checked the gas gauge. And neither could the truck. Fuck a duck. He couldn't even run away without screwing up.

What he needed was a drink.

A horn blared annoyance at him. He swerved onto the shoulder, and a Corvette sped past, the driver offering a middle finger salute. Charm groused something creatively unflattering about the guy's parentage, checked his mirrors, and pulled back on the road.

Of course, it would be just his luck if Ellie reported the damn truck as stolen. He slammed his hand on the steering wheel. He didn't steal it! He borrowed it.

His anger yielded to regret. One lousy day. He couldn't keep it together for one lousy day. Christ, it was like being sixteen again. All the judgment and disappointment he'd felt back then had come rushing back, and he'd acted exactly like he had then. "When are you going to learn to think before you act, Freeman?" he said out loud. The only response was the squeak of the truck's suspension, or what was left of it, as it bounced through a pothole.

Unsure what else to do, Charm drove into the Walmart lot and parked at the far end, near a smoke shop and a liquor store. There were more cars in the lot than there had been earlier. Funeral was over, so life went on. Back to bargains and bulk items. The marquee under the Walmart sign wished the citizens of Collier a happy New Year and offered a ten percent discount on space heaters. A billboard across the street said, "Congratulations, Ray Forbes, winner of the Washburn Cup." Charm had no clue what the Washburn Cup was, but the sign had lots of bright colors and fireworks, so it must have been important if someone had rented a billboard simply to congratulate the guy.

Forbes. Hadn't the kid said something about somebody named Forbes? Remembering Lucas sent a flush of shame to Charm's face. God, why had he told the kid he would get him the dog? Why hadn't he listened to Ellie? Hell, the kid himself said she didn't like the dog. Charm groaned. Could he have screwed this up any worse?

One of the Walmart patrons walked past him on the way to her car and shot him a suspicious glance. She whispered something to the man with her, and he turned back and squinted at him. Charm sighed. God, he hated small towns. Bunch of damn busybodies.

He fired up the truck and pulled out of the lot. He needed a drink. Several drinks. His current wallet-less situation meant the liquor store was a no-go, so he knew of only one solution. *Please God, let Brother Jack's still be there.*

God, who had proven to be nothing if not capricious in the last thirty-four years, was apparently in a charitable mood because the bar in which he'd spent so much time during his formative years was still there, three miles south of the new red light on the main highway. Considering his financial situation, Charm hoped he might find a familiar face also in a charitable mood.

Brother Jack's sat at the edge of a cornfield in what could rightfully be called the middle of nowhere. The good churchgoing folks of Collier tolerated it because it was far enough away that strangers passing through might not associate it with the town but close enough that even the most pious could slip in for a pint on a Saturday night. No food, no music, just beer, liquor, and pool. At sixteen, the last made a perfect escape from the simmering conflicts at home. The bar's owner, a wiry Brooklyn import named Buster, turned a blind eye to Charm's frequent underage visits even during school hours as long as Charm stuck to pool and didn't drink. Smoking was okay, but a beer in his hand got him booted fast and good. Not that it stopped him.

The knots in Charm's gut loosened as soon as he exited the truck and relaxed further with each step toward the door. Odd that a gravel parking lot could feel more like home than being with his mother and sister. More cars filled the lot than he had expected in the middle of a Tuesday afternoon. Post-funeral crowd maybe.

When he stepped inside, the scent of grilled burgers made his stomach growl. Food? Apparently, Brother Jack's had changed. Not visually — long and narrow with dim lighting and an abundance of dark wood, seating on the left, bar on the right. Same crappy green vinyl booths and scarred wooden tables, but as many of the patrons looked like suburbanites as they did weary farmers.

Charm had been right about the funeral: a group of men in Sunday best made toasts at the bar. In fact, it appeared everyone had likely attended the service, except maybe a teenager who was feeding himself french fries and guzzling soda without taking his eyes off his laptop screen. A laptop? Jesus. Brother Jack's had turned into Starbucks.

He ducked his head and made his way through the crowd at the bar. He used to have to walk down a narrow hall past the bathrooms to get to the back room, but sometime during the years he was gone, the wall between that room and the dining area had been torn down. Probably to give some visibility into what was happening back there, he surmised, stepping out of the way as the bartender barreled past.

"Boudreaux!" the bartender snapped. "What'd I tell you about them trick shots?"

Charm looked past him to a dissimilar pair at the pool table. Each wore a dress shirt and slacks, but the resemblance ended there. One towered over the other, dark skin, long limbs, and sharp angles a contrast to the other's pasty complexion, rounded edges, and rumpled clothes. The latter used his shirttail to clean the end of his cue, leaving a bright blue streak. "Don't jinx me, Max." He painted a new layer of blue on the tip. "I got ten bucks on the line."

The last of Charm's tension gave way. Jimmy Lee Boudreaux had that effect on people. A short, pudgy exterior hid mischievous soul. Where Jimmy Lee was, a certain degree of chaos was soon to follow, and that meant fun or trouble, depending on which side of the altercation you were on.

Jimmy Lee had placed the eight ball next to the hole in the end pocket to his right. The cue ball sat near the rail, two-thirds of the way to the end pocket on his left. Between the two lay a wall of four balls set end to end, perpendicular to the rail. *Jump shot,* Charm guessed by the way he was sighting his cue.

"Your ass is mine if you tear the felt on that table," the bartender said. "You ain't paid me for the last one yet."

Jimmy Lee looked momentarily chagrined, then brightened. "If I make this shot, I can make a payment."

His buddy scoffed. "You been trying to make that shot since college."

Charm stepped forward. "He's been trying since high school." All eyes turned toward him. "Never could shoot pool worth a damn." He took the cue, but rather than pop the cue ball over the obstacles, he banked it off the left rail with significant backspin. Instead of angling up the table, the cue ball arced around the wall of balls, as if drawn by a magnet to the bottom right pocket. The eight ball dropped with a satisfying *clunk.* "No felt tearing required."

His audience broke into applause and laughter. "I defer to the master," Jimmy Lee said. He grasped Charm's hand and pulled him into a hug. "Welcome home."

"Takes a pro to make that shot," his tall friend said.

Something roughly the size of a grizzly bear's paw engulfed Charm's hand. He peered into the giant's smiling face. "Good God, Bird, what have they been feeding you?"

Henry Gannaway Jr.'s bony stature and hooked nose had earned him the nickname "Bird" in fifth grade. The nose hadn't changed, but the rest of him had grown. A lot. He stood at least six-eight, and his lean frame now resembled a jungle cat more than a sparrow. His stature wasn't all that made him stand out in Brother Jack's, though. He was, at least at first glance, the only African American man in the place.

Bird drew him toward the bartender. "Max, meet Charm Freeman, Collier's prodigal son and famous world traveler."

"And huckster," came a voice from the corner. The legs of a stool scraped on the wood floor, and a figure carrying a mug emerged from the shadows. "Don't forget that part of the story."

Charm's smile held firm. "Now, Oscar, I gave up the carnival life years ago." He held up his palms in surrender. "Professional huckster no more."

Oscar Strickland studied his beer, wiped a smudge from the rim, then took a long drink. When he finished, his lips turned up in a smile that didn't reach his eyes. "Who said anything about professional?"

Jimmy Lee threw his arm around Charm's shoulders. "Christ, don't start." He and Bird grabbed their drinks and steered Charm to the nearest booth. "Mags, more beer!" he yelled to a passing waitress.

Bird slid in beside Jimmy Lee, folding his long legs into the cramped space underneath. "I don't guess we have to ask what brought you to town."

"Yeah, tough about Jake," Oscar said. He ignored a glare from Charm and dragged a chair from a neighboring table to the end of the booth, turned it backwards, and straddled it. "He was a good guy."

Jimmy Lee tipped his glass to their absent friend and took a healthy gulp. "Saved my bacon on more than one occasion."

"How's Elle doing?" Oscar asked.

"She's…Ellie." The tightness in Charm's chest was back. He

swiped Jimmy Lee's beer and took a swig. "Just as stubborn as she was at twelve. And just as angry."

Jimmy Lee shook his head. "That's the grief talking. She hasn't been angry since she married Jake."

"So, Freeman, if you're not a carnie anymore, what have you been doing with yourself all these years?" Oscar asked. "And how long are you staying?"

Charm looked sharply at him. "Just tonight." He hesitated, then lied, "I've been traveling, mostly."

"Is that code for homeless?"

"He's been traveling all over the world, like he said he would," Jimmy Lee burst in before Charm could reply. "China and Everest and shit like that."

Oscar's eyebrows raised, and he looked Charm up and down. "You've climbed Everest?"

*Shit, shit, shit, shit.* Charm sipped his beer and resisted the urge to suck in his gut. "Just to base camp. I'm not a climber."

"You win the lottery or something?"

"Nope." Charm kept his voice light. "You'd be amazed at how cheap you can travel. Hostels, Europass. All you need is a backpack and a passport." The beer made the lies easier.

"So you took a backpack and rode Eurail to the Everest base camp? Was that via the north or south side?"

Charm met his eyes with a smile. Thank God he'd been rereading *Into Thin Air.* "No Eurail. Through Khumbu on the Nepalese side of the mountain. American outfit hired me to guide tourists to the summit. Work with the Sherpas, keep the people happy, that sort of thing."

"Yeah, that sort of thing." Jimmy Lee glowered at Oscar. "Mags! Where's that beer?"

A tray with four tall mugs and a basket of popcorn appeared in front of them. "Don't get your panties in a wad, Jimmy Lee," said the waitress. "You're a long way from sobriety."

Jimmy Lee relieved her of the tray. "Put Charm's beer on my tab." He lifted his mug in a toast. "A welcome home present. Hey, Freeman, you remember my sister, Maggie, right?"

Charm had been too eagerly finishing off the first beer to notice the waitress at first, but now he looked up and blinked. "Magpie?" Only a splash of freckles across her nose remained of the skinny kid he had known. She resembled her brother, except her hair was worn long and smooth in a ponytail instead of short and chaotic, and her extra pounds were — he leaned back to get a better look — much better distributed.

The young woman laughed. "No one has called me that since I was ten."

"That's the last time anyone else got a word in. Ow!" Bird flinched away, rubbing the shoulder she had punched.

"Shut up, Henry." She tilted her head to the side. "The last time I saw you," she said to Charm, "you were threatening to float my Hermione doll down Fox Creek."

"That's because you were spying on me and Jessica Taylor." He appreciated the way her Brother Jack's T-shirt stretched across her breasts. Excellent advertising. Then he noticed how she had relaxed against Bird and how his arm had slipped around her. Their left hands, adorned with matching silver rings, intertwined. "You two are…" He motioned back and forth.

"Married," she confirmed. "Five years."

"Long years," Bird said. "Ow!" She had thumped him that time. "What about you?"

"Normal years, I'd say. Last year was pretty quick, all things considered." He sipped his beer, willed his heart to slow its sudden drumbeat, and hoped Maggie would get called away. That kid with the laptop probably needed a refill.

She rolled her eyes. "Are you married?" She drew out the word as if he had trouble understanding. "Living with someone? Dating?"

"Nope. Free agent. Is the food any good here?"

Jimmy Lee ignored his question. "What about that French chick?" He tried to shove a handful of popcorn into his mouth but scattered most across the table. "Sandy? Sandra? Something?"

*Sandrine, his laughing dark-haired angel.* Charm watched Jimmy Lee herd the stray popcorn kernels into a pile. She used to do that — make piles of crumbs at the table, then brush them into her hand

and put them in a tiny, careful heap on the corner of her plate. It's what she was doing the first time he saw her. *She laughed when he commented on it. "I suppose I should try to blame it on being French, but truly it is simply me." Her lack of self-consciousness captivated him. She extended her hand. "I'm Sandrine."*

He pushed the memory — and the pain — away. "Ancient history." He took a long drink, and when he set the mug down, his usual mask of nonchalance had clicked firmly into place. "So, if you're up for a good time tonight, Magpie…" He grinned and ducked to avoid the popcorn Bird threw.

"Dude, that's my sister," Jimmy Lee groused.

Maggie laughed. The door opened, and she waved to a couple who entered. "Have a seat anywhere. I'll be right with you," she called. In a lower voice, she mused, "They're early. Must be the funeral."

Charm squinted at the couple. At first glance, they looked like everyone else. He was mid-fifties or so. She was younger, forty maybe, and trying hard to look even younger. Dressed down compared to the people who'd come straight from the funeral. But they stood out. Others noticed it too. Much of the conversation in the bar had stopped when they came in, and people watched as they bypassed the tables and made their way to the group at the bar, where they were greeted enthusiastically. "Who are they?"

"Ray and Emerson Forbes." Maggie gathered the tray and empty mugs and stood straight. "Y'all need anything else?"

Jimmy Lee drained his glass and dropped it on her tray. "More beer."

"How'd I guess?" She winked at Charm and headed back to the bar.

He turned his attention back to the couple. "Forbes. The kid mentioned a Forbes. Something about a dog."

"Yeah, that's him." Bird craned around to see them. "Holier-than-thou type, moved here about five years ago. Always has to have the best of everything. Best cars, best house."

"And best dog." Oscar abruptly stood up. He dug a couple of bills out of his wallet and tossed them on the table. "Y'all have a good evening." Without another word he strode from the restaurant, nodding curtly to Ray Forbes as he passed.

Charm watched him go. "What was that about?"

Jimmy Lee shoved another handful of popcorn into his mouth. "Oscar's the one who talked Forbes into buying that dog. It's some kind of huntin' dog from New Zealand or Australia or somewhere. Oscar convinced him it could run field trials here and be worth a lot of money in stud fees. Only when it got here, he couldn't do a thing with it."

"So Oscar works for Forbes?"

"Worked. Past tense. Forbes wasn't thrilled to have dropped a ton of money on a dog that couldn't be trained to do what he wanted."

"I don't get it. What's the big deal? Aren't there dogs like that here? Why import?"

"Dog's a rare breed — a curly coat. And curlies don't run field trials. Oscar said there's, like, one up in Michigan or Minnesota or something running in…Derby? Qualifying? I don't remember what Oscar said. Not Open."

Open must be the most competitive. Charm made a mental note to ask about it later. "So how'd the kid get him?"

"Not sure exactly. Forbes tried other trainers, but the dog was a complete washout. I mean, he may have been good wherever he was from, but American field trials are a whole different game, you know?" Charm didn't know, but whatever. "So anyway, somehow Forbes ended up hiring Jake to train the dog."

"Jake was a field trainer?"

"Nope. He'd trained a dog or two of his own but nothing competitive. No clue why Forbes would hire him."

A raucous cheer erupted at the bar. Judging from the smirk on Forbes's face, Charm assumed he had just bought a round. *Nothing like spreading a few dollars around to make yourself feel superior. Rich bastard.* "So what happened to the dog? Ellie said it was in the accident."

Jimmy Lee shrugged. "To my knowledge, livin' in Forbes's kennel."

Interesting. Charm mulled that information as he nursed his beer and watched Forbes. Unlike the others who had clearly come straight from the funeral, Forbes and his wife wore casual clothes.

But not inexpensive ones. Not many of the farmers in Collier sported two-hundred-dollar Timberland work boots.

The door rattled again, this time as a group of women came in, their laughter floating past the crowd up front to the back of the bar. Charm recognized one as the woman he'd seen in Ellie's kitchen. He kicked Jimmy Lee under the table. "Hey, who's that?"

Jimmy Lee and Bird both turned around. "Which one?"

"The hot one — tall, Black girl."

"That's Angeline," Jimmy Lee replied. "She's from Holly Springs. Her brother…what's his name?"

"Marcus Brown," Bird said.

"Right. Marcus Brown. You remember him, right? He was their quarterback when we were in high school. Anyway, she teaches over at the elementary school."

Angeline and her friends crowded into a booth near the door. Charm watched her hold the entire table enthralled with an animated recounting of some anecdote. The woman closest to her in the booth had to duck more than once to avoid Angeline's flying hands. He suppressed a grin. Those lively hands were sexy as hell. As if she felt his gaze, she looked past her friends and met his eyes. She paused no longer than it took her to draw a breath and flicked a wave his direction, then went back to her story.

Charm suppressed thoughts of Sandrine and appreciated the view at Angeline's table a while longer, suddenly regretting he was in town only one night. Remembering why he had come to town in the first place shifted his attention back to Ray Forbes and the dog in his kennel. If the dog was still in the kennel, it was probably fine, and Ellie was worrying about nothing.

The conversation at his table had turned to high school football. He tuned it out and sat back, an idea brewing. Maybe he'd be able to make it up to Ellie and her kid in one fell swoop.

"Another beer, Charm?" Maggie had appeared with a tray of frothy mugs.

He traded her his empty. One more, to celebrate his great idea. This trip to Brother Jack's had been unexpectedly fortuitous. He lifted his beer in a toast. "To lucky coincidences."

# CHAPTER 4

This was the first night Elle hadn't cried herself to sleep. Crying would take energy she didn't have. The first wave of visitors found excuses to leave shortly after Charm's dramatic exit, but others stopped by throughout the day and well into the evening. It had been after eight thirty before her mother firmly escorted the last of them to the door, and after checking on Lucas once more, she herself finally left with a grudging, "Call if you need me."

Right. Like Elle didn't have enough problems. Her head spun with them. Problems like how to heal a nine-year-old's broken heart — and broken body. How to run a farm single-handedly. And how to pay for her husband's funeral.

*My husband's funeral.* She ran the phrase through her head a couple of times, tasted it, but no involuntary sob burst forth, no righteous cursing or blaming God, no shudder of fear that curled her into a self-protective ball. Just emptiness and exhaustion. Maybe they'd buried her heart along with the man she loved.

The clock flipped to 1:37, and a twinge of annoyance pierced the numbness. Where the hell was Charm with her truck? Charm. Despite her current frustration, the corner of her mouth turned up in an involuntary smile. He had called her "Ellie," as if she were still the ten-year-old little sister who worshipped him.

The familiar chug of her truck's engine and the crunch of tires on the gravel driveway interrupted her reverie. *Finally*, she thought, and muscles she hadn't realized were tight began to relax. She settled into her pillow but had no more than shut her eyes when sudden repetitive blares from the horn drove her to her feet. "Christ on a cracker!"

Flashing back to the day the police came to tell her about the accident, she sprinted down the hall and stairs and, with a swipe at the switch for the porch light, out the front door. Multiple scenarios flashed through her trauma-scarred mind, each more terrible than the last. *Not again, not again, not again….*

The pickup turned sharp left onto the lawn and rattled toward the house. Elle froze at the edge of the front porch and shielded her eyes against the glare of the headlights. With a squeak and a series of clunks, the old truck came to an abrupt stop inches from the steps. Still blinded, she had to squint to recognize the lanky figure climbing out of the front seat.

"Charm?"

"Wait till you see what I've got." He grabbed her arm and pulled her down the steps to the back of the truck. "Ta-da!"

Frosty grass crunched under her bare feet. Still trying to figure out the emergency, she shifted her weight from one foot to the other and stared at the inky lump in the truck bed. This? This was why he woke up everybody in the county? This was why he scared her to death? "What the hell are you doing?"

"Making your son's dreams come true." He tugged on a rope, and the inky lump stood and transformed into a haggard-looking dog.

Charm's voice was a bit too jovial. She peered at him. "Are you drunk?"

He poked a finger in her chest. "You have a gift for the irrelevant. Focus on the obvious." He gestured to the dog again and repeated, "Ta-da!"

The retriever she'd last seen just before Christmas stood

motionless, head hanging as if it lacked the energy to lift it. She wouldn't have recognized it as the same dog if it weren't for his distinctive curly coat. "What's he doing here?"

"I talked to Mr. Forbes, and he was happy to help."

"I bet he was." She skirted around the back to get a better look. Too dark to see much, but he seemed smaller than she remembered. A loop of rope tethered him to the truck.

Her brother patted her shoulder. "You don't have to worry. River came through the accident fine. Except for a couple of little, minor issues."

Elle untied the makeshift collar. "You don't tie a dog in the back of a pickup like this. You want him to hang himself? Couldn't Forbes loan you a crate?" She opened the tailgate and patted it. "Come on, dude. Let's get you in the pen. It's too frickin' cold to deal with this tonight." River twitched an ear but made no move to jump down.

Charm stepped in and set him on the ground. "See, about the crate and the pen. That's the issue. It seems after the accident he has a thing about small spaces."

She arched her eyebrow. "He's a hunting dog that can't be kenneled?" River, oblivious to the discussion about him, sniffed the ground and then looked toward the house, ears pricked. He trotted up the stairs, used his paw to open the screen door enough to get his nose in, and disappeared inside. Elle stalked after him, trembling now from anger instead of fear or cold. "Idiot!"

Charm followed close behind. "What's your problem? I'm trying to help."

She whirled around, sending him stumbling back against the porch rail. "By giving me more to do? Who's going to take care of that dog? Who's going to train him? Lucas? He can't even get out of bed."

He glared. "Maybe this'll give him a reason to." He pushed past her and stomped inside.

Elle filled her lungs with cold air to tamp down flames of temper in her gut. *That dog. Why did it have to be that dog? If it weren't for that damn dog, Jake would still be alive.* Tears spilled down her cheeks, and a wave of overwhelming defeat nearly dropped her where she stood.

"Oh, Jake. I don't think I can do this."

A sound floated down the stairs and out the front door. Her breath caught, and she listened. A giggle. Lucas's giggle — the first laugh she'd heard from him since the accident.

Fierce protectiveness rose in her chest. If she didn't do it, who would? She sniffled, wiped her eyes on her sleeve, and banished the desire to hide under her blankets back to whatever dark place from which it had emerged. She could do it because she had to do it. And if that dog made her son happy, she guessed she could deal with that too.

* * *

Despite the late night, Elle woke early. Barely five thirty, dawn not yet a hint in her east-facing window this time of year, but duty loomed no matter how much she wanted to sink back into her blankets. Morning chores used to be shared among the three of them: Jake fed the large animals, Lucas milked the goat and took care of the chickens, and she made breakfast and lunches.

Neighbors had covered the farmwork since the accident, but she'd told them yesterday she was ready to take it on again. Simultaneously dreading the magnitude of the work and anticipating the opportunity to do something, anything, other than focus on the accident, she slipped out of bed and into the shower and let the warm water wash away the last of the sleep fog. Lost in the mental organization of the tasks ahead, she was halfway down the stairs before a bark pulled her up short. River. Damn it. She had completely forgotten the dog, who had climbed into bed with her son and settled in like he belonged there.

Lucas's voice drifted into the hallway. "Mommm…"

She sighed and turned back. The dog tried to push past her when she opened the door, but she blocked him with a glare and a well-placed knee.

Lucas peered up from his pillow with bleary eyes. "River needs to pee."

*Then take him*, she wanted to say. *Or tell Charm to take him. He's the one who brought the mutt here.* But she swallowed her recriminations and grabbed the dog by the collar. "Go back to sleep."

River stood tall for a retriever, but not so tall that a woman of Elle's height could easily lead him by the collar. They slid and stumbled their way down the stairs to the front door where he waited with single-minded focus, nose pressed into the crack between the front door and the frame, until she managed to turn the deadbolt and pull the door open. Her fingers tightened barely in time to keep him from dashing out. Damn dog. If he got loose in the flat early morning light, she'd never find him.

He made a second dash attempt on the porch stairs, and she grabbed at the railing to catch herself. The stressed wood groaned and swayed. She managed to keep her feet but lost ground to the dog determined to pull her to the closest tree. The rope from the night before lay where they had left it — in the back of the pickup parked on her front lawn. A quick knot turned it into a serviceable leash, freeing River to do what he wanted, namely lift his leg on her favorite oak.

When he finished, the energy that had nearly sent her tumbling ass over teakettle vanished. He sniffed disinterestedly at the tires of the truck, dropped his butt to the ground, and waited. Odd. The week before Christmas, River had bloodied Lucas's nose in an ill-timed bolt after one of the rabbits that typically dotted her lawn at this hour. Today he pricked his ears when one hopped around the corner of the house but didn't so much as whine.

Something wasn't right. Elle squinted at him, trying to decipher what it was, but all she saw was a black, curly-haired dog waiting to go inside. She obliged, delivering him to Lucas's room where he climbed, one long leg after another, onto Lucas's bed, stretched out the length of the boy's torso, and closed his eyes with a sigh. Without bothering to order him off, she shut the door and headed downstairs. Waking Charm to help with chores occurred to her as she passed his door, but she dismissed the thought with little more than an uncharitable grumble. This was her house, and Charm wasn't going to be here after today.

In the kitchen, the coffeepot sat cold and empty. Jake used to set the coffee maker up before he came to bed so he could fill a thermos on the way out the door. The carafe held enough for the thermos plus one cup, but he always left her two, one for her to drink while making breakfast and one for her drive to work. Exactly the right amount every day.

She picked up the carafe, stuck her nose inside, and breathed deep, the faint scent of a thousand pots of coffee conjuring the ghost who made it every bit as much for her as for himself. The memories swirled around her until the imperious neigh of a hungry horse pierced the fog. Animals before coffee. Setting up the coffee maker at night would have to go on the daily to-do list.

She pulled on her heavy Carhartt jacket, tugged a wool cap down over her ears, and exchanged her tennis shoes for muck boots. Just drizzle so far this week, but the forecast promised wet days ahead. Better safe than sorry. *Gloves, gloves, gloves.* She checked her pockets and the floor and the cabinet above the washer. No gloves. No worries though. The physical labor would keep her hands warm.

She repeated that thought to herself one hour and a new bruise on her knee later as she wrestled a recalcitrant goat with a zero-tolerance policy for icy hands on her udder. To make it worse, even as the damn goat kicked and danced and avoided Elle's cold hands, the animal bleated incessantly because her udder was too full.

After a lucky strike to the other knee and a short (very close) debate with herself about having goat for dinner, Elle took the only option left to her: she put both herself and the goat in time-out and cried on a hay bale while her hands warmed under her shirt. After a few minutes of deep breathing, she tried again. By eight o'clock she'd managed to milk the goat without bloodshed and finish feeding the remaining animals.

As she worked, she added to her mental to-do list. Her neighbors had kept the place going since the accident, but they had focused on the things that had to be done right away, not the small-but-critical tasks that rapidly piled up when neglected. *Things Jake would have done.* She banished that thought. *Not going there. Jake isn't here. I am, and I can do this.* Chickens clucked contentedly as they pecked at scratch she'd tossed for them. *I did do it.*

Mostly. Water troughs needed to be scrubbed out and refilled, but that would have to wait for another day. Today she'd have to settle for topping them off. She stretched and rolled her shoulders and looked toward the house. Lucas would be awake again soon if he wasn't already. Water could wait another hour. Time to make breakfast.

*But first,* she thought as she stripped off her outerwear, *coffee.* Finally. While she waited for the heavenly nectar to brew, she thumbed through a dangerously high stack of mail collecting on the end of the counter since…when? Since the accident? Christ on a cracker.

She scooped the pile into her arms and dumped it in the center of the kitchen table. Junk mail? Easy sort: straight into the recycle bin. Sympathy cards, on the other hand, needed energy and personal attention. She stacked them unopened in a pile to her left to go through later. Finally, only bills, correspondence from the insurance company, and myriad official-looking letters remained in front of her. With a deep breath, she dove in.

Two medical bills on top. She tried not to wince at the amounts due. God bless health insurance. Their high deductible would hurt, but they could manage. Probably. She made a mental note to ask about payment plans. Next, a utility bill. She opened it and stared at it, puzzled. "That doesn't make sense," she said out loud. She set it aside and opened the letter from the bank below it. Her stomach dropped.

Feeling ill, Elle pushed back from the table and scooted the chair to the desk in the corner Jake had used as an office. She flipped through the checkbook, but it didn't tell her much. Damn it. She was going to have to tackle The Beast. "The Beast" was the not-so-loving nickname she'd given to the old PC Jake used, purchased when he was still in high school. It ran Windows ME and not much else. That suited Jake fine. He could check email and access the internet, track his hay and cattle production in an Excel spreadsheet, and keep the family books in an ancient version of Quicken.

Elle opened the latter. What the dinosaur program lacked in bells and whistles, it made up for in straightforward data. It took her only a couple of minutes to find specific expenses and view their history.

Which didn't make sense. She clicked through. None of it made sense.

She wasn't sure how long she stared at the screen before Lucas's voice pierced her focus. She blinked and came back to herself. Lucas called her again. "I'm coming," she shouted back. She powered down the computer, shoved the bills into a desk drawer, and rose on trembling legs.

"I'm hungry," Lucas announced when she got upstairs. He was sitting up in bed playing tug with River using one of the nice black socks he wore to church.

She ignored the sock. "Your uncle will make breakfast for you. I need to run an errand." She held up a hand to stop the coming complaint. "It's an emergency. I'll be back as soon as I can. You aren't going to starve to death." Lucas set his mouth in a pout and probably would have complained anyway, but Elle shut the door before he had a chance.

She strode down the hall and into the guest room without knocking. Charm lay sprawled across the bed wrapped in the patchwork quilt and wearing, at least on the body parts she could see, the clothes he'd worn the day before. A pillow covered his eyes to keep the sunlight streaming through the window from disturbing him. Obviously closing the drapes confounded her brother as much as getting undressed and under the covers.

"Charm." She tapped his ankle. When he didn't respond, she gave his leg a shake. "Charm!"

He startled awake mid-snore, thrashed loose of the quilt, and lifted the pillow from his face. "Wha——? Ellie? What the fuck?" He squinted against the light. "Christ, my head hurts. What time is it?"

She swallowed the urge to drop the clock from his nightstand on his head. "I have to run an errand. I need you to watch Lucas."

"What? Lucas? No. No, I can't watch…anybody." He pulled the quilt to his chin and curled into a sleeping position. "I'm not staying. I'm leaving as soon as…when I wake up…"

Elle pulled the quilt off, ignoring his protest. "I don't have time for this. Did you come to help me or not?"

He growled but grudgingly cracked open his eyes.

"I need you to watch Lucas for a couple of hours. Starting now."

"Can't Mom do it?"

She arched her eyebrow. "Seriously?"

He managed to grin. "Good point." He stretched and rolled to his back. "Okay. What do you need?"

"I have to go into town. Lucas hasn't had breakfast yet and may need help getting dressed." She turned and started out the door, then stopped. "Oh, and the animals haven't been watered yet. Just top off the water buckets and drain the hose when you're done."

His groan followed her down the stairs. She was in her truck and out of the driveway before it occurred to her that she hadn't thanked him.

* * *

The only bank in town, the Citizens Bank of Collier, established 1880, resided in a brick building on the north edge of the town square, between the town's only realty office and one of its many antique shops. The old square had undergone revitalization in recent years as the town's population grew, resulting in a mix of original businesses catering to the everyday needs of the locals and trendy shops trying to cash in on the weekend antiques hunters.

Elle drove up fifteen minutes before the bank opened and parked in an angled space in front. Normally, she would have popped into the café around the corner for a chocolate croissant or, if the weather was nice, taken a walk around the landscaped park in the center of the square. Today she drummed her fingers on the steering wheel and watched the front door until Bud Yarber, the bank manager, unlocked it.

"I hate doing this, Elle," he said a few minutes later, after he'd shut the door to his office and rolled back to his desk.

As long as Elle had known him, which was pretty much her entire life, Bud had been "the guy with one leg." She remembered her father whispering to her when she was little that Bud had lost his leg in a combine accident, but to her he was the bushy-haired guy on crutches who gave out lollipops. Losing his leg hadn't slowed him down much, at least not by the time Elle knew him, but as years passed, his hair got thinner, his belly got bigger, and he elected to use a wheelchair more and more often. Elle found herself watching him and wondering if this was a vision of Lucas's future.

Bud pecked at his computer's keyboard and squinted at the screen. "I hate it," he repeated, "but I don't have any choice. Your mortgage is six months behind." He turned the monitor around so she could see it.

She refused to look. "This is impossible. Jake would have told me."

He looked sad. "I don't think he meant to keep it from you. Men need to feel like they can provide for their families. I expect his pride was hurt."

"His pride? I'm going to lose my home because of his pride?" Anger drove her to her feet, and she paced in front of his desk. Where would they go if they lost the house? What would they do without the farm's income?

"No. No, I'm not going to let this happen. There has to be a way to stop this." Tears spilled onto her cheeks, and she brushed them away. "You had to be working with Jake. Things didn't get this bad overnight."

"We've been working on it for a year and a half, ever since —"

"Those damn storms." She rubbed her temples. Eighteen months ago a series of storms with multiple tornadoes had swept through the county. No human lives lost — mainly property damage — but they lost half their herd and most of their corn. Jake had assured her they had enough in savings to make it through. "Give me the same deal you gave Jake."

He shook his head. "Jake had an income —"

"Jake had a farm, the same farm I have."

"You have medical bills and, I'm sorry to say it, a crippled son."

"He's not crippled!"

Neither his voice nor his gaze wavered. "Injured, then. Any cash you have is gonna get eaten by doctors, and your time will be taken by your son. Cows and crops don't grow themselves."

"You haven't even given me a chance. What do you have to lose this time of year? It'll sit on the market for months." She saw a glimmer of acknowledgment. "Jake's life insurance payment is coming. I'll pay the mortgage plus half every month. Be current in a year."

Bud rubbed the back of his neck. "I've got board members I'm accountable to. They won't —"

"Six months, then. Give me six months, and you save the cost of foreclosure. You know you can't sell it now anyway." Her voice dropped to a whisper. "Please."

Indecision and sympathy warred on his face. Finally, he gave a curt nod. "Six months. Bring it current and stay current. You fall behind, and I won't have a choice."

Unshed tears caught in her throat. "Thank you," she managed to say.

Every eye watched her when she slipped out of Bud's office. She schooled her features into a polite mask and walked calmly to the women's restroom. As soon as the lock clicked, her knees gave way.

The enormity of her situation sucked the breath from her lungs as she sank to the floor. Jake had admitted things were "tight." Things weren't tight. They were absolutely *drowning* in debt. And she had *lied*. There was no life insurance. Jake had let the policy lapse last year.

She hugged herself and rocked back and forth, her breath coming in short, desperate gasps. *Don't fall apart. We have a second chance. Just breathe. Breathe.*

A sudden knock refocused her. "Are you all right?" a kind voice called in.

Elle wiped her cheeks. "I'm fine," she replied, hoping the tremble in her voice wasn't obvious. "I'll be right out." She climbed shakily to her feet, stepped to the sink to splash cold water on her face, then studied her reflection. The face in the mirror looked...defeated. That wouldn't do. *What would your mother say, Elle girl?*

She blotted her face dry, ran her fingers through her hair to bring some semblance of order to her curls, and rubbed her finger over her lips to give them some color. Then she turned the corners of her mouth up in what she hoped would pass for a pleasant smile. Ignoring the eyes following her, she made her way to the front door of the bank. *Just a little longer.*

The door opened, and she stepped aside to allow two women to enter. Elle groaned inwardly. *Oh no, not Gert —*

"Elle!" Gertie Pritchett's voice, easily an octave higher and a hundred decibels louder than anyone else's, screeched when she caught sight of her. "How are you doing?" She grabbed Elle's hand and patted it in an enthusiastic show of sympathy. "How's your precious little boy? I was just telling Janelle that your sweet, sweet family has been at the top of our prayer list ever since that awful accident."

"Absolutely," her companion, Janelle Hinton, said earnestly. "It's positively tragic what happened to Jake. Everyone's talking about it."

*I bet they are,* Elle thought, but she kept the ungracious thought to herself. As church organist and secretary, Gertie felt led to direct the church's prayer chain. And the gossip chain. It wouldn't do to give her any more fodder than the accident already had. "I appreciate your prayers, but we're doing just fine. Lucas gets better every single day."

"Such a miracle," Janelle said clasping her hands together in a display of piety. "And you're so blessed to have your brother come to town."

And there was the target of the whole conversation. Charm. Her life was falling apart, and all these women cared about was the reappearance of her prodigal brother. With great effort, Elle kept her expression neutral. "A true blessing." She squeezed Gertie's hand and tried to look sincere. "So sorry to cut this short, but I have to get back to Lucas."

She exchanged polite goodbyes with the women and walked out of the bank. "You let us know if there's anything — anything at all — we can do!" they called behind her.

One foot in front of the other to her truck. *Just keep it together.*

*Good. Back the truck out and drive. Just drive.* She didn't know where she was going. It didn't matter as long as she could escape the oppressive sympathy oozing at her from every person she passed.

Her truck drove automatically to the one she always relied on to give her strength. He wasn't at the house where he belonged, of course. He had a new place in the cemetery. She parked where the limo had been the day before, but rather than going to the grave, she stayed in the truck and did what she couldn't do at the bank or at home: she screamed.

"I hate you!" she railed when she was able to form coherent words. Cries of rage tore at her throat. "Why?" She slammed her fists on the steering wheel. "Why, why, why?" Her fists pounded the window, the steering wheel, and the seat beside her again and again until the only energy she had left reduced her to bone-shaking sobs.

When the sobs faded to sniffles, she stumbled out of the pickup and made her way to the grave. Her knees buckled, and she collapsed next to the mound of dirt. She managed to pound the dirt one time before succumbing to another wave of tears.

When even crying was too much effort, she stretched out on her back next to the mound and stared at the sky. Rocks, or maybe just little clods of dirt, poked uncomfortably under her left hip and right shoulder, but she didn't bother to move. Yesterday, the overwhelming scent of lilies had made her gag. The floral scent had vanished, replaced by the clean scent of freshly turned earth.

After her emotional outburst, nothing remained but an odd sense of peace. A distant part of her still wanted to yell and scream and pound on the dirt. He deserved that and more for the state he had left them in. But she just stared at the sky. Maybe she'd yell more later. In a little while she was going to have to get up and be strong and deal with this new disaster. And all the old disasters. But none of that had to happen right this minute. Right now all she wanted was to lie where she was and be as close to her husband as she could.

- 60 -

# CHAPTER 5

Shirtfront soaked and water dripping from his ears, Charm stomped up rickety steps to the side porch. "Top off the water buckets," he grumbled. He paused on the doorstep, tried to squeeze out his shirt, and swore under his breath, the words forming frosty vapor-like puffs. He dug his flask out of his back pocket and took a healthy swallow. It was too damn cold for this.

The temperature inside wasn't much better. *Jesus, hasn't Ellie ever heard of heat? Even Mom —* but he didn't get to finish the thought. A shrill voice rang out and pushed everything else from his mind: "Help! Uncle Charm, help!"

He acted. Imagined scenes of blood and mayhem drove him up the stairs three at a time. *Fall from bed. Dog attack. Fire.* Into his nephew's room, braced for the horror awaiting him.

An unharmed Lucas was sitting up in bed, arms crossed, glaring. When Charm burst in, Lucas's mouth dropped open. "What happened to you?"

"Your hose is a menace."

The boy nodded sagely. "Been there."

Charm scanned the room, still trying to identify a threat. Nothing appeared out of the ordinary. Mostly empty dishes lay on a tray shoved toward the foot of the bed, a glass of orange juice untouched on the nightstand. A video game was paused on the TV, the controller abandoned beside him. Charm frowned. "What's wrong? Why did you yell?"

Lucas stuck his lower lip out in a pout. "You left me alone. I've been stuck up here for hours."

"I set up your Xbox thirty minutes ago. I brought you a juice refill ten minutes before that and served you breakfast ten minutes before that."

"River's bored."

Charm arched his eyebrow. The retriever lay on his side on the floor next to Lucas's bed. At the sound of his name, his tail thumped twice on the hardwood. "And what do we do about that?"

"He needs exercise. Carry me outside so I can play with him," he ordered.

"What am I, a horse? You've got crutches."

"It hurts, and I'm not allowed to do the stairs."

Non-weight-bearing exercise only, Charm remembered his mother mentioning to someone yesterday. Ellie owed him a cold six-pack when she got home. His stomach lurched a bit, and he gave it a mental pat. A little hair of the dog would set it right. Dog. River. *Focus, Freeman.* He picked up the crutches and held them out. "I'll help."

Had the boy been unable to get to his feet or continued to complain about the pain, Charm might have given in and carried him, but Lucas's sullen manner disappeared as soon as he was on his feet. "Come on, River!"

"Wait." Charm peered critically at the boy's pajamas and bare feet. "Shouldn't you get dressed first?"

"Why? I spend my day in bed." He grabbed his robe from the bedpost and used a crutch to pull his slippers out from under the bed. "Happy now?"

"Thrilled. Do you need to pee? I'm not carrying you back inside in five minutes so you can pee."

"You sound like Mom," Lucas groused, but he let his uncle help him down the hall to the small bathroom they shared.

"Do you need help?"

"Do you?" Lucas slammed the door in his face.

Charm grinned. "And they said parenting was hard." River had followed them and now stood with his muzzle against the bathroom door. The dog glanced back at him and wagged his tail once, then pressed his nose in the crack under the door and exhaled.

"Hey, does this dog have a leash?" Charm called.

"I think Mom used a rope. It's in my room."

The rope, tied to a collar, lay on the dresser amid a stack of game cartridges, a plant that desperately needed water and sunlight, and half a dozen wads of paper Lucas had probably tried to toss in the garbage can. No water handy, but Charm opened the blinds and, after a moment's consideration, raised the window.

Lucas's room was one of two on the front of the house. As Charm had noticed the day before, rather than the road, the house faced the driveway and a pasture beyond. To the left were the barn and the various animal sheds he'd familiarized himself with earlier. A cool breeze brushed his face. It wasn't that much colder outside than in, and a few minutes of fresh air would greatly improve the — he sniffed — aroma of nine-year-old boy.

As his last good deed, Charm brushed the paper wads into the trash and looked around for anything else that should join them. A brightly colored piece of paper sticking out from under the pillow on the bed caught his eye. Candy wrapper. He smoothed out the green foil, guessing the name before he saw it. *Andes mints.* Jesus, he hadn't had these since he was a kid. They were the special candy his mother put out for guests. Only occasionally did he and Ellie get to eat one. Of course, he knew where she hid the box, so he might have had a few more than his share. Several of the green wrappers were stuffed into the crack between the mattress and the headboard. Charm pulled them out and saw a glint of silver. A phone?

"Uncle Charm!"

Lucas's voice startled him, and he stood up, silver object forgotten. He tossed the candy wrappers in the trash and strode to the bathroom. "Ready to go?" He fastened the collar around River's neck.

Lucas held tight to Charm's shoulder and grimaced as he hopped, carefully and with Charm bearing most of his weight, from stair to stair. "So if you're my uncle, how come — ow — how come I've never heard of you?"

Ellie hadn't even mentioned him? "I've been gone a long time, and…I wasn't good about staying in touch."

"How long?"

"Eighteen years." At the bottom of the stairs, Charm paused. "Hang here a second." He made sure Lucas had a grip on the banister, then dashed forward and opened the front door.

"Did you have a fight?" Lucas asked when they continued their trek.

"Not with your mom." Charm turned them toward the picnic table.

"Then why didn't you call her?"

Charm let River explore a bit and considered how much to tell his nephew. "When I was a teenager, I had a really big fight with our dad, and I ran away from home. When you run away, you don't call your family."

"Ever?" The boy thought about this for a moment. "I don't think I could ever get so mad at my parents I wouldn't talk to them. What was the fight about?"

"Traveling. My dad and I used to dream about traveling all over the world. It was our thing, you know? Did you have a thing like that with your dad?" Without waiting for the boy to answer, Charm continued. "But my dad stopped dreaming, and he thought I should stop too. I didn't want to."

"Did you travel?"

Charm bent down to look him in the eye. "I joined a carnival."

Lucas's eyes opened wide. "Cool!"

River lunged to reach a rhododendron, and the duo paused their conversation to let him sniff and lift his leg. Charm took his first good look at the dog. Not much to look at. Black. Tall. Ribby. Kind of like a skinny lamb. Too skinny. Charm cocked his head. There was something off about the dog, but he wasn't sure what. He knew one thing, though. For a dog that was bored, he seemed entirely disinterested in being outside. Pee opportunity aside, instead of running around and sniffing, he seemed content to follow the kid and lie at his feet.

Charm helped Lucas get settled at the picnic table. "What kind of dog is that anyway? A labradoodle?"

"No." The boy sounded annoyed. "He's a curly-coated retriever from New Zealand. He's gonna be a *champion.*"

Charm frowned, trying to picture the dog trotting around a show ring.

As if he could read his mind, Lucas clarified, "A field champion. He's a retriever. Dad and I are" — his voice caught — "were…Dad and I were training him for a field trial." His voice wobbled. "That was our thing."

*Shit, shit, shit.* Charm struggled for something, anything to say. "Your dad had a dog when he was your age."

The boy blinked through his tears. "You knew my dad?"

"We grew up together. He was my best friend." The truth was, Charm couldn't remember a time when he hadn't known Jake. They'd met in preschool and made a fast, rough-and-tumble friendship on the playground. He had only one clear memory from that age: Jake punching Lamar Barnes after Lamar knocked Charm off the slide. Good times.

"What was he — what was he like when he was a kid?"

Probably shouldn't mention the punching incident. "He was funny. Told jokes a lot. Bad jokes."

Lucas grinned. "I tell bad jokes too."

Charm looked him in the eye again. "I don't doubt it."

The boy erupted into something that was a mix of giggles and sobs, and River put his front paws on the bench and pushed between them to lick his face. Lucas buried his face in the dog's neck. River leaned into him for a moment, then extricated himself and flopped at his feet.

Lucas took a deep breath and straightened his back. "Was it a hunting dog?"

That movement, steeling himself like that, reminded Charm of Ellie. Of her strength. The kid regarded him with eyes that reminded him of Jake, but the stormy combination of pain and anger and, oddly, hope were all Ellie. Too old for a little boy.

Lucas tilted his head and lifted his eyebrows, waiting. Had he asked him something?

"You said my dad had a dog. Was it a hunting dog?"

Charm sat beside him. "Nah. It was this little ten-pound mutt. Ugliest thing I've ever seen. Weird snaggle teeth and a tongue that hung out the side." He screwed up his face to illustrate. "Smart though. Your dad had taught him a shi — a bunch of tricks."

Lucas wiped away the last tear. "My dad was a real good trainer. None of the others could train River, but my dad could." Deep breath. "Now I'm gonna do it. I have to."

Charm studied his hands. "I don't know much about dogs, but if you want some help —"

"No!"

The sharp tone brought his head up. The color had drained from the boy's face.

"No!" Lucas slammed River's rope to the ground to punctuate his words. "You can't!" He flailed at Charm, his fists landing harmlessly against his chest. "You can't do it!"

Charm jumped out of reach. "Hey, calm down."

"It's our project — mine and my dad's. Just go away. Go away!"

Charm backed away. "I-I think I forgot to water the horse." He fled.

The chestnut gelding nickered when he appeared in the barn. Charm paced and ran his fingers through his hair. What the hell? Ellie was going to kill him for upsetting the kid. Maybe he should simply leave like the kid said. *I can't leave. Ellie isn't home yet.* If she would kill him for upsetting him, she'd draw and quarter him for leaving him alone. He swore, dug out his flask, and took a quick swallow. Who in their right mind would leave him alone with a kid? *The sister I owe everything to, that's who.*

Charm groaned his frustration and grabbed and flung the first thing he could put his hands on — an empty feed bucket sitting on a square hay bale. The bucket slammed into some sort of tractor attachment that looked to Charm like a gaping metal mouth.

A large portion of the old barn overflowed with all manner of farm equipment and tools of destruction. The bucket should have done nothing more than bounce off, but the steel contraption was leaning against another piece of equipment — with wheels. One shifted, then the second, then began a Rube Goldberg–style chain reaction. Charm watched, mouth hanging open, as equipment clattered and fell around him, culminating with the tip of a ladder smashing into a huge pegboard of tools.

In a final crescendo, the entire thing collapsed with a deafening crash.

Before Charm could do more than stare at the carnage around him, a wail rang out. "Uncle Charm!"

The sheer anguish in his nephew's voice spurred Charm back outside. Lucas waved and pointed toward the field beyond the barn. "River!"

The dog no longer lay at the boy's feet. Heart pounding, Charm sprinted in the direction Lucas had pointed, using a thankfully sturdy post to vault the barbed wire fence, and saw…nothing. He looked around. Nothing but some disinterested cows toward the road. No black dog. He detoured through a gate and jogged back to his nephew.

"I don't see him. What happened?"

Tears streamed down the boy's face. "There was a loud bang" — Charm flushed and felt a pang of guilt — "and he got scared and ran away. He ran that way." He pointed into the field again.

Damn troublemaking dog. "I didn't see him, buddy. I'm sure he'll come back…"

"You have to find him. There's a swamp that way. He could get eaten by alligators. Or he'll get lost. Or get hit by a car." He grabbed Charm's arm and tugged him closer. "You have to find him, Uncle Charm, please."

*He's all I have left.*

The unsaid words stabbed Charm in the gut. "Okay, where should I go?"

"Other side of the pasture, through the fence, there's a trail."

Charm glared at him. "I'd better not get eaten by alligators," he grumbled, but he took off at a jog. After a couple of steps, he turned back around. "What about you?"

"I'm fine. You're wasting time!"

Charm ran. A cascade of blackberry vines partially concealed the trailhead, a dirt path just about the width of a nine-year-old boy. The occasional sneaker tread or paw print confirmed Lucas and River had come this way in the past, but he had no idea whether any of the tracks were new. They all looked the same to him. Daniel Boone he was not. He called, listened, and called again. Nothing. Not even the cracking of underbrush. He pushed forward, calling River's name again and again.

One swamp, two pastures, and three barbed-wire fences later, Charm stopped to catch his breath. His heart pounded, not only from exertion but also from rising panic. How did he even know the dog had gone this way? The trail had split back near the swamp. Maybe he'd turned the other way and gone toward the road. A vision of the dog lying dead on the pavement churned his stomach. Maybe he'd seen a rabbit and not followed the trail at all. Trail. What dog in his right mind followed a trail? He was a dog for Christ's sake.

He started forward again, and then stopped. This was stupid. He pulled out his flask, shook it, and groaned. What a time to hit empty. He shoved it back in his pocket and kicked at the ground. He wasn't going to find River out here. He'd probably already gone home. *But what if he hasn't?* Throat aching, Charm yelled the dog's name once more, and heard…something.

He froze in place and listened. Nothing. He shouted again, but the overgrown field he stood in seemed to hold its breath with him. Then the sound came again. A rustling, then a cry, not quite howl, not quite bark. Charm sprinted down the trail toward it, calling River's name.

The field turned to scrub cedar. Where was he? Charm pushed his exhausted legs faster, ducking under branches and zigzagging through close-packed trees.

"River? I'm coming, River. Where are you, boy?"

A strangled yelp and violent thrashing guided him off the path into a tangled mass of winter-dormant underbrush. *Where, where?* A flash of movement and distinctive curly black fur caught his eye.

The rope that served as leash had snagged around the post of yet another barbed wire fence. Old and unmaintained, the fence had become a trellis for kudzu, and the dog's efforts to free himself had served only to tangle him in a Gordian knot of leafless vines and rope. River wheezed and thrashed again, less violently this time. He was strangling to death.

Charm dashed in and fell to his knees. "Hold on, boy. I've got it. Just hold on."

But he didn't have it. Pulling at the vines or rope elicited more yelps and struggles and forced the dog's head into an unnatural position. He would have to cut it. His hands flew to his pockets. Nothing. With what? He scanned the area. Maybe a sharp rock or...

"Use these."

A pair of scissors appeared in front of him. He blinked and looked over his shoulder at the person offering them: his mother.

"Where did you..."

"You're in my backyard. I was getting something to free him with."

Charm blinked at her for another moment, then looked past her. Sure enough, not fifty feet ahead, just beyond the next bend in the path, the trees gave way to a chain-link fence and what appeared to be the backyard of a suburban home.

His mother crowded in beside him and wrapped her arms around River's chest and midsection. "He's in a hell of a state." She turned her head to avoid an errant branch. "What happened?"

"Some equipment fell, and he freaked." River flinched at the first touch of the scissors. "How'd you know he was back here?"

"Heard him. Sounded like he was being eaten by a bear."

Bears, alligators — Mississippi had become a dangerous place. The body beneath his hands trembled, and drool soaked the dog's chest. With each snip, freed legs scrambled against the dirt in an attempt to flee.

"Lucky he happened to end up here." He shot her a sideways glance.

She snorted. "Lucky for you. Lucas needs this dog. We need to call him and let him know he's safe."

A picture of Lucas sitting on the picnic table flashed through Charm's mind. Suddenly the air felt very cold. He paused his cutting. "Oh, shit."

"What?"

"Lucas is still outside. We were tossing that retrieving toy thing —"

"Finish this up. I'll drive you back."

He bent his head to his work. "Ellie's gonna kill me."

"Probably."

"Thanks for the support." One more snip. "Okay, that's everything but the rope holding his head. Can you hold him if I cut it?"

"Can you save a few inches above the loop? I've got a leash in the house."

That part of the rope angled back into the thickest part of the tangle. He forced the blades in as deep as they would go and sawed at the rope. When it broke, River gagged and barked and threw his body sideways. Charm grabbed him. "Get the rope!"

As she touched it, River twisted his head and pulled backward. *Screw this.* Charm scooped the struggling dog off his feet. "Jesus, how much does this mutt weigh?"

"Just get him inside the fence."

Charm expected him to bolt again when he set him down, but the dog shook himself and trotted around the yard sniffing in corners. His mother whistled, and River pressed his cheek against her thigh. She fondled his ears.

"Looks like he'll be okay. Let me get the leash and my key, and I'll drive you back."

River jogged ahead, arcing away from the brick patio to a set of outdoor stairs to a door over the garage. "Bob and Alva Matheson own the house," she said, as they trailed behind. "I watch the house when they travel, and they cut me a deal on the rent on the apartment."

She must have sold the house after his father passed away. But that wasn't what his brain focused on. "They travel?" Jealousy twanged in his gut. He remembered Bob Matheson as the janitor at his middle school.

"Alva is the queen of travel bargains. It's amazing how many places they've been able to go. I guess you can do anything if you put your mind to it." She opened the door. "Come on in. I won't be a minute."

Far less. It wouldn't take more than ten steps to explore the entire apartment — a far cry from the sprawling farmhouse they'd lived in when he was a boy. A small kitchen filled two-thirds of the back portion. A door in one corner led to what he assumed was the bathroom. The front half did double duty as living room and bedroom. A pull-out sofa, still pulled out, functioned as bed. *My, how the mighty have fallen.*

"Sorry for the mess," she said, rushing to close it up.

"It's fine."

Photos covered the walls and adorned flat surfaces. Family photos, mostly from what he called the "happy times." Not all, though. Pictures of his father stared at him from every angle. Impossibly young in some, a laughing man Charm barely recognized. The man he remembered in others, still laughing when Charm and Ellie were young, then grim and old before his time. Some Charm recognized not at all, pictures from the last decade of his father's life. An aged man, bent and angry in most, but incongruously smiling in others. Charm's gut twisted, and unexpected, unwanted tears filled his eyes.

He roughly brushed them away and covered them with a sniff and a cough. "You ready?"

His mother held up a leather leash and nodded. "Get the door behind you, please."

As he turned to grab the knob, his gaze fell on a bowl of candy wrapped in familiar, bright green foil. Interesting. He snagged a piece and followed her to her car. River climbed slowly into the back and lay with his head between the front seats.

"How often do you see Lucas?" Charm asked conversationally, once they were underway. He unwrapped the candy and popped it in his mouth.

She tilted her head and pursed her lips. "Not often enough. Eleanor doesn't trust me."

He snorted. "Do you blame her?"

"Yes, I do." She sounded somewhat surprised, as if she hadn't thought about it before. "She's holding on to a grudge she should have let go of years ago."

An old anger crawled under his skin, an itch he'd never been able to scratch. "The people who wronged us don't get to decide when we let go of our grudges."

"Your father was angry and in pain. I thought you'd understand that by now."

His gut twisted. "If by 'angry and in pain' you mean drunk and mean, I absolutely understand."

"He never laid a hand on you," she said coldly. "Stop exaggerating. Besides you —"

Charm grabbed the wheel. "Watch the road." He steered the car to the right of the center line. "Ellie doesn't need to deal with another accident." Convinced he wasn't going to die in the short term, he continued their conversation. "I what? I antagonized him? I brought it on myself? That's called gaslighting. He was a drunk."

Eyes firmly on the road, she leaned sideways and sniffed. "If you're not careful, people might think you are too."

Charm's mouth dropped open. "Ellie got me out of bed to take care of her kid. Sorry I didn't have a chance to shower. You know what? Never mind."

He crossed his arms and slouched against the door, painfully aware of the flask poking into his lower back. Yes, he liked to drink. But he never got sloppy, never missed work, never acted out. He was not an alcoholic. He was not his father. He would never be his father.

There was a 2:30 bus to Memphis. If Ellie was back, he was going to be on it. Wrong direction, but at least he'd be out of godforsaken *Collier*. His mind sneered the name. Eighteen years he'd played the "what if" game. What if he hadn't run away? What if he'd come back? What if he'd stayed in touch with his sister — or brought her with him in the first place? He was done with that shit. As soon as he got on that bus, Collier and everyone associated with it would be history.

"Uh-oh."

Charm looked up. They were turning into Ellie's driveway, and Ellie herself was standing in the front yard. She did not look happy. His mother paused at the end of the driveway. The two of them regarded his sister for a long moment.

"I don't think I'll stay," his mother said finally.

He nodded slowly. "That's probably a wise choice."

"Good luck."

No sarcasm colored her tone. He glanced at her and saw the opposite: empathy. He grunted and exited the car.

River climbed between the front seats and followed him. Charm caught him and snapped the leash on the collar before he could head back toward the road. *All I need is for the mutt to get hit now.* When it became clear the dog wanted nothing more than to get to the house, he dropped the leash and let him go. River broke into a trot and beelined for the porch. Charm wished he could do the same.

Ellie stalked toward him, hands balled into fists at her side. "What the hell were you thinking?" she demanded without preamble. "You left my son alone outside? In his pajamas? In January?"

"He told me he'd be fine." That sounded wrong even to his own ears. He tried again. "The dog freaked out. I thought I would catch him really quickly." That part wasn't exactly true, since he hadn't the foggiest idea where the dog had gone, but it sounded good. "I didn't mean to leave him alone. I didn't think —"

"You didn't think. There's a shock." She spun on her heel and marched toward the house. "You didn't think. Jake didn't think. Jake and that damn dog." She spun to face him again, and he nearly crashed into her. "I hate that dog." She backed him up with a finger in the chest. "I wish I'd never seen that dog."

He opened his mouth to speak, but she was off toward the house again. He jogged to catch up. "What is it with you? *That dog* lights your kid up from the inside out."

She paused on the porch stairs and shook her head. "And what would have happened to that light if you hadn't found him? How could Lucas deal with that on top of everything else?"

River sat at the door, waiting for someone to open it. Ellie trudged the last few feet and let him inside. She closed the screen behind him and rested her head against it. "Damn it, Jake," she whispered. She pounded her fist against the doorframe. "Damn it, Jake!" she yelled. "This is all your fault."

Charm reached for her. "Ellie…"

She jerked away and brushed tears from her cheeks. "He filled Lucas's head with this nonsense." She paced, pulling at her curls. "God, I hate him. I really hate him."

"No, you don't."

"I do! Everything is falling apart, and it's Jake's fault. He left a farm I can't run. Bills I can't pay. A son I can't reach because of a promise I can't fulfill. He left me —" Her voice broke with a sob. "He left me…."

He reached for her again, but she stepped away. "I can't." She took a shuddering breath and disappeared into the house.

Charm sighed, leaned on the porch railing, and desperately wished his flask weren't empty. Even his mother wouldn't begrudge him a nip in this situation. He groaned and buried his face in his hands. He'd really screwed up by getting River for the kid. *Couldn't take the time to think it through, could ya, Freeman?* One fuckup after another. Exactly like old times.

Ellie would be a lot better off when things got back to normal, and the first step toward that was him getting out of her hair. A short goodbye, and he could hoof it to the bus station. Or get Jimmy Lee to pick him up. Whichever.

Decision made, he headed into the house to find his sister. He found her in the kitchen obsessively wiping water spots off the clean dishes from the dishwasher. She would pull out a dish, hold it to the light, scrub furiously at imagined spots, hold it up again, and scrub again until she deigned it clean enough to go in the cabinet. He leaned against the doorframe and watched her clean dish after dish.

"Are you just going to stare at me?" she snapped finally.

"When you were a kid, you used to rearrange your books."

She lowered the glass she had been peering at and turned to face him. "What?"

"When you were pissed. You would rearrange your books over and over. By author. By title. By height. By color. You were creative."

She turned away and scrubbed at the glass again. "I'm not a kid anymore."

He didn't reply, simply waited and watched her scrub.

After two pots and a serving bowl, she said matter-of-factly, "We're behind on the mortgage and a bunch of other things. We may lose the house."

"Oh, Ellie."

She shrugged. "There was some bad weather a couple of years ago, and we lost a lot of cows and most of our crops. Jake…didn't tell me how bad it was."

"He was trying to protect you."

She glared and dropped into a chair at the table. "So I've been told."

He slid into a chair across from her, angry on her behalf. Even though he understood Jake's reasoning, it was still a shitty thing to do. Now Ellie couldn't even properly mourn her husband because she had to deal with this. Empathy replaced the anger. His situation in St. Louis had kept him from mourning Sandrine, hadn't it? Or that's what he told himself. That there was too much on his plate to deal with it. "What are you going to do?"

She sighed. "I have six months to get current on the mortgage."

"Can you do it?"

"Probably not," she said bluntly.

"Savings?"

She shook her head.

"Insurance?"

"No life insurance. Catastrophic medical, but the premium was astronomical. By itself, we could have managed, but with everything else…." Her voice trailed away. "First thing tomorrow, I'll talk to my boss about increasing my hours."

He blinked. "You have a job?"

The corners of her mouth turned up. "Yes, I have a job. Lots of farm wives do. I work as a clerk in the county clerk's office up in

Rolling Fork. Money isn't great, but it provides some benefits, gives us a bit of on-hand cash through the year, and covers my tuition."

"Tuition?"

She flushed. "I've been taking some classes at a community college down in Vicksburg," she mumbled. "Anyway…" She refocused on their conversation. "Maybe I can work some overtime and make some extra money."

"What about Lucas?"

She grimaced. "Mother can take care of Lucas."

"Oh, come on, the world isn't ending. Don't do something crazy."

She managed to laugh. "Nothing crazy." She took a deep breath. "We'll make it. No matter what, we'll make it."

Work full time, run a farm, take care of an injured kid — he could only imagine what rehab would be like. No, nothing at all crazy. "I can help," he heard himself say. *No, no, no! Shut up! Get on the bus!* "I can move in here and help with the farm and take care of the kid." *Don't listen to me! I left the kid outside this morning. Mom is better than me.*

She took a quivery breath. "But what about your traveling?"

"Forget my traveling," his mouth, which had clearly divorced itself from his brain, said. "I could maybe get a job in the evenings to help with cash too."

"No. I can't ask you to do that too. That's too permanent." She took a deep breath. "If you can stay for only a few months, long enough for Lucas to get back on his feet and me to catch up the mortgage, that's enough. More than enough. Thank you, Charm." She barely managed to get the last word out before tears spilled over her cheeks.

The look in her eyes reminded him of the way she used to look at him when he would distract their father, redirecting his wrath from her to him. He wondered how she had coped once he ran away. "You're welcome," he said quietly. "I owe you."

She gazed at him for a long moment, and then nodded. "Oh God," she said suddenly, sitting up straighter. "I should check on Lucas. I left him upstairs to get dressed on his own."

"He said he spends the whole day in his pajamas," Charm said indignantly as they rose to their feet.

She chuckled and wiped her face. "First rule of parenting: Double-check anything kids tell you. They're experts at spinning things in their own favor."

"Duly noted." He turned her by her shoulders and pushed her gently toward the sink. "Wash your face and finish what you were doing…with, perhaps, a bit less spot removing. I'll check on him."

The smile slid from his face the moment he was out the door. What had he done? Stay in Collier? Take care of her kid? His mind replayed their conversation. What had she said…six months? He counted on his fingers. July. Halfway through the summer. Jesus.

Lost in his thoughts, he might have walked past Lucas's room if River hadn't whined. "You okay, kid?" He pushed open the boy's door.

Lucas, dressed in a sweatshirt and a pair of pants torn to accommodate the brace, sat in a chair next to the window, gazing outside. River sat next to him, his head resting on the boy's thigh.

"Kid?"

"I'm fine. Go away." His voice was thick, like he'd been crying. *Poor kid. Must have really been scared his dog was lost.* "You want some help getting into bed?"

"I can do it. Leave me alone!"

Charm frowned. The dog was back. Why was the kid pissed? He watched the kid use the windowsill to push himself into a standing position, and suddenly it hit him: the windowsill. Of the open window. That looked out over the front porch. Where his mother just lost her shit. *Fuck. He heard everything.*

Lucas used furniture to balance himself as he hopped to the bed. Getting his body on the bed was easy; getting his broken leg up was less so. Charm jammed his hands in his pocket to keep from helping him. The boy grimaced as he wrestled it up and got it situated on a stack of pillows. "Told you I could do it," he said when he was done.

"Yep, you did. I bet you can do lots of things." He watched the lanky retriever climb onto the bed and curl up beside the boy. Maybe this retrieving thing would be a way to pay back the debt he owed

Jake. Really pay it back. "You know, I was thinking. What River needs is a chance to get back to business. Some real retrieves." The boy's hand stroked the dog's head possessively. "I could help with that if you want. It would still be your project. I'd be your legs. For a while. Until you can do it on your own."

Lucas didn't look at him. "Mom doesn't want River around."

"You let me worry about her. Deal?"

For a long moment the kid stroked the dog's head and didn't speak. Then he nodded. "Deal."

They shared a brief smile, and then Charm backed out of the room and shut the door. As soon as it was closed, he sagged against it. What had he gotten himself into now?

# CHAPTER 6

*Hell.* He'd gotten himself into hell itself, he decided, when Ellie dragged him out of bed and down to the kitchen at seven thirty the next morning. They needed to talk about this morning thing.

A trip to Brother Jack's the night before had resulted in an opportunity to chat further with Angeline and more than a few "welcome back" beers, which served to push Ellie's situation and his promise to her to the back of his mind. Those worries came roaring back as soon as his head hit the pillow, and even the significant amount of alcohol he had imbibed couldn't grant him the respite of sleep. He had finally slipped into a restless doze when Ellie had demanded his presence at breakfast.

"Charm? Charm!"

Charm jerked. "What? I'm awake." He checked — yep, still sitting upright at the kitchen table. That counted as awake.

"You were snoring," Lucas said.

Charm turned his head — just a bit. Lack of sleep had ratcheted his hangover up to a twelve. His nephew, dressed in rumpled pajamas and with hair sticking straight up on one side, looked as grumpy as Charm felt. Charm squinted. "You have a milk mustache.”

“I do not.” But the boy swiped his sleeve across his mouth anyway.

Ellie glared at Charm and waved a skillet. “Did you hear anything I said?”

Not really. She yammered way too much for this hour of the day. “You’re going to work?”

She rolled her eyes and forked scrambled eggs from the skillet onto two plates. “I said I spent last night looking for a better job. I checked out the Mississippi job website.” Bacon and toast joined the eggs. “Not a lot of positions open right now.” She set a plate in front of Lucas.

He frowned. “I don’t want eggs. I want donuts. Why can’t Grandma watch me?”

The boy’s whine clawed at Charm’s hangover-sensitized nerves. He rubbed his temples. “Shut up, kid, or I’ll send you over there.”

“It would be better than you!”

“All right, you two. Let it go.” Ellie plopped the second plate in front of Charm and returned to the counter.

He glanced at the food and winced. The greasy scent of bacon had made the early morning trip downstairs almost bearable, but now the thought of eating made his stomach churn. He poked at the eggs and wondered if he could manage a bite. He noticed Lucas slipping some of the eggs to the retriever lying next to him.

Ellie continued her story. “This girl, Marilyn, quit right before Christmas.” She filled a travel mug with coffee. “I’ve been there almost as long as she has — longer if you don’t count the time I took off when Lucas was born — so I figure I have a good chance of getting that position when it opens. I’ll ask my manager this morning.” She glared at her son. “Lucas, eat. That’s not for the dog.”

The boy wrinkled his nose and popped the bacon he had been about to give the hopeful dog into his own mouth instead. “He needs it! We’re going to train him.”

Ellie froze. “What do you mean?”

Even half asleep, Charm caught the tone in her voice. “Nothing.” He shot a significant look at Lucas. “We’re just going to do some retrieves. He's a retriever."

The boy looked like he was going to complain, then looked away and stuffed toast in his mouth. "Just retrieves," he mumbled.

She glared at Charm. "Just retrieves. That dog has caused enough problems in this household. Understand?"

"Got it." He kicked at Lucas's good ankle under the table.

"Got it," the boy said.

Elle grabbed a mug from the cabinet. "Charm, how do you take your coffee?"

He blinked. Finally, words he wanted to hear. "Black. Please, God."

The last of the coffee filled a mug that she placed into his hands. He breathed deep. *Thank you, thank you, thank you.* A sip. Manna from heaven. His brain slowly began to function. "You want a new job? I thought you were going to ask for extra hours."

She sighed. "My job doesn't pay enough. I'm going to see if I can get Marilyn's job for a few more hours and more money." She rinsed the skillet and wiped off the stove. "I've got to get going. I fed the animals, but the goat needs to be milked as soon as you can get out there" — she ignored his groan — "and the water buckets need to be scrubbed out and refilled. Pens need to be cleaned too. I left you a list on the fridge.

"I should be home by four," she added as she shoved her phone in her purse and grabbed her keys. "Can you make sure Lucas takes his medicine at lunch?" She headed out without an answer.

Two seconds later the door opened again, and she rushed back in. She kissed her son's forehead. "I love you. I'll see you when I get home." She headed out again. "Listen to your Uncle Charm. And eat your breakfast." The door slammed behind her.

Lucas scraped his eggs into the dog's mouth. "I want donuts."

Charm pushed the plate away and rested his forehead on the table.

* * *

Elle shut the truck's door and rested her forehead on the

steering wheel. After a moment, she sat up and took a deep breath. *I can do this.*

The bills, the mortgage, the deal with the bank. It had hounded her last night. A dream about debt collectors taking her farm and leaving them homeless had ruined the few minutes of sleep she'd managed to get. That wasn't going to happen, not to her son. She had a plan now. She was going to save her farm — and her son.

She started her truck and headed down the driveway. *Yes, sir. I can do this.*

* * *

Elle tried to remind herself of that a few hours later. Word she was back had spread quickly through the Sharkey County administration building, and an endless stream of sympathetic well-wishers had stopped by to pay their condolences.

The latest was the pair of sheriff deputies who had been first on the scene of her husband's accident. The raw pain in their apologies for not being able to do more for her family broke through the fragile facade she had managed to erect, and she spent twenty minutes crying in a supply closet — the only place she could escape the attention of others.

When she emerged, she was grateful to find the counter busy and the rest of the office empty. She slid behind a desk and picked up the first in her stack of records requests, a stack that had grown exponentially since she left. "Doesn't anyone but me work on these?" she muttered, just as one of the women from the counter turned to drop another on the pile.

The woman rolled her eyes sympathetically. "Girl, don't get me started. You and Marilyn gone, people out for Christmas, ain't nothing gotten done in here. And you know the county council won't approve ten minutes of overtime, no matter how backed up it gets." Elle winced, feeling a door shut on her hope for additional hours. Her coworker made a moue as three more people joined the line in front. "Glad you're back. Hope you're rested 'cause they're about to work you like a dog."

*Great.* Public court records, arrest records, marriage licenses, judicial records, business liens, real estate taxes — her office handled them all. Sometimes the question could be answered immediately by the people working the windows at the front. Other times they simply collected a form and a fee and sent it back for more research. But, she acknowledged, that research, tedious at the best of times, was exactly what she needed today.

"Elle? Could I see you for a minute?"

Elle looked past her computer to see her supervisor, Dovye Curtis-Jackson, beckoning from her office doorway. Elle took a moment to grab a sheet of paper she had printed earlier and slipped into Dovye's office.

The office contained the same inexpensive utilitarian desk, chair, and commercial gray carpet as every other walled office in the building (other than those of the various judges based there), plus several nondescript metal file cabinets and two equally nondescript bookcases, stuffed to overflowing with manuals and paper. But the institutional sameness ended there. There were healthy plants in the window, a smattering of knickknacks, and an ergonomic chair behind the desk. Three of the walls were painted a soothing sage color, and the fourth was a surprising terra cotta. On this wall hung an arrangement of framed family pictures, a showcase of dark smiling faces at weddings, graduations, celebrations, and other moments of family joy.

The office was as much a mix of efficiency and style as the woman herself. Dovye — a diminutive African American woman called Miss Dovye by anyone who knew her, including the mayor and, Elle had heard, the governor — had kept the Sharkey county clerk's office running smoothly and efficiently for almost thirty years.

Miss Dovye waved her to a seat. "How are you holding up?"

Elle perched on the edge of a chair, suddenly cognizant of crumbs from her rapidly eaten toast on her shirt and feeling decidedly unkempt, as she usually did in her supervisor's presence. "It's easier when I actually get to work. I appreciate the sympathy from everybody, but I need to think about something other than the accident."

"Want me to keep people out?"

"No. Thanks, but no. People need to do this. Let's let them get it out of their systems." She cringed. "I sound horrible, don't I? I should be grateful. I mean, I am grateful —"

Miss Dovye waved her off. "No. You're fine. You're overwhelmed, and you have every right to be. Are you sure you don't want to take some more time off?"

Elle shook her head. "No. I wish I could, but my brother is taking care of Lucas, and we need the money. I wanted to talk to you about that..." She shifted in her chair. "Marilyn left a few weeks ago, and I'd like to apply for her position." She pushed the paper she had grabbed on her way in toward her supervisor. "I looked up the job description. See? I meet the qualifications. I've been here long enough, and I do most of this stuff now —"

"I have no doubt you can do the job. But I'm not sure now is the right time —"

"But —"

Miss Dovye held up a hand and stopped her. "For *either* of us." She paused, then continued. "We're not ready to fill Marilyn's position. New year, new budget. Nothing is likely to come open for at least a month and maybe not until the end of the quarter."

Elle nodded. "But when it does come open, I can apply?"

"You can apply. I can't promise. Elle, this position has a lot more responsibility, and you're a single parent now."

"Yolanda and Sierra are single moms." Miss Dovye's expression didn't change. Unspoken words hung between them: *But Lucas is disabled.* "I can do it —" Elle said, hating the shaking in her voice.

"You said your brother is helping you. How long will he be here?"

Elle dug her nails into her thighs. "Indefinitely." She forced her voice to steady. "I won't pretend there won't be an adjustment period. There will be doctor's visits and physical therapy, but I can do it. I can handle the job."

"That job is only a few more thousand dollars a year. With taxes that's only a hundred dollars extra in your paycheck."

Elle blinked. *Surely not.* "I can do it."

Miss Dovye took a deep breath and sat back and regarded her for several long moments. "There's at least a month before the position is posted. Let's see how it goes."

Elle expelled a breath she hadn't realized she was holding. "I won't let you down," she said, rising on trembling legs. Miss Dovye didn't speak as Elle exited the office and made her way back to her desk.

Not exactly what she'd wanted, but it had gone okay, hadn't it? Elle stared at the form in front of her, but the conversation with her supervisor spun through her mind. It was okay. She could do this. She just had to show them she could do it. The only way out of this mess was to keep moving forward, no matter how miniscule the steps.

*Lucas. Lucas needs this.* Her throat tightened as she thought of her son, so fragile now, so lost without his father. Thank God for Charm. If there was any bright spot in all of this, it was knowing her brother would keep things going on the home front.

** * **

"Uncle Charm!" Lucas's voice echoed down the stairs to the living room.

"I'll be up in a minute," Charm called back for at least the fourth time.

"You keep saying that."

"If you'd quit bugging me, it will eventually be true." No retort followed, but Charm guessed it was only an interlude. His nephew was nothing if not persistent. *And bored.* A twinge of guilt almost sent him upstairs, but what he was doing was important.

Charm tilted the bottle of Jameson he'd found in Ellie's liquor cabinet and trickled the golden whiskey into his flask. "Have to be careful," he said to the dog lounging at his feet. "It's sacrilege to waste so much as a drop of this divine creation."

River's attention swiveled toward the door, and he leapt to his feet with a bark. Heavy boots stomped on the welcome mat, and the front door opened, sending a blast of cold air in from the entrance hall. "Anybody home?"

"In here." Charm took a quick swallow from the bottle, savoring the sweet burn on its way down. He was placing the liquor back on the shelf when Jimmy Lee strolled in, blowing on his hands to warm them.

"I hope you're sharing that," Jimmy Lee said. "The wind's really kicked up out there."

Charm glanced through the front window and grimaced. The bare trees swayed, jerked, and danced in the gusts, and the midafternoon sky promised rain. This dog training thing was getting better and better. "Where have you been?" he asked. "I thought you were gonna be here around lunch."

Jimmy Lee worked only occasionally, which made him the ideal partner for this little foray. Jake had never been sure how Jimmy Lee paid his bills and speculated his moneymaking activities might not be wholly legal. Ironic since his best friend, Bird, was a sheriff's deputy. Charm didn't really care what Jimmy Lee did with his free time since he was willing to help him with this fool's errand.

River gave Jimmy Lee's shoes a thorough examination and politely sniffed his hand when offered but otherwise adopted a disinterested look, even when the newcomer rubbed his ears and knelt for a closer look. "So this is Forbes's famous import? Looks more like a French poodle than a retriever."

Charm glanced at the entrance hall, hoping the words hadn't carried upstairs. "Don't say that in front of the kid. You'll just piss him off. He said it's a" — he snapped his fingers until he remembered — "a curly-coated retriever. Jake promised Lucas this dog was going to win a field trial, so we're gonna make sure he does." *As long as Ellie doesn't find out.*

Jimmy Lee rose to his feet. "You know, Jake was a great guy, and I don't want to speak ill of the dead, but he could be a mite" — he searched for the word — "over-optimistic."

Not nearly as over-optimistic as a non-dog-person helping a crippled kid train said dog. "What exactly have I gotten myself into? 'Cause I haven't got a fucking clue."

Jimmy Lee snorted. "You volunteered to train a weekend ball

player for the NBA."

Charm's stomach sank. "That bad?"

"According to Oscar, River was a really good hunting dog. A really, really good hunting dog. Best he'd ever seen. That's why he thought River might have a shot to compete. But when he got him here, River washed out. His style of hunting was simply too different."

"Was that a curly issue or a New Zealand issue?"

"Neither, really, though curlies don't usually compete in field trials. It's a hunting versus competition issue. A weekend pickup game versus pro ball. Similar, but the precision and skill and pressure at the pro level make it a whole different ball game — so to speak. Field trials are full of Labs that have been linebred for generations to do this one thing. Occasionally you see Chesapeakes or goldens, but even those are underrepresented. Black male Labradors win field trials."

"So I'm wasting my time?"

Jimmy Lee shrugged. "You're making a kid happy. And who knows — maybe Jake really did know something we don't."

Charm thought for a moment, then shook his head. "I don't guess it matters. I promised Lucas I'd help, and he really needs this. Did you bring your shotgun?"

"On the porch."

"Great. Let's get going on this. Grab it, and we'll meet you out there." Charm jogged up the stairs two at a time to Lucas's room. "Ready?"

"I've been ready," he said crossly. "For hours."

Charm gave him a quick once-over anyway to be sure Lucas's idea of ready matched his. Or Ellie's. Kid wasn't freezing on his watch. Again. "Got your crutches?"

Lucas wiggled the crutches and pulled on his jacket. "Are we really going to train River, or are we just doing retrieves like you told Mom?"

*Right to the point there, kid.* Charm considered how to best frame the answer, then finally sighed and bent over to look him in the eye. "Sometimes what your mom doesn't know won't hurt her."

Lucas's eyes lit up. "Or us?"

Charm grinned. "Or us. Do you think you can get to the head of the stairs on your own, or do you need to lean on me?"

The boy swung the leg with the brace to the side and struggled to his feet. "It would be a lot faster if you carried me."

"Your mom says you should be getting used to those crutches."

"What mom doesn't know won't hurt her."

Charm snorted. "Touché, kid." He turned around and squatted. "Grab hold."

Lucas wrapped his arms around his uncle's neck. "What does *touché* mean?"

Charm stood up and wiggled his shoulders to be certain the boy was holding tight. "It means you're a smart ass."

Ellie might not have approved, but carrying Lucas was significantly more time effective, particularly since they had only an hour or so before Ellie was due home. Charm repeated that limitation when Lucas complained about sitting on the porch while he and Jimmy Lee did the actual training.

"This is *my* project." Angry red splotches rose on Lucas's cheeks. "You said you were only going to help!"

Charm resisted the rather strong urge to hand over the leash and adopted his most reasonable tone. "We're not trying to take it over. I promise. It's just that..." He searched for a convincing argument.

"You know what you're doing," Jimmy Lee said. "Your Uncle Charm and I? Total newbies. We need some practice, so we can be as good as you are. As good as River needs us to be."

The suspicion remained etched on Lucas's face, but he didn't voice another protest, so Charm blundered forward. "You and your dad had been training him, right? What had you done so far?"

Some of the rebellion faded from Lucas's eyes as he thought back. "River was already trained to hunt. Dad said he needed to learn to do it like we do here in America."

"What does that mean?" Jimmy Lee asked.

"Like he doesn't always run in a straight line. And he doesn't run through stickers and mud."

That didn't sound terribly unreasonable to Charm. "What did

you *do* when you trained him? Just shoot a bird and have him bring it back?"

Lucas eyed him scornfully. "We weren't ready for live birds yet. Those cost money. We use bumpers. We did singles and doubles and marks and blinds, in lots of different ways. Only on land, though. We were starting to test water. We'd done a few triples, but we needed some extra help for those." He brightened. "One time, there was this duck —"

"Why don't we toss a…what did you call it? A bumper? And see what he does," Jimmy Lee said. "It's been a while. Let's see what he remembers."

Charm nodded. "That sounds good." Lucas rolled his eyes, clearly unimpressed. "Where should we do it?"

Jimmy Lee scanned the yard. "How about right out here? We've got a couple acres to work with."

The chase the day before flashed through Charm's mind. "Nope, I veto that one. I'm not running him near the road."

"Okay." Jimmy Lee looked around, his eyes eventually settling on the area to the east beyond the barn and outbuildings. "How about that hay pasture back there? We can angle him away from the road, plus there's a fence."

Charm considered it a minute, then nodded. "That should work. Hey kid, where can we get some of those bumper things?"

The steel-gray clouds in the sky were no match for the storm on the boy's face, but he finally said, "The barn. There's a cabinet with a bunch of them. Rubber with knobby things and a rope tied to one end. About this long." He indicated with his hands.

"Perfect. Now you have to watch us. We'll need you to tell us what we're doing right and wrong." Charm patted his leg to get River's attention. "Come on, buddy." He and Jimmy Lee strode toward the barn, the dog padding disinterestedly behind them.

Jimmy Lee hefted his shotgun to his shoulder and leaned in so Lucas wouldn't overhear. "You know anything about field trials?" he asked.

"Not a whole lot, no," Charm admitted.

"I did some reading before I came over. You're talking blind retrieves up to a quarter mile away. You'll be competing against the best linebred Labs in the country." They stepped into the barn, took a moment to orient themselves, and headed to a cabinet near a fenced area Charm guessed had been River's kennel.

"Why don't you do hunt tests instead?" Jimmy Lee continued. "Lots easier. Put a junior hunter on him. Lucas won't know the difference."

Charm snorted. "He broke his leg, not his skull. We're not going to fool him like that. Did you hear him back there? He knows a lot more about this than we do." He opened the cabinet and scanned the contents. Oh yeah, a hell of a lot more. Whistles, lots of knobby oblong things with rope tied to one end — the bumpers, he assumed — duck decoys of different types, a starter pistol, a couple of leashes, some camouflage canvas rolled up, and other equipment he couldn't begin to identify.

"How many of these do we need?" he asked, poking at one of the bumpers. "And what color?" White, orange, black, and white-and-black patterned. This couldn't be simple, could it?

Jimmy Lee grabbed three white ones. "There are more of these, so let's use them. Let's get this over with." He headed toward the field without waiting for a response, irritation evident in every step.

Charm sighed. He wasn't terribly thrilled with the situation himself. He jogged to catch up. "Anyway, maybe Lucas isn't dreaming. Jake had faith in this dog."

"It takes more than faith to win. You're setting that kid up to fail."

Charm faced his friend and stood tall. Despite his own misgivings, when he spoke, his voice was firm. "This is all that kid has left of his father. He *needs* this. If you don't want to help, road's that way."

Jimmy Lee glared at him a moment, then shrugged. "What do you want me to do?"

They walked through a pasture gate, and Charm gestured toward the far end of the field. "Head out to the top of that little rise there. That should give us some good visibility. Shoot the gun, and then toss one of these." He handed him the bumpers.

Jimmy Lee squinted at the area Charm had indicated. "Isn't it kind of far? Maybe we should start closer for the first few runs."

Charm cleared his throat and studied the mud on the tip of his Pumas. "Yeah, well, he has problems with loud noises. I want to give him some distance from that shotgun." He looked anywhere but at his friend, but still felt the weight of his disbelieving stare.

"He's gun shy?" Jimmy Lee's voice was about an octave higher than normal.

"He's not gun shy. He's just…go on out in the field."

His friend made a strangled sound and stomped off toward the far end of the pasture. Charm took a deep breath and knelt beside River. "Okay, buddy. Are you ready?"

The dog had already figured out what was happening. His body vibrated with tension, his focus on the man with the shotgun marching to the other end of the field. He whined softly and shuffled his feet as Jimmy Lee got ready to shoot.

"Here it comes, bud," Charm said softly.

Despite the distance, the shot rang out like a small explosion. A moment later, the bumper flew through the air. "Go get it, fella! Fetch!" He looked down, expecting to see the dog racing across the field, but River was neither beside him nor in front of him. He spun around to see the dog clear the gate and bolt for the house.

Jimmy Lee appeared next to Charm as the dog disappeared inside. He rested his hands on his knees and tried to catch his breath. For a moment the two of them just stared. Then a snort burst out of him. He waved off Charm's look of betrayal and patted him on the shoulder, almost choking on the laughter he was holding back. Finally, he shook his head and trekked back to the house.

Charm swore under his breath and watched his friend — *rotten, ex-friend!* — help Lucas inside. In search of that damn dog, of course. *What else can freaking go wrong?* The sky opened, and the rain that had been threatening began falling in frigid sheets. He sighed.

Auspicious.

* * *

As she pulled into the driveway, Elle felt much like she had on Lucas's first day of school, except she was the one coming home this time. She was several hours later than she had expected she'd be. Wanting to make a good impression and knowing she needed to take Lucas to physical therapy tomorrow, she had worked late. Finally, though, she was home and could spend some time with her son.

Had Lucas been all right without her? Did Charm make him a nutritious snack? Was his leg hurting? She parked in her usual spot, ducked her head against the spitting rain, and cut across the lawn to the side door. After a day back in the real world, the need to hug her little boy made her heart ache.

Laughter and loud voices drifted out. "I'm home," she called. She paused to wipe her feet and hang her purse and keys where she could find them in the morning. Charm's voice drifted out. "…view of the jungle when we finally got to the top of the pyramid was amazing…" he was saying.

Ooh, a travel story! "Which pyramid?" she asked, walking in.

She stopped in the doorway and stared at the chaos that had once been her kitchen. Sink overflowing with dishes, leftovers from the funeral spread across the counter, fridge door not quite closed. The kitchen table had transformed into a gambling den for food addicts. Lucas, Charm, and Jimmy Lee were embroiled in what appeared to be a raucous game of poker. "Poker chip" had been taken literally, and the pot was made up of a combination of Cheerios, pretzel sticks, and Cheez-Its. The participants each wore a ball cap and sunglasses. Charm and Jimmy Lee chewed on cigars — thankfully, not lit — and her son had a pretzel stick mustache.

"A Mayan one in Belize," Charm said. He tossed cards on the table. "Gimme two."

"Hi, Mom!" Lucas said cheerfully. He counted the cards and handed them to his uncle. "Uncle Charm cheats!"

Indeed, most of the snacks were in a disordered pile to Charm's right. He lifted a hand in objection. "Not a cheat! Just a very good bluffer."

Elle stared. She'd left a list. How could this be happening? She left a *list*.

Jimmy Lee started to rise. "Elle, I want you to know how —"

"Don't!" Her tone was sharp enough to get everyone's attention. "Don't say it. The next person who tells me how sorry he is will become an immediate candidate for organ donation." She took a deep breath and tried to tamp down the rage bubbling like lava in her gut.

The men exchanged glances and surreptitiously pulled off their hats and glasses. "On that note, I'll say my goodbyes." Jimmy Lee slid back from the table and headed to the living room, pausing scarcely long enough to nod to Charm before fleeing. A moment later, the front door clicked shut.

"Hey, what about the game?" Lucas asked.

Charm set down the cigar and pushed back from the table. "I think the game's over, kid. Why don't I take you upstairs, and you can get into your pajamas and play some video games." He helped the boy stand, and then turned so he could loop his arms around his neck. No crutches. Of course.

Elle automatically began cleaning up the containers of leftovers. Food in the fridge — door firmly closed — dishes in the sink. A glance at the list on the fridge confirmed what she'd already guessed: hardly anything was marked off. A hot tear rolled down her cheek, and she swiped it away. There wasn't time to feel sorry for herself. She brushed the poker "chips" into a trash can and gathered up the cards.

Okay, she did feel sorry for herself. She slammed the trash can into place and stalked back to the sink. All she wanted was to spend some time with her son. Was that really so much to ask?

She was rinsing the last plate when Charm appeared in the kitchen again, dressed in clean clothes and pulling on his jacket. "Where are you going?" she asked.

"Meeting the guys at Brother Jack's." She stared at him in disbelief. "What?" he asked, sounding sullen.

She suppressed a dozen furious answers to that question. "I could use some help around here."

Now it was his turn to look disbelieving. "I've been helping all day. Who do you think took care of your kid? I fed him dinner, by the way. You're welcome."

She blinked. "He can't walk. How labor intensive could he be? I don't suppose you found time to do a load of laundry during your busy day. I can see you didn't have time for the dishes. Jake used to —"

"I'm not Jake."

"No. You're not."

"Mom!" Lucas hollered from upstairs.

Elle glared at Charm, then walked to the doorway. "I'll be up in a few minutes, sweetie." She looked back at her brother. "Charm, I need real help around here. Not another child to take care of."

She walked back to the sink and didn't acknowledge him again. A few moments later she heard the side door slam. She answered by slamming a pan into the soapy water. "I can do this. I can do this," she said over and over.

She finished the dishes, then went out and fed the animals. She cleaned out pens and scrubbed out buckets and apologized to them that it wasn't done earlier. The chickens clucked contentedly, and the baby goat followed her around and butted her affectionately. At least they didn't hate her. Hopefully her son wouldn't either. There were only a few more things on the list, and then she could go up and spend some time with him. Finally.

It was almost ten before she finally climbed the steps to the second floor. "Lucas, sweetie?" She peeked into his room. The boy lay sprawled on his bed, snoring softly, broken leg supported on a pillow, one arm over his eyes, the other draped across River. His video game flashed "Game Over."

Elle swallowed her disappointment and turned off the TV and the light next to the bed and sat down next to him. He didn't stir. "It's going to get better, Lucas," she whispered, gently brushing a curl from his forehead. "I promise." She pressed her lips to his forehead, tucked the blankets around him, and slipped out, heart heavy.

She crawled onto her bed, too tired to wash her face, much less shower. The thought of doing all this over again tomorrow and the next day and the next... Her new normal.

On her nightstand, a photo of her and Jake and Lucas gave silent, unending testimony of everything she had lost. She picked it up and brushed fingers over the surface, wishing she could touch the people, the lives, within. "I miss you so much. Why did you leave me?"

A soft scratching noise got her attention. Setting the picture down, she looked toward the hall. "Lucas? Are you okay?"

The door swung open a few inches, and River stuck his head inside. He inched in, wagging submissively, and rested his head on the edge of her bed.

She groaned. "Oh, no. I do not need sympathy from a dog." She tossed a pillow in his general direction. "Just get out of here!"

River sniffed at the pillow, then crept around to the far side of the bed and climbed up. He curled into the space behind her knees, laid his head on her hip, and sighed.

Elle gazed at the picture on her nightstand. Those smiles. Those happy people. They were gone. Everything in that picture was gone. She swept it off the nightstand, and it hit the floor with a crash.

The tears finally came.

- 96 -

# CHAPTER 7

*Three weeks.* Hard to believe he had been here only three weeks. It felt more like three months. Charm slammed the posthole digger into the ground, twisted it, then levered the handles apart to scoop out a chunk of dirt. Farm life sucked. Glorified babysitter and hired hand. And he thought life had been bad in St. Louis. At least there he only had to deal with his own grief and failure. Now he was surrounded by grief 24/7, and failure had bigger consequences.

In the years since he'd helped on his father's farm, he had forgotten how much work there was to do — and to be honest, he didn't know how to do the chores on this farm anyway. His dad had raised soybeans, not corn, not hay, and not animals of any kind. Winter had been a time of rest when he was growing up. But *rest* wasn't in Ellie's vocabulary. According to her, winter was when you caught up on all the things you were too busy to do the rest of the year. Like this fence work.

The fence looked fine to Charm. Yeah, sure, there were a handful of rotting posts, but they hadn't fallen down or anything. No cows had pushed through. But Ellie said the old posts had to be dug out and replaced and the wire restrung and tightened. And since he really did want to help her out, that's what he was doing. Sort of.

Digging out the old posts was hard work. So, he'd gotten creative. He sawed the old posts off at ground level and dug new holes just inside the fence line, next to the old ones. In his opinion, he deserved extra points for getting the job done faster and making it easier.

He slammed the digger into the ground again and again, the blisters on his hands a silent testament to his hard work. At least the endless January rain had softened the ground for him. The rain had also made it easier to put Lucas off when he wanted to train River. Mostly. They had tried again a few times with the same disappointing result. How the hell were they going to train that dog for a field trial if they couldn't even get him to retrieve in the backyard?

The sun on his back reminded Charm that as they moved toward February, the rain had finally given way to blue skies. It wasn't a lot warmer, but at least it was drier. That meant Lucas was going to want to try again. Had Ellie not picked him up an hour ago for physical therapy, he'd have been yelling out the window, wanting to do it now. *Thank God for PT.*

Charm took a breather, blew on yet another blister building on his palm, and peered into the hole. Deep enough. Who cared anyway? Wasn't like they were tying the cows to the fence posts. He hefted a large round post and dropped it in, then packed loose dirt around it, tamping it down as tight as he could. He stepped back and looked down the row. Maybe it wasn't quite as straight as it used to be, but the job was getting done. What more would Ellie expect from free labor?

Probably more. Probably a fence line as straight as a Nebraska highway. As straight as the life Ellie wanted him to live. As straight as Jake would have strung it.

His stomach flip-flopped. The specters of Jake and their money woes lurked in every corner, haunted every conversation. The pile of bills on the desk in the kitchen grew taller every day. The cash Charm had brought with him was long tapped out, and his credit card was worn thin from overuse. And savings…well, saving wasn't really compatible with his worldview. He was going to be surviving on free rounds from strangers at Brother Jack's pretty soon. He wiped sweat from his brow and started the next hole. Ellie was getting paid today. Maybe that would ease the pressure.

The crunch of tires on gravel interrupted his reverie. A newer F-350 rumbled up the drive. He squinted until he recognized the driver, then returned to his digging with renewed ferocity.

Oscar Strickland rubbed Charm the wrong way. Always had. Oil and water since Oscar had spread the rumor that he caught Charm kissing Amanda Williams in the coat closet in first grade. It was true, mind you, but it still wasn't any of his business. It was bad enough Oscar was at Brother Jack's most evenings. *Why is he here?*

The truck pulled into the grass next to him, and Oscar got out. No greeting, just leaned against his truck and waited for Charm to acknowledge him.

Charm didn't bother to look up. "Long way from town." The posthole digger hit a rock. He slammed it down again and again, trying to get around or through it. His frustration grew with each clank of metal on stone.

From the corner of his eye, Charm saw Oscar casually kick at a clod of dirt. "Came to see how things are going."

Charm scanned the property. Animals fed and watered. Yard straight. New fence going in. "Going fine. Thanks for stopping by." He returned to his digging.

Rather than leave, Oscar lit a cigarette and took a couple of puffs. After a minute or so, he said casually, "Heard you're having trouble with that dog."

Ah. So that's why he had made the trip out. "Jimmy Lee has a big mouth."

"Jimmy Lee feels sorry for the kid. Doesn't want him hurt."

Charm parked the posthole digger in the ground and looked up. "Why does everyone think training River will hurt him? He loves that dog. He loves working with him. Training is a connection to his father."

Oscar leaned toward him, his pretense of a lazy demeanor forgotten. "I liked Jake. Liked him a lot. But he wasn't a trainer. I don't mean to speak ill of the dead, but he'd have failed in the end.

The mutt is a washout."

"You couldn't do it, so nobody can?" Charm translated.

Oscar narrowed his eyes. "I recognized the truth and cut my losses."

"You mean you got fired." He squared up and tilted his head. "You jealous we're doing something you couldn't?"

"Look." Oscar took a deep drag from the cigarette, and when he spoke again, his volume was carefully normal. "The dog…River…is a nice hunting dog. He's a *really* nice hunting dog, but he ain't no field trial dog. I admit it — I was wrong when I talked Forbes into buying him. You and Lucas can chase your tails all you want, but that's not gonna make that dog more than he is. Let it go, and let the kid have his perfect memory." He took one more puff, then dropped the butt, killed the ember with his bootheel, and headed back to the driver's side of the truck. "Tell Elle I stopped by."

Every muscle in Charm's body tensed. Ellie? What did she have to do with Oscar? "Why would I do that?" he asked suspiciously.

"We're neighbors." Oscar enunciated each word slowly and clearly as if Charm might have trouble understanding. "I've known her all my life. I'm…checking…in…on…her. That's what neighbors do." Charm glared at him. Oscar rolled his eyes and opened the truck's door.

Charm leaned on the digger. "Hey, tell me something." The animosity from a moment before was gone. Oscar paused. "How did River end up with Jake?"

Oscar hesitated, then shut the door and faced him. "Nobody else wanted him. He couldn't take the pressure of a regular training program. Ran hot, too soft, couldn't keep weight on. Talent's useless without control. Forbes went through every trainer in the area, and finally just stuck him in the kennel. Maybe Jake saw him as an opportunity to expand his skill set. I dunno."

Charm considered all this, and Oscar opened the door again. "But he's talented?"

Oscar glanced his way and snorted. "Yeah, he's talented." He started to get in the truck, then stopped. "Do you want help?" The offer seemed to explode out of him, and he cringed after he said it.

Charm felt a modicum of empathy. He'd made a couple of those please-don't-say-yes offers recently himself. He swallowed his sarcasm. "We've got it under control, thanks."

Oscar shrugged and this time got in the truck. "Tell Elle I stopped by," he repeated. He hesitated and nodded toward the fence posts Charm had set. "Don't worry. You'll get the hang of it."

Charm growled and glared balefully as Oscar headed out. *What was that about?* Not for a moment did he believe Oscar had stopped by because he was a good neighbor. But was the real reason River…or Ellie?

The truck honked as it made a left out of the driveway, and Oscar waved at an older Ford sedan turning in. Charm groaned and swore several colorful epithets. His mother. He really couldn't catch a break today, could he? He leaned against one of his recently set posts to wait and swore again when it shifted against his weight. He had straightened it and was tamping the dirt more firmly when she parked on the drive near him.

"Ellie took Lucas to physical therapy," he said when her door opened.

"Hello to you, too, Charm." His mother reached across to the passenger seat and picked up several books. "Yes, it's a delightful day, and it's wonderful to see you too."

The innocent-sounding greeting stabbed at his heart. He doubted she'd ever been glad to see him. Maybe when he was little. Maybe before his father became a raging drunk, and she chose to provide the alcohol that fueled those rages instead of standing up for the son who was the target of them. The old pain flickered into anger.

"I see. Okay, we'll play it your way." He transformed his face from a scowl into the charming smile that had earned him his nickname so long ago. "Hello, Mother. It's nice to see you. Is there something I can do for you?"

Her answering smile almost looked genuine. And friendly. The longing in his heart extinguished the anger with a whoosh.

"I came to make a trade," she said.

Of course. Couldn't be a polite social call. He finished straightening the post and began gathering his tools. "What do you want?"

Her features took on a serious expression. "Information."

Whatever he'd expected, it wasn't that. "What kind?"

"I want to know how my grandson is doing."

Considering how often Lucas talked about his grandmother, she had been conspicuously absent in the past few weeks. That hadn't hurt Charm's feelings, but now that he thought about it, it seemed strange. Charm hefted the digger onto his shoulder. "It's lunch time," he said in explanation and headed toward the barn. In reply to her request, he said, "Why don't you ask Ellie?"

His mother trailed through the grass behind him, still carrying her armload of books. "I have. She gives me facts and platitudes and tells me not to worry. I want to worry. He's my grandson."

Another flare of anger. Charm stacked the tools inside the barn door and stalked toward the house. "You didn't worry when I ran away at sixteen. You didn't even care enough to look for me."

"Is that what you think?"

The question was so sincere that he stopped and turned back. His mother stood near the barn door, staring at him. His heart pounded in his chest. He opened his mouth to reply, then resumed walking to the house. He paused at the steps to the side porch.

"You coming?" he asked without looking back. "I'll make a sandwich."

River met him at the door, tail gently wagging. Charm gave him a pat and headed into the kitchen, his mind churning. It wasn't just what he thought. It was a fact. *Wasn't it?* He was pulling plates out of the cabinet when River woofed to let him know his mother had come in.

"Hello, Mr. River," she said. The dog stuck his nose out and sniffed her, then deigned to let her rub his ears.

Cutlery followed the plates. "We have two kinds of chicken, sliced roast beef, and meatloaf. Leftover. From the wake. For sandwiches, I mean. There's more in the freezer." *You're rambling, Freeman.* He shut his mouth and grabbed chips and sandwich bread.

"I'd like that." Her voice was softer than he ever remembered hearing it. "I'll have whatever you're having."

He motioned for her to sit at the table. "What do you want to know?"

She set the books down and sat in Ellie's chair. "How's Lucas doing — really?"

Charm took roast chicken, lettuce, mayo, and sliced Swiss from the fridge and considered the question. "Misses his dad. Misses his mom. Misses his friends. Some kid — Matthew? Mark?"

"Marty."

"— came over for a few hours last week and played video games, but the guy seemed really uncomfortable while he was here. I didn't hear them fighting, but Lucas was pissed off when he left."

"Marty is a tool," his mother declared dryly, and Charm couldn't help but snicker. "Lucas told me he has to let him win anytime they play video games, or Marty cries and accuses him of cheating."

"Lucas tell you that on his shiny silver cell phone?" Charm asked slyly.

"Does Eleanor know about that?"

He shrugged. "Not from me." He cut each sandwich in half and dumped a handful of chips on each plate. "But I'd be surprised if she doesn't. Water, milk, or lemonade?"

"Milk, please." Her eyes took on a faraway look. "You know, Jake is the one who bought that cell phone, not me."

He grabbed a couple of glasses from the dishwasher. "Really?"

"He didn't think it was fair to keep me and Lucas apart simply because Eleanor and I don't always get along. When she was busy, Jake would sneak Lucas over to my house for a couple of hours, or Lucas would run over through the fields."

Charm grinned. "So that's how River ended up in your backyard."

"Guilty."

He poured milk in the glasses and began moving the food to the table. He handed her a paper towel to use as a napkin. "What else do you want to know?"

"How's Eleanor holding up?"

Charm slid into the chair across from her. "Overwhelmed, I think. Not that she'd admit it."

His mother folded the paper towel and placed it in her lap. "Oh, no, she would never admit such a thing. I'm glad she has you to help her out."

He looked sharply at her, wondering if she was being sarcastic, but she was relaxed and focused on her sandwich. "Yeah, well, I'm trying."

"Harder than you expected?"

He shrugged. "Hard to live up to a dead man."

"Ah." She nodded, and he saw what looked like sympathy in her eyes.

They lapsed into silence and ate their sandwiches. Charm wanted desperately to ask her what she'd meant earlier. Had she looked for him? All of a sudden, it seemed so important, but he choked when he tried to form the words.

"Are you all right?" she asked, looking up.

"Fine. Just ate too fast." Charm tossed the last bite of his sandwich to River and got up to rinse his plate. "You said something about trading?" he asked, remembering their initial conversation.

"Oh, yes." She wiped her mouth and tapped the stack of books on the table. "These are for you."

"Books?" He picked up the top one and peered at it.

"On retriever training for field trials. They're library books, so don't lose them."

He sighed. "Is there anyone in town who doesn't know about Lucas's little project?"

"Yes — Eleanor. I told Jimmy Lee if she finds out, I'd have him cut off at Brother Jack's."

Charm felt ill. Maybe the goodwill they had just shared was misguided after all. The wicked witch had evil, evil powers.

She continued, "If you're going to help Lucas, do it right. There's also a binder there with the current rules for AKC field trials."

"AKC?"

"American Kennel Club."

Charm frowned. "Why did you do all this?"

"I want my grandson to be happy."

He set the book down. "I don't know if that's going to happen," he said. "I don't know what to do. We're not making any progress." He looked at the retriever speculatively. "I'm starting to wonder if there's something more than my own ineptitude."

"You'll figure it out," she said. She got up and rinsed her own dish. "I should go before Eleanor gets home and finds me meddling."

Charm watched her walk to the door. He glanced at the clock — 12:45. "You know," he said hesitantly, "Lucas's physical therapy appointment will be over by one. She's going to drop him off here by one fifteen and head out immediately. If you wanted to come by, I mean." An olive branch.

She met his eyes and nodded. "Thank you, Charm."

Wordlessly, they walked together back to her car. She popped the trunk and dug around until she found what she was looking for. Leather work gloves. "These were your father's. I keep them here in case I need to change a tire. Looks like you need them more than I do."

Charm wanted to say no, wanted to throw them away, but his fingers wrapped around them.

His mother nodded and closed the trunk. She paused for a moment and gazed out at the fencerow he was building. She started to get into her car, then stopped and looked back at him. "The fences you build here, Charm? Just remember they're going to last even after you've gone." She touched his arm, then got in and drove off without another word.

* * *

$743.23.

Elle stared at the amount deposited into her account overnight. Her paycheck for the last two weeks was $743.23. The outstanding mortgage, the *current* mortgage, the stack of medical bills not covered by her so-called "insurance," *food.* It wasn't enough.

Brown-skinned fingers sporting coffee-colored acrylic nails with gold French tips dangled a fast-food bag between Elle's face and the computer monitor. Without looking up, Elle took the bag and breathed deep. Fried chicken nirvanaYou are a goddess, Tan. "esha." She took a moment to minimize the banking info on her screen, then spun her chair around to face her benefactress.

Tanesha Johnson, a woman of great size and great heart, dropped herself into a nearby chair. "Two-piece spicy with extra honey-butter biscuits. Just like you like it."

Elle reached for her purse. "Let me pay you back..."

"No need, no need." Tanesha dismissed her with a flick of her manicured nails. "I can hear your stomach growling from across the room on days you take Lucas to rehab."

Elle took a bite of a biscuit and savored it. "Physical therapy, please. Rehab sounds like he's a drug addict. I've got enough problems without that image hanging over me."

Tanesha laughed — a deep full laugh that dispelled dark thoughts like sunlight burned away morning mist. Elle smiled, grateful to feel the ever-present worry dissipate a tiny bit. Those bits mattered.

"Oh girl, I'm sure you do," Tanesha said, cheeks flushed with amusement. "How's that sweet boy doing?"

Elle snorted. "Hating me for making him do his exercises one minute and whining that I never spend time with him the next. If he's like this at nine, I can only pray for Jesus to return before he becomes a teenager."

Tanesha fanned herself and rocked back and forth. "Ain't that the truth, ain't that the truth!" Her face took on a more serious expression, and she gave Elle a comforting smile. "Tell me, though. How is it *really*?"

Elle pulled a plastic knife out of her drawer and began deboning the chicken breast to build herself a biscuit sandwich. *How is it?* Six sessions into PT, and Lucas still fought like she was driving him to the gallows before each appointment. Both the doctors and his physical therapist had yelled — okay, not yelled — stressed emphatically that he had to do the exercises at home every day. And there was Charm. Her gratitude for his presence and help warred with frustration and jealousy. Yes, jealousy. She had to work while he got to spend his days bonding with her son.

"Exhausting," she said finally. "I feel like I'm drowning. I take Lucas to PT, but Charm gets better results by bribing him with that" — she managed to swallow an expletive — "dog. Charm is trying harder around the farm, but his definition of 'done right' ranks somewhere between my 'barely started' and 'Are you kidding?'"

"Oh, honey, that's a man for you," Tanesha commiserated.

*Not Jake.* Elle banished that thought and continued. "So instead of spending my evenings with my son, I spend them re-doing the things Charm *almost* did during the day." She took a bite of her sandwich. Heaven. Pure heaven. "I have too many biscuits. Help yourself."

"I had three with lunch," Tanesha said, but she picked the crusty top off one and popped it in her mouth with a moan of happiness. "Have you tried showing him the way you want it done?"

Elle cringed and nodded. "Didn't go over well. Told me I was anal retentive."

"Are you?"

"Probably." They laughed, and she watched Tanesha pull bits of fluffy white biscuit and nibble at them. "I really ought to cut him some slack. At least he's keeping Lucas busy with that *training* project" — she emphasized with air quotes — "I told them not to do. The one they think I don't know about."

"Sounds like they listen 'bout as well as my kids. Would you believe James and Malik tried to hop on a moving train the other day?" Disgust sent her voice up an octave. "James is twelve. I expect nonsense like that from him, but Malik is only eight. I tanned their hides so bad they won't even play with a model train till they're grown."

Elle couldn't help but snicker. "I think Charm was about eight the first time he hitched a ride on a train. Or, at least that's the story Mom tells. She says that's when she knew he was going to be a traveler." Her smile faded. Tying Charm down in Collier wasn't fair. If only she didn't need his help so badly.

Tanesha squeezed her hand. "Tell me what's really got you so down. I could see it on your face when I got here."

Elle hesitated. "Money," she finally admitted. "I just…" She gestured at the office around her. "I don't think we're going to make it." Her eyes filled with tears.

Tanesha shook her head and patted Elle's hand. "Don't you believe that for a second. Have you asked for help? There's agencies…"

Elle blushed and shook her head. "We're not that bad yet."

Tanesha shook her head. "Pride goeth before a fall. Or so I've heard. So, what *are* you going to do?"

Panic swirled in the pit of her stomach. What *was* she going to do? Her head spun. As she tried to still the chaos that threatened to overwhelm her, her gaze fell on a flyer taped to the outside of the fast-food bag. A Help Wanted flyer. Deep breath.

"I guess," she said, "I'll fight harder."

Tanesha looked at the bag and then back at her. "No. You're not going to spend your evenings working at a fast-food place for minimum wage." She thought for a moment. "You live down in Collier, right?"

Elle nodded.

"Let me make a call."

# CHAPTER 8

Y ou got a second job?" Charm's razor froze mid-swipe, plans for his evening at Brother Jack's temporarily forgotten as he swiveled to stare at his sister.

Ellie glared at him and glanced nervously down the hall. "Keep your voice down. I haven't told Lucas yet." She stepped inside the bathroom and shut the door. "I didn't have a choice," she said in a hushed voice.

Charm opened his mouth to ask a question, then held up a finger to pause the conversation. He finished the last of his shave and wiped his face clean, then motioned her to follow him downstairs. He grabbed his jacket on his way through the entrance hall and tossed it over a chair when they reached the kitchen.

"What job?" he asked, grabbing two beers from the fridge. He offered her one, but she waved it away. He set it on the counter. *Might need a second.*

Ellie leaned back against the counter, arms crossed against her chest. "Waitress at Collier Caboose, that restaurant on the square."

"Where the old train-stop buildings used to be?"

She nodded. "Evenings to close every day except Friday and Monday. The manager is the brother of one of my coworkers."

"Starting when?"

"Tomorrow." She wouldn't meet his gaze.

"What about Lucas?"

She paced to the far end of the kitchen and back again. "Nothing changes. His PT and doctor visits are scheduled over lunch."

Charm's stomach tightened. "I meant at night."

She stopped moving and looked at him, then dropped her gaze and resumed pacing. "I don't know yet," she muttered.

Relief she hadn't asked him to give up his evenings at Brother Jack's grated against guilt that he wanted relief from days spent with a nine-year-old. Perversely, irritation overrode both the relief and the guilt. Her selflessness was so damn *irritating*. He chugged his beer and tossed the bottle overhand across the room into the trash.

"So, your plan is to work full-time for the county, spend nights working for some restaurant, and in your spare moments ferry your kid around?" He opened the second bottle. His eyes met hers — red and swollen with tears dammed up behind her own frustration.

"What do you want me to do, Charm? I have bills to pay. Those beers you're guzzling cost money."

*Ooh, right to the heart.* "So, how did it work before? I assume you haven't always lived on the edge of bankruptcy."

"Not to my knowledge," she said darkly. "We raise beef cattle. Some corn. Some hay. We'd make enough through the year to pay the bills and keep us going. Like a lot of farm wives, I worked because my job provides health insurance and a bit of predictable cash for the lean times or unexpected expenses." She stopped pacing and sagged against the counter, as if the weight of her life burdens were too much to bear. "Two years ago, a summer tornado took out most of our stock and damn near all our corn. Jake said we would be all right, and I believed him."

And clearly wouldn't make that mistake again, Charm concluded. "Didn't you sell cattle last year?"

"Yeah, some, but we've been putting a lot of our profit back into the herd, trying to get back to the numbers we were at before. We're still not quite there, and we didn't plan for all this." She waved toward the bills piled up in the corner.

Who would have? Charm rolled the beer bottle between his fingers and considered possible solutions. "You're right," he said.

"Usually," she said dryly, "but about what specifically?"

He finished the beer and deposited it in the trash, less colorfully this time. "These beers cost money. I cost money."

"I don't want you to leave, Charm —"

"Hadn't considered it. I'll get a job tending bar at Brother Jack's. It won't keep you from needing a second job, but it'll cover my expenses." *And my beer.* He pulled on his jacket.

Ellie shook her head. "I draw the line at having my son spend his evenings in a bar."

"Wouldn't be my first choice either." Nothing like a nine-year-old kid to tank a social life. Charm pulled a butter knife from a drawer and checked his hair and teeth.

Ellie arched her eyebrow. "Why are you primping?" She batted her eyes. "Is there something you and Jimmy Lee want to share?"

He snorted. "Angeline usually stops by on Thursday nights." Satisfied with his reflection, he turned back to her. "Anyway, I wasn't thinking about taking Lucas to the bar."

"He can't stay home alone either."

He watched her carefully. "What if Mom stayed with him?" Her eyes got big, and he held up his hands to ward off an explosion. "It's not ideal. I get that. But we don't have a whole lot of options unless you want to take him to the restaurant with you. We need the money, and you know it."

She growled under her breath and glared.

"It sucks," he said. "The whole thing sucks right now. But we're gonna get through it."

"Promise?"

Her tone was light, but Charm heard the uncertainty below it. Even Superwoman wasn't all-powerful all the time. He kissed her forehead and pulled her into a hug. "I promise."

That promise weighed on him as he drove to Brother Jack's a few minutes later, banishing thoughts of beautiful Angeline to the back of his mind. *Will we get through it? What if we truly can't raise the money Ellie needs? What will happen to Ellie and Lucas then? Where will they go?*

Maybe he should get a daytime job, as well. He needed to buy some new clothes and shoes. Honestly, he was going to need a car too. No, he doubted his mother would want to take Lucas all day *and* all evening. Maybe when Lucas was able to go back to school.

Of course, if he were working, he might be able to convince Lucas to give up on the idea of training River. Even as Charm thought it, he knew that wouldn't happen. Training River was the buoy keeping Lucas afloat. Ellie grasped at her plan, her strategy, the to-do list that inched her toward the finish line. Lucas had River. And Charm would be damned before he let Lucas fail.

Charm strode into the smoky darkness of Brother Jack's and scanned the room. He had begun to recognize the regulars, and it seemed like a typical Thursday dinner crowd. Oscar sat at one end of the bar, sharing close conversation with a woman Charm didn't recognize. All of the bar seats were taken, and a group of farmers — Charm recognized Ray Forbes in the middle — crowded the center area. *First things first.*

He made his way to the end of the bar and laid a hand on Oscar's shoulder. "Hey. You gonna be here a few minutes?"

Oscar barely spared him a glance. "I hope not," he said with a flirty smile at the woman next to him.

Charm ignored that. "Hang around. I need to talk to you. It's important." Without waiting for a reply, he called out to the bartender. "Hey, Max, can I talk to you?"

Max Webster, a round man on the far side of fifty, glanced up from the mug of beer he was filling from a silver tap. Without pausing the conversation he was having with Ray Forbes's groupies or spilling a drop of beer, Max nodded and jerked his head toward the kitchen. Charm slipped around the crowd and ducked behind the bar and into what a sign designated as an employees-only kitchen.

Jimmy Lee's sister, Maggie, entered at something close to light speed behind him. "On your right!"

Charm pressed himself against the wall to keep from being run over. "Geez, Magpie."

"This is a working kitchen, not a rest station." She grabbed a ticket and loaded prepared plates onto a tray.

Max entered from the bar, wiped his hands on a towel hanging near the door, and habitually scanned the activity buzzing around him. "Turtle, them dishes are piling up. Let's get 'em done and out of the way." He motioned to Charm to follow him. "What can I do for you?"

Max's brusque tone matched Maggie's. Dinner rush maybe wasn't the best time for this, but too late now. "I want to come work for you. Closing bartender. Whatever nights you want."

Max reviewed a ticket from the kitchen line. "Maggie, you're up! Don't let this soup get cold."

"God forbid," she said, loading the soup and several plates on a second tray. She hefted both and accelerated back to the dining area.

Max looked sideways at Charm while he reviewed the next ticket. "Who says I need another bartender?"

Charm grinned. "You do. You hate working close, and your wife hates that you do it."

Max grimaced. "Where are the fries for this burger? And it needs a side of blue cheese." He abruptly sped toward the freezer, and Charm had to jog to keep up. "Who says you're the one I should hire? Bar regulars don't always make great bartenders." He met Charm's eyes. "They tend to drink up my profits."

Charm kept his gaze steady. "I'll pay for anything I drink."

"Damn straight you will." Max shuffled some frozen patties from a box to a shelf. "You got any experience?"

"Some. I worked a couple of restaurants in St. Louis. Waited tables. Backup bartender."

Max tossed empty boxes toward the back door and shut the freezer. He turned and regarded Charm for a long minute. "Well, you're personable enough, and the women sure like you. All right, I'll give you a try." Before Charm could thank him, he added, "You want to drink your paycheck, that's fine with me as long as you don't start fights and don't get a DUI. You drive drunk, and I'll fire your ass, understand?"

Charm kept his voice steady. "Yes sir. I understand."

"Be here at four tomorrow. We'll do some paperwork, and then we'll do the first shift together. Tending bar here means you do any job in the front of house that needs doing."

Charm smiled and backed toward the door to the bar. "Thanks, Max. I owe ya!" The voices and overloud jukebox in the bar drowned out any response. *Maybe this will ease Ellie's load a little.* He thought about the empty wallet in his back pocket. *With maybe a little left for me.* Ellie surely wouldn't begrudge him a little entertainment money.

"How's your nephew doing?"

The question prodded Charm from his thoughts. Ray Forbes beamed at him. "Good. He's doing good," Charm said. He nodded politely and tried to circle the group gathered around Forbes. Needed to get to Oscar before he took off.

Forbes motioned expansively. "I was just telling my friends about how I loaned my imported retriever to Jake. He wanted so much to be a field trainer — just needed a little help. I was happy to do it, of course."

Charm plastered a polite smile on his face and nodded. "Yes, that was very generous of you." *To loan a dog you couldn't train to an inexperience trainer.*

"And when I heard how much little Luke loves that dog, I knew I had to give him to you." A murmur of approving voices swelled around him, and Forbes preened like a peacock.

*Privileged ass.* Despite the annoyance digging at his spine, Charm had played this role too many times to betray his emotions with so much as a flicker of a frown. "Oh, yes sir, we're incredibly grateful for your generosity. Lucas" — he emphasized the boy's name — "spends about every waking minute with River. He hopes to train him for field trials, like his father wanted."

Something, a shadow, passed over Forbes's face.

Charm froze but didn't let his expression waver. "Of course," he hastened to say, "there's little chance of that."

Forbes's face brightened again. "Of course not. But I'm so glad that *my* dog" — he emphasized the possessive — "makes the little boy so happy."

Forbes turned to one of his friends then, and Charm was able to nod his goodbyes. Something about Forbes didn't sit right with him.

His dad would have said *"If Forbes were a horse, I'd be wary in the saddle."* As focused as Charm was on getting to the far end of the bar where Oscar, thankfully, still chatted with the unfamiliar blonde, he still mentally noted that the memory of his father hadn't been accompanied by a wave of pain or anger. *Maybe there was hope.* "I need to talk to you," Charm said when he reached Oscar.

Oscar didn't even glance up. "I'm busy, Freeman."

Charm checked out the woman. Mid-thirties. Too much makeup. Bedazzled jacket from the eighties. *Jesus, Oscar, set some standards.* "Consider it a favor for Ellie."

Oscar's gaze flickered toward him, then back to the woman. "Give me sixty seconds, sweetheart." He grabbed Charm's arm and steered him out of earshot. "What?"

"I think there's something wrong with River."

Oscar nodded to the bedazzled woman and held up a finger to assure her he would be back in a minute. "You pulled me away from a lonely woman to talk about a dog? I'm gonna beat the crap out of you later." He kept the smile on his face, but his tone sounded ominous.

"It's important."

Oscar sighed and pulled a container of chewing tobacco from his shirt pocket. "Your obsession with that mutt isn't healthy." He tucked a bit of chew in his bottom lip. "What's wrong?"

"When you had him, did River like to retrieve?"

Oscar stared at Charm like he'd grown three heads. "He's a retriever. Of course, he did."

"I didn't ask if he *could.* I asked if he *liked* it."

"He's a working retriever. He lived for it." He frowned. "Are you saying he won't retrieve?"

"Runs the other way."

Oscar blinked at him for several seconds, then shook his head. "He's just gotten lazy. Them curly dogs don't have the same drive as field-bred Labs."

"What do we do about it?"

Oscar looked around for something to spit in. "Refresh his collar conditioning." He lifted a hand to get Maggie's attention.

"Hey, Maggie, you got —" She dropped out of warp speed to hand him an empty Coke can from the table she had just bussed.

"What's collar conditioning?" Charm asked.

Oscar spit in the can. "E-collar. *Electronic* collar. It's how hunting dogs are trained. Let me guess. You haven't got one."

Charm ignored his exasperated tone. Barely. This "make nice" crap was tough. He shook his head. "No clue. Lucas didn't tell me to use one."

Oscar sneered. "Why you letting a ten-year-old tell you how to train a dog?"

Nine-year-old, but probably shouldn't mention that. *Crap, crap, crap.* Charm had no idea how to do this on his own. Maybe Jimmy Lee…nah. He disregarded that idea. Jimmy Lee was up for adventure, but he knew less about training dogs than Charm did. There was only one option. And it really, really hurt. He gritted his teeth. "Can you help us?"

Oscar regarded him for a long moment. Charm could practically see possible responses — all of them sarcastic — swirling in Oscar's mind. and he steeled himself to resist a snarky comeback. Oscar finally rolled his eyes. "If I say yes, will you let me get back to my girl?"

Charm swallowed his opinion about said "girl." *Not the time, Freeman.* As if rewarding his self-control, Angeline and a friend walked through the front door. Charm made eye contact with her, and she flashed a bright smile. Even though he'd gone there expressly to see her, a twinge of guilt still tightened his gut. *Sandrine is gone. She would want me to keep living.*

He patted Oscar on the shoulder. "Won't interrupt again." He started toward Angeline, then turned back. "Tomorrow?"

Oscar rolled his eyes. "If it doesn't rain."

Charm grinned. Two things on his list accomplished, and the third was waiting for him. Best of all, he had a possible solution to his issue with River. Yes, this was turning into a fine night indeed.

# Chapter 9

I t rained.

And it rained the next day. And the next. When the rain finally stopped for a few days, Oscar was traveling for work. By the time he returned, so had the rain. Of course. Charm didn't remember Mississippi being this *wet* in winter. Later in the month, the weather gods threw in tornadoes. Twice he had to haul Lucas and the dog into the basement. Fortunately, neither tornado hit Collier directly, and neither did much damage, except to Charm's attitude.

The storms directly reflected the mood of the household. Charm spun from chores to babysitting to work with little time for anything else, which didn't exactly endear him to Angeline, who moved on to someone "more present."

His schedule was nothing compared to Ellie's, though. In late, out early. The only time he saw her was when Lucas had an appointment with a doctor or physical therapist, and those moments weren't exactly happy family time. Lucas *hated* those appointments the way Charm hated fixing fences, even this week when he was finally allowed to put some weight on the leg. Nope. The kid tried yelling and then tears to escape the appointments, and when those failed, he settled on simple rebellion: he refused to cooperate.

Charm had considered adopting one or two of those strategies himself. He was now on his third re-do of the fence line — the cows had made it clear why the fence posts needed to be sunk deep and the wire strung tight. It didn't help matters that when Ellie had asked their mother to pitch in with Lucas, Dot had, to Charm's irritation, all but moved in. Jesus. Living with his mom and sister at thirty-four. *What a winner you are, Freeman.* The least she could have done was take over the house chores and free him up to have some kind of life, but she'd actually laughed when he suggested it. She *did* take over the meals. Hot food was nice, and since the bounty from the wake had run out, he and Lucas had basically lived on peanut butter and tomato soup. Cooking wasn't Charm's forte.

To Charm's surprise, after the initial adjustment, his mother added stability to the household. Good thing, too, because he needed a break from childcare. Lucas whined and sneered and challenged, and Charm returned like for like. Not only was Charm living with his mom and sister, but he'd also regressed into a prepubescent child.

His mother had also helped him find an ancient Crown Victoria that would have made him feel like he was driving a police cruiser had it not been painted neon green. Ah, well, beggars couldn't be choosers. It got him to work and back, even if it did smell like old turnips. He named it Vlad.

The last week of February was fast approaching when the skies cleared, the weather warmed, and Oscar finally agreed to work with River. Thank God. Maybe they could finally turn around this shit show of a month.

* * *

"I still think we ought to give this one more try." Oscar shook the electronic collar. It was dripping with mud — like all of them. Well, like Oscar and Charm. Lucas would have been clean and dry had he not been hanging from Charm's back.

River growled. Whether it was actually toward the e-collar, Charm couldn't be sure, but he tightened his leash anyway. "I think you'll lose a limb if you try to put that thing back on that dog."

It had taken two attempts for Charm to determine definitively that collar conditioning wasn't the issue. At eleven that morning, the group had traipsed into the pasture behind the house to refresh his collar conditioning. "The collar," Oscar explained, "is just to reinforce a command the dog already knows." River knew how to retrieve; he had, in Oscar's opinion, gotten lazy. "I took this dog through the whole collar-conditioning program myself," he said. "We should be able to run through it very quickly, start to finish, and get him retrieving again."

River sat quietly while Oscar fitted the collar. Rather than jumping into retrieves, Oscar first ran the dog through a series of obedience commands. River came, sat, heeled, and stayed with precision, no correction needed, even when Oscar tried to trick him into making a mistake. To Charm, it didn't look like River had the interest or energy to make a mistake. Despite the flawless performance, Charm couldn't shake the feeling that something wasn't right.

Oscar seemed nonplussed by River's responses. Unable to find a fault, he moved to the next step, and that's where they discovered a problem. He knelt beside River and held out a bumper. Without hesitation, River grabbed it…and then dropped it. Oscar was so surprised, he didn't correct the mistake.

"That's weird," he admitted. "I never had a problem with him dropping bumpers." He picked up the bumper and held it out again. River grabbed it cleanly, and then dropped it. The instant his mouth opened, Oscar corrected him. The dog flinched and yelped.

"You hurt him!" Lucas cried.

Oscar frowned. "No, I didn't. It's not turned high. He shouldn't have reacted like that." He took the collar off and examined the prongs, then put it around his own arm and tested it. "It's fine. Must have startled him." He didn't sound entirely convinced but refastened it around the dog's neck.

Something was wrong. Charm could feel it. "Oscar, wait —"

Too late. Oscar offered the bumper, River took it, and River dropped it. Oscar hit him with a correction, and this time the dog jerked and screamed like he had been set on fire. He pulled backward, broke away, and bolted. Lucas burst into tears.

Charm swore and sprinted after the dog, imagining a chase like the last time River had gotten away from him. Fortunately, this time the dog went only a hundred yards or so to the far side of the small stock pond that provided water to the pasture. Thick brush behind him more or less trapped him in that small area. Unfortunately, the cows had turned the area around the pond into a mud pit.

"You go around left," Oscar said. "I'll get him from the right."

Had it not been for the mud, it would have been a stellar plan. Charm remembered trying to catch a greased pig at the fair when he was about Lucas's age. Trying to catch River in this mud was worse. First, the mud sucked his shoes off, then it left him flat on his back staring at the sky. At least Oscar ended up in the pond. Charm did, too, but seeing Oscar do a face-plant in the brackish water made the whole experience worth it — until Lucas whistled, and River trotted right to him and waited patiently for him to snap the leash on.

That was the end of the training session.

"You don't understand," Oscar said as they made their way back to the house. "This isn't *normal.* I've trained this dog. With an e-collar. He shouldn't have reacted like that."

Charm made a noncommittal noise. His misgivings about the session currently took a back seat to his irritation with being a pack horse. How had Oscar ended up with only the e-collar while he carried Lucas and the bumpers *and* had the leash of a clearly unrepentant dog?

Lucas hadn't moved on so quickly. "You hurt him!" he wailed from Charm's back.

"I didn't. I'm telling you, he knows how this works. Something else is going on." Oscar veered off the path to avoid a puddle, not that he could have gotten wetter. Or muddier. "Maybe we should ask Tim Layton. He's training Forbes's dogs now."

"No!" Lucas said. "This is my project, and I don't need him. You guys just don't know what you're doing."

"Oh, like you two were doing so great on your own." Oscar glared at the boy. "But you know what? If you want to do it yourself, that's fine with me. I quit."

"That's enough, children!" Charm snapped. Oscar turned his glare on him. Charm guessed Lucas was glaring too. Instead, when Lucas spoke, his voice shook.

"You're not giving up, are you, Uncle Charm?"

Charm navigated them through the pasture gate and shut it behind them. He considered his response carefully. "I'm not giving up," he said, "but we have to be realistic. This dog may not be cut out for field trials."

"He is! Dad said he was." His nephew's voice quavered and his volume rose. "My dad wouldn't lie to me! River only needs a chance. Please."

The raw desperation in the plea tore at Charm. Lucas's grief for his father was now inextricably bound to River and this project. *Oh God, what happens if the dog doesn't win?* The idea sat like lead in his stomach. Had Ellie been right? Was he setting Lucas up to fall even harder?

Beside him, Oscar came to a sudden halt. "Uh-oh."

Charm stopped and looked where Oscar was looking. Ellie stood on the front porch, arms crossed, eyes blazing fire Charm could see from a hundred feet away. "I think we forgot something."

"Physical therapy." Lucas sounded matter-of-fact. Even gleeful.

Charm made a silent promise to hang the kid upside down from the barn rafters for an hour or two. Ellie had started tapping her toe. "We'd better face the music."

"Who's we?" Oscar pulled his muddy cap lower on his forehead. "You're on your own, Freeman." He strode to his truck without looking back.

"Coward." Charm looked back toward Ellie and wondered if he could make it to Oscar's truck before he drove off. Instead, he gritted his teeth and marched to the house.

"I'm not seeing this," Ellie said without preamble. "Tell me I'm not seeing this. We have a PT appointment in fifteen minutes. What the hell happened, Charm?"

"Drive-by mudding." He walked past her.

Their mother met them on the porch and took River's leash. "I'll take care of this one."

"Thanks." He headed upstairs, Ellie on his heels. "Cool your jets, Ellie. All he has to do is change his clothes. He wasn't rolling in the pigsty."

"Do you think this is funny?" she demanded. "I don't have time for this."

Lucas released his grip on Charm's neck and slid to the floor, landing awkwardly on one leg. "You never have time for anything!" He half hopped, half limped into his bedroom and slammed the door.

Ellie stared. "He walked."

Charm snorted. "He's pissed off enough to fly."

His sister opened her mouth, and Charm squared off, ready for battle. But she gave a sharp shake of her head and turned away. "We'll talk about this later," she promised and followed Lucas into his room.

Charm shook his head. "Can't wait."

* * *

Elle slipped into Lucas's bedroom and quietly shut the door behind her. He pointedly ignored her and hopped from closet to dresser gathering clean clothes. She bit her lip to squash the urge to tell him the doctor wanted him to use a crutch rather than hop.

Anger clenched Lucas's jaw as he set about the task of getting undressed. The muddy shirt was stripped off and tossed near a laundry basket. His jeans were tougher. He pushed them down as much as he could and, using the dresser for support, tried to wiggle and stomp his feet to get the pants the rest of the way off.

"Let me help…" Elle offered.

"I can do it. You don't have to do everything for me."

She bit her lip and stepped back. "I can see that."

Lucas stomped the jeans the rest of the way to the floor, then sat on the edge of his bed and pulled a clean shirt over his head. "You're never here. And when you are here, you treat me like a defective baby."

"You're not defective. Or a baby."

"Why aren't you ever here anymore?" He clenched his fists. "The only time I ever see you is when I have a damn rehab appointment."

"Don't swear," she corrected automatically.

Lucas snatched the only thing he could reach — the remote for the TV — and threw it to the floor. "Damn! Damn, damn, damn!"

Elle grabbed his shoulders like she was going to shake him but instead pulled him to her. His slender body stiffened and struggled, and he flailed at her, screaming to let him go. She tightened her hold. "I've got you," she whispered.

The boy collapsed against her and sobbed, weeks of pain and anger pouring out. They sank to the floor together, and she crooned and rocked him as she had when he was a toddler.

"I'm so sorry," she murmured. "I hate being away, Lucas. I hate having to work."

He looked up, eyes swollen and cheeks blotchy. "Quit."

Elle hesitated, and he pushed away. "I can't," she said as he used the bed to pull himself up. "We have bills to pay." She rose to her feet.

"Dad had bills to pay, but he still had time for me!" He swung his broken leg onto the bed and curled forward to try to hook the clean jeans over his foot. He missed and tried again. When missed the third time, Elle caught them and slid them on his leg. Lucas jerked the pants out of her hand. "I said I can do it!"

She signaled her apology and stepped back, racking her brain to figure out some way to soothe him. With the troublesome leg back in the jeans, it took Lucas little time to finish dressing. Without speaking, he limped past her and made his way to the bathroom where he combed his curls — a challenge under the best of circumstance, but she appreciated the effort — and made a passable attempt to remove the mud on his chin and hands.

"I'm ready," he said finally, his voice dull and subdued.

Elle took a deep breath. "Why don't we skip physical therapy today?"

He blinked and looked suspicious. "Won't you get in trouble?"

Elle smiled. "Probably. But we're late anyway, and they'll get over it."

"What about work?"

"I still have to work." When his face fell, she added, "But I have an hour and a half, and it's all yours. To do anything you want."

His eyes widened. "Even play with River?"

She managed to keep the smile plastered on her face. "Even play with River." Lucas threw his arms around her, and she hugged him tight and kissed his head. "Just do me a favor," she said. "Use your crutches."

* * *

Charm escaped outside, glad that Lucas's little scene had distracted Ellie before their tiff had blown up into a real argument. Okay, yeah, he had forgotten the appointment, but he did it to help her kid. That had to be worth something, even if it did involve training the dog she had expressly told him not to train.

He traipsed around the house and found his mother next to the side porch spraying mud off the aforementioned retriever. She glanced at Charm through the top of her glasses and waved the hose his direction.

"You look like you need this more than him."

"I decided in the moment that retreat was a wiser tactic than a shower." He took the hose and River's leash and assumed the dog bathing duty.

His mother settled herself on the steps. "So I guess I don't need to ask how the training session went."

He grimaced and focused the spray on River's back paws. "Something's not right. Oscar said he wasn't like this before. He used to be retrieve-crazy, and now he doesn't want to pick up anything." *Well*, he corrected mentally. *Pick up but not hold.*

"Time for a trip to the vet?"

Charm winced. "Yeah, Ellie's working two jobs and can't pay the mortgage. I don't think vet care for a dog she wishes didn't exist is gonna be an option. At least not when we don't know for sure it's medical."

Dot fell silent for moment, then slapped her thigh. "Then I guess I'll pay for it."

He stared. "Why would you do that?"

"Because Lucas is my grandson. Besides, if there really is something wrong with that dog, it would be cruel not to fix it if we can."

Charm squinted, decades of suspicion overriding any gratitude he might have felt. "And if that fix costs thousands of dollars?"

"Don't create problems that don't exist." His mother pushed herself to her feet. "I'd better go make some lunch for Lucas and Eleanor."

"They're late for rehab. They're not gonna have time for lunch."

"We'll see," she said brightly. She winked and sauntered up the stairs and into the house.

"Being a grandmother has softened you!" he called after her. He shook his head. Bemused, he muttered, "Done lost your mind."

He was still shaking his head and mumbling under his breath five minutes later when Ellie came down the stairs with a towel. By this time he had finished with River and was spraying the worst of the mud off himself. He eyed the towel. "Good timing."

She settled on the steps where their mother had been minutes earlier. "It's actually for him," she said with a jerk of her chin toward River, but she handed it over anyway. The retriever had already shaken off most of the water and was now alternately rolling and rubbing his face and shoulders in the grass.

Charm plopped down beside her and dried his face and hands anyway. "I don't think he'll mind. I take it you're not going to PT?"

"Not only are we not going to PT, but I have volunteered to spend an hour playing with that dog." She sounded disgusted by the idea.

"Oooh, that bad?" Charm made a kiss noise to get River's attention and motioned him over.

"I think my son hates me."

"He doesn't hate you. His whole world has crashed in on him." Charm rubbed the retriever's head with the towel. "He's lost his dad, he's lost school and his friends, you're working two jobs, and he's stuck with this weird guy he's never met."

"That's the worst," Ellie said.

"Totally." The siblings grinned at each other. Charm continued drying River for a moment, then asked as casually as he could, "I'm curious. Why didn't you raise a stink about us going behind your back to train River?"

She made a noise in her throat and shot him a glare, but she couldn't keep the corners of her mouth from turning up. "I love my son, and I love you, and I didn't want to discourage you from doing something together. Even if it does have to be a project with this dog."

River decided he'd had enough drying and presented his butt for scratching.

Ellie absently scritched the itchy spot right above his tail. "So what do I do now?" she asked.

Charm noted that she knew exactly where that itchy spot was and how River liked it scratched. "What you've been doing. Put one foot in front of the other. Lucas will be okay. He needs time."

She nodded, and they fell silent, watching River butt dance in ecstasy. Time, Charm reflected. It was all about time. Lucas needed time to grieve. Ellie needed time with her son. He himself would kill for some time away from farm chores.

"I have an idea," he said. "Next week is Mardi Gras."

She arched an eyebrow. "You would know that."

He ignored the jibe. "Biloxi has a pretty good parade. Let's go. Next Tuesday. No work. We drive down in the morning, back that night."

"You want me to call off work to drive four hours — each way — for a parade."

"Nope. I want you to call off work to spend a day having fun with your family." He bumped her with his shoulder. "Whadda ya say?"

She looked at River. Entranced by the delightful butt scritchies, River had now dropped into what Charm referred to as "upside-down pretzel dog." Butt still in the air, his front half on the ground twisted onto his left shoulder, as if he were trying to roll over for belly rubs. He craned his neck as much as possible to grin up at them, and his tail wagged furiously.

Ellie rose to her feet and headed inside. "Your dog is weird."

Charm chuckled. "He's not my dog."

She didn't respond.

He jumped to his feet and followed her, River at his heels. "Ellie? He's not my dog…"

# CHAPTER 10

Considering his luck with weather, Charm half expected a blizzard, or at least rain, to blanket southern Mississippi on Fat Tuesday. Instead, the storm had brewed in their kitchen. A six-pack of beer in the cooler wasn't asking much, but Ellie refused. Then she insisted on driving because she didn't believe he was entirely sober.

Charm reasoned he was close enough, but Ellie wouldn't budge, so he topped off his flask and settled into the passenger seat to doze. By the time he, Ellie, and Lucas arrived in Biloxi, it was near lunchtime, and any early frustrations had yielded to the excitement of being away from Collier.

"Well, isn't this a diamond in the Cracker Jack box?" Charm drawled when they lucked into a primo picnicking spot at the edge of the beach about halfway through the parade route. The parade wasn't due to start for another hour, which meant it would probably be a couple of hours before it got to them, but families packed the beach between the Gulf and US 90. Sunny skies had edged the temperature into the low sixties, but the breeze from the Gulf was both chilly and pervasive, so most people were dressed warmly.

Charm leaned back on the blanket they had brought and filled his senses with Biloxi. The beach, like the route itself, sported festive green, gold, and purple decorations, the colors of Mardi Gras Biloxi shared with New Orleans. Jazz music blared all around them. He closed his eyes and breathed deep the briny scent of the water, a scent, truth be told, he didn't particularly like. People spoke of "fresh ocean air," but apparently, he hadn't been to the right oceans. In his opinion, the beach smelled like algae and rotting fish.

Ellie poked him and offered a peanut butter and jelly sandwich wrapped in waxed paper. "What are you thinking about?"

The flaps on the sandwich formed neat triangles. Exactly how their mother used to do it. "The smell of home," he said. "I wintered here for several years after I left Collier. When the carnival wasn't operating."

She unwrapped a sandwich and handed it to Lucas. "Why here?"

"Virgil lived here." At her blank look, he clarified, "Virgil Wade. The owner. I stayed with him during the offseason." Charm unwrapped his own sandwich and took a big bite, not really tasting it. He was sixteen again, asking the grizzled carnival owner for work, keeping his famous smile plastered on his face as he claimed skills he didn't have. "I lied about my age when I applied for the job. He knew it, knew I was a runaway, but he took me in anyway. Carnivals are full of strays looking for family."

He grinned. "Virgil was this wiry little dude about six inches shorter than you. Had a wooden leg and a matchstick temper." He snorted. "Kicked my ass with that wooden leg plenty of times too. But he taught me everything I know about selling."

Charm took a deep breath and swiped a hand over his face. "He died a few years ago. Pretty sure his wife still lives here." Damn salt air was irritating his eyes.

Ellie screwed up her face. "Virgil Wade. I swear I've heard that name before." She shook her head and unwrapped her own sandwich. "Why'd you leave the carnival?"

"Virgil kicked me out." Over a decade had passed, but still a cacophony of emotions flooded through him when he voiced the words. He fell silent, remembering.

"Why'd he kick you out, Uncle Charm?" Lucas prompted.

Charm blinked. Damn. He'd forgotten his nephew was listening. He looked Lucas directly in the eyes and tapped his temple with his index finger. "He said I was way too smart to work for a carnival forever. So he sent me out to follow my dreams."

"And you traveled around the world and saw cool things?" The boy's eyes were wide and his cheeks slightly flushed.

Lucas's enthusiasm for Charm's stories usually encouraged Charm to paint them even bigger and more exciting. But a flash of himself as a boy, listening, rapt, to his own father's stories sobered him. Where had those stories gotten them? He tugged one of the boy's curls and smiled a bit sadly. "Something like that."

Before the boy could respond, Ellie tugged his sleeve. "Hey, Lucas, look over there."

The boy's head swiveled in the direction she was pointing. "A pirate!" A short distance away, a man in an elaborate costume pulled handfuls of Mardi Gras beads from a treasure chest and tossed them to passing children. "Beads! Can I get beads?" Lucas was already using a crutch to pull himself to his feet when Ellie nodded permission. He lurched off in a half hop, half run. Still a long way from tossing his crutches, but night and day from the sullen, resistant boy a week ago.

"You okay?" Ellie asked Charm.

Her kindness felt like ground glass in his gut. "Fine," he said. "I get a little maudlin when I think about the old days." It sounded good, and she seemed to buy it.

Ellie's eyes drifted back to her son. He had joined a throng of children clamoring for the strings of brightly colored beads. Despite watching Lucas's smile, the corners of her eyes wrinkled with concern. Hard to blame her. "Nice to see him having fun," Charm said casually.

She nodded and tore her gaze away. "He *is* having fun. Thanks for dragging us down here."

He patted her hand, happy for the change in subject. "You can always count on me to help you slack off." He grabbed a bag of chips and stuffed three in his mouth. "So what's your deal with Mom? I know why I have issues, but what about you?"

Ellie checked the group of children again, located Lucas standing to the side comparing beads with two other kids his age, and then responded. "She didn't want me to marry Jake. And after I did it anyway, she tried to talk me out of having children."

Charm's mouth dropped. *How could she not love Jake?* Jake had never told him that. Another wave of emotion, this one guilt. After all that Jake had sacrificed the night Charm left, his mother hadn't thought him good enough for her daughter? And Lucas? "But she loves Lucas," he managed to say.

She shrugged, clearly unaware of the tumult her revelation had caused. "I know. Didn't say she made sense. Speaking of..." Ellie leaned closer. "I heard a rumor that Madam Cold Heart paid for a vet visit."

Charm chuckled. "It's true. Drove all the way to Vicksburg for it."

"Was it worth the cash?"

He raised one eyebrow. "Apparently Lucas's cherished retriever is suffering from PTSD."

Ellie stared. "Post-traumatic stress disorder?"

Charm stole some of her chips. "That's what the vet said." He grimaced and wiggled his hand. "There's no real test for it, but he said it explained the sudden noise shyness."

She pushed her paper plate over to him. "But why won't he retrieve?"

"Broken jaw."

"What!"

He nodded grimly. "Hairline fracture healing nicely. Two molars really messed up, though. She's taking him in to get those pulled today."

Charm could see the conflicting emotions as she processed what he'd told her. "You mean, he was in pain —"

"Hey, Mom! Can I go to the pier?" Lucas's arrival was heralded with a spray of sand from the crutch he motioned with.

Ellie took a moment to brush the grit off her jeans and the anger from her face. When she looked up, her voice was carefully neutral. "Where?"

Lucas pointed down the beach at the narrow wooden platform jutting out over the Gulf of Mexico. "The pier. With Olivia." He motioned to a freckled redhead about his age standing a few feet away. The girl wiggled her fingers in greeting. "Her and her family are going to walk down there. Can I go?" Twenty feet farther away, a woman — Olivia's mom, Charm presumed — stood with a man and three other children, all freckled and red-haired. The woman raised her hand and smiled warmly.

The corners of Ellie's mouth turned up, and she returned the wave. "I suppose," she said, after a moment of consideration. "Don't make a nuisance of yourself." He was off without even a goodbye. Ellie watched him go, a smile that didn't quite meet her eyes plastered on her face. Charm could feel her anxiety building. "It's nice to see him with other kids," he said.

She half laughed and looked down, embarrassed. "You must think I'm ridiculous."

"No. I think you're a mom who almost lost her son."

A breath of relief escaped her, and some of the tension left her shoulders. Still the worry didn't entirely leave her eyes.

Charm cocked his head and glanced toward the pier. "Why should he have all the fun? Want to take a walk?"

She laughed but climbed to her feet and waited for him to take off his shoes. "Does this make me a helicopter mom?" she asked as they meandered a discreet distance behind the family.

"Eh, I'll give you a pass."

She bumped him with her shoulder, and Charm had a sudden flash — a happy one this time — of how she used to do that when he teased her as a kid. Well, sometimes she did. Other times she punched his arm and yelled for their mother. He had missed his sister.

As parade time drew nearer, more individuals filled the strip of white sand. Charm steered Ellie away from the road, toward the area where waves lapped at the shore and some of the braver children built sandcastles. Every so often Charm and Ellie had to retreat to the drier sand when a larger wave threatened to soak their feet. The late-February sun warmed his face, but it was much too early to wade in the Gulf.

"So why *did* he kick you out?" Ellie asked, switching back to their conversation about his carnival past. "Virgil. Why'd he fire you?"

"I told you. He said carnival life wasn't good enough for me. He didn't want me to turn into him."

"Was he right?"

Charm didn't answer. *Was he?* It hadn't felt like it. It had felt like losing his family a second time. Charm had thought Virgil was joking at first — until Virgil had shoved $500 into his hands. Severance. A huge amount for a twenty-year-old still paid under the table. Charm had thrown the money back at him and raged at the unfairness. Begged for another chance, not even sure what he'd done. Broke down. Then stumbled to his trailer to pack four years of a vagabond's life. His stuff fit in a duffel. Five stages of grief in about fifteen minutes.

Through it all, even when he entered Charm's trailer and tucked the bills into his bag, Virgil had remained quiet and resolute. Charm could still hear him say, "You're too comfortable."

It had taken years for Charm to understand what Virgil had meant, what he had offered. This was what Charm had wanted when he left home on a stormy night when he was sixteen. He could do anything. All he had to do was decide. And act.

*Was Virgil right?* Charm glanced sideways at his sister. "I haven't decided yet."

"You traveled everywhere. That must count for something," she said.

Traveled. Telling Lucas fanciful travel stories had been a way to distract the boy, to entertain him. But when Ellie mentioned them, the stories felt more like lies than fairy tales. Why hadn't he told her the truth the very first day? *This has to stop.* Charm realized he'd stopped walking and Ellie was staring at him.

"You okay?" she asked.

"I haven't traveled anywhere," he blurted. "I haven't been past St. Louis."

He waited for an angry outburst about lying, but instead she looked puzzled. "What about the stories?"

"Those weren't my stories. They were Sandrine's. Mostly."

"Who's Sandrine?"

Charm winced. He hadn't meant to mention Sandrine. *I guess today is a day of confessions.* "A woman I...dated." Loved. Wanted to marry. A traveler who had finally convinced him to make the jump. "She's gone now." *Let it go, Ellie.*

"Gone where?"

He looked at the Gulf. "She died. Car crash. In Paris."

*He stood next to the security line at the airport as long as he could. "Go home," she said with a laugh. "I'll be fine. I'll see you next week in Paris. We'll talk every night."*

*He kissed her one last time. "Promise?"*

*"I promise!"*

*Another kiss, and he reluctantly walked away.*

*"I love you!" she called after him.*

*He turned around to call back, but she had reached the front of the line and was showing her boarding pass. Something she said made the typically serious agent smile, and she walked through. He waited and watched her put her carry-on things on the belt and take off her shoes. Sixty seconds more, and she was through. She looked up as she slipped her shoes back on and waved. Then she was gone.*

"I'm sorry," Ellie said.

Charm blinked and managed a smile. "It's all right."

They started walking again. "That's why you came here?" Ellie guessed.

"No. I came because I owed it to you and Jake to step in and help out. But...that's why I stayed. I don't have a lot to go back to anymore."

Perhaps sensing they'd spent enough time on depressing topics, Ellie turned them back toward the road and led them into a sea of people and vendors selling food or Mardi Gras trinkets. She picked up a doodad made of yarn and waved it at him. "Need a purple, green, and gold dreamcatcher?"

"Not today." He cocked his head and regarded her seriously. "What about you?"

She leaned back and arched an eyebrow. "Noooo. I don't need a dreamcatcher."

"No. Sorry. I meant, what are your dreams? When I left, you wanted to be an astronaut."

She set the dreamcatcher back where she'd found it, and they continued down the row. "I was eleven. I prefer to be on Earth these days." Her voice had gotten tense. Maybe a little annoyed. But Charm pushed ahead anyway.

"You have to have a passion for something," he said, warming to his subject. "You were going to school."

She scowled and waved her hands as if trying to brush the subject out of the air. "That was nothing. Night school. Prelaw."

"That's not nothing."

She turned to face him, her jaw tight, and snapped, "What difference does it make now, Charm? Dreams don't pay the mortgage."

"Hey, Mom! Come look!"

Lucas's voice echoed through the crowd. Charm and Ellie looked, and he waved to them from perhaps fifty feet away. Apparently, they hadn't been as stealthy as they thought.

Lucas and his friends stood in front of three small wooden booths with glass fronts. Inside each, Charm discovered, was a white chicken who would play a game with you for the bargain price of fifty cents. In the booth nearest Lucas, an electronic tic-tac-toe board filled most of the back of the booth. A sign at the top encouraged them to try their luck against the world's smartest barnyard fowl.

"Look at this cool chicken!" Lucas held out his right hand. His left held a partially devoured deep-fried Twinkie. "Can I have some money?"

"I hope you thanked them for that," Ellie said, digging through her purse.

"Mommmm." But his annoyance wasn't enough to turn down the quarters he wanted.

"All I have is a five," she said, producing a crisp bill. Lucas's face fell.

"Uh…" Charm dug in his own pockets and pulled out a wadded

up-single. "I got a buck. No coins. Sorry."

"Do you folks need change?" The owner of the voice, a bored-looking young woman in jeans and a light jacket, stepped around the end of the exhibit. Charm automatically flashed the winsome smile that melted women's hearts like butter. She just held out her hand.

"Tough crowd," he muttered. He handed her the dollar bill, and she dropped four quarters into his hand. "Thanks." He gave fifty cents to Lucas, who dropped them in the coin slot, and the game began.

The chicken went first. It pecked the lower left square and an "X" appeared. It was Lucas's turn. "Don't play the center square," Charm said.

Lucas's hand hovered over the exterior game pad. "Why?"

"Because I want to see how smart this chicken is."

Lucas shrugged and chose the upper left square. An "O" filled the spot. The chicken chose the upper right. Lucas blocked her by selecting the center.

Charm laughed. "She won."

Sure enough, the chicken blocked Lucas's win by selecting the lower right, giving herself two ways to win. Lucas could block only one. When the chicken pecked the winning square, the game flashed its colorful lights, and the chicken received a few bits of rough ground corn.

"She's really smart," Lucas said.

Charm narrowed his eyes thoughtfully. "She sure is." He glanced over at the attendant, who looked as bored as ever. He tried his smile again. This time she looked pissed off. He cleared his throat. "Excuse me. Do you know anything about these chickens?"

The woman shrugged. "What do you want to know?"

"How does it work? What's the trick?"

She glowered and pointed at the sign above the exhibit. "World's smartest chickens."

"Can I do it again, Uncle Charm?"

Charm ruffled the boy's hair. "Nah, kid, the parade will be here soon. We should go find a spot near the road." As Ellie and Lucas headed back down the beach, he turned to the bored-looking attendant. Resisting the urge to point out that her attitude had cost the owner a repeat customer, he pasted on a polite smile one more time and asked, "You know anything about the company that builds these?"

She gave a loud, aggrieved sigh and disappeared behind the booths. A few seconds later she returned carrying a backpack. After another few moments of rooting around, she handed him a business card.

Charm squinted at it.

Brainy Beasties

Tallulah, LA

S. Clark, proprietor

Brainy Beasties. He tucked the card into his pocket. "Thanks for the scintillating conversation," he said and hurried to catch up with his family.

The parade was just as he remembered. A hundred themed floats, give or take, many of them blaring New Orleans jazz; lots of loud, happy people, many of them edging past tipsy; and lots of Mardi Gras beads, many of them ending up around Lucas's neck. By the time the King and Queen had passed, the boy had amassed dozens of the colorful strands.

Ellie and Lucas slept on the drive home, giving Charm a welcome respite from the boy's chatter and a chance to process his own day. Their mother, Jake, Virgil, Sandrine. Snippets of related and unrelated memories circled through his mind.

Miles of highway passed unseen as he replayed his conversations with Ellie. What she'd said about their mother didn't make sense. Their mother adored Lucas. And Jake. Pieces were missing from the story. *What had been going on with Jake? How much does Ellie know about the night I left?*

"I slept through most of it." Ellie's voice was thick with sleep. "I didn't wake up until the sirens." She shifted and curled up against the door.

"Sorry. Didn't know I was talking out loud." He focused on

what she'd said. "What sirens?"

She shrugged and, with a glance behind her to be sure Lucas still slept, waved off his concern. "Police and ambulance, I guess. Blue and red flashing lights. Sirens. I don't remember much. Mrs. Turner from down the road came and got me."

Charm stared at her, puzzled, then remembered himself and turned back to the road. His mouth opened, then closed. "What are you talking about?"

She blinked. More awake now. "Don't you know what happened that night?"

"Dad was drunk. We fought. I'd had enough." He recited the facts slowly, the pictures playing like a movie in his mind. "I packed a backpack and called Jake to come get me."

Jake had hesitated. Out with the football team celebrating a big win — his win. Four sacks and a shutout and more than a little pissed Charm had missed it.

*"I don't care. I'm done. I can't be here anymore." Charm crouched lower in the space between his parent's bed and the wall and held the receiver close to his mouth so he wouldn't be overheard. Boisterous voices in the background made it difficult to hear. "I only have to say goodbye to Ellie, and then I'm out of here."*

*"Charm, just wait till tomorrow —"*

*"No!" Charm put his hand over the receiver and listened. His father still ranted and grumbled downstairs. Probably didn't hear him. "I'm going to be on the next bus with or without your help." He hung up then, not giving Jake a chance to talk him out of it.*

*Charm hooked his backpack over his shoulder and crept to the bedroom door. Still quiet. Taking care to avoid the squeaky spots in the floor, he crept to his sister's room. Lights off, but the moon shining through the slats of her blinds gave him enough light to see her curled up under the blankets.*

*"Ellie?" She didn't respond. His stomach dropped and tears threatened. How could he leave her here? He sat gingerly on the edge of her bed. "I've got to go, Ellie. I'm so sorry."*

*She stirred but didn't open her eyes. He sat there a moment or two more, then tiptoed to her window and raised it. One leg over the sash, then he paused and took one last look behind him. Stuffed animals haphazardly dumped on the floor. Schoolbooks stacked on her nightstand. Walls decorated with posters from* her latest favorite movie, *The Incredibles*. She'd already announced her plan to be Violet for Halloween.

"Remember. No capes, kid," he said softly, then slipped through the window to the porch roof.

He'd swung off the porch roof dozens of times. The darkness made no difference this time. Once on the ground, he shifted his backpack once more and trotted off toward the road, not giving his home so much as a backward glance.

Threatening clouds were slowly obscuring the moon, but it still provided enough light for him to navigate the road. No traffic to worry about out there anyway. On the rare occasion he heard a vehicle coming from the direction of his house, he dashed into a field or ditch to hide. Twenty minutes later, just as fat raindrops began to fall, a familiar truck approached from the direction of town, passed him, and turned around.

"Get in," Jake said, wrenching the Blazer's passenger door open from the inside. The old truck was used when his dad bought it, and Charm had never known that door to open right. The vehicle smelled like sweat socks and fast-food burgers.

"I couldn't tell Ellie goodbye," Charm said as soon as he was inside.

"You want to go back?"

"No. I'm never going back." He paused. "My dad's gonna lose his shit."

"I'll make sure Ellie's okay," Jake said. Charm liked that about Jake. He didn't wait to be asked, simply did what needed to be done.

The old Blazer rumbled into town, and they parked on the square in view of the bus station. "Ortmann is selling tickets. Think he'll give me crap?"

Jake shrugged. "Probably. But if you look like you're supposed to be there, he'll sell you a ticket. Where are you going?"

"Not here," Charm said darkly.

Jake jerked his chin toward the glove box. "Open that."

The door opened with a squeak, and a fat envelope tumbled out. "Jesus effing Christ!" Bills. Twenties. Lots of them. "What are you, a drug dealer?" But Charm knew what it was. Four years of mowing lawns. Jake's future. "No. I can't take this."

Jake scowled. "Don't piss me off, Freeman. Just take it." He grinned then. "Besides, everybody knows I'll score a free ride once the scouts see me."

Charm scowled back, mostly because Jake expected it, and shoved the cash into his backpack. The dashboard clock said 11:25. "I'll call when I get *somewhere. Only you. And maybe Jimmy Lee. Nobody else." Time to go. He wrenched open the door. "I owe you," he said, sliding out.*

*"Cut that shit out," Jake said dismissively. His voice sounded choked, like it was hard to talk.*

*"No." Charm's voice was serious. "I owe you." He shut the door and started toward the bus station. After a few steps, he turned and yelled back, "I'm good for it!"*

"I called Jake a couple of weeks later to let him know I was okay," Charm said. "He said Dad was pissed, and the cops were looking for me."

"Jake left some things out." Ellie sounded irritated. Charm got the feeling that if Jake had been there, she would have smacked him in the back of the head. "That night changed everything." She gazed outside and didn't say anything for a few moments. When she did speak, her voice was as far away as the memories. "Dad lost it when he realized you'd gone. Mom said once that he bellowed like a bull moose. I don't know how I slept through it."

Charm snorted. "He bellowed every night."

She turned her gaze to him. "But this time Mom got hurt."

"What!" Charm's voice was overloud, and in tandem, they looked back to see if Lucas had awakened. He hadn't. Like mother, like son. "The son of a bitch beat her up?"

"I asked her once, and she said no. She said they were arguing on the stairs and she stepped wrong. Said he didn't lay a hand on her."

Charm growled. "Probably covering up for him."

"I don't know. I know she spent three days in the hospital, and I spent a week with the Turners."

He slammed his hand on the steering wheel. "Bastard!"

"Dad was different after that." She thought for a moment and then spoke slowly, as if voicing ideas she hadn't expressed before. "I think initially he blamed you. If you hadn't run, they wouldn't have fought. Or maybe just because you got out." She waved her hand, dismissing those conclusions. "Jake was right, though. Dad *was* pissed at first, and he did have cops looking for you. But he got over it."

"Forgot I ever existed?" Charm asked bitterly.

"No. Stopped blaming you and started blaming himself."

"Thought he didn't do it."

She shrugged. Any emotion she had tied to the night had clearly been worked out long ago. "I don't know. All I know is he didn't yell after that. He still drank, but he stopped yelling."

His father's face as Charm had last seen it, flushed and angry, filled his mind. Mean, drunken slurs spit at him one after the other. Reeking of booze and farm, sweat streaming down his forehead. Then, suddenly, Charm remembered his father's face as it had been before. Before the alcohol. Before the screaming. Nose red from too much sun, rather than too much whiskey. Eyes that crinkled when he smiled. Quick to laugh at his own stupid dad jokes.

Charm's heart beat faster. *What if Mom was right? What if he yelled because I pushed him? What if it really was my fault?*

"What about Mom?" he asked. "Did she look for me?"

Ellie looked at him for several endless seconds without speaking. "I don't know," she said finally.

They drove in silence the rest of the way home. Lucas woke when they turned onto their gravel drive, and their mother and River met them at the vehicle. Unable to face his mother at that moment, Charm ignored the cheerful family chatter and focused on getting the cooler and other flotsam they'd taken with them. Ellie sent her son in with his grandmother and hung back with Charm.

She relieved him of part of his burden and bumped him with her shoulder. He grinned despite his somber mood. "Thank you," she said, as they meandered toward the door.

"For what?" He bumped her back, and she laughed.

"For helping us feel normal for a day. It felt really good."

Charm looped an arm around her shoulder and gave her a squeeze. "Felt good to me too."

# CHAPTER 11

It took Charm a few minutes the next morning to figure out what was different: no hangover. How novel. Perhaps he had no physical need for "hair of the dog" that morning, but he still enjoyed a nip to face the day, and orange marmalade rocked a breakfast martini. He sipped, sighed with happiness, and allowed himself a moment to reflect on the especially curvy bartender who had shared this particular recipe. Their evening together had been as delightful as the drink. Maybe he'd look her up again when he got back to St. Louis. She worked somewhere downtown. Or was it the riverfront? Wherever.

The screen door squeaked open and banged shut, distracting him from his thoughts. He poked his head into the utility room and saw his mother exchanging her farm boots for her regular shoes. His stomach clenched a bit, and the entirety of his conversation with his sister came back to him.

*"What about Mom? Did she look for me?"*

*"I don't know."*

His mother smiled, and he had a sudden flash of her kicking off rain boots next to the back door of the house he'd grown up in and then suggesting they make hot chocolate. "You're up early," she said, bringing him back to the present.

*Which one are you? The one who made me hot chocolate, or the one who let me go without a second thought?* Her head tilted quizzically, and he remembered she'd asked him a question. "If nine can be considered early, I'm the early bird on a worm hunt."

"And what worm would that be?" They relocated to the kitchen, where she side-eyed his breakfast martini and began putting away its ingredients.

Charm put the gin back into a cabinet deemed out of Lucas's reach. "Internet. Maybe a library?"

His mother snorted. "Say no more. I'm going to poke my eyes out with a stick, if I ever have to look something up using Jake's old computer again." She tapped her chin and thought for a moment. "Rolling Fork has the closest library. If all you need is internet, though, you can go to my apartment. I've got a laptop and satellite internet. Not the fastest, but it gets the job done."

"That'll work."

"What are you looking for?"

Charm dug the business card he'd gotten from the parade vendor out of his pocket. "Information on a chicken trainer," he said, reading the information on the front once again. His mother's face took on an expression he couldn't identify. Shock? Surprise? But before he could ask her about it, Lucas swung into the kitchen, Ole Miss ball cap askew on his head, River at his heels.

"Hey, Uncle Charm!"

"Hey, kid! Whatcha up to?"

"Grandma says River can't do real retrieves yet" — *Ah*, Charm remembered, *the tooth extractions* — "so she's taking us to the park."

"And shopping," she confirmed, smiling fondly at the boy. "Someone goes back to school next week and needs clothes that fit."

Lucas groaned, but Charm wasn't sure whether it was at the thought of school or shopping. Charm didn't care for either himself, but he knew Lucas was, not so secretly, excited about seeing his friends again. The past two months had been tough on everyone, but especially on the lonely little boy. No matter what Ellie thought about the dog, River had been a godsend, and Charm shuddered to think about how heartbroken the boy would be if he ever lost him.

"Oh, crap," Charm said suddenly. His mother looked up questioningly. "You're going to use your car. I was going to ask to borrow it. Vlad busted a belt."

"If you hurry, I can give you a ride to my apartment," she said. "It's not far out of our way."

"Brilliant. I appreciate it!" Charm sprinted upstairs to grab his wallet and phone. "Shotgun," he called, tagging his nephew on the way to the car.

"Hey!" Lucas launched into a faster gear.

His mother just shook her head, and Charm heard her mutter "children" under her breath. There was no real battle for the front seat, despite a taunt or two tossed back and forth, and the excursion got underway. Only a couple of minutes later, Charm climbed out into his mother's driveway with her key in hand and a promise he would call when he was ready to come home. He felt like a prepubescent teen being dropped off at a friend's house. He took the stairs to her garage apartment two at a time.

The laptop was tucked against the wall at the end of the kitchen peninsula. Charm moved it to the small table and turned it on. While it booted, he pulled out the business card. Brainy Beasties.

It didn't take much Google-Fu to determine there wasn't much to learn about Brainy Beasties online. No website, but the Better Business Bureau in Tallulah, Louisiana, had a business by that name with no complaints, no reviews, and no rating. It did, however, have an address and phone number, which he jotted on the card. A reverse lookup revealed the number matched a landline registered to a Smokey Clark — S. Clark, Charm presumed. More googling revealed Smokey was fifty-nine and related to a Dulcie Clark, but nothing terribly useful.

Charm picked up his phone to call, then set it back down. What exactly would he say? *Can you train my hunting dog like you trained a chicken?* He grabbed himself a soda from the fridge and paced while he considered his painfully short list of options. None of them thrilled him. To distract himself, he wandered around the apartment.

Unlike the first time he'd been here, the sofa bed was neatly tucked away and the coffee table in its right place, both staged as though his mother expected company. This was the South; maybe she did.

The photos covering the walls attracted him the most. Before, he'd focused on pictures of his father, but photos of her family and friends throughout her life dotted the walls, as well. She with her mother, both dressed in their Sunday finest, shielding their eyes against the sun. A Halloween party, his mother a preteen dressed as a scarecrow. Laughing with girlfriends, probably during college. A life before him, even before his father. What had her dreams been?

That reminded him of Ellie, and he returned to the table. Setting thoughts of chicken trainers aside, he focused on his second task, law schools and prelaw programs in Mississippi. Nothing in Collier of course. She said she'd been driving to Vicksburg. What would it take to get her back into school?

He had fallen down a rabbit hole of applications and financial aid when his phone rang. His mother. To his surprise, more than two hours had passed. He gratefully accepted her offer of a ride home.

"May I borrow your car?" he asked without preamble when she and Lucas arrived. Mud streaked the boy's cheek, and grass stains discolored his shirt. River snoozed on the seat beside him and barely noted when Charm folded himself into the front seat. Looked like a good time was had by all.

"I suppose," his mother said, backing out of the driveway. "Do you have an errand to run? We could do it now."

"No, I need to run to Louisiana."

She pressed the brake hard. "Louisiana!"

"Just the other side of the river," he assured her. "I'll probably only be gone a couple of hours." His mother looked thoughtful and resumed driving. At least she hadn't said no.

Lucas leaned over the front seat. "Can I go?"

"Not this time, sport." Um, probably. He looked back at his mother. "You don't mind watching him a couple more hours, do you?"

She blinked. "No, of course not." She sounded distracted.

"You sure?" Charm pressed, not sure how to read her reaction.

"Positive," she said. "But fill the tank when you bring it back."

Done. After a brief stop at Ellie's, where he surreptitiously topped off his flask, Charm hit the road to Louisiana. Tallulah, he discovered, was a small town in Madison Parish, just off I-20 maybe twenty miles from the Mississippi border. He stopped briefly at the Love's Travel Stop to get his bearings, then headed south out of town on Highway 65. Brainy Beasties had no sign, but the address matched, and when he followed the long driveway in, he saw barns and enclosures that suggested something more than the average farm. The lion dozing in one well-fenced area pretty much cemented that theory.

Charm parked in a small paved lot at the side of a modest farmhouse and scanned the area. A gray truck, but no other cars, no people working. Were they closed? There was no obvious office space, so he followed a gravel walkway past some sort of unpruned, thorny shrubbery to the front of the house and knocked. After a few moments, he knocked again. When he knocked a third time, the door jerked open, and standing before him was the woman from the pier.

Only long years of practice on the carnival midway kept Charm from rolling his eyes. Of course, she worked here. *Give her the benefit of the doubt, Freeman. Maybe she was tired yesterday.* He smiled. She waited without speaking. Maybe she didn't recognize him.

"Hi. We met yesterday on the pier —" he began.

"I know. What do you want?"

Charm hoped this girl wasn't their regular receptionist. He kept his smile firmly in place. "Is Smokey Clark here?"

"My father isn't seeing anyone. Can I help you?"

Her father. This must be Dulcie Clark. Charm took a deep breath and barreled forward. "My name is Charm Freeman. I live...sort of...well, temp — never mind. I live in Collier, Mississippi, about an hour from here. I have a project I need help with."

A miniscule light of interest flared in her eyes. "What kind of project?"

"We're training a dog for a field trial —"

The flicker of interest died. "We don't work with dog trainers," she said flatly and shut the door in his face.

Charm stared, open-mouthed. *What the fucking hell?* He forced back his anger and knocked again.

She jerked open the door a second time. "Are you deaf? We don't work with dog trainers."

He glanced at the parking lot. "Looks like you don't work with much of anyone." He put a hand against the door to keep her from shutting it. "I'm asking for your help. Can't you at least hear me out?"

She glared at him, then stepped back and opened the door enough for him to enter a spartan living room. Not uncomfortable, he decided. Just not…personal? At least not to her — to Dulcie. The walls were full of photos of all sorts of animals doing all sorts of things, from dolphins in the open ocean responding to trainers in boats to ravens flying toward targets.

Most of the photos featured a Black man. Smokey Clark, maybe? Some included Dulcie, but clearly the animals were the stars. Missing were family photos, except for one. By itself on a low bookcase was a photo of Smokey, a blonde woman, and a toddler with Dulcie's eyes. There was something familiar about the woman. Charm wanted to look more closely at the photo, but Dulcie didn't seem like she would appreciate the intrusion.

She had positioned herself near the door, arms crossed, and stood waiting. "Well?" she asked finally.

Charm opened and shut his mouth a couple of times, suddenly unable to recall the pitch he had practiced in the car. How could he express how important this was? How fragile his nephew was? "A couple of months ago, my brother-in-law was killed in a car accident." No reaction. "Before the accident, he and my nine-year-old nephew were training a dog for a field trial. It's really, really important to the boy that this dog wins a field trial."

"A field trial, I take it, is some sort of dog sport?"

*Yes, yes, yes. A sport that's everything to that nine-year-old boy.* "Yes. It's a hunting competition."

"Are there no professional field trial trainers out there?"

"Yes, there are, but Lucas doesn't want to work with them." *That didn't sound good.* "Besides the dog has already washed out with most of them." He mentally face-palmed. *Idiot. That sounded even worse.*

Dulcie cocked her head. "So you want me to work with a nine-year-old to train a dog that no one else can train. And how much are you going to pay me for that privilege?"

Charm felt his face redden, and he looked at his feet.

"That's what I thought." Her voice had, for the first time, taken on a gentle tone. "Look, I'm sure you and your nephew are fine people. But we don't train dogs for sports. Most of our projects have lives on the line, not ribbons."

"Life-or-death chickens?"

Her lips tightened. "Those chickens are steady income that pays the bills." The gentle tone had vanished. "You're asking me to work for *months* on a project for no pay. I'm sorry, Mr. Freeman. I hope you and your nephew find someone to help you."

And that was that. Charm thanked her and let himself out the door. She wasn't being unreasonable, he admitted to himself as he pointed the car toward home. What idiot — other than him — would volunteer to spend months training someone else's dog for free? He grabbed his flask from the glove box and took a healthy swallow. Reasonable or not, the rejection irked him.

"The worst part," he said to his mother when he got home an hour later, "is that I have to tell Lucas that we're out of luck." He dropped dejectedly into a chair at the kitchen table. "I knew this was a long shot, but it was the only long shot I had left."

His mother placed a glass of sweet tea in front of him and sat across from him. "Are you sure she had the authority to make that decision? What about her father?"

He shrugged. "Didn't see him. She said..." He thought for a moment. "She said he wasn't seeing people. Or something like that." He dug the business card out of his pocket and tossed it on the table. "I guess that's that."

"Hmmm." She picked up the card and studied it. "Well, don't give up quite yet, at least not until you've talked to Oscar again. Or asked Eleanor to talk to him. He would walk over knives for her."

Charm's eyes widened, and he sat up. "You know about that?

What's the deal with him and Ellie?" He leaned back and squinted suspiciously. "You're not going to tell me they had an affair, are you?"

"Charm!" She sounded scandalized. "Of course not. Jake and Oscar competed for Eleanor in high school. He never really got over his crush. I expect he'll ask her out as soon as she's ready to start dating."

"Ugh." Hopefully Ellie believed in a really long mourning period.

His mother rose from the table and gathered her purse and keys. "What time do you have to be at work tonight?"

Charm glanced at the clock. Three fifteen. "Not until seven. Why?"

"I need to run some errands. Do you mind watching Lucas and covering dinner this evening?"

"Pizza it is!" Charm climbed to his feet. "Where is he anyway?" The house was quiet, he noticed suddenly. Too quiet for a newly active nine-year-old boy. "Get tired of him and lock him in the basement?"

"We stopped by the school and picked up a stack of assignments. He's supposed to be upstairs doing homework." Organized and ready to go, she turned back to Charm and smiled. "My guess, then, is he's upstairs playing video games with a headset on so I can't hear him." She headed for the door. "It's your job to be bad cop. Make sure he gets a good start on the math."

Charm walked her to the door and watched until she was out of the driveway. Then he topped off his flask once again and ran upstairs to see what game he and Lucas were playing this afternoon.

# CHAPTER 12

Dear Lord, she hadn't even looked in the mirror. *I look fine,* Dot Freeman reassured herself, and besides, if she didn't go now, she'd probably lose her nerve.

Dot typed the address she'd memorized from the back of the card into the navigation app on her phone. How did she ever survive without an app like this? Not that she needed it, of course. She excelled at navigation, but paper maps or printed directions were annoying to keep track of while driving. An in-car nav system like she'd seen in the Walton's new SUV last time the minister's wife took her to lunch would be even better, but who could afford a new car these days?

Not entirely convinced she wasn't about to make a huge fool of herself, she pointed the car toward Louisiana. The app, in a Jamaican accent she'd chosen to remind her of Smokey Clark, told her each turn well in advance, freeing her mind to remember the last time she had seen him.

Smokey Clark. After all these years.

Would he even remember her? Would it matter if he did? The question made her so anxious, she lamented the lack of a paper map. At least navigation would have distracted her.

Her heart pounded as she drove onto a long driveway and parked next to a small house. The house itself was nondescript and indistinguishable from dozens of others she'd passed. Winter landscape did it no favors. Her gaze scanned the various pole barns and enclosures that made up the rest of the facility. Sterile. Empty. Well-maintained, though. Somewhere she could hear chickens clucking, but she couldn't see them. The only animal she could see was a male lion curled up in a cardboard box, which made her smile.

Dot got out of the car and straightened her clothes. Her hands trembled, which annoyed her. Stiffening her shoulders, she marched to the front door and knocked.

A young woman opened the door. "Look —" She stopped short and stared at Dot. "Um." She leaned out, looked at Dot's car, then back at Dot. "Who are you?"

The woman's discomfiture amused Dot. Charm clearly knew how to make an impression. Well, so did she. "I'm looking for your father," she said, ignoring the woman's question. No doubt this was Dulcie Clark. Last time Dot had seen Dulcie, she had been a toddler. That was right after the funeral for Ava — Dulcie's mother and Dot's best friend.

Dulcie straightened. "He's not available," she said firmly.

"He is to me," Dot said and breezed past her.

"Hey!"

Dot didn't pause. From somewhere in the back of the house, jazz music played. With Dulcie close on her heels, Dot followed the sound to a bedroom and pushed open the door. On the far side of the room, a large man looked through a massive collection of vinyl albums, his back to her. Before she could say a word, Dulcie grabbed her.

"What do you think you're doing? Get out of here, before I call the police!"

The man turned at the commotion, eyes wide with surprise. Dulcie tried to pull Dot back into the hall.

"Let me go!" Dot protested.

"Dream on, you crazy —"

"Stop!"

The tone, more than the word, froze them in their tracks, and they looked at Smokey. He stared at Dot and she at him. He had aged, of course, though his dark Jamaican skin didn't show it nearly as much as hers did. Hair that had been jet black then was shot through with gray now, as was his beard. A few deep lines gave his face character and made him more distinguished than handsome, but she could still see the young man who swept her best friend off her feet with his bravado — and with his music.

She saw recognition flicker in his eyes, and she smiled. She nodded toward the turntable. "How about playing 'Blue Train'? Coltrane always was my favorite," she said.

The corners of his mouth twitched, and Dulcie's grip loosened. "Papa?" Waves of confusion and irritation radiated from the girl.

He waved Dulcie off, but his eyes didn't waver. "Dot."

One word, but with it came a flood of understanding. A word, forced and muddy. Posture not quite straight. His smile higher on the left side.

Smokey Clark had had a stroke. She took in the rest of the room then. Recliner facing a window. Rolling table, like the hospital tables that extend over the bed, stowed against the wall. A walker and a cane near it. Myriad bottles of prescription medications arranged on the dresser next to a pitcher of water.

The room of someone who had been ill for a while.

Dot walked into Smokey's arms and hugged him. The arms that wrapped around her trembled and lacked some strength, but there was no reservation. She looked in his face and patted his cheek tenderly, then turned to Dulcie. "Don't worry about us. We have a lot of catching up to do."

If Dulcie had been a cat, she'd have hissed, every bit of fur standing on end. "Don't tell me —"

"Dulcie!" Muddy speech or not, Dulcie fell silent. He glared at her until she looked down. "Make tea."

She shot a look of pure venom at Dot but disappeared from the room. Dot bit her lip to hide her smile.

"I'm sorry…" he managed to say. He waved, clearly dismayed by his struggle to speak.

Dot shook her head. "Nonsense. Do you think this bothers me? Means I get to talk more, and we both know how much I love to talk about myself."

His eyes twinkled. It was an old joke. Neither of them had been able to get a word in when Ava was around. Vivacious — electric — Ava burned bright. Dot patted his cheek again and pointed him to the edge of the bed. "Sit. I'll get the record."

The collection filled a set of shelves near the turntable. Overfilled. Nearly all jazz. Some blues, probably because Ava had liked it, but jazz flowed through Smokey's veins. He had been playing jazz with a friend in a club in New Orleans the night he met Ava. She had fallen for the suave musician, but it was his brain, not his music, that made it more than a vacation fling. Smokey Clark had a master's in animal behavior and trained animals for a company based in Arkansas.

Dot glanced over her shoulder with a smile as she thumbed through the collection. "When my son mentioned a chicken trainer, I guessed it was you."

He let out a short bark of laughter. "N-not…many…of us." Despite the struggle, the words were intelligible enough for her to understand.

"No." She held up the Coltrane album she had suggested earlier. "This one all right?" He nodded, and she replaced the album currently on the turntable. "It's been a long time since I used one of these," she confessed as she carefully positioned the needle. Sweet tones filled the air, and she closed her eyes for a moment to soak them up. "This is still my favorite."

She opened her eyes, and Smokey motioned for her to sit beside him. She gazed at him for a long moment, the lost time an ache in her heart. "I'm so sorry I didn't stay in touch," she said. He tried to wave her off, but she shook her head and persisted. "No, no, I should have. Ava would have wanted that. And you needed help with Dulcie."

"T-Too…far." Smokey and Ava had lived in Arkansas then.

He was right, but that hadn't made it easier. Dot had been there when the cancer took her best friend, and she had stayed through the funeral, but she couldn't stay longer. Eleanor, she remembered, was only a couple of years older than Dulcie and hadn't been in school yet. Her family had needed her.

Dot nodded and dropped her head, lost for a moment in the pain of an old wound ripped open anew.

"W-Why…are you…here?"

She looked up surprised, then laughed. "I came to visit an old friend and to ask for help."

"Help we can't give," Dulcie said sharply. Smokey and Dot looked in unison as the young woman swept through the door carrying a tray laden with a steaming teapot, two cups, and sugar. She slammed the tray on a table, rattling the cups.

"Dulcie!" Smokey admonished.

She ignored him and focused her ire on Dot. "Look, lady, I don't know who you are, but you can't push your way in here and beg for us to work for free."

Smokey roared. "Dulcie!"

Hands on hips and eyes flashing, Dulcie was every bit a dark-haired version of her firecracker mother. "No! I'm the one who has to do the work, and I refuse to donate months of my time to a…dog trainer." She said the term like it was a slur.

"That's enough!" Smokey's words weren't crystal clear, but Dulcie swallowed her protest. Smokey took Dot by the shoulders. "W-What is…about?"

Dot felt Dulcie glaring at her. "I'm sorry. My son came here earlier today to recruit help. He doesn't know anything about…" She gestured between the two of them. "He saw your chickens at the Biloxi parade yesterday. Dulcie turned him down because we have no money to hire you, and she has every right to be annoyed with me."

"Why…need help?" Tenderness in Smokey's voice communicated more than his words ever could.

Dot ignored Dulcie and told him the whole story, beginning with Jake's deal with Forbes and ending with discovering the retriever's injuries. "We're at our wit's end," she concluded. "The dog will be healthy soon, but I think Charm has figured out that there's a lot more to training for a field trial than he knows."

"Why is it so important?" Dulcie grumped. "It's not like there's a cash prize or anything." Dot and Smokey looked at her, and she blushed. "I looked it up after he left."

Dot considered the question. "I don't know," she said finally. "But it's all Lucas has thought about since his father died." She paused again, thinking of the light in her grandson's eyes when he talked about River. "It's important," she said again.

Dulcie nodded, and Dot could tell she chose her words carefully. "Even so, we can't help you."

"Dulcie…"

This time it was Dulcie who held up a hand to stop her father. "I'm the one putting food on the table here. This project will take months, and it's not going to pay any bills. I'm sorry. I can't do it."

As Dulcie spoke, a light went out of Smokey's eyes, and he looked down. He looked infirm, weak, when moments ago he was simply an older version of the man she remembered. Her eyes drifted to the chair facing the window. Worn fabric spoke of many hours spent there. *How long ago did Smokey have his stroke?* Dot imagined it must have hurt the proud man she knew to cede control so completely to someone else, even his daughter. *This isn't how Ava would have wanted her husband to live out the end of his life.*

"I agree completely," Dot said. Dulcie blinked, surprised. "It wouldn't be fair to you," Dot continued. "You have to take care of paying clients and keep the business going."

Dulcie seemed shocked, but she nodded. "Thank you for understanding."

Dot took the hands of the man sitting next to her. "Will *you* help me?" she asked.

The room reacted as if she'd asked him to bungee jump naked. Smokey's eyes went wide. Dulcie snapped, "Are you insane? He can't!"

Dot rose to her feet and faced Dulcie squarely. "You just said you were running the business. I expect he has plenty of free time on his hands, and it *is* right up his alley."

Dulcie's face loomed inches from Dot's. "Look at him! Are you trying to kill him? He *can't* do it."

"That's not for you to say."

"I'm his daughter!"

"And Smokey is an adult of sound mind." Dot turned to face Smokey again. He hadn't moved or said a word, just stared at her. "I'm not part of this" — she motioned to the room — "I don't know your health history, what the doctors have told you, or what you can or can't do. If you say you can't do it, I'll accept that and promise to visit every week. But I want to hear it from you."

"You need to leave," Dulcie said, grabbing her arm.

Dot pulled loose. "I can find my own way out." Smokey still hadn't spoken. Dot pulled a pen and old receipt from her purse and scrawled her phone number and Eleanor's address on the back. She held it out to him. "We won't lose touch again."

Smokey took it and gazed at it. Sensing Dulcie was about ten seconds from throwing her out via the window, Dot headed to the door.

"W-Will…you m-make…lemon…icebox…pie?"

Dot paused and grinned back at him. "Every damn day. You need some meat on your bones."

* * *

Incessant banging followed by equally unrelenting barking pulled Charm out of a deep slumber. He groaned and buried his head under a pillow. Door. Dog. He swore a slew of creative phrases taught to him by his tribe of carnie pals and sneaked a peek at the clock.

Eight thirty.

In the morning.

He groaned aloud. "Somebody get that!" he yelled. The knocking continued. "Anybody!" The bar closed at two. It had been pushing three before he crawled into bed. The ensuing five hours hadn't completely renewed his sobriety, and it certainly hadn't been enough for him to awaken bright-eyed and bushy-tailed.

More banging. Okay, okay. He rolled out of bed with a thud,

wrapped a quilt around his shoulders, and headed downstairs, pausing only to read a note taped to his door. His mother and Lucas were grocery shopping. Lovely. He crumpled the note and dropped it.

*Bang, bang, bang.*

*Bark, bark, bark.*

The noise rattled in his inebriated, sleep-deprived brain like a whole crew of carpenters remodeling his skull. "I'm coming, I'm coming." He jerked the front door open. "What the f —" He stopped. The girl from Louisiana — Dolly…something — stood on the porch. Behind her stood an older African American man leaning on a cane. Charm stared at them, then looked around them, trying to figure out why they were on his porch.

"Can I help you?" he asked finally.

Dulcie removed her sunglasses and looked at him from his face to his bare toes then all the way back up. "Get up, buttercup. It's time to train your dog."

# Chapter 13

An hour later Charm stood on the front porch watching Dulcie and Lucas and tried to figure out how "We don't work with dog trainers" became "Time to train your dog" overnight. Literally. The older guy was Smokey Clark — he'd figured that out. And somehow his mom knew him. Anyway, Charm assumed she did, since she had Smokey settled on the porch swing, blanket across his lap, eating pie.

But Dulcie. She'd been clear about her opinion of working for free. Frankly, he felt the same way. So why was she here? Considering the glare she shot his way, he was pretty sure it wasn't voluntary. But she had been friendly enough to Lucas when he and his mother arrived home a few minutes after Dulcie and Smokey turned up on the doorstep, apparently to his mother's surprise. At least he wasn't the only clueless one.

Charm had excused himself to shower and get dressed, and when he returned, plans had been made, and they all traipsed out to the front yard. He'd have to follow up with his mom to find out what he'd missed. She had settled on the swing next to Smokey with her own piece of pie and a peculiar, self-satisfied smile. That cat had eaten a whole cage of canaries. They were going to have a long talk later.

"Are you going to join us, Mr. Freeman?"

Some Southern accents drip with honey. Hers dripped with sarcasm. *What is this chick's deal?* He pasted on his best smile and said, "Call me Charm." He trotted down the stairs into grass still wet with morning dew and extended his hand.

She stared at it for a long moment, then finally, grudgingly, stuck her long brown fingers in his and gave his hand a barely there shake. "Dulcie."

Point to Charm. Charm moved to stand next to his nephew and waited.

The handshake might have thrown Dulcie a moment, but this was her stage. She paced slowly in front of them, a drill sergeant sizing up new recruits. "Forget everything you think you know about training a hunting dog. I don't train that way. I train differently than any retriever trainer you've ever seen before."

"Why doesn't anyone else train this way?" Charm asked, genuinely curious.

Dulcie narrowed her eyes. "Because they don't have my education or my experience."

Half of his brain recognized that he had, however unintentionally, pushed her into a defensive position. The other half controlled his mouth. "And yet, they still succeed."

"Did they succeed with this dog?"

Point to Dulcie. He didn't reply. When Dulcie started pacing again, Lucas tugged on Charm's sleeve. "Why are you being mean to each other?" he whispered.

"Because she's an arrogant bitch," Charm whispered back.

Dulcie stopped and smiled at him. If she'd had fangs, she'd have bared them. "If you want my help, Mr. Freeman, I'm here free of charge on two conditions. First, you do as I say. We either do it my way, or I'm going home now."

*This is for Lucas. This is for Lucas. This is for Lucas.* Charm had a feeling that was his new mantra. "And second?"

"Second, that dog doesn't compete until I say he's ready."

Weird that she prioritized that as high as "Do it my way." *Why?* he wondered. Charm couldn't, offhand, think of a reason to protest, so he shrugged and nodded. "Fine."

Satisfied, Dulcie unzipped a duffel bag and pulled out myriad objects, including one he recognized. "Damn dog trainers always rush the training. If you can't deal with it, you're welcome to find another trainer." She shook the plastic bumper in his direction. "Are we clear?"

*Jesus Christ. What a power trip this chick is on.* He glanced at Lucas, who watched him with wide eyes. "Crystal," Charm said.

"Okay. We're going to start with simple ground-to-hand delivery. I'll put the bumper on the ground —"

"Ground-to-hand?" Charm interrupted. "With all due respect, *Miss* Clark, this dog is way past that."

"Then this part should go fairly quickly, shouldn't it?"

Charm glowered. *This is for Lucas. This is for Lucas. This is for Lucas.*

Dulcie sighed and held up a hand in truce. For the moment, anyway. "Duck retrieving is a fairly simple chain of behaviors done over and over in a huge variety of scenarios. If there's a problem with the basics, then we'll never get the hard stuff solid. So I'm going to start with the simple component skills and test each piece before putting them together. If River is solid — and I have no reason to believe he isn't — this part will go very fast and will be nothing more than a good reminder for him. Make sense?"

It made a lot of sense, not that Charm was particularly eager to tell her that. But he didn't want her to think he was stupid either, so he grudgingly said, "It does."

"Good." She smiled at Lucas. "Let's train."

* * *

Charm accepted his second beer from the waitress and ignored the look his mother shot him. Yeah, sorry, but he'd gotten through two interminable hours with Dulcie. He'd earned some hoppy refreshment. He took a long swig and let some of his irritation drain away.

They'd gotten to Brother Jack's at just the right time to grab one of the two large booths. Charm hadn't ever sat in one of these. Too difficult to slide in and out. Fortunately, Lucas had demanded to sit next to his new best friend, so Charm and his mother had one half all to themselves. Well, themselves and Lucas's crutches. The lunchtime air at Brother Jack's lacked the ever-present smokey haze it featured at night, and it smelled more of grilled meat than booze. Different crowd of people too. A feeling of being out of place niggled at him. He took another deep draught from his mug.

Across the table, Smokey and Dulcie dug into their hamburgers and fries, oblivious to his discomfort. His mother had chided him for bringing everyone to Brother Jack's — "There are other places to eat in Collier, Charm" — but he got an employee discount here. Honestly, he'd have made them sandwiches at home, but he'd used the last of the bread when he got home last night. Last of the peanut butter too.

They had talked training since they sat down, which he supposed made sense, but still, it was tiring. She had been especially interested in the PTSD diagnosis.

"The doctor said it was a hypothesis," Charm admitted. "No way to actually test for it."

"And ultimately irrelevant. The solution is systematic desensitization. To be honest, I don't find either the noise shyness or the issue with small spaces terribly concerning," Dulcie said.

Charm arched his eyebrow. "Gun-shy bird dogs don't do terribly well in the field."

She rolled her eyes. "I'll email you a protocol when I get home that will teach him to love a crate. Start today, and work on it a little bit every single day. Next time I come, I'll bring a DVD with gun sounds and a second protocol. Again, you do a little per day, every day. We progress at his pace. It may take longer in his case, but it doesn't matter. We have plenty to do."

"Are you going to come train every day?" Lucas asked, eyes shining.

Charm shuddered at the thought.

Dulcie bit a fry in half and shook her head. "We've found it's beneficial to allow time for latent learning."

Lucas looked confused. "Huh?"

"River needs time to think about what he learned," Charm translated.

Dulcie looked at him in surprise. "That's right."

Charm popped a fried mushroom in his mouth. "Not as dumb as I look."

She cocked her head and studied him, then turned back to Lucas. "How about three days a week? Monday, Wednesday, Saturday?"

"What time?" Charm asked. "Lucas has physical therapy at twelve thirty on Mondays and Thursdays, and he's going back to school soon."

"Please don't train without me," Lucas begged.

"How about midafternoon? Three or so works for us," Dulcie said.

His mother touched Charm's sleeve. "Speaking of physical therapy, did you tell Eleanor where we are?"

"Yep. Texted her before we left the house." He drained his beer and signaled to their waitress for another. He didn't recognize their server, which surprised him. She must work only first shift. He checked her out as she walked away. Maybe he'd introduce himself later. He refocused on the conversation with Dulcie. "We're not taking you away from your paying customers, are we?" Charm asked.

Dulcie busied herself with her burger. "No." She cut the burger into quarters, then took a deep breath and met his eyes, her cheeks bright red. "We haven't had a lot of business since my father had his stroke. The trainers didn't like working for a woman."

Smokey frowned, but Dulcie didn't notice. His mother did. She met his eyes, and they shared a long, significant look. Charm waved his fingers toward them. "So, what's your deal?" he asked. "Clearly you know each other."

Now it was his mother's turn to flush as her significant look transformed into an almost shy smile. "We've known each other for a very long time." She thought for a moment, and then told her story. "My best friend when I was growing up was a wonderful girl named Ava. Her mother died in childbirth, and the whole town helped raise her. She was everything I wasn't — beautiful, vivacious, brilliant. I have no idea why, but in fourth grade, she befriended mousy me."

Charm bit his tongue. Too easy.

"Ava and I were inseparable growing up, and after graduation we went to college together. Will and I dated in high school, and when his father passed away in my sophomore year of college, I dropped out to get married and help him with his family's farm. That summer Ava met Smokey, and they fell in love." A shadow crossed her face. "The people of Collier weren't as accepting of mixed-race couples back then. Ava got angry and never came back. She and I remained friends, but we didn't see each other much after that."

She got quiet and looked at the table. "Charm, you were a little younger than Lucas is now, when Ava was diagnosed with breast cancer. By the time they found it, it had metastasized. I stayed with her for several weeks toward the end."

"I remember you being gone," Charm said. "Dad didn't know how to make anything but grilled cheese."

She smiled sadly. "No, he didn't. But those grilled cheese let me spend time helping my friend before she died." She looked at Dulcie. "You were a toddler, hardly more than a baby, when your mom was diagnosed. You wouldn't remember me being there."

"I-I…remember," Smokey said. "G-grateful."

A somber mood had descended over the table. Smokey and Charm's mother seemed sad, no doubt remembering the woman who had forever linked them. Dulcie gazed at her plate, lost in thought. Even Lucas was subdued.

Just as Charm opened his mouth to change the subject, the restaurant door swung open, and Ellie rushed in. She scanned the room, spotted them, and hurried over.

"There you are. Are you ready?" she asked Lucas. She glanced at her cell phone. "I'm running late. Why did you guys go out?"

Charm rose to his feet. "The cupboard was bare. Let me get him a to-go box." He walked backward toward the bar and yelled back to them. "Dulcie, Smokey, the crazy woman is my sister, Ellie."

"Elle," he heard her say. He grabbed a container from behind the bar and returned before they'd finish introducing themselves. Ellie simultaneously nodded politely to Dulcie and Smokey as their mother explained who they were and rushed Lucas to gather his crutches and get ready to leave. Charm transferred the boy's lunch into the box and passed it over to Ellie.

"Hey, Elle."

The table turned to look at another newcomer: Oscar Strickland. As the group of men he had come in with pushed a couple of nearby tables together and signaled for menus, Oscar stood a few feet away, John Deere hat in hand, shuffling his feet nervously. He looked remarkably like a teenage geek about to ask the head cheerleader to prom.

"How are you?" he asked awkwardly. "It's good to see you and Lucas out and about."

Ellie managed a smile as she herded Lucas toward the door. "Doing fine, thanks. Sorry — we're late — nice to see you!" And she vanished through the door.

Oscar seemed to take this as a positive sign, because when he turned around, his face shone with a beatific smile. Charm rolled his eyes. Oscar's expression turned sour, and had Charm's mother not been present, Oscar probably would have flipped him off.

The expected social niceties taken care of, Charm tilted his chin toward one of the men Oscar came in with. "That Forbes's trainer?" *Tim Layton*, if he recalled correctly.

Oscar looked around. "Yeah, and a couple of the other trainers from around here. Hey, Layton!" All the men looked over. "This is Charm Freeman. He's trying to train that curly dog."

The men exchanged snorts and knowing looks. "Good luck," Layton said in a tone that suggested training River would be anything but.

Dulcie scowled. "What does that mean?"

Charm groaned inwardly. *Here we go.*

"No disrespect, Miss," Layton said patronizingly. "We've all worked with that dog. He's not cut out for field work."

"Why is that?" she persisted.

Layton ticked off the issues. "Too hot. Can't keep weight on him. Too soft for corrections. Too easily distracted. Too lazy to hold his line."

"Those sound like training issues to me. I thought you were professionals," she said with a sniff.

"Dulcie!" Smokey snapped.

Layton's expression darkened, but he kept a civil tone. "We are. And it makes better business sense to work with dogs who have a chance of winning the prize than it does to waste time with a dog that doesn't have the aptitude."

Charm slunk down in his seat. Great. His chicken trainer had just pissed off the only people in town who could give them real insights into retriever field trials. Judging by the looks on their faces, they had now washed their hands of the whole situation. Charm wished he could too.

# CHAPTER 14

Elle rubbed her temples. She should have taken the whole week off. Then maybe *something* would have gotten done when she was out. Well, to be fair one thing had been done. Wrong. It had been done very wrong, and people were pissed — at her. She'd spent all day yesterday trying to fix that, and now she had to get to her towering stack of incoming forms — *Really, people. Couldn't anyone have helped?* — before it physically toppled under its own weight. But first, she needed to get through her email.

She scanned the subject lines, and one from her manager, Dovye, about the position she had applied for jumped out. Her stomach dropped as she read. Position filled, yada, yada, yada. Guess when she stopped putting in that unpaid overtime so she could work at the restaurant, Dovye had decided she couldn't hack it. *Maybe if I had this job, I wouldn't need to work at the restaurant, you old biddy.*

She sighed. Been at work ten minutes, and she had sunk to the level of name calling.

"Elle, can you help meeeee?" The whine implicit in the request grated, and Elle didn't bother to wipe the scowl from her face when she looked up. A new admin, one Tanesha had not-so-graciously named Hot Pants due to her fascination with shiny gold pants two sizes too small, blinked at her through thick false eyelashes and waved a stack of papers. "I can't remember how to enter these."

Of course not. Because before this job Hot Pants had never turned on a computer. How on earth could anyone living in the US not have computer skills? Elle kept that observation to herself and explained for the third time how to log in and locate the records she needed to update. *Christ on a cracker.* Her whole job was computer-based. What had Dovye been thinking?

"But I don't understand," Hot Pants said helplessly. "Can you walk me through it all again?" Elle banged her head on her desk three or four times, then resigned herself to getting nothing done.

A few minutes after noon, Elle's phone chimed, and she pulled up a text from Charm. "Oh, shit," she said out loud. Hot Pants had the nerve to look offended. "I'm late picking up my kid. Gotta go!" She had completely spaced rehab. How could she forget that? More guilt, more irritation. She grabbed her purse from her desk drawer and sprinted for the door, Hot Pants calling, "Who's going to help me with these records?" in Elle's wake.

It took three tries to get the truck to start. At least no one had to give it a jump. This time. *How long before the damn alternator gives out altogether?* she wondered as she turned onto the highway. Instead of turning toward their house when she reached Collier, she kept the truck pointed south.

Picking up Lucas at Brother Jack's wasn't truly out of the way. In fact, it was probably faster than picking him up at home. But she was in the mood to be irritated. Eating out cost money they didn't have, even if Charm got a discount. Unless the food was free, it wasn't enough of a discount.

Elle barely noticed the strangers at the table, even when introduced to them, and would have forgotten them entirely had Lucas not rambled on about them and the training session with River during the whole drive. *River, River, River.* "Can you talk about something else?" she snapped as she maneuvered her truck into a space marked compact. Why were so many spaces marked compact when everyone drove trucks and SUVs?

The physical therapist's office was located off Race Street in

Rolling Fork, near the hospital. Elle still shuddered when she passed a hospital, even though this wasn't where Jake died. He and Lucas had been hurt too badly for a little community hospital like this. They had been transported all the way to Baptist in Jackson.

Lucas shoved one last, oversize bite of hamburger into his mouth. "Do I get to quit physical therapy since I'm going back to school?" he asked. "I'm walking gooder now. I bet I'm off crutches soon."

Well, she'd asked for a different subject. "Don't talk with your mouth full, and hurry up," Elle said, coming around to his side of the truck to help him. The boy set the mostly empty container on the seat and slid out, holding on to the door until his mother fished his crutches out.

"Come on, we're late," she said, pointing him toward the door.

He didn't move. "Why are you being so mean? Everybody is yelling today, and I don't know why."

Equal measures of remorse and frustration wrapped around her heart and squeezed. "I apologize. I'm flustered because I'm running late, and it has been one of *those* days." She dragged out "those" and waggled her eyebrows at him. He laughed, and the guilt eased.

"So can I quit PT?" he asked again, swinging toward the door.

"Nope."

For all that he complained about physical therapy, Lucas was too eager to show off his progress to dwell on that particular disappointment. Thank goodness. Her patience might not have survived a typhoon of nine-year-old emotion today.

Lucas really was improving by leaps and bounds — literally. The physical therapist said he'd probably be off the crutches in a month. So hard to believe this was the same boy who hadn't been willing to put weight on his leg a week ago. An image of him in his hospital room, swathed in bandages, distraught after learning his father had died, popped into her head. They'd come so far.

By the time PT wrapped up, her equanimity had been mostly restored. A bad morning doesn't mean a bad day!

It took four tries to start the truck.

Then Hot Pants met her at the office door.

By four thirty, when Elle arrived at her waitressing job at the Collier Caboose, a headache had settled in her temples. The Caboose catered primarily to tourists who visited Collier's antique shops. *It's Thursday. Surely, Thursday will be quiet.*

"Elle!" Her manager, Louis, a stick-thin African American man who resembled his sister not a bit, breezed past her with a stack of menus before she could say hello. "You and Marcia are the only servers on tonight. And we got no runners." He breezed past her again, this time carrying plates. "Everyone who worked last night got food poisoning." Past her again, this time with a bucket of dirty dishes. "And no. It wasn't my food." She stared until he passed her yet again. "Why are you just standing there? Get a move on, girl. We got a tour bus arriving in five minutes."

"On Thursday?"

He stopped and stared. "This is the first day of Antiques Weekend. Did you forget?"

*Christ on a cracker.* Collier held a huge antique show and auction on the first weekend in March every year, the equivalent of Black Friday for many of the town's shop owners. She used to bake pies for the bake sale they held on Saturday, and she and Jake and Lucas would spend that whole day on the square. It was one of their favorite family outings of the year. How had she forgotten?

Tears burned her eyes. No, she wouldn't cry. She wouldn't. She swallowed, put her head down, and strode to the kitchen. She could do this. *Just focus.*

The tour bus arrived in a whirlwind of activity, and it was packed. Cranky seniors packed two twelve tops. Separate checks, of course. Then the regulars spilled in. Elle spun from table to table, taking orders, delivering food, topping off drinks, working like her mortgage depended on it. Which, of course, it did.

"Whatcha got for me, Tony?" she asked, pushing through the swinging door that separated the bright kitchen from the dimly lit dining room.

The long-time assistant manager usually greeted her with a smile, but even he had no cheerful words tonight. "Order for table thirteen is up."

A seven top — exactly what she needed to complement her twelve top — with a husband, wife, and five kids. "Can you help me run?"

He scowled but began throwing plates onto trays and hefted his with little trouble, even grabbing both folding tray stands near the door. Elle struggled a bit under the weight but didn't have time to complain. She led the way through the sea of tables toward her table.

"Hey, can I get my check?" a man called to her over the din of hungry diners as she passed.

"Be right with you." She squeezed past Marcia, who managed to give her a sympathetic eye roll, and arrived at the table. "Here we are," she said, waiting for Tony to set up a tray stand and then, thankfully, setting down the tray.

She stepped out of the way to let Manager Louis walk by with menus and a gaggle of church ladies including Ruth Walton and, oh God, Gertie Pritchett. "Elle, you've got a new four top at table four," Louis said under his breath, offering the family she was serving a smile.

"I had the chicken nuggets," said a little girl missing her two front teeth.

"Yeah, the hamburger is mine," said her brother, a boy near Lucas's age with a buzz cut.

"Right." Elle switched the plates and checked the ticket for the owners of the other dishes.

"I wanted mayo," the boy said, looking under the bun.

"I'll get that for you," she said. Steak to dad. Catfish to mom.

"Hey, Elle! The check?" The man who had called to her on the way out of the kitchen waved to get her attention.

"Just a moment," she called back. More chicken nuggets, another hamburger, and some macaroni and cheese.

*Thunk.* The little girl without her front teeth knocked her Coke over, and the table erupted into chaos. The little girl burst into tears — her dinner was drenched. Her siblings slung jeers and jibes, and her parents alternately scolded her for her carelessness and told her to stop crying. Elle grabbed napkins and tried to mop up the mess as best she could.

"I'll bring you a new plate as quick as I can," she told the sobbing girl.

A hand settled on her shoulder, and she turned to find Gertie Pritchett beaming at her. "Elle, how's Lucas doing?" she asked. "We've been praying for you at church every Sunday. You'll let us know if there's anything we can do for you, right?"

Elle stared. "Do? You want to do something?"

The little girl's wailing grew louder. The man across the restaurant called her name and waved again.

Elle put her hands over her ears and yelled, "Shut up! Just shut up!"

The restaurant din dropped to silent in a moment. All eyes stared at her.

"I'm in the middle of hell, and you ask what you can do?" Tears spilled over her lashes. "Why don't you go to the grocery store for me? Why don't you fix my alternator or mow my field or take Lucas to rehab? Thank you very much for your thoughts and prayers, but your praying isn't putting food on my table!"

Gertie's mouth had dropped open. *Oh God.* Elle looked around at the shocked faces. Some people had frozen in place with forks halfway to their mouths. *Oh God. Oh God. Oh God.* She put her hand over her mouth and took two steps away — away from Gertie, away from the table of horrible children.

Then she ran.

* * *

Night had fallen when Elle drove into the driveway and let the truck's engine sputter to silence. Trucks weren't supposed to do that. This was probably more than the alternator. It was probably something expensive. She rested her head on the steering wheel for a few moments, then wiped copious tears and snot on her sleeve, and trudged toward the house. Out of habit, she reached for the railing to steady herself, and the rickety wood, cracked and loosened by too much of Lucas's acrobatics, chose that moment to snap in half.

It was the proverbial straw, and the camel's back broke. For a moment she stared at the railing in shock, and then her anger bubbled over like lava from Mount Saint Helens. With an inarticulate scream of rage, she wrenched a piece of the broken wood loose and swung it again and again, smashing the railing until not a piece remained standing.

*Smash.* "I…" *Smash.* "Hate…" *Smash.* "This…" *Smash.* "House!" *Smash.*

Strong arms wrapped around her from behind and tried to pull the wood from her hands. She screamed and struggled. "He never fixed anything!"

"I know," Charm said.

She turned and sobbed into his chest. He walked her away from the house to the picnic table. A glance back told her why — Lucas stood in the doorway, his grandmother trying and failing to pull him back inside. *Lucas.* She leaned against the table and cried harder. "I did something stupid. I lost my job —" It occurred to her that Charm should be at Brother Jack's right now. What if she had caused him to lose his job too?

"No, you didn't. Marcia called and told us what happened. It's been two hours — where have you been?"

"Driving around." Sobs choked her. "It's all falling apart. I'm falling apart."

Charm squeezed her shoulders. "You're not. You're just overwhelmed."

She shook her head. "I can't do this anymore. I can't."

He gave her a little shake and made her look at him. "You can." She focused on him, desperately wanting to believe him. "Ellie, you're the strongest person I've ever known. Even when we were kids."

She exhaled a shuddering breath. "I don't want to be strong. It was Jake's job to be strong." She looked back toward the house. "I bet Snow White's castle didn't fall down around her ears."

Light words that caused a surge of resentment. Memories…all the times he was off training River or off at a neighbor's house…cascaded over her. Insignificant moments that suddenly added up into something weighty. "He should have been here. If he'd been home where he belonged this wouldn't have happened, and we wouldn't be in this mess."

Guilt twisted her gut even as the words left her mouth. She anticipated Charm's protest and waved him off. "I know, I know. Not fair."

He shifted to lean on the table next to her and bumped her with his shoulder. "You've earned one or two emotional outbursts."

Elle squeezed her eyes shut and rubbed her temples. "Change the subject. Talk to me about something normal. The new people helping with River."

"They train chickens."

She opened her eyes and stared at him. "That's…not normal." She couldn't help herself: she snickered. And then giggled. And then laughed until she could barely breathe. "Wait," she said when she could speak. "Are these the people from the fair?"

Before Charm could respond, a pair of headlights cut the darkness as a car turned in the drive. "Who's that?" he asked.

She shrugged. The sedan parked close to the side door, and a woman got out and went to the trunk. Elle squinted to identify her in the darkness, then her eyes widened. "Oh my God, that's Gertie Pritchett." Her cheeks burned, as memories of her meltdown at the restaurant flared anew. She and Charm crossed the yard. "Hi, Gertie."

Gertie turned and set two bags of groceries in Charm's arms, then two more in Elle's. Elle's mouth dropped open. "Oh, Gertie, I'm sorry. I didn't mean for you to do this…"

Gertie laughed. "Gracious, I know that." She shut the trunk and headed back to the driver's door. "I'd have done it ages ago if you'd asked." She got in and shut the door, then rolled down the window. "Honey, this is only a down payment."

And with that, she backed up, turned around, and drove off into the night, leaving them open-mouthed and speechless.

* * *

Elle pulled Lucas's door mostly closed, leaving it cracked enough that River could come and go as he pleased. She hadn't reached the stairs before the dog nosed the door open and joined her. "Well, come on then," she said in a gruff voice she didn't mean. He huffed at her and wagged his tail, and she scritched his ears before heading downstairs.

"Lucas is asleep," she announced, walking into the kitchen. River followed and busied himself sniffing for crumbs under the table.

Charm looked up from the dish he was drying. "Is he okay?"

Elle slumped into a chair at the table. "Yeah. Just a little scared. It's not every day you see your mom have a breakdown. Fortunately, he was easily distracted by questions about your chicken trainers." She waved vaguely toward the sink. "Y'all don't have to do those. I'll finish them up."

Her mother pulled a pot from her sink of soapy water and rinsed it. "Not much left. We got the groceries put away, and these few dishes are the last of supper. Oh" — she turned — "do you need dinner?"

Elle smiled and shook her head. "No. I'm good. Thank you for cleaning up." She looked down. "Thank you — for everything."

Her mother's eyes widened a bit, then she turned back and busied herself with the remaining dishes. "Charm told me what Gertie said. What did she mean by down payment?"

"I have no clue," Elle said, sitting straighter. "We saw her at church and various functions, but I've been racking my brain, and I can't think of anything that would have resulted in any sort of debt."

"Maybe something to do with Jake?" Charm mused, accepting a pan from their mother.

Elle shrugged. "Maybe. No idea."

"Truly bizarre," he said. He placed the pan in its proper cabinet. "Okay, folks, I'm out of here."

"Where are you going?"

"Work. No reason to miss a night since you're okay." He paused. "You're okay, right?"

"Oh. Yeah." She looked down. "I-I was afraid I'd screwed up

your job too."

"You haven't screwed anything up. Not your job or mine. You're allowed to be human, Ellie." He grabbed his keys and headed for the back door. "Tell her," he called back to their mother.

"You're allowed to be human," she repeated obediently.

Elle snorted. "Am I?" she asked seriously and not a little sadly. She pushed away from the table and opened the fridge. Maybe she would have a sandwich after all. "There's so much at stake."

To Elle's surprise, her mother turned her to face her and then hugged her. "You and Lucas are going to get through this," her mother said. "It may not look the way you expect it to, but you'll survive. You're going to be okay, Elle."

The use of her preferred name made Elle's eyes fill with tears. She rested her head on her mother's shoulder and let herself be comforted, if only for a little while.

# CHAPTER 15

As the days of early March stretched later and early April flowers gave way to a world of deep green in late May, Charm grew more and more frustrated with Dulcie. She knew her stuff. Unfortunately, to his great annoyance, she knew she knew it, and she didn't hesitate to tell him so.

Charm might have been able to ignore that if she weren't also bossy as hell. She gave him more commands — "Stand there," "Throw that," "Pick that up," "Put it back down" — than she gave River, and "Thank you" wasn't in her vocabulary. If he balked, she threatened to quit, and Lucas would plead for him to apologize. So Charm gritted his teeth and did what he was told.

*The months haven't been all bad*, he reluctantly admitted to himself. Lucas and Smokey had bonded, and each had motivated the other to work harder and get better. Smokey's body had gotten stronger, his balance better each day he worked alongside Lucas and his daughter in the field. His speech wasn't perfect, but it was a hundred times better than it had been when they'd shown up on Charm's porch. In March, X-rays had shown Lucas's femur had healed well and completely, and he was finally allowed to ditch the crutches. A slight limp — temporary — was the only sign he'd been injured.

Even River progressed quickly, as Dulcie had predicted he would. His retrieves got longer and more challenging. His training simply didn't *look* like Charm expected it to, and that bothered him. Lots of repetitions, odd ones. When she moved to new terrain, Dulcie didn't even start with a retrieve. Instead, she wasted time with simple recalls.

"I don't understand," Charm complained when she told him to set River up on the other side of a pond for a recall rather than just tossing a bumper. "River has only so much energy. Why are you throwing it away on something that has nothing to do with retrieving?"

"S-Straight lines," Smokey said. "Competition retrievers —"

"Do you remember when we talked to the other trainers at Brother Jack's?" Dulcie interrupted. Charm nodded and glanced at Smokey. He sighed and walked away from them. Dulcie didn't seem to notice. "They said he was 'too lazy to hold his line.' Do you remember that?"

Charm shrugged. "Maybe. So?"

"River isn't lazy. He wasn't trained to run in a straight line." At his still confused expression, she explained, "I did some research. In the United States, field trial dogs are linebred to run in a straight line, no matter the terrain. Is there a briar patch in the way?" She gestured at the small pond. "Is there water in the way? A normal hunting dog would take the easiest, most energy conserving path. But competition dogs are required to hold their line, or they will be penalized. I tested River. What those trainers perceived as laziness was smart energy conservation."

Charm watched the dog stick his nose in a rabbit warren and come up sneezing. "Does that mean he can't win a competition?"

"Nope. It means that my job isn't to teach him to retrieve birds. He already knows how to do that. My job is to teach him to run in a straight line. So first we do straight line recalls in both directions. Then we graduate to bumpers and birds and all the other factors. Make sense?"

It did, and he appreciated her taking the time to explain it. As he started to thank her, she added, "Can you do what I asked now?"

And the moment of goodwill popped like a bubble. Despite all the good things that happened in the past few months, this chick got on his nerves.

* * *

"…and then she said, 'Oh, we'll train in the mornings, starting at eight, from now on. Because I'm the queen! And I decree it must be so!'" Charm's Dulcie imitation made Jimmy Lee and Bird chuckle over their beers.

He himself didn't feel much like laughing. Lucas was now out of school for the summer — before Memorial Day no less. Charm swore he hadn't gotten out until mid-June when he was a kid — and Dulcie had declared all training sessions would happen in the morning now. Okay, yeah, afternoon temperatures roasted vegetables on the vine, but damn it, he didn't fall into bed until three most of the time.

"Did you tell her you work nights?" Jimmy Lee asked. He drained his beer. "Can I have another?"

"Yeah. She said they could do it without me. Hang on — " Charm refilled his buddy's beer, then migrated to the other end of the bar and served a pair of women dressed for a Friday night manhunt. On his way back he refilled the mugs in the usual group of hangers-on surrounding Ray Forbes.

"Could they?" Bird asked, continuing their conversation when Charm returned. "Do it without you?" Bird sipped his beer more slowly than Jimmy Lee and positioned himself so he could watch the rest of the bar while he drank. It was a habit he acquired working as a sheriff's deputy in the next county over. Charm occasionally wondered if Bird had gotten a job in a different county so he wouldn't ever have to arrest Jimmy Lee. Not that Jimmy Lee was a criminal. As far as Charm knew. Jimmy Lee did know things that weren't common knowledge.

Charm focused on Bird's question. He shrugged. "Maybe. Smokey has been doing more hands-on stuff lately. Planting bumpers. Manning the mechanical bumper-thrower thing."

"It's called a Winger," Oscar Strickland said, pulling up a bar stool and joining them. "You got Guinness on tap tonight? Pour me one."

Charm drew the requested pint and set it in front of him. "A stout? I thought you preferred ales. I need to talk to you, by the way. Do you know anything about tractors?"

Oscar glowered. "I'm a man of many moods. I know enough to be dangerous. What about them?"

"It's time to do the first cutting on the hay field. I have no idea how to attach the different thingies —"

"Implements."

"— implements to the tractor." *Or what to do with them*, he added to himself. His only experience with tractors was with soybeans, not hay. Completely different. But he could figure that out later.

"So are you going to quit?" Jimmy Lee asked, switching back to their original conversation.

Oscar perked up. "Ooh. Are you quitting?"

"Not bartending," Charm said. "Training River. And no, I'm not quitting. I said I'd do this, and as long as I'm here, I will."

Bird focused on that. "As long as you're here? Planning on leaving?"

Before Charm could reply, his phone chimed. He dug it out of his pocket and checked his messages. He swore. "Do you recognize this address?" He stuck his phone under the nose of each of his friends in turn.

Bird took it and frowned. "That's east of here in Yazoo County. That area makes Collier look like Atlanta. What's that for?"

"Dulcie wants to train there tomorrow." A second message came in, and he read it. "She says, 'Bring hands.'" He looked up hopefully.

Bird downed the last of his beer and waved him off. "Nope. I'm working. And speaking of, I'd better get home." He pushed away from the bar and headed toward the door. "If you hear 'Dueling Banjos' tomorrow, I'd get the hell out."

"Funny," Charm said. He looked at the two remaining.

"I've got another commitment," Oscar said.

Jimmy Lee shrugged. "I'm free, but I don't want to stand in the middle of some god-forsaken field and take orders from that b —"

"I'll buy you a beer."

He looked unimpressed.

"Two beers."

He cocked his head, smiled, and waited.

"Three beers."

"Okay, what time?"

Charm grumbled under his breath but tapped on his phone. "Eight. I sent you the address."

"Hey, Freeman! We need more beers down here!"

Charm met the eyes of Ray Forbes. "Yes, sir."

"A round for all the gullible gents around me," Forbes announced when Charm arrived.

"You want in on the action?" Tim Layton — apparently one of the gullible gents — asked.

Charm pulled out several bottles and topped off a couple of mugs. "What action would that be?"

"We're wagering on whether Goliath wins at Vicksburg again this year." At Charm's blank look, he explained, "Most of the field trials in the South occur early in the year. February. March. There's only one that happens in the summer. That's Vicksburg in August. If Goliath wins, it would be his fifth year in a row."

"And a record-breaker. Don't forget that!" Forbes added.

Charm lifted a glass and tipped it to Ray Forbes. "Ah. Good luck, sir."

"He doesn't want to bet because he's betting on that curly dog," one of the men said. Charm recognized him as one of the trainers who had been at the table when Layton met Dulcie back in the spring.

Forbes looked up from his glass. "What's that?"

"Nothing," Charm said quickly. "Lucas is still dreaming about River competing in field trials."

"Such a valuable animal" — Forbes's voice boomed across the bar — "but I was happy to help the little boy in any way I could."

"Yes sir. We're very grateful." Charm backed away, careful to keep his smile plastered in place. When he reached the end of the bar, the smile faded, and he exchanged a significant look with Jimmy Lee and Oscar. Forbes was going to be trouble if Lucas ever tried to compete with that dog. And Charm had no idea what he could do about it.

Oscar edged closer to the bar. "Hey, Freeman. Do you think Elle would go out with me if I asked?"

Charm poured himself a drink.

* * *

Eighty-seven degrees at eight in the morning and humidity that made a simple walk feel like a swim through soup. God, Charm hated Mississippi. Four hours of sleep wasn't enough to deal with this shit. *Get over it, Freeman. Only thirty-seven days left, and you can get out of this hell hole.*

July first. That's when he planned to leave. He'd been thinking about it, but when he got the text last night, the decision was final. He'd promised Ellie six months, and that was close enough. Even criminals got time off for good behavior.

"You're weaving," Lucas said.

Charm straightened the truck. "Avoiding a pothole. Where the f…heck are we going anyway?" Bird was right. This place put the boon in boondocks. Yazoo City sparked a couple of long-ago memories when they drove through, but he'd never, as far as he remembered anyway, ventured south into the countryside. And now having been here, he didn't see the point of ever doing it again. Thank goodness he'd driven Ellie's truck instead of his cheap-ass sedan. The truck might be temperamental now and then, but these roads would have destroyed what was left of Vlad's suspension.

"There they are," Lucas said, pointing down a dirt road, their vehicles barely visible in the distance.

They turned off the main road, bumped along the dirt road, and finally pulled into a fallow field. Jimmy Lee had beaten them there — and looked no happier (or any more awake) than Charm felt.

"Nice of you to join us," Dulcie drawled.

"I didn't know I'd need an Indian guide and a compass to find this place." Charm opened the back of the pickup and released River from his crate. The program Dulcie had given them had worked wonders with River's crate issues. He absolutely loved his crate now. Not that he'd tell Dulcie that. "Out," Charm ordered.

As they tramped through tall weeds with tangles of briars that grabbed at their ankles, Charm saw immediately why she had chosen this place.

Dulcie had found a hill.

The lowland plains of western Mississippi lay as flat as the plains of Kansas — rich farmland kept fertile by the frequent floods of the many rivers, creeks, and tributaries riddled throughout. Central Mississippi, in contrast, was comparatively hilly. Not mountains, mind you. Rolling hills, long gentle slopes. But Dulcie had found a rare beast. A wide, fairly tall, fairly steep hill with brush, but no thick stands of trees.

Charm looked it up and down. "You dragged us to hell and gone for this?"

Dulcie ignored him. "We're doing a pattern blind." She and Lucas stood in the center of the field. At varying distances, radiating out from that spot, she had planted bumpers. If the layout had appeared on a clock face, bumpers had been placed up the hill at roughly ten, twelve, and two o'clock and behind them in the flat field at four, six, and eight o'clock.

"Lucas, I want you to start with this one." She turned him toward the one at four o'clock and pointed. "Then work your way around clockwise. The ones here on the flat should be an easy warm up."

She looked back at the others and motioned toward the remaining bumpers. "Dad, you, Charm, and Jimmy Lee position yourselves by the ones on the hillside. No more than twenty feet from the bumper. I need you to be able to pick it up if necessary." Picking up the bumper meant River couldn't reward himself with the retrieve if the run hadn't been to Dulcie's exacting standards.

Smokey took the bumper at ten o'clock. Helping Dulcie in the field had restored a great deal of his strength and balance, and he jogged up with no difficulty. Jimmy Lee scrambled to the one at twelve o'clock, and Charm tromped out to the bumper stashed at two o'clock — the longest run of the day, an easy hundred and fifty yards ending about thirty feet from the crest of the ridgeline.

He concealed himself behind a bush. A thorny bush. He scratched at his ankle. Probably got chiggers from that long grass too. And damn it, he'd left his flask in the glove compartment. No way he was hiking all the way back to his truck. Probably.

As Dulcie had expected, River retrieved the first few bumpers with no issues. Clean lines, fast finds, even faster returns. The ten o'clock retrieve, the first on the hill, was fairly short, the bumper positioned less than halfway up the hill. River retrieved it cleanly, as he had the others.

*Good.* Charm used his sleeve to wipe away sweat that threatened to drip into his eyes. *Maybe we'll be out of here early.*

The first sign of trouble came with the twelve o'clock bumper. It lay on a steep line directly up the hill, about twenty feet from the top. River powered himself up the hill, *past* the bumper, all the way to the top and turned around. Dulcie blew her buzzer, and Jimmy Lee popped out and grabbed the bumper.

"Call him back," Dulcie said to Lucas. Then to Jimmy Lee, "Wait until he's in position, then toss it to the same location. We'll do it as a mark."

The boy blew the whistle around his neck three times, and River ran back to him. Lucas waved him into heel position without offering the "happy bumper" he used to reward successful retrieves. Then he gave the cue that told the dog to look for a falling object to retrieve: "Mark."

Dulcie pointed a starter pistol in the air and pulled the trigger. River shuddered a bit, but didn't move from his spot, his eyes scanning the area in front of him. Jimmy Lee tossed the bumper. The dog visibly tensed, like a runner on his starting line.

"River." The dog's name cued him to pursue the retrieve. He exploded up the hill, powering himself up the slope with his hindquarters. His momentum took him a half stride past the bumper, but he stopped, turned, and grabbed it and started back before Lucas had even given the three tweets on his whistle. Charm smiled at the little party when River dropped the bumper in Lucas's hand.

"Let's do it again. Same line, as a blind. Jimmy Lee, put it lower. About halfway up the hill. Same line," Dulcie repeated. She turned Lucas and River around, so River wouldn't see Jimmy Lee plant it.

Charm watched. Twice the bumper had been in the same place near the top of the hill. The challenge initially had been to control his speed. Now it was memory. A lot of dogs would blow right past the bumper, heading to the spot they remembered it being in before.

River nailed it on his first try.

Charm sat a little straighter. His turn now. Finally. *Come on, buddy. Let's nail this one, too, and go home. A hundred and fifty yards. You can do this in your sleep.* Distance was a sticking point between him and Dulcie. Field trial marks could be four hundred yards — almost a quarter mile — and she had focused almost exclusively on these shorter marks. That choice had been the topic of more than one argument.

Lucas lined River toward the bumper and sent him. The line took the dog diagonally across the hill. He held his line solidly for the first two-thirds of the run, then began drifting to the top. The same instant Charm realized the dog was off his line, Dulcie sounded her buzzer. "Try again."

"You want a mark?" Charm called.

"Nope."

They repeated the exercise, same result at roughly the same point. Again, she sounded her buzzer.

"Oh, come on!" Charm groaned.

"Again!" Dulcie said.

This was such bullshit. "You don't call a dog in for fading on a hill," he said, stalking down the hill. "They all do that. Whistle-sit him and recast."

"And lose unnecessary points," Dulcie said dryly. Charm gave an aggrieved sigh. "If you know better, you're welcome to take over."

For a tenth of a second, he considered saying yes. How many times had they had this argument — or a nearly identical one? What would she do if he snatched that whistle and set the dog up himself?

She'd leave. And she wouldn't be back.

Dulcie Clark held all the cards.

Charm clenched his jaw and trudged back to his bush. He sulked through the rest of the training session. Dulcie persisted with her methodical plan, and by the time they quit for the day, River held a steady line on the diagonal of the hill. They would, of course, have to keep practicing — so sayeth Queen Dulcie.

Charm ignored the wrap-up discussion and got the truck started and the air conditioning blasting. No amount of air conditioning could cool the anger churning inside him. *Thirty-seven days. Thirty-seven fucking days.*

Lucas climbed in a few minutes later. "You okay, Uncle Charm?"

"River in his crate?"

The boy nodded. Charm pressed the gas so hard the back wheels spun. Lucas grabbed the door handle and hung on as the truck bounced and rocked through the ruts baked into the dirt road. The tires screeched when they turned onto the main highway. *Road,* Charm amended. Nothing this dinky got to be called a highway.

"Why are you so mad?" Lucas asked in a small voice.

"Because she's fucking nuts."

"She's not nuts!"

"That's not how you train a hunting dog. Mark my words, kid, that dog won't *ever* compete." *Damn it, where's my flask?* He reached across his nephew and dug around in the glove compartment. "She's wasting time on stuff nobody worries about instead of adding distance. It's distance he's going to need in a real trial." *There. Finally.* He fumbled with it in his lap trying to get it open. "A damn quarter mile of distance."

"You can't drink and drive!" Lucas snapped.

Charm waved the flask at him. "I'm not drunk. This is just…to clear my head." Finally got the cap off. "Trust me, you'll understand when you get older." A pothole sent the whiskey down his shirt. "Crap!"

"Look out!"

A horn blared, and Charm refocused on the road. And swerved.

# CHAPTER 16

Elle burst through the side door and swept through the kitchen, past her mother, at a jog.

"What are you doing here?" her mother asked.

"Spilled coffee all over my restaurant uniform this morning," Elle called back. She took the stairs two at a time. Was her spare uniform up here? *Christ on a cracker.* It was in the laundry. She ran back downstairs.

"I spilled coffee," she repeated. "Please tell me the clothes are clean."

"Clean but not folded." Her mother held up sliced deli meat. "Would you like lunch?"

Elle dug through the dryer until she found the white blouse she sought. "No time, thanks. I've got to get back to work." A few wrinkles. It would do. Maybe they would come out if she hung the blouse in the car until she needed it. She grabbed a hanger. "Was that Charm in the field? I didn't think he knew how to run the mower."

"Not Charm," her mother said. "Oscar."

Elle paused. She looked through the glass in the door to confirm, then walked into the kitchen. "Why is Oscar mowing our pasture?"

"It needs to be done."

"I know that, but why —"

A horn, distant but growing closer, interrupted her. She and Dot both looked toward the front of the house. "Dear Lord, now what?"

They made it to the front door in time to see Jimmy Lee's truck turn into the driveway, honking the entire time. He drove onto the lawn and skidded to a stop in front of the porch.

"What the hell?" Elle demanded, walking to meet him. "I don't need ruts in my lawn, Jimmy Lee."

He rolled down his window. "Hop in. There's been an accident."

* * *

Memories assaulted her. Overwhelmed her. Jake's truck mangled, parts strewn across road and field. Emergency lights, blue and red, creating a disorienting strobe effect in the darkness. Interminable drive to Jackson. Hospital waiting room, staffed with jaded nurses there to manage, not soothe. *"You can't go back there. We'll tell you when we know more."* Horrible, burnt coffee. Uncomfortable chairs. Her husband swathed in bandages, swollen face unrecognizable.

Jimmy Lee was speaking to her. She looked at him, but the words didn't make sense. *Not again. I can't do this again.*

Emergency lights appeared in the distance. Blue. Not red. What did that mean? She stopped breathing. Police. And a tow truck. She drew in a gulp of air. No ambulance. She took in the scene all at once. A sheriff's car and several individuals, including Lucas and River — thank God — stood on the left side of the road. Her truck sat on the left side of the road, the tow truck snugged up close to its front. Charm leaned against the truck's open door talking to an officer — was that Bird? — who was searching the front seat. Everyone stopped and looked her way as Jimmy Lee pulled over and parked.

"Lucas!" Elle was out and running almost before the truck had stopped.

Charm intercepted her. "He's fine. Nobody's hurt."

Elle pushed him aside. "Lucas!"

"Mom!" The boy broke away from the group and half limped, half ran to her.

Elle knelt, and he buried himself in her arms, sobbing. "Are you all right?" She alternated pushing him back to look at him and pulling him close to hug him. Tears left his eyes swollen and red, but otherwise he seemed unharmed. Physically. "What happened?" She looked past him to the people who had been taking care of him — Dulcie and Smokey. *Thank you.*

"All we did was drive into a ditch. Everybody's fine," Charm tried to assure her.

She rose and faced him in one swift movement. "Were you drinking?"

He stammered.

She stepped toward him. "Were. You. Drinking?"

Across the road, Bird backed out of the cab of the truck and held up an open flask. "Charm, we need to talk."

Charm visibly paled, and he looked back at Elle. "That's not what it looks like."

Hot tears flowed down her cheeks. "How could you?" She grabbed Lucas's hand and River's leash and ushered them toward Jimmy Lee's truck.

"I'm not drunk!" His voice pleaded with her to believe him.

She whirled and advanced into his space. "How could you risk my son?" She shoved him back — hard. "He's all I have left!"

Elle scooped Lucas up and marched to the truck. As Lucas and River clambered in, she looked back. Bird had Charm by the arm, preventing him from following her. "I knew I couldn't count on you."

"Ellie! Ellie, wait!" Charm called desperately.

Jimmy Lee closed the door and looked at her.

"Let's go," she said.

# CHAPTER 17

Bird released his grip on Charm's bicep and pointed to his cruiser. "Go wait right there."

Charm did as he was told. Thank God, he hadn't drunk from the flask. When did he close the bar? He did some math. He shouldn't have any alcohol left in his system at this point. *It was an accident. A simple accident. Could have happened to anyone.*

Bird and the tow truck operator spoke in low tones. The tow truck operator pointed at the ditch and the front of the truck, and together they bent down and looked under the front of the truck. The tow truck operator pointed at something under there, and Bird nodded. Charm chewed his lip and watched. Hopefully he hadn't damaged the truck too badly. Repairs cost a fortune. Maybe Jimmy Lee knew somebody who could fix it cheap. If Jimmy Lee was still talking to him.

Jimmy Lee had been the first one to arrive after Charm drove into the ditch. Really that's all it was. Not really an *accident.* He got too far to the right and ended up in a shallow ditch. No big deal. The other guy didn't even stop. This was getting blown all out of proportion.

Self-righteous indignation flared. If Jimmy Lee hadn't wasted time getting River out of the crate — seriously, he was *fine* — Charm wouldn't even be in this mess. Surely one of them had a spare shirt. They could have tossed the flask and his whiskey-soaked shirt, and no one would have been the wiser. But no. By the time Jimmy Lee and Lucas finished fussing over that dog, Dulcie and Smokey had driven up. They'd called the tow truck and the cops.

Charm heard Bird tell the tow truck operator to "Hold up," then he checked both ways and jogged across the street. Dulcie stopped him before he reached the car.

"May we go?" she asked in a polite voice Charm hadn't heard before. "We didn't see anything. Just stopped to help."

*Yeah, you were a huge help.* Charm scowled. If she hadn't been such a know-it-all, he wouldn't have been pissed off in the first place. *It's your fault all this happened.*

Bird nodded and thanked her, and she walked away without even glancing toward Charm. Bird watched her and Smokey return to their truck and nodded to them as they drove past. Then he glared at Charm and walked to his trunk. Charm crossed his arms and waited. Less than a minute later, Bird returned with a Breathalyzer.

"Oh, come on! Don't ask me to do that," Charm protested. "I'm not drunk."

Bird grabbed him by the front of his shirt and slammed him against the doorframe. "You know what you are? You're a goddamn jackass! I'm trying to help you here."

Fighting Bird was like arguing with a bear. "How's beating the crap out of me helping me?"

Bird released him but didn't step back. "I'm not beating the crap out of you, though I might consider it if there wasn't a witness." The tow truck guy wandered to the other side of the vehicles, whistling aimlessly. "I'm trying to get you to stop your pity party and listen for two seconds."

Charm looked anywhere but at his friend. "I'm not having a pity party," he muttered.

"Oh, please. It's all over your face. You've convinced yourself that you're the victim here."

"I'm being treated like I'm some sort of monster. All I did was drive into a ditch."

Bird pointed behind them. "Look at the skid marks. You barely missed that pole." He switched and pointed ahead of them. "And if you'd gone fifty feet more, you'd have slammed into *that* telephone pole."

Charm looked where Bird pointed and felt the blood drain from his cheeks. He'd been so angry, he hadn't even seen the poles. Images of what could have happened swirled around him. Lucas. He could have killed Lucas. Ellie's words whispered in his ear: *"He's all I have left."*

Bird attached a plastic mouthpiece and pressed the power button on the Breathalyzer. "This is how this is gonna work. You're gonna take this test. Your truck is drivable. Blow clear, I write you a ticket for careless driving, and you drive out of here."

Thirty seconds before, Charm would have sworn on a stack of Bibles he was sober as Pastor Walton on Sunday (or any other day, probably), but now his hands shook too hard to hold the device.

Bird held it for him. "Blow hard and steady. You're gonna hear a tone. Don't stop blowing until that tone stops."

Charm nodded then hesitated. "What happens if I fail?"

"Then the truck gets towed, and I haul your ass in on DUI, reckless driving, and pissing off everyone who knows you."

Charm nodded again and blew. And blew. And blew. Finally, the tone stopped, and he drew in a deep breath. *Please be clear.* After two more lifetimes, or fifteen seconds, Bird peered at the device and said, "Point zero one. You're clear."

Charm sagged against the car. Vindication tasted a lot like luck.

Bird gave a thumbs-up to the tow truck driver, who waved and drove away. "Go home," Bird said flatly. "If you still have one."

Charm looked up. Would Elle kick him out? God, he'd fucked up. "What about the ticket?" he asked. Bird just glared. *Oh.* "See you later," Charm mumbled, heading for the truck.

"I hope not," Bird called after him.

Charm glanced back and nodded. Message received. The last place he needed to be was Brother Jack's.

The truck, he discovered, reeked of whiskey and pulled to the right. He'd knocked the alignment all to hell. How much would that cost to fix? Less than a ticket or bailing it out of police impound, he guessed.

He rolled down the windows, pointed the truck toward home, and tried to figure out how to get himself out of this fuckup to end all fuckups. Groveling and sucking up didn't seem adequate. Only a few hours before, he had been counting the days until he could leave. Now, faced with the possibility, the thought of leaving filled him with a rush of emotion. *Lucas still needs my help,* he told himself.

Charm's sedan, which Ellie had been driving that day, was nowhere in sight when Charm arrived home. Some of the knots in his guts loosened; he didn't have to face his sister right away. His mother's car was where he expected, and to his surprise, Dulcie and Smokey's truck was there. Great.

He pulled Ellie's truck into its usual spot near the barn and turned off the engine. Deep breaths. *It'll be okay. I can do this.* Two more minutes of deep breathing, and he climbed out of the truck. Thirty-nine steps later he walked through the front door.

Conversation in the kitchen stopped.

Charm tugged nervously at his shirt. His shirt. His whiskey-soaked shirt. Not the impression he wanted to lead with. Three hours in Mississippi heat and humidity hadn't left him fresh as a daisy either. Shower first.

Twenty minutes later, he stood at the bottom of the stairs again, cleaner but no more eager to face his family. *Let's get this over with.* He walked into the kitchen as nonchalantly as he could manage. All eyes at the table turned toward him. His mother and Smokey on one side, Dulcie on the other, Lucas at the far end. All stared at him. River rose from his place at Lucas's feet and ambled over to greet him, tail wagging.

Charm busied himself rubbing the retriever's ears. "Hey, buddy," he crooned. *At least River has forgiven me.* "Ellie at work?" No one answered him. He swallowed and rubbed River's ears harder. The scent of cooked onions and grilled meat permeated the air. He tried again. "Something smells good. Any left for me?"

"We thought you'd be in jail," his mother said.

"I wasn't drunk."

Lucas pushed back from the table. "You can have my lunch. I'm not hungry." He patted his leg. "Come on, River."

And just like that, Charm's one friend in the room whirled away and trotted back to the boy's side. Lucas limped past Charm without so much as a sideways glance.

"But you were drinking?" His mother's tone was more accusing than questioning.

Possible replies spun through his head. Ways to spin the situation to lessen his culpability. "I had a flask, but I hadn't drunk from it."

"How did the accident happen?"

More possible replies. He settled on the truth. "I was angry. I was distracted, and I swerved to miss an oncoming car."

"Hmph." His mother touched Smokey's arm. "I'd better check on Lucas." He nodded, and she rose. "Excuse me, Dulcie," she said politely and left in search of Lucas. She didn't glance at Charm as she passed either.

Charm sighed and gathered Lucas's and his mother's plates from the table. "I'm sorry I messed up your meal," he said to Smokey and Dulcie. "And…everything else." His mother and Lucas hadn't really finished. He decided to leave their plates on the counter in case they came back and turned his focus to putting away the leftovers. Suddenly he stopped and looked at Dulcie. "Can I take you to lunch?"

Dulcie looked down at the food in front of her and then back at him with a raised eyebrow. "I just ate."

"I know. But I need to talk to you." He hesitated, then added, "Please."

Dulcie exchanged a glance with her father, then shrugged. "Whatever." She picked up her plate and her father's as she rose.

"I'll take those," Charm offered.

"I've got them."

He stepped back and looked for something to do. "Would you like a slice of pie, sir?" he asked Smokey.

Smokey smiled. "I certainly would. Thank y-you."

Glad for something to do for someone who didn't seem openly hostile to him, Charm rushed to place a clean plate and fork in front of him and dug a lemon icebox pie from the freezer.

Dulcie took the pie from his hands and cut her father a small slice. "You don't need to eat so much of this," she scolded. Smokey's smile turned to a grimace. She ignored that and handed the pie back to Charm to put away. "We'll be back in an hour or so," she said. "Do you need anything?"

"We'll be fine," Smokey said, waving his fork at her. "Take your time." His assurance didn't seem to fully satisfy her, but she shrugged her readiness to Charm and headed out the back door.

He hesitated. "Let me grab my keys, and I'll join you," he called to her rapidly disappearing back. He waited until the door slammed shut, then tiptoed back, grabbed the pie from the freezer, and set it on the table. "Enjoy!" he said in a stage whisper. Smokey chuckled and saluted with his fork.

Charm was still smiling when he joined Dulcie at Elle's truck.

"What are you grinning at?" she asked suspiciously.

"A joyful life." A waft of whiskey smacked him in the face when he opened the truck's door. Dulcie's nose wrinkled. "Ummm…it's not so bad with the windows open," Charm said.

She rolled her eyes but climbed in and cranked the window down. "Where are we going?" she asked, as he turned the truck around.

"Brother Jack's."

She snorted. "Is that really where you need to be right now?"

*Not in the least.* He turned out of the driveway. "I need to talk to Max."

They drove to the bar in silence. The knots in Charm's stomach grew tight again as they got near and finally parked. They walked in together, and he pointed to an empty table toward the back. Before he could say anything, a voice roared from the bar: "Freeman! Get your ass back here!"

Max's face looked like his shirt collar was three sizes too small. Charm nodded. "Shouldn't take me more than five minutes," he said to Dulcie. "Want to split something? Order whatever you want, except the nachos. They're horrible." He didn't wait for a reply before weaving through the tables to the far end of the bar.

The speed of the Collier rumor mill was truly impressive. Charm wondered if Jimmy Lee had told Max himself or if he'd just posted it on Facebook. He followed Max into the kitchen.

"I told you what would happen if you drove drunk," Max snapped.

"I didn't drive drunk." His calm reply surprised even Charm. "You can ask Bird. He gave me a Breathalyzer, and I blew clear."

Max looked confused, but he'd worked himself into a fit of righteous anger and didn't show signs of being ready to give that up. "I heard you totaled your sister's truck and half killed your nephew."

Now it was Charm's turn to get angry. "Of all the ridiculous…I drove the truck here, and Lucas isn't even bruised. Don't believe everything you hear, Max."

Max rubbed the back of his neck. "Well…maybe. What did happen?"

"I did something really stupid," Charm said matter-or-factly. "I was mad and hungover, and I drove into a ditch. I wasn't drinking, but frankly, if it had happened two minutes later, I would have been." It was the first time he had admitted that out loud. He looked away from Max, not wanting to see the anger in his eyes. Or the compassion. Definitely not the compassion.

"I need to quit, Max," Charm continued. "You gave me a real good opportunity, and I appreciate it, but I gotta get away from the bar for a while."

The big man sighed. "That's a tough decision, but I understand. Don't worry about your scheduled shifts. I'll cover 'em." He stuck out his hand. "Good luck. I'll give ya a reference if you need one."

Charm managed a wan smile and thanked him, genuinely grateful for the kindness, then wove his way back through the tables to where Dulcie sat, his mind churning with the repercussions of what he had done. Right decision, but they needed his income. What would he do now? He slid into the chair across from her. "You order?" he asked.

She nodded. "What did you want to talk about?" No beating

around the bush. No small talk. No curiosity about what happened in the kitchen.

Charm fixed his gaze on her and tilted his head. "Why don't you like me?"

Her eyes opened, and her jaw dropped. "Wow. And here I thought you were going to apologize."

"I might get around to that." Maybe. From his point of view, she wasn't entirely without culpability herself. "But I'm curious. You disliked me the second you laid eyes on me on that beach. I want to know why."

"Bruise your ego?" He didn't rise to the bait. She scowled at him and didn't say anything for a long minute, but he could almost see the possible responses cross her face like shadows. Finally, she said, "It was your smile."

Now it was his turn to frown. Thinking about it, he realized every time he had flashed his trademark smile — the one that wooed women better than chocolate and wine — she had snarled like a wolverine.

"I've seen so many people like you," she continued. "Rich white guys who think a woman should flop on her back and part her legs simply because they *smile*." The word dripped with venom.

Charm blinked, not entirely sure where to go with that. "Rich? We're so buried in bills, we work — or worked — three jobs between us, and our mother has practically moved in to take care of Ellie's kid. That day on the beach was our only day off in two months. All I did was ask for change. Politely."

"And then you showed up at the house begging for free help."

"I *asked* for help. And when you said no, I did *not* argue —"

"No, you sent your mommy to do it for you —"

"No. I had no idea she knew your father. I didn't know that until you showed up on my doorstep the next day. Which you made clear you'd never do. So why did you?" Their voices had gotten overloud. Other people were listening.

"My father," she spat. "Stubborn bastard would have done it without me if I hadn't."

"So?"

Her eyes opened wide. "Have you seen him? He can barely walk."

"Have *you* seen him? He keeps up with you in the field every damn day." And the slurring and pauses had almost disappeared from Smokey's speech.

Dulcie blinked, but before she could respond, a waitress placed a large order of nachos on the table. "What would you like to drink, hon?" the waitress asked Charm.

A beer. Or six. "Sweet tea," he said with a grimace. He scooped a healthy portion of the cheesy goodness onto a plate.

Dulcie watched him savor his first bite. "You said you hated the nachos."

"What can I say? You're predictably contrary." He smirked and took another bite. "Go ahead, have some. They're awesome." He glanced up in case she decided to come over the table at him.

She managed to keep her seat, but her dark eyes flashed. "Is this why you asked me here? To fight?"

"Actually, no," he said. "As entertaining as this is, I want to figure out how to get along. We don't have to like each other, but we have to work together."

"Why ask me?" She dragged a chip through guacamole. "You're the one who has to challenge everything."

"I ask *questions*. Why are *you* so threatened by that?"

"I'm not threatened by questions. But I get irritated when people like you can't accept that a young Black woman might actually know what she's talking about." She gestured with the chip so violently, guacamole flew onto a nearby table.

"People like me? What people? *Rich white guys?*"

"No," she grumbled, at least having the decency to look abashed. "Not just white guys. Not even just *guys*. People at school. People I worked with. I'm good at what I do, and no one wants to give me credit for that." She slumped in the chair, arms crossed across her chest, looking like a teenager rebelling about an early curfew.

Charm managed not to roll his eyes. "If you treat everybody else the way you treated the trainers here, I don't blame them. You don't discuss. You don't ask questions to learn. You talk at people and try to make them feel inferior. Eh eh —" He held up a hand and stopped her outburst before it started. "I've seen you do it. You're smart, you're educated, and you *are* good at what you do. Doesn't mean you know everything."

"I never said I did."

"But you act like it."

Dulcie glowered and pushed back from the table. "Well, this has been fun. But I need to get back."

Charm didn't move. "Not without a truce."

She paused, then scooted back. "What kind of truce?"

"No fighting. No sniping. No baiting. No sarcasm."

"Are you gonna ask questions?"

"Unless you prefer I screw up the training."

She made a show of trying to decide. "What do I get out of it?"

"No fighting. No sniping. No baiting. No sarcasm. And since I just quit my job, someone more rested and less cranky."

She shrugged and tried to look unaffected. "Done. Can we go now?"

Charm tossed some money on the table and followed her out. They drove back to Ellie's house in silence, each lost in thought. Rather than parking, he pulled the truck up to the side door to drop her off. Dulcie hesitated before getting out.

"What are you going to do now?" The antagonism had left her voice.

"In the short term, I'm going to see if I can figure out how to get the stench of whiskey out of this truck." She managed a small smile. "Then I've got to find a job. You don't happen to know any used car lots around here?"

"'Fraid not."

"I can sell the hell out of a used car."

"I don't doubt it." She extended her knuckles. "Good luck."

Fist bump. "Thanks."

He watched Dulcie leave the truck and walk inside the house. Not friendship, but a start. A chance. He hoped other people in his life would give him the same chance. And he hoped to God he didn't screw it up.

# CHAPTER 18

Cleaning the truck wasn't as bad as Charm had feared. The old truck had vinyl seats, and not much whisky had hit the floorboard. A good scrub with Clorox wipes and Febreze got the worst of it. Problem one solved.

According to Google Maps, Collier didn't have a used car dealership. Rolling Forks had three, but only one was big enough to interest him. Vicksburg, forty minutes to the south, had a good number and was probably a good bet. If he struck out there, he'd try Greenville, about an hour north. Maybe. Might be too far to justify the gas and car maintenance.

The dealer in Rolling Fork wasn't hiring. Of course not. That would be way too easy, and Charm had screwed up way too much for easy, so on to Vicksburg. His car rattled its way down Highway 61, the temperature gauge crawling upward in the Mississippi sun. Not even summer yet, and the air conditioning struggled to keep the car at something less than sauna temperatures.

No luck at the first or second dealership, and by the third, anxiety began to poke and dig at the edges of his mental plan. What if he couldn't find a job? Would it be better for him to leave now and go back to St. Louis? Was he more burden than help?

Even if their mom took care of Lucas, Ellie couldn't work two jobs and run a farm by herself. She *couldn't*. Charm had muddled through the farm chores during the spring. More or less. Sometimes a lot less if he were being honest — and, at this point, why not be honest? He lacked skill. He lacked knowledge. No telling how many things he should have done that he didn't know to do. But even his amateur attempts were more than Ellie could have done while working two jobs. *What will Ellie do when I leave?*

"Mr. Freeman?" Charm blinked and pulled himself out of the tornado of questions that swirled in his mind. A short, round man with slicked back hair but a remarkably nice suit stuck out his hand. "I'm T-Bo Dupre, the manager. Want to step into my office while I look over your application?"

A cautious sort of hope nudged at Charm's heart as he followed the man to a dingy office with a metal desk, a metal guest chair, a metal filing cabinet, a metal fan, and dangerously tall stacks of paper on every surface. Someone forgot to tell Mr. Dupre this was the computer generation. Charm pictured the chaos that would result if someone turned on that fan. A plaque on the desk informed Charm what he heard as "T-Bo" was spelled *T-h-i-b-a-u-t*. Huh. Live and learn.

Mr. Dupre took his time reading Charm's application. As the minutes ticked by, Charm's nervousness grew. He squirmed a bit in his chair and wished he had his flask. Just a nip of whiskey would have settled him. A calendar on the wall featured a sports car and a nearly naked girl. Charm focused on it, not because of the girl, but because the photo featured a banner advertising the calendar's sponsor — Budweiser. A banner with a mug of frothy beer. Charm gritted his teeth and shifted again. He glanced at Mr. Dupre and found him staring at him.

"Your application says you've been working at a bar up near Collier." Despite his Cajun name, Mr. Dupre's accent was all Vicksburg. "Why you lookin' to change?"

Charm cleared his throat. "Yes, sir. I have been. But my brother-in-law passed away a few months ago, and I've been helping my sister with her farm and her son. Closing a bar at three doesn't work with the family dynamics." He flashed his most winsome smile.

"So, it didn't have anything to do with your drinking?"

The question was so direct that all Charm could do was stammer. "M-my drinking?"

Mr. Dupre dug his wallet out of his back pocket and pulled out a bronze coin. An AA recovery chip. "Two years sober." He glanced at the calendar, then back at Charm. "I've been around long enough to recognize a thirsty guy."

Charm clenched his teeth and swallowed the words that jumped into his mouth. *Who the fuck does this guy think he is?* He needed a job, not a sponsor. When he spoke, he kept his tone carefully modulated. "You're right. At three o'clock on a steamy June day, yes, I saw the picture of that beer and thought, 'Damn, a beer would be good,'" he said. "That thought, Mr. Dupre, even coupled with a job as a bartender, doesn't make me an alcoholic." He leaned forward, eyes blazing. "Just because you can't handle a drink doesn't mean no one else can."

Without giving Mr. Dupre a chance to respond, Charm stalked out. *This guy doesn't even know me. How dare he judge me?* He clenched his fists but kept them pinned to his sides to keep from smashing something, anything, as he made his way to his car. *Where does this guy get off?* He got in the vehicle and slammed the door, then loosed a tirade of expletives.

*He thinks I'm a drunk? I'm a bartender. I can show him a drunk.* Charm backed the car out of the space and headed for the exit. His father was a drunk — the bitter, vicious words he spoke when drinking poisoning everyone around him. Anton Brown, a Brother Jack's regular, was a drunk, crying in his beer five nights a week about the wife that left him. Max had to drive him home most nights. And there was that other guy. Charm snapped his fingers trying to remember his name. That guy who was in jail now because he ran a stop light and killed somebody.

Those people were drunks.

Charm paused at the exit to let a police cruiser pass. The officer glanced his way, and Charm took a breath to rein in his rage. All he needed was to piss off another cop today. Or to wreck this car.

Enough job hunting. Tomorrow he'd hit the rest of the dealerships in Vicksburg and, if necessary, make the drive up to Greenville.

He stewed during the drive. As Brother Jack's drew closer, Charm fought the urge to stop. What he wanted — maybe even more than a beer — was a sympathetic ear. Unfortunately, he doubted he'd find one there. Jimmy Lee and Bird had made their position clear. So, with a shaky sigh, he drove past the bar and continued to Ellie's house.

According to his phone, it was a bit shy of four when Charm parked near the barn. His mom's car was the only other vehicle in the driveway. Ellie had a shift at the restaurant that night. Dulcie and Smokey probably left ages ago. Just his mom and Lucas then.

He didn't reach for the door handle, not particularly anxious to go into a house where he wasn't wanted. Too hot to sit in the truck, though. If he was going to be hot and miserable, he might as well be productive. Early for the evening feed, but he'd been out all day, and there were plenty of farm chores to be done.

The tractor sat in a different place than he'd seen it this morning. Oh. The fields had been mowed. More to feel guilty about. The tractor and all its attachments made Charm uncomfortable, but he was willing to learn if someone would teach him. He guessed Ellie thought him too much of a screwup and instead asked someone else to come do it. Or maybe she figured he wouldn't be around long enough to do it. Whoever had done it had removed the drum mower and replaced it with some sort of attachment Charm didn't recognize.

A sick feeling settled in his stomach. Was Ellie going to kick him out when she got home? Not that he'd blame her. But despite his grumpiness this morning, he really, really wanted to stay. Well, the best way to change her mind was to show himself to be invaluable on the farm. So he dove in.

After spraying the mower clean, Charm scrubbed clean the troughs and buckets used to feed and water the various animals. While the water buckets refilled, he picked out the horse's stall and paddock, then tackled the messy job of cleaning out the chicken coop. By the time he was done, it was time to feed.

This time of year, the cows and their calves ate mostly grass and hay. The hay was in round bales, placed in their pasture as needed. Square-baled hay for the horse and the goats was stored in the barn. On the first floor, a half dozen pallets, laid side by side along one wall, could hold nearly a hundred bales. That hay was used daily until gone, then it was replenished from bales stored in the loft. By the end of summer, the loft would be stuffed with a thousand bales, which would get the horse and goats through the cold weather.

They were almost out of hay on the first floor, so Charm headed into the loft. Not much left up there either. Good thing the first cutting of the season lay drying in the pastures. A hole in the loft floor over the pallets made it easy to toss the bales down. He'd go down and stack them in a few minutes.

With the hay gone, Charm explored the rest of the loft for the first time. Newer boards stood out among the dark, aged ones; Jake had ensured the old structure remained solid. Large objects — lots of them, covered with tarps and cloths — filled a great deal of the space not used for hay storage. Charm brushed cobwebs off the nearest tarp and pulled it off.

Boxes. He read the labels he could see. Fine china. Will — books. Dot — memorabilia. *Oh,* he realized. This must be the stuff from the family home. His mom must have stored it here after his dad died.

He pulled off the next tarp and was surprised. Furniture — and not furniture he recognized from the old house. The good pieces from there were in Ellie's house. What was this? Under the tarp there was some sort of wooden cabinet. A nice one. There was a bed frame with beautifully carved finials under another tarp. A dining table and chairs under another. Different styles. Beautiful pieces, though. Why was all this hidden in Ellie's barn?

"Charm!" His mother's voice rang out across the yard. "Dinner's ready."

Charm didn't answer. Lucas's face when Charm had walked in at lunch flashed into his mind. The boy couldn't even look at him and then had left without eating. Charm pushed the memory away and looked under the next tarp. Where had all this furniture come from? Maybe from Jake's folks? But Charm remembered their house, and their style was more 1970 garage sale.

The ladder-stairs to the loft squeaked, and he glanced over to see his mother climbing up. "Good Lord, a person will melt like bacon grease in this heat. What are you doing up here?" she asked, fanning herself.

"What is all this?" Charm asked, gesturing to the furniture.

"Things from the house. I never could bring myself to go through it all."

"No, the furniture. This wasn't in our house."

"It's your dad's furniture."

Charm frowned. "What do you mean? What furniture?"

"Oh, Charm. Surely you remember. When you were little, you used to spend hours with him in his shop, watching him carve and build."

He blinked at her. He hadn't remembered…until that very moment. There had been a shop in their old barn with tools — hand tools — where his father had repaired and refinished old furniture and created new handmade pieces. Why had he forgotten that? The scent of sawdust tickled at the back of his mind. When he was young, he would sit on the edge of a worktable and watch his dad patiently carve and sand and rub at a chunk of wood until it transformed into something polished and beautiful.

As he'd gotten older, his dad had put tools in his hands. Charm could feel the heft of the wood and the clumsiness of the knife. He couldn't see the shape within like his dad could. He tried to give it back, but his father guided him, coaxed him. His effort hadn't been as skilled as his father's, but Charm remembered how proud his dad had been.

That was where they had talked, where they had planned their trips. "There was a map on the wall…" he said.

She nodded. "A big world map with pushpins showing all the places you wanted to go."

He and his dad had spent so much time there, and then…they didn't. One day the door was locked. He remembered asking his father about it, and his father had yelled at him. Charm didn't ask again, and he didn't remember ever going in there again. He ran his hand over the smooth grain of the table, trying to will long-forgotten memories to the surface.

"What happened to the shop?"

She shook her head. "Your dad locked it up when he couldn't do the work anymore. He was an artist. Losing that…broke him."

How old had he been when his father had locked the shop? Older than Lucas definitely. Eleven, maybe? Charm focused on the first thing his mother had said. "Why couldn't he do the work anymore?"

His mother gazed at him quizzically. "His rheumatoid arthritis made it impossible. The drugs weren't as good then, and we didn't have insurance to pay for them anyway. It took his ability to carve first. Then his ability to use hand tools. Eventually, it took the farm."

Rheumatoid arthritis? His father had rheumatoid arthritis? Charm didn't know that. Had he known then? Ever? He didn't think so. So many things he *did* remember began to make sense. "That's why he drank," he said.

She nodded, her eyes reflecting pain — his father's, Charm's, her own. "At first it helped with the pain. Then it helped him forget. The arthritis took everything from him."

Charm compared the father who had guided his hands through his initial, clumsy attempts at carving with the one who had yelled at him, belittled him, and sworn with every inch of his vicious countenance that Charm would never escape Collier, never achieve his dreams. "No," he said. "The arthritis took a lot. The alcohol took everything."

His mother nodded, then shook herself to dispel the gloom that had settled over them. "I can't stand this heat another minute. Dinner is ready."

He shook his head. "You go on. I'm not hungry."

"Starving yourself isn't going to fix the problem."

He thought about Lucas waiting at the table. "I'm less…thirsty when I work," he said finally.

"Suit yourself," she said, her voice softening. "There will be leftovers when you get hungry."

Charm nodded and watched until she disappeared into the house. Then he covered the furniture, set thoughts of his father aside, and went to stack hay.

# CHAPTER 19

Elle sat on the front porch swing, sipped a glass of sweet tea, petted River, and soaked in the feeling of not working. Oh, she would have to go in to the restaurant later, but at least on Saturday and Sunday, the first half of her day had a tad more flexibility. The scent from the roses planted along the front of her house permeated the humid air, and the heat made her body feel languid. A long to-do list awaited her, but right now, Lucas and his grandmother were grocery shopping, Charm was turning hay in the field — she needed to thank Oscar for attaching the tedder to the tractor and coming back yesterday to show Charm how to use it — and she was going to flexibly lounge on this porch for a while.

She closed her eyes and let her body absorb everything around her. Jake had built this swing. They used to snuggle up here when the evenings got cool. She sighed and opened her eyes. Cuddling with River wasn't the same, and damn it, he was too hot. She ordered him off the swing and told him to settle on the porch. He obliged, his elbows making a loud *thunk* when he lay down. He panted, and his tail gave two thumps before he put his head down and closed his eyes.

Her mind drifted. The retriever inevitably brought thoughts of her husband. Was Jake disappointed in her? Two jobs and money from Charm, and she wasn't making a dent in their debt. Damn it. This was Jake's dream, and she wasn't going to lose it. But how could she keep it after Charm left?

Charm. There was another bug in the salad. It had taken everything she had not to mama-bear his ass after that stunt he pulled. The memory still made her seethe. How could he risk her son like that after everything they'd been through? But Lucas grudgingly admitted Charm hadn't had anything to drink (yet), and she'd confirmed his sobriety with Bird. And, she had to admit, he was trying hard to make it up to her.

He'd quit working at the bar — quit drinking entirely as far as she could tell — and started working harder on the farm. The truth was, she couldn't run this farm without him. Whether she forgave him or not, she needed him. And whether she needed him or not, he had promised her only a few months, and they were pushing into June. Considering everything that had happened, she couldn't see him staying much longer.

A horn distracted her from her thoughts. River barked in reply. "Hush," she said, and he stood and wagged his tail. She glanced toward the road and waved at the mailman. *Oh good, more bills*, she thought cynically. But she hauled herself off the swing, told River to wait where he was, and walked to the end of the driveway anyway. She had just opened the mailbox when another car honked and turned into the drive. More barking from River. She waved again — this time at Bird. Without bothering to look through the mail, she hiked up the driveway to greet him.

"Charm's in the field," she said. River trotted up and stuck his head into Bird's lap when he opened the car door. All that training and the dog couldn't hold a stay for five minutes.

Bird flashed a grin, scratched River's ears, and unfolded his lanky body from his car. "Not here to see him," he said. "I'm here to replace your alternator." He unlocked his trunk and took out a tool chest.

"Why?" she asked.

"I was under the impression you needed one." He opened her

truck's door and popped the hood.

She leaned against the truck and watched him disconnect the battery and lift it out of the engine compartment. "Gertie said something about a down payment."

Bird dug a pry bar and a wrench out of his tool chest and finagled around until he was able to remove the two bolts holding the alternator in place. "Jake never had a lot of money," he said as he worked, "but he was always helping out somebody with something. The Pritchetts haven't cleaned their own gutters since Bubba fell off the ladder trying to put a Santa sleigh on the roof."

Elle blinked. "I was in high school when that happened."

He loosened another bolt and removed a belt. "I don't reckon there's a person in town Jake didn't lend a hand to at one time or another. I guess paying you back now really is a sort of down payment."

All the times Jake was off "running an errand" or "helping with a project" — all the times she had been frustrated because he wasn't right where she needed him the moment she needed him — had he been helping other people do what they couldn't? He hadn't said a word. "Why didn't he tell me?"

He lifted the old alternator out and set it on the ground. "It wasn't really tellable, I guess." He rested his forearms on the vehicle and tried to put his thoughts into words. "To Jake, helping people was as everyday as putting his pants on."

Tears burned her eyes. She nodded and squeezed his arm in thanks, then, after a quick call to River, headed back toward the house. Dear, sweet Jake. How could she have not recognized all that he did? Pride and love for the man he'd been — and sorrow that she hadn't recognized it when he was alive — filled her heart. Then followed a moment of missing him so much, her heart felt like it might shatter.

The depth of the grief surprised her. Over the past months, the pain had faded to the dull ache of a missing limb. Phantom pain in the night when her body sought the man who made her whole. But here and there in the light of day, she would see something, hear something, smell something that brought Jake to mind so vividly that the grief flared fresh, tearing off the scab of a wound just beginning to heal.

Elle swiped the tears off her cheeks. Jake was gone, and the best way to honor his memory was to save this farm. She had a lot to figure out.

She swung by the porch to grab her glass of tea and then made her way into the kitchen, River at her heels. She flipped through the mail. Mostly junk mail. *Does anyone actually read this crap?* She stopped and frowned. At the bottom of the stack was an oversized mailing envelope with a return address of the admissions office at Ole Miss. Admissions office? Did Charm want to go to college?

She considered opening the envelope but managed to put a hold on her curiosity. It wasn't addressed to her. Still, a bit of envy nudged at her heart. Ole Miss had arguably the best law school in Mississippi. She glanced at her schoolbooks, still stuffed into the corner with the computer, and sighed. Law school — any school — had again become a dream deferred, perhaps forever this time. Running this farm by herself and getting a law degree were entirely incompatible.

The side door squeaked as it opened, and a moment later, her mother walked in, carrying bags of groceries. Elle dropped the mail on the table and went to help. "Lucas getting the rest?" she asked, taking some of the bags and setting them on the counter.

"Lucas is at Noah Thompson's house playing the new Spider-Man game." Dot shook out her hands to restore circulation. "Charm is getting the rest of the groceries." As if in reply, the side door banged open, and Charm clomped in, laden with bags.

Elle took some of those as well. "How did Lucas end up at Noah's?"

"We ran into him and his mother at the market. Althea invited him. I thought it would be okay."

"Fine with me. He misses his friends during the summer." Elle unloaded fresh vegetables into the crisper. "When's he coming home?"

"Althea suggested that he spend the day and come home after dinner. Around seven?"

Elle paused. "I'll be at work. Can you pick him up?"

Before she could answer, Charm said, "I can do it." He handed her milk to go in the fridge. "I need to go to the hardware store anyway."

"Oh, thank you, Charm," their mother said. "I need to run some errands in Vicksburg, and this frees me up to do that."

"Works for me," Elle said, switching from the fridge to canned goods in the cabinets. "Take your time, Mom."

"If I'm here too much, just tell me," her mother said a little coldly.

Elle blinked, startled, and turned around. "That's not what I meant —"

"Oh cool!" Charm's exclamation interrupted her. He had made his way to the table and was tearing open the oversized envelope.

Elle looked at her mother wanting to explain, but curiosity got the better of her. She peered around him as he pulled out a glossy folder adorned with coeds with remarkably white teeth. "You never told me you want to go to college."

"I don't. These are for you." He held them out to her.

She didn't take them. "What?"

His eyes brightened with excitement. "Ever since that day in Biloxi, I've been thinking about what you said about wanting to go to law school. So now and then when I got the chance, I researched different schools." He held up the materials. "I have a whole slew of this stuff from other schools upstairs. It's really late to apply for this fall, but I think Ole Miss is probably your best bet."

Every bit of envy vanished, replaced by a seething anger. "Are you out of your ever-lovin' mind?" The light in his eyes faded. "What fantasy world do you live in? You think I'm gonna commute from here to Ole Miss every day?"

He had the grace to look embarrassed. "I was only trying to show you some options. Your dream doesn't have to die —"

"*You're* one to talk about dreams —" She bit back what she was going to say and tried to rein in her temper. "After eighteen years you come back to help me, and your solution is to uproot me and my son to follow some pipe dream. How would I pay for it? I'm working two jobs now and barely managing to keep a roof over our heads."

Charm dropped the folder on the table. "I may not know anything about achieving my dreams, but I sure know what it's like to regret not trying."

"Yeah, you're the king of not trying," Elle snapped.

Instead of biting back, a look of defeat settled over him. "Yeah. I guess so." He pushed the folder to the middle of the table and left the kitchen.

"Charm, wait," Elle called, but he didn't return. She growled in frustration.

Her mother sidled up to the table and looked through the folder. "He's right, you know," she said quietly.

Elle turned to stare at her. "Excuse me?"

"This farm isn't your dream. It was Jake's."

"It was *our* dream," Elle corrected, her anger flaring again. The mental discussion she'd had with herself on the porch minutes earlier nudged at her memory, and she pushed it away. *Struggling isn't the same as failing.* "What is it with you guys? Why don't you believe in me?" Unexpected tears burned her eyes.

"Oh, Eleanor." Her mother's tone had turned dismissive. "Don't be ridiculous."

Anger turned to rage. "You have never believed in me! Never!" Tears spilled onto her cheeks. "Not when I wanted to marry Jake. Not when I wanted to have a baby."

Her mother stared at her, mouth agape. "Is that what you think?"

"I know it," Elle said. "None of my choices are ever good enough for you."

Her mother sank into a seat at the table, shaking her head. "Oh, Elle, no," she whispered. "That wasn't it at all."

*Oh, no.* There would be no revisionist history. Elle had lived under the weight of her mother's disapproval for a decade. She sat across from her mother and leaned forward to look her in the eye. "Don't pretend you wanted me to marry Jake. Don't pretend you didn't try to talk me out of having children." Ten years of resentment bubbled out. "Why did you do that, Mother? Were you afraid I'd be like you?"

The words were said out of spite, barbed and pointy, intended to stab deep. Elle expected anger, protest, even cold dismissal. Instead, her mother looked right at her and said simply, "That was exactly what I was afraid of."

Elle sat back, opening and closing her mouth like a fish, unable to find a retort. Finally, she managed to say, "I'm nothing like you."

Her mother pushed back from the table and stood. "You're exactly like me." And with that, she grabbed her purse and left.

- 216 -

# CHAPTER 20

Ellie's words stung. Charm paced around his room, driven by the specter of yet another failure. *No matter how hard I try…*

He stopped by the window and gazed at the farmland beyond. Corn, in this direction. Still-small plants in neat rows planted only with the help of a neighbor. The implements for the tractor mystified and intimidated Charm. Some help he was. Lucas could run this farm as well as he could. Probably better.

What use was he here, really? He'd promised to help Lucas train River, and he had. Or had he? He wasn't even the one who talked Dulcie and Smokey into helping — that was all his mother. Really, he'd never been *that* helpful, and now he was no more than a glorified pair of hands. Lucas didn't even want him there now. And who could blame him? Dulcie and Smokey would see the project through.

Neighbors helped with the farm; their mother watched Lucas; Charm didn't even have a job anymore. It hit him with a sinking feeling: he wasn't needed here.

It was time to leave. Time to go back to his waste of a life in St. Louis where he could lose himself in memories of Sandrine and what could have been. He hadn't thought of her often since he'd finally talked about her with Ellie. Now the pain settled on him, fresh and raw. Damn it, he wanted a drink.

Outside, Charm paused on the front porch to adjust to the sauna-like wave of humidity. Nope, not even Mississippi weather was going to keep him here anymore.

"Where are you going?" asked a voice from his right.

Ellie sat curled up on the porch swing, River stretched out on his side at her feet. "I thought you left," he said. Then he answered her question. "Just out."

"To the bar?"

Whether he deserved it or not — whether accurate or not — the accusation hurt. The pain must have shown on his face because she sighed and apologized. "I shouldn't have said that."

He could pack later. Leave early tomorrow. He nodded and started down the steps.

"Charm, wait." He paused and looked back. "I'm sorry about before too." She tried to smile. "If it makes you feel any better, Mom agrees with you."

Okay, curiosity piqued. "About what?"

"School, I guess. Honestly, I'm not sure. I...might have blown up at her."

"Imagine that," he said dryly. He hesitated a moment longer, then joined her on the swing.

"She said that she and I are alike."

"I'm so sorry."

Ellie snorted. "That's bullshit, right?"

"I never thought about it," he said. It occurred to him that their physical similarity had been the first thing he noticed on that ride from the cemetery to the church so long ago. But that was normal mother-daughter stuff. Ellie, he assumed, meant something deeper. "You're both widowed farm wives."

She cringed but nodded. "Yeah, but Dad didn't die until you and I were adults. He wasn't old, exactly, but it wasn't like Jake. And he didn't die in an accident."

No. His father had slowly drunk himself to death. Technically he'd died of heart disease, but Jake had told him that the heart disease was probably caused by the alcohol. How come knowing that didn't make Charm want to drink any less? The thought of a shot of whiskey burning its way down his throat made him restless, like ants crawling under his skin.

"I've got to get going," he said, standing up.

"Where are you going?" At his raised eyebrow, her cheeks flushed. "I'm not accusing you of going to Brother Jack's. I was just wondering what you were doing this afternoon."

He didn't answer her right away. What did he want to do — really? He gazed out at the farm. That hay was going to need to be baled soon. "Job hunting," he said finally. "There are still some used car dealerships in Vicksburg I haven't tried."

"Thanks for that." She squinted up at him. "It won't be forever. I'm going to figure this out."

Funny. When she mentioned not needing him forever, his stomach did flip-flops. He started down the stairs, then paused again. "Hey, Ellie? I'm really sorry."

"I know."

"I wouldn't hurt Lucas for the world."

"Not intentionally," she said steadily. "But all the good intentions in the world wouldn't have brought him back."

He nodded. "I guess it's true — God takes care of children and fools." Ellie didn't smile. "I won't let you down again."

"You don't have to do this alone, Charm," she said. She grinned wryly. "I've recently discovered that asking for help can work miracles."

Maybe for her. Maybe for Lucas. Miracles tended to run in short supply for Charm. He could handle it himself.

* * *

By Monday, Charm felt a bit better. Lucas had begun talking to him again, and both Jimmy Lee and Bird had texted him. Most importantly, the ants under his skin and the thirst clawing at his throat had receded. Some. Training at nine thirty instead of eight o'clock didn't hurt either.

He recognized the address Dulcie texted him as one of the places she had found to train water retrieves. Rivers, streams, creeks, lakes, ponds, and swamps filled the Mississippi delta and most of the western half of the state. Generally, trees bordered (or filled) the lakes and ponds that weren't purely seasonal, but a few were open enough to use for training — as long as you cleared the area of snakes and the occasional alligator.

This location — they referred to it as a lake, even though technically it was a widening of one of myriad streams in the area — was an odd shape with edges that randomly jutted in or curved outward and featured tall grasses and fallen trees, most of which were pushed to the south end by the current. It was precisely the right width to do retrieves both in the water and through the water to the other side. Though trees grew around the south edge, the water opened into wide expanses of fallow field on both sides. In short, it was one of the best locations for training in the area.

Apparently, they weren't the only ones who thought so. Charm spotted Dulcie's and Jimmy Lee's trucks as soon as he and Lucas reached the field. However, three other trucks, two equipped with silver dog boxes, were parked in the same area.

"Who's that?" Lucas asked, sitting up to get a better view.

Charm parked and squinted at two men working with a sleek chocolate Lab a short distance into the field. "Looks like Forbes's guy, Tim Layton."

Lucas sat even straighter. "Cool! Is that Goliath? My dad said he's the best field trial dog ever." He caught his breath. "Except for River."

Charm grinned. "Except for River."

They climbed out, and Lucas hopped into the back to get River from his crate. Jimmy Lee dropped in beside Charm as they walked to join Dulcie and Smokey, who stood nearby watching Layton and his team. "How you doin'?"

"Good."

Smokey nodded a greeting. Dulcie smiled at Lucas and ignored Charm, as usual. Charm peered out at the field. Goliath was positioned on a long, oblique angle to the water, an easy couple hundred yards away from the farthest of three men Layton had stationed as white-coated gunners at various places in the field on the other side of the pond.

"How long have they been here?" Charm asked. He didn't particularly mind waiting. True, the day would get hotter, but at least he wouldn't have to beat the grass for snakes. Or alligators.

Dulcie's gaze didn't waver from the field. "Dunno. We've been here half an hour. That dog's good."

Their voices must have carried over the flat field because Layton glanced over. "My second string is good. Goliath is phenomenal." He glanced at River. "Hang on to that curly dog. I don't want him to interfere with us."

Lucas scowled but wrapped an arm around River's neck and tightened his hold on the leash. River whined.

Layton smirked. "Hold tight. I heard he doesn't like loud noises." With that, he checked with the man handling Goliath, got a nod, and raised his hand to confirm they were ready.

The chocolate's body tensed, and his head swung back and forth as he scanned the field for a bird. A shotgun blast sounded across the water near the northwest corner of the field followed by a thrown bird. Layton glanced at River, but he sat rock still, unfazed by the gun, just as rapt on the bird as Goliath.

Seconds later, there was a second shotgun blast toward the middle of the field and a second thrown bird.

And then there it was — a live flyer. It took off at an odd angle, low and hard to see from where Charm stood. There — it had curved over the south end of the water. Less than five seconds after the release, a shotgun blast felled it into an area of tall grass and fallen branches. In the water? On the ground nearby? Charm couldn't tell.

A triple. Goliath would have to remember where all three marks fell and retrieve them one at a time. Charm whistled softly and knelt down to watch Goliath's run. This was way harder than anything they'd ever asked River to do. Goliath whined and danced at the start line, desperate to get his prize. The handler lined him up for the live bird. It was the most valuable bird, the go bird, and Goliath clearly remembered where it fell.

But he couldn't find it.

Charm wasn't sure exactly where the bird had ended up, and apparently neither was Goliath. Trees, thick grasses, and downed limbs made the area hard to search. The lake itself had all that plus a current, thanks to the creek that fed and emptied it. Get caught in the wrong place, and it was possible to be pulled under a downed tree or get otherwise hung up and drown.

Goliath didn't hold his line. He swam, skirting the edge of the tall grass, and crossed to the other side. He searched. Hard. He scented high and low, entered the water, then came out again, convinced the bird was on land. Was it? Charm wasn't sure.

Layton grew tense.

River whined again and strained against Lucas's arms. "River could find it," Lucas said.

"Not a chance," Layton replied.

Dulcie shook her head. "It's too far. River isn't ready for that. Slow and steady, remember?"

Goliath's search widened, and he headed further into the field, switching to the second bird. The handler whistle-sat him and signaled him back toward the area where the live flyer fell. He went back into the water this time and swam into the tall grasses. A few seconds later, though, he popped out and returned to the bank. Layton groaned.

Goliath kept searching and again was unsuccessful. When he tried to switch to the other bird a second time, Layton hit him with a correction. "Somebody help him!" he yelled.

Before anyone in the field could respond, River had had enough. He leapt up and back, breaking Lucas's hold and then powered *backward*, ducking his head. Lucas managed to hold his leash for a couple of steps, but the retriever ducked out of his collar. "River!" he yelled, as the dog broke loose.

"Hold that mutt!" Layton's face flushed red with anger and embarrassment.

"Lucas, use your whistle and call him back," Dulcie said.

"No." Charm blocked his nephew's hand and stayed the action.

Everyone looked at him. His eyes didn't waver from the retriever streaking toward the pond. "Sometimes you just have to do what you were meant to do."

River plunged into the water and disappeared into the grass. Every few seconds a bit of black would be seen among the cattails, or his head would pop up as he scrambled over a log.

Then he disappeared.

"Where's River?" Lucas asked after a few seconds. Charm shook his head and stared at the area he'd last seen him.

On the other side of the bayou, one of Layton's men ran toward the water. "I think he went under," he yelled, waving his arms and pointing.

Charm stood but hesitated. What should he do? Lucas clutched at his hand. Then, the moment Charm made up his mind to run to the water, Dulcie shouted, "Look!"

River's head popped into sight from a stand of thick grasses. In his mouth was a dead mallard. Lucas gave three sharp tweets on his whistle, and the dog paddled to the edge, climbed out, shook once, and sprinted toward them.

The watchers — except for Tim Layton — erupted into applause.

Lucas pulled on his uncle's shirt to get his attention. "I don't understand. Why couldn't Goliath find it?"

Charm shrugged. "I don't know. His angle was different. Maybe he couldn't see it. Maybe the current pulled it under one of those logs, and he couldn't smell it."

Lucas surged forward a few steps to meet his dog, who dropped his prize into the boy's waiting hands. Lucas tossed the duck at Layton's feet, then hugged his sopping wet pet.

Layton glared at them, then signaled his team. "Wrap it up!" By this time, Goliath had returned as well. Layton slipped a lead over his head and stalked off.

To Charm's left, Jimmy Lee giggled like a schoolgirl at Layton's rapidly disappearing back. To his right, waves of anger rolled off Dulcie. Charm ignored them both and squeezed Lucas's shoulder. "They're leaving. Let's get to work." He met the boy's gaze and held it for a moment. *Don't make a fuss about this.* Lucas looked confused, but he must have gotten the message or at least understood the seriousness in his uncle's expression, because he didn't crow about River's achievement when he walked over to Dulcie and Smokey to find out where to set up.

Jimmy Lee lacked that sense. He grabbed Charm's arm. "That was epic. You've *got* to come to Brother Jack's tonight and tell everybody what you did to Layton."

"I didn't do anything to Layton, and I'm on the wagon," Charm said.

"So, don't drink," Jimmy Lee said with an eye roll. "Come shoot pool with us. You're not going to let me tell this story, are you? At least consider it."

Charm didn't answer.

* * *

"…and Layton —"

"Mr. Layton," Ellie corrected.

Lucas waved a piece of broccoli for effect. "…and Mr. Layton didn't know that we've been working really hard to cure River of his fear of big noises, and he couldn't believe it" — his voice shot up several decibels there — "when River didn't move a muscle when the shotguns went off." He paused to use the broccoli to scoop mashed potatoes into his mouth. "River did really good, didn't he, Uncle Charm?"

"Yep, he did," Charm agreed, more focused on his pork chop than his nephew's story. This was at least the third time he'd told it since Ellie had gotten home. Probably not how she wanted to spend her night off. Ellie's night off brought to mind Jimmy Lee's suggestion of stopping by Brother Jack's. Should he go? Could he manage it? He felt pretty good, and he missed his friends. They wouldn't let him drink. Well, Bird wouldn't.

"Uncle Charm, what does *honor* mean?"

Charm blinked. He had lost track of Lucas's ramblings entirely. "What?"

"Mr. Layton said River didn't know how to honor. What does that mean?"

"Oh. Um, I think it means he has to be able to sit and watch another dog retrieve a bird without interfering."

The boy cocked his head. "Why hasn't Dulcie taught him that?"

"Well, for one thing, we only have one dog." At Lucas's stricken look, he added, "I'm sure it's on her to-do list. Slow and steady, right?"

Lucas brightened. "Right." He turned back to his mother and grandmother, still waving the same piece of broccoli. "So, he shouldn't have retrieved Goliath's duck, but everybody clapped anyway, because it was the best run anyone had ever seen ever!"

"Stop playing with your food and eat it," Ellie said.

Lucas dropped it on his plate with an aggrieved sigh and pushed at it with his fork. "I don't like broccoli. Maybe River likes broccoli." At the sound of his name, the retriever got up from his spot near the door to the living room, tail wagging expectantly.

"That's for you, not River," Ellie said, a note of warning in her voice.

"But Mom, he needs a special reward." He handed a piece to the dog who sniffed and then gently took it. He lay down and set the vegetable between his paws. Picked it up, mouthed it, then set it down again.

Charm stuffed a bite of pork chop in his mouth to hide a smile. Apparently, River was no more thrilled with broccoli than his young master. From the corner of his eye, he caught Ellie ducking her head to hide a smile too. Maybe he shouldn't go to Brother Jack's tonight. Ellie was going to be home. What they needed was a good family night. All five of them. Popcorn. Monopoly. He'd opened his mouth to suggest it, when his mother spoke.

"Did I hear you say on the phone earlier you're off tomorrow morning?" she asked Ellie. "Charm, please pass the potatoes."

He passed the bowl across the table. "Trade you for the rolls."

Ellie got to the rolls first and held the basket out to him. "Yes," she replied to her mother. "I have an appointment with Bud at the bank at nine tomorrow."

That got Charm's full attention. He met her eyes, but Ellie shot a significant look toward Lucas and changed the subject.

"A friend from work called," she said in a bright voice. "She invited me to a movie in Vicksburg tonight. You don't mind watching Lucas, do you, Charm?"

There went game night. "I was thinking I might go out tonight too." He took another bite of his pork chop, aware of their gazes on him.

Ellie and their mother glanced at each other, then back at him. Their thoughts practically broadcast through the silence. Their concern. Their lack of trust.

*That's what it is,* Charm groused inwardly. *They don't trust me.* "I'll be with Jimmy Lee and Bird," he said, answering a question they hadn't asked. "We might not even go to Brother Jack's."

More silence. Then his mother asked, "Do you think that's a good idea?"

"It'll be fine," Charm said. Why did they always doubt him? It was one night. Among friends. To celebrate a pretty damn big accomplishment they didn't even appreciate.

They looked at each other again. "Charm..." Ellie began.

"I'll be fine," he said firmly. The discussion was over.

* * *

The parking lot of Brother Jack's smelled like hamburgers and beer. Charm sat in Vlad, windows rolled down, for a long time, debating whether to go in. Now that his self-righteous bravado had passed, he was unsure. No. He was scared.

As he sat there, several cars came in and parked. No one left. Monday night wasn't as crowded as Friday or Saturday, but since most of the other restaurants in town closed on Mondays, Brother Jack's pulled a decent crowd for dinner. A few people noticed him. One or two waved, but no one came over to chat. That could be done inside out of the heat.

The heat, and Charm's lack of desire to melt like soft-serve ice cream, finally pushed him to make a decision. He got out of the car.

With each step: *I'll be fine, I'll be fine, I'll be fine.* He paused at the door. *Last chance, Freeman. Call it good and go home.* Ridiculous, another part of his mind argued. Why shouldn't he enjoy an hour socializing with his friends? Socializing didn't have to mean drinking. If nothing else, he'd tell his story and then leave.

He went in.

Jimmy Lee's voice rose over all the others. "— and then this curly haired nobody dog goes right past Forbes's champion, who's doing nothing but swimming in circles at this point, and goes right to the bird. Had to be a quarter-mile run."

So much for telling his story. "Oh, probably not that far," Charm said.

"Charm!" Jimmy Lee pulled him into his group of four. The others joined in the welcome, eliciting a genuine smile; Charm had missed these people.

*I'll be fine.* He settled onto an offered bar stool and looked around for Bird. Bird would keep him on the straight and narrow.

"Beer, Charm?" a red-haired waitress asked.

He shook his head. "You don't usually work Monday nights, Tabitha. Where's Maggie?"

Jimmy Lee grimaced. "Tripped on something out back when she was taking out the trash. Broke her wrist. Bird is driving her to the hospital in Rolling Fork."

"That's too bad," Charm said. He should leave. Now. He licked his lips. Jimmy Lee had already told the story anyway.

Oscar pushed into the circle. "Hey, y'all. What's up?" He nodded to Charm. "Freeman."

Charm nodded and stood. "You can have my stool," he said. "I just stopped by to say hi."

Jimmy Lee grabbed his shoulder. "Not until you tell Oscar what that curly dog did today." He signaled to Tabitha to bring Oscar a beer.

"Yeah, tell me," Oscar said, a note of sarcasm in his voice. "Did your superstar manage more than a hundred yards today?"

Oh, no, no, no. Not after what River accomplished today. The people around Charm chuckled. He grinned, warming to his rapt audience. "It was more like two hundred yards, and he handed Goliath his ass."

His audience hooted and banged their bottles and mugs on the bar. Someone pressed a beer into Charm's hands. His breath caught, and he stared at the frothy liquid. *Tell the story. Just tell the story.* But he couldn't. His mouth filled with cotton. He tried to swallow. A sip to wet his mouth. A sip wouldn't hurt.

He took a drink…and nothing happened. The world didn't end. He didn't implode. He wasn't overcome by an uncontrollable lust for alcohol. He took a second swallow and smiled. "Ladies and gentlemen," he said to the bar at large. "Let me tell you a tale about a woebegone retriever and his very own Goliath."

As the story spilled out, with only minor alterations and exaggerations, Charm's anxiety faded, and his body hummed with the energy of the people around him. Oscar played his part, accepting the good-natured ribbing with a combination of grace and snark. Before the first telling had even faded, one of the local trainers who hadn't been at the field walked in, prompting a second telling and a second beer.

Charm was well into the fourth retelling when Layton and his men came in.

"Fluke, fluke, fluke," Layton proclaimed loudly when Jimmy Lee pulled them to the center of the bar and offered to buy them a "condolence round." Then began a good-natured debate of viewing angles and wind direction and the importance of honoring.

"All I know," Charm said, getting everyone's attention, "is that River retrieved a bird that Goliath didn't, and in my totally unqualified opinion, that makes him the better dog."

Instead of erupting into cheers and jeers, as he'd expected, the group got strangely quiet. He frowned and realized they weren't looking at him, but, rather, past him. He turned to see a puzzled-looking Forbes standing in the doorway.

Charm smiled and opened his arms expansively. "Mr. Forbes! We were just talking about your dog. Wait until you hear what happened today."

# CHAPTER 21

The crunch of tires on gravel sent Elle, clutching a towel and still wet from the shower, dashing to the window in time to see her mother's sedan come up the driveway and park. *Oh, thank goodness.* She'd thought it might be Charm sneaking out before she could talk to him.

Okay, *sneaking* wasn't fair. Charm could come and go as he pleased, and he had no idea she wanted to talk to him. Well, not really talk to him. She wanted to see if he was hungover. Simply wondering about it made her feel guilty. Didn't she trust him? Yes, he'd been out late — he wasn't home when she'd gotten back from the movie, and he'd slept in this morning. But that didn't mean he'd been drinking. He could have been hanging out with his friends. Maybe they went to a movie like she did. Or maybe he'd spent the evening with a girl. A girl would be a good thing, she decided. Someone to occupy him and keep his mind off drinking.

She sighed. Enough worrying about Charm. She had a bank meeting to get ready for. The reflection staring back from her makeup mirror looked…tired. Older. *Where did those wrinkles come from?* She rubbed at her forehead and alternately raised and lowered her brows. Perpetual surprise seemed to be her only solution. She sighed and relaxed her face, and the wrinkles returned. Great. Maybe Bud would think she was older and wiser and be more inclined to work with her.

Now to make the rest of her look like a serious professional. Hair first. Her curls generally had a mind of their own, particularly in this humidity, but after tackling them with a little gel and a few minutes of finger styling, she figured she wouldn't scare small children. Makeup was easier. New wrinkles aside, her skin was clear enough that she could get by with moisturizer and no foundation or powder. Most days she put on a bit of mascara and lip gloss and called it good. Today she added some eyeliner and a bit of subtle, neutral eyeshadow. She carefully examined the result from each side and then stuck out her tongue and made a face. It would have to do.

Her closet held no more miracles than her makeup bag. She tapped her foot and considered her options. No jeans. No khakis. Nothing she would normally wear to work. Too…dowdy. She pulled a sundress from her closet, held it against herself in front of her full-length mirror, then discarded it onto the bed. The sunshine-colored dress was entirely appropriate for the day, but not the occasion. It made her seem too carefree to be running her own farm. Bud had known her since she was a girl, but it wouldn't do to remind him of that today. Today she needed to show the bank manager her mature side.

That didn't leave a lot. The life of a farm wife didn't provide too many opportunities for power suits. Didn't provide the budget for power suits either. She pulled out a navy pencil skirt and looked at it in the mirror. *This could work.* Especially since she had a great pair of matching heels and purse. But what to wear with it? Long sleeves out of the question — too bad because she had one nice white blouse that would have looked great. Oh — there! Her maroon blouse. Boat neck, sleeves that ended just above the elbow, and tailored enough to tuck in without bunching or fitting weirdly around her boobs. Perfect.

She dressed quickly, added some simple jewelry as a finishing touch, and admired the result in her full-length mirror. Not bad. But did she look like someone capable of making smart financial decisions?

When she had seen Bud five months ago, she had been blindsided, unprepared, and emotional. Not now. She picked up a folder from her desk. Hours spent on Jake's old computer poring through bills and expenses and income had resulted in spreadsheets and lists and numbers and options. She knew what they spent and why, where their income came from, and where they had potential for income in the future. She was ready. *I better be.*

She glanced at her phone. *Christ on a cracker.* She was also late. She grabbed the purse from the back of the closet, gave herself a final once-over to be certain she hadn't forgotten anything critical, and trying not to break her ankle in the heels, rushed down the stairs to the kitchen. River trotted in from the porch, followed by her mother and Lucas.

"You're late," her mother said, hefting a load of groceries onto the counter.

"Grandma says we can make brownies," Lucas announced.

Elle kissed him on the head. "Save me one. Mom, leave the receipt for the groceries on the table, and I'll grab you some cash while I'm out." She transferred her wallet from her everyday purse to the navy one and kept moving toward the door. "I'm going from the bank straight to the office, and I'll go from there to the restaurant, as usual."

"Do you have your uniform?"

"Shit. Lucas?" The boy raced off, River at his heels. "It's on the back of my bathroom door," she called after him. She couldn't help but grin. Five months in, and no sign her son had ever been injured. If only they'd all been that lucky. She shivered to dispel a sudden feeling of gloom. "Brownies, huh?" She kept her tone light. "Where was all this baking when I was nine?"

Her mother stiffened. "I did the best I could."

Elle cocked her head. "I wasn't implying otherwise." Lucas ran in and thrust her uniform at her. "Oh, thank you, sweetie." No time to figure out why her mother was upset. Uniform, folder, keys, wallet, phone. Everything in hand, she headed to the door. "Y'all be good today."

The screen door banged shut on their goodbyes. She glanced at her phone. If she hurried, she wouldn't be more than five minutes late. Hopefully, Bud wouldn't hold that against her. As she reached for the door handle on her truck, a vehicle turned into her driveway. *Now who is this?* She didn't recognize the truck at first. It was big, an F-350 king cab, brand-new. When it pulled up beside her, her stomach clenched. Ray Forbes.

Elle forced a smile, as he climbed out of the cab. "Mr. Forbes. What a pleasant surprise. Forgive me, but I'm late for an appointment at the bank."

He smiled, revealing a row of even, unnaturally white teeth. "I won't keep you, Elle. I just came to see how your son is doing. Terrible accident."

*Five months ago.* She opened the door to her truck, hoping he would take the hint. "Yes, it was. He's doing much better, thank you. The dog…River…has been a miracle for him."

"How is that dog?"

An innocuous question, but the knot in her stomach tightened. "He's fine. I'll invite you back sometime to see him. I've got to get to this meeting —"

"I was wondering when I could get him back."

The words slammed into her with a whoosh that knocked the air from her lungs. Her own words echoed in her ears: *"What if Lucas lost him?"* When she could draw a breath, she straightened and turned back to him, her voice carefully neutral. "Get him back? I was under the impression he was a gift. What would you need with a dog who can't hunt?"

His smile widened, and those white teeth flashed like weapons. "But he can hunt, can't he? According to your brother, he beat my best dog just yesterday."

Elle forced herself to return the smile, even as the cold fear turned to raging fury. "I expect your dog had a bad day," she said, tossing the folder and her purse into the cab of her truck.

"It's funny," he continued, ignoring her attempt to end the conversation. "My wife, Emerson, begged me to buy River when Oscar told us about him. She'd seen those curly dogs on TV and thought there might be some sort of market for the puppies since they're so…unique. Never actually thought he'd be able to keep up with the Labs."

She blinked. "I'm confused. If you didn't think he'd be any good in the field, why'd you hire Jake?"

He laughed — a full, deep laugh. "I didn't hire him. He approached me — on commission, so to speak — and I didn't have the heart to turn him down, even if I did think it was a fool's errand. Of course, according to your brother, Jake might have been right after all. Too bad he didn't get the chance to prove it. Might have been a new business for him."

The final, missing piece of the puzzle clicked into place. If Jake had been successful, not only would Forbes have paid him, but other people would have too. *So he could pay the mortgage.*

That bit of clarity didn't change the current situation, though. "Mr. Forbes," she said in a slow drawl hewn of honey and oak, "I don't know what happened on that field yesterday. I wasn't there. I do know my brother's a drunk.

"That dog is in training, that's true," she continued, "but try to correct him, and he runs screaming for home. Charm and Lucas have talked about entering him in a trial at the end of summer, but as far as I know, that's only talk. Kinda like what goes on down at that bar." She held up a finger and stopped him before he could interrupt.

"So, if you want to take a dog who looks more like somebody's spoiled poodle than a field retriever and enter him in a trial, I think you should go ahead and do it. Even if it will break a little boy's heart."

Forbes looked away first and shuffled his feet. "Well…I wouldn't want to do anything to hinder your boy's recuperation. I suppose there's no harm in letting the dog spend the rest of the summer here." He turned to leave, then hesitated and turned back. "But don't misunderstand, Miz Gibson. The dog belongs to me. If he can hunt, he will do so from my kennel with my trainer." He smiled. "Have a good day."

Elle gave a short nod, but her gaze didn't waver. She watched him climb back into his truck and didn't move until he'd turned around, driven down the driveway, and disappeared from sight.

Then the rage erupted in a primal scream. *Charm!*

She stalked back to the house, a staccato crunch of gravel at every step. Her mother pulled Lucas to the side, wrapping an arm protectively around his chest when the screen door flew open. He, in turn, clutched River. The tears on his face left little doubt he had heard.

"We'll figure it out," Elle managed to say as she passed, her own tears flowing now. Lucas's distress further inflamed her righteous anger. *How could he do this?* She didn't break stride until she threw open the door of Charm's room.

The door thunked against the wall, but Charm, wrapped burrito-like in their grandmother's patterned quilt, didn't so much as flinch. Elle grabbed the edge of the quilt and pulled as hard as she could. "You bastard!"

The stench of stale beer exploded from the cover as Charm, dressed only in boxers, rolled and crashed to the floor, arms and legs flailing. Now he was awake. "Ow! What the —" He climbed to his feet. "Ellie, what the hell —"

She ran at him and shoved him hard, sending him backward against the bed and to the floor again. "You son of a bitch!" She kicked at him, but he scrambled sideways and managed to get to his feet. Before he could speak, she came at him swinging. He caught hold of her arms.

"Have you gone completely bat-shit crazy? What the hell is wrong with you?"

"Forbes!" she yelled. "Forbes came to the house looking for his dog."

He looked bewildered. "River? Why?"

"Because he can *hunt.*" She shook her head, new tears spilling down her cheeks. "You son of a bitch. You told him." Blood drained from his face. She jerked loose and stalked away, willing herself not to say hurtful words she couldn't take back.

"If I hadn't, Layton would have —"

She whirled. "But Layton didn't. You did! You did because you were drunk. You're a drunk just like Dad was."

"That's not fair. I'm nothing like him!"

Pity and disgust intertwined in her gut. "You're exactly like him." The door slammed in her wake.

* * *

Charm stared slack-jawed at the door for a long moment. Shame and fury from being compared to his father warred with a sinking feeling she might be right — and the horror of what she had told him. *Oh God. What did I do?*

He paced and pulled at his hair. *What did I do, what did I do?* Only vaguely did he remember Forbes arriving at Brother Jack's the night before. The alcohol haze muddled his memory. He should have known better — he *did* know better. He'd seen that look in Forbes's eyes when River was mentioned. How many times had he downplayed River's recuperation and healing? He'd known in his gut that Forbes would take River back as soon as he found out he could hunt.

The recriminations came at a furious pace. Why did he go to Brother Jack's? Why didn't he drive away instead of getting out of his car? Why didn't he leave when he realized Bird wasn't there? Why did he accept that congratulatory beer?

Beer. His stomach roiled, and he barely made it to the bathroom before throwing up.

What started with cheap tequila drunk from the bottle behind the carnival trailers, turned into whiskey sipped from his flask during the day to make the tedium of daily life more bearable and beer through the evening and into the wee hours at a bar with his friends. Or strangers. It didn't matter. Bad news? Drink. Rotten day? Drink. Great day? Drink.

His usual excuse, the one he had used since he was a teen, whispered in his ear: *As long as I can work and function, it doesn't matter, right?* Images of his family, lines of deep disappointment etched on their faces, swatted that excuse as if it was a mosquito. What had he done? And why, even now, sitting on a bathroom floor, mouth tasting of vomit, having destroyed what he'd worked for, did the desire for "just one more" claw at him?

Shaking, he climbed to his feet and rinsed his mouth. *No more.* He stumbled back to the bedroom and pulled on jeans and a shirt that reeked of cigarettes and bar food. Where was his duffel? He found it under his old white Pumas in a corner of the closet in his bedroom and stuffed it with all the clothes within arm's reach — far more than the single change of jeans, three pairs of underwear and socks, and three clean shirts he'd started with five months ago. He wrestled to close the zipper and finally pulled out several shirts and left them on the floor. Ellie could send him what he left behind. Pumas on without taking the time for socks, wallet shoved in his back pocket, and he was out.

"Charm, wait!" His mother's voice called out after him as he strode to his car. He didn't break stride, didn't pause. Just tossed his duffel in the passenger seat, gunned the engine, and drove away. *They're better off without me. I'll check in again in another twenty years.*

* * *

A mile down Highway 61, almost at the new Walmart, Vlad blew out a sidewall. The bright green sedan rolled into the parking lot with an irritating *thwap, thwap, thwap* and sputtered to silence in a space far from the store. At that moment, Charm envied Bruce Banner his ability to hulk out into a big green monster and smash everything in his vicinity.

Still-very-human Charm stomped to the trunk and pulled out a spare that was probably original to the car — and flatter than the Mississippi delta. Wouldn't have mattered anyway. There was no jack or lug wrench. He threw the tire on the pavement.

What the fuck? All he wanted was to leave, to go back to St. Louis and his crappy job with no future. *Just let me leave.* Well, Vlad wasn't taking him anywhere like this and, even if Walmart sold tires, he didn't have the funds for a new tire, a jack, and a lug wrench. Fuck it. He'd leave the green monstrosity here. Right here.

And get to the bus station how? No way he was walking in this heat and humidity. He needed to call someone. Not his mom — that was a guilt trip he didn't want. Obviously not Ellie. Jimmy Lee. He'd call Jimmy Lee. This was all his fault anyway. Charm swore out loud and stomped back to the front seat to get his phone.

Which was on his nightstand back at Ellie's.

He roared his frustration to the heavens. Done, done, done. He stormed across the parking lot, past the doors to Walmart, and into the liquor store. He grabbed the first reasonably priced bottle of whiskey he saw — Evan Williams — tossed a twenty-dollar bill on the counter, ignored the protests of the cashier, and stormed back outside, very nearly running over an older lady on her way in. She squawked, and he paused long enough to physically set her to the side, and then headed not to his car, but east, away from the highway.

He turned north out of the parking lot and continued two blocks to the first place he had visited the day he'd arrived in Collier: the cemetery. No funeral today, no line of cars. Only grass in need of mowing, trees in need of pruning, and lines of lonely headstones. He cut through at an angle, knowing where he was going this time. He stalked to Jake's grave — and past it to its neighbor.

William Freeman
1963–2017
Peace in Death.

*"Peace in death" be damned.* The whiskey bottle tumbled from Charm's fingers as he snatched a fallen branch and charged the headstone with an inarticulate growl. Again and again and again, he slammed the branch against the stone until the branch snapped and sent him spinning to the ground. Rocks, dirt, grass — anything he could reach, he flung at the headstone — until there was nothing left to throw.

The headstone still stood, not even a little crooked. Mocking him. He cried out and kicked at it. Once. Twice. It tilted, just a bit. Charm leaned back on his elbows, brought his knees to his chest, and kicked with both feet. The headstone listed at an odd angle backward but didn't fall.

Charm almost laughed. A standoff with a man six years dead.

He wiped at the tears that blurred his eyes and saw it. Several feet away, sunlight glinting off the glass. The whiskey. He wiped the back of his hand across his mouth and stared at it only a moment before crawling to it. He grabbed the bottle, but hesitated. He shouldn't. A want — a need — rose in him, ripping through his good intentions and willpower like claws through tissue paper. His trembling fingers twisted at the top; his hands shook as he brought it to his lips.

No. Not this time.

"I'm not you!" With another strangled cry, he threw the bottle at his father's headstone. The bottle shattered in an explosion of glass and amber liquid. "I'm not you."

He buried his face in his arms and sobbed.

His father didn't reply. When Charm couldn't cry anymore, he sat and stared at the headstone, wishing that if his father wouldn't capitulate, he would share some wisdom that would get Charm, his son, the heir to his legacy of alcoholism, out of this mess.

What did he expect, coming back to Collier? What did he think had changed? *Everything*, he reflected. *Everything has changed.*

Except for him.

His instinct was still to run, to escape rather than fight. Which way is the highway? When's the next bus?

Sandrine had almost changed that. Or, he had almost changed for her. When she died, he thought he would die too. His dreams right there — so close his fingertips could have grasped them if only he'd closed his hand — and it was all jerked away. The emptiness of his life almost overwhelmed him when she was gone.

After Sandrine's death, Jake's death felt like a siren pulling him back to Collier. Charm owed him and Ellie so much. But finally, he could admit even to himself that owed debts weren't why he came back. He returned because he had nowhere else to go.

And, he admitted, Collier had welcomed him. He hadn't wanted it to. He wanted to justify his choice to leave at sixteen and justify his quick exit after the funeral. But Collier…everything about it drew him back. His sister's need. The broken nephew who looked so much like Jake. The friends who embraced him as though he'd been gone only a day, not a lifetime.

Not that being here was easy. The farm. And Lucas. And Dulcie. Every damn day one of them tested him and pushed him and enraged him.

The bus to freedom was a mile away. If he jogged, he could be there in fifteen minutes. Running away would make his life so much easier.

But it wouldn't make it fuller. Memories from the past five months enveloped him. Attending the parade with Ellie and Lucas. His mother and Lucas making pies for Smokey. Sitting on the front porch and enjoying the sunset with his sister. Reconnecting with old friends. Making new ones.

At some point that damn farm had become home, and no way in hell was he walking away now.

Even as he thought it, the doubt crept in. Lucas would never forgive him. They were going to lose River, and it was all Charm's fault. If only he'd gotten some sort of paper from Forbes officially transferring ownership. But he hadn't, and if he was being honest, he knew Forbes never would have done such a thing. As long as there was a chance that River could bring him any sort of prestige (or money), Forbes wasn't letting him go.

A hand settled on his shoulder, startling him out of his thoughts, and someone settled beside him.

"Oh, Charm," his mother said softly.

He glanced at her, then looked away and wiped his face. "How'd you find me?"

"That woman you nearly ran over at the liquor store was Gertie Pritchett." *Woman who brought groceries*, he filled in mentally. "She got worried when she saw the state of your car and called me. I dropped Lucas and River at her place and have been driving around looking for you ever since."

"I've been talking with Dad," Charm said.

His mother glanced at the cockeyed headstone. "I can see that."

"Why did he give up?" he asked. "I mean, I know he was sick, but why…why didn't he fight?"

She considered her answer for a long minute. Finally, she sighed.

"Your dad's whole life was a dream deferred. Those travel dreams started young. He was a craftsman — good with his hands — and he dreamed of using that skill to finance travels around the world." She chuckled softly. "Big dreams for a farm kid from Mississippi, huh?"

Charm pictured his father the way he used to picture himself: holding a duffel and nothing else, boarding a plane for Europe, ready for any adventure. Pain fluttered along the edge of his soul, not so much because of failing as because of letting his dreams wither untouched on the vine. It was always there. Always whispering what could have been. "Why didn't he go?"

"Life. Obligations to his parents. Obligations to us. No matter how many plans he made, there was always something. He kept trying, though, kept planning — you were wonderful because you shared those dreams with him — but every setback took something from him. When he was diagnosed with rheumatoid arthritis…he broke. He wasn't as strong as you."

Sadness rose inside him, both for his father and for himself. "I thought it was my fault."

"No. No, Charm. Not at all. Losing you was the biggest regret of his life. Even more than the loss of his dreams. It changed him. He wasn't the same after you left."

"Then why didn't he look for me and bring me home?"

She squeezed his hand. "He had police looking for you for years."

No. No, Charm couldn't believe that. "Jake would have told him where I was."

"I wouldn't let him."

The words were like a slap. He stared, mouth agape. All those years…it was his *mother* who had kept him apart?

Her eyes softened. "Charm, if you had stayed in Collier, you would have been pushed into taking over the farm. That life would have killed you."

"Being on the streets could have killed me!"

"It could have. That's why Jake told me where you were as soon as you contacted him."

He blinked. "You knew?" *And didn't come after me?*

She touched his arm to still his protest. "Jake came to see me in the hospital after you left and confessed his part in your disappearance. I had guessed, but it was nice to get confirmation. I might have guilted…okay, threatened him into keeping me in the loop when you got in contact with him."

"You didn't tell Dad?"

She shook her head. "When Jake told me you'd gotten a job with a carnival," she continued, "I did some research and made some calls. Eventually I tracked down Virgil Wade. Virgil offered to get the police to bring you home, but I told him no. I asked him to keep an eye on you and keep you safe. We talked every month or so, the entire time you were with him. It broke my heart — and scared me to death — to let you go, but I truly believed you had a better chance out there than here."

Charm mulled this for a minute. "At the end…when Virgil kicked me out…did you ask him to do that?"

His mother shook her head. "No, that was Virgil. He felt like you'd become too comfortable. I wanted you to stay for exactly that reason. But" — she waved her fingers — "it was his carnival."

"What about after that?"

"You were an adult by then. I still got updates from Jake, but I left you to make your own life without my interference. I made sure Jake told you when your dad died. I hoped maybe you'd come home after that."

But he hadn't. So much hurt, so much anger. Had Sandrine not died — and Jake right on the heels of it — he likely wouldn't have ever come back.

His mother slipped her arm through his and squeezed his hand. "It's your choice, Charm. What do you want?"

One bus ride and he would be back in St. Louis. No more farmwork. No more early morning training sessions. His voice quivered. "I want my family."

She nodded and smiled tenderly. "Then let's go back."

He shook his head. "I ruined everything."

"You threw a fox in the henhouse, for sure. But it's only ruined if you don't try to make it right."

"Lucas will never forgive me."

"Lucas has already forgiven you," she said. "He and I had a long talk. He was angry, but he recognizes there was no way he could have run River in a field trial without Ray Forbes finding out. I think you'll find his anger is exactly where it should be — on that ass threatening to take his dog away."

Five months of wanting to leave, and now his heart broke with the thought. "I don't want to lose them," he whispered.

His mother wrapped her arms around him, and he let himself be held and comforted the way he had as a child. She kissed his head. "Then don't let go."

# Chapter 22

As his mother had predicted, Lucas met him on Gertie Pritchett's front porch with a hug and tears of righteous indignation toward Ray Forbes. The boy leaned in close. "He's a butthole," he said. Charm bit his cheek to keep from laughing. Or crying.

He glanced to the back seat frequently as they drove home. Despite the bad news, Lucas played tug and the usual car games with River. Only once did he see the boy's smile falter and his fingers clutch the dog's fur. River sniffed Lucas's ear, then lay down and rolled over to get his belly scratched. River had the right of it: no matter what happened, for right now they were together and happy.

Having finally given himself permission to love his family, Charm decided love shared a lot with heartbreak. It hurt.

"Eleanor's back from the bank," his mother noted as they turned into the drive. Ellie sat on the front porch swing. They parked and then walked as a group to see her. She smiled, but her eyes were red. Something was wrong.

"Hi, sweetie," she said brightly, holding her arms open for her son.

He hugged her. "Why are you crying, Mom? Is it because of

mean old Mr. Forbes?"

Her smile faltered, then was fixed more firmly. "I've had a hard day."

Charm touched his nephew's shoulder. "Hey, why don't you take River inside? I think you guys have had a hard day too."

"No. I want to stay and listen."

The adults shot glances at each other above his head. "I need to get started on dinner," his grandmother said. "Why don't you come in and help me?"

"No." Lucas crossed his arms. His tone was uncharacteristically emphatic. "I'll just go in and listen from the window. You might as well let me stay. I live here too!"

Ellie snorted. "Nine going on fifteen. When did you become a teenager?" He didn't budge. She sighed and motioned for him to join her on the swing. She gathered her thoughts for a moment, then said to Lucas, "I had a meeting with Mr. Bud at the bank today. We're losing our house."

Their mother's breath caught. Lucas glanced at his grandmother, then back at her. "What does that mean?"

"It means that we have to move."

"Move to town?"

"Maybe. Maybe away to a city where I can get a better job."

"Why?" He sounded horrified, and color had drained from his cheeks.

"It costs a lot of money to keep the farm going. Without your dad, I don't make enough." Her voice thickened with unshed tears. Lucas frowned as he tried to process what she'd told him. Ellie looked at Charm. "I walked Bud through all my ideas for raising cash in the short term, but he said those would impact my ability to stay caught up in the long term."

Lucas shook her arm to get her attention. "We don't have to move," he said. "When River wins the field trial —"

"Winning a field trial won't fix this," Ellie said firmly.

"No, you don't understand." Lucas's voice grew louder, and his grandmother stepped in and took hold of his arm. Even as she guided him toward the door, he protested, "Dad said when River wins, our troubles will be gone!"

The screen door swung shut, and Lucas's voice faded away as his grandmother steered him somewhere other than the front porch. Ellie groaned and buried her face in her hands. Charm sat beside her and wrapped an arm around her shoulder.

"What are you going to do?" he asked.

"I don't know." She picked up a folder from the swing. "I knew we weren't making much progress on the mortgage debt, but I thought surely one of these plans would convince him that eventually I would." She took a deep breath, finding the words physically painful to say. "Bud is going to file the foreclosure paperwork in thirty days."

Charm took the folder and scanned the pages. "He hasn't filed yet. That's good. You still have some options."

Her voice took on an angry edge. "I'm losing my home, Charm. What kind of options do I have?"

He squinted toward the road. "Well…" He gestured down the road toward town. "Just down there, developers are building new subdivisions." He pointed the other direction. "Up that way, the land is owned by one of those big farming conglomerates." He motioned away from the road. "And on this side of the road, you have farming neighbors who might appreciate increasing their buffer between either of those options. Seems to me like you're sitting pretty."

Elle's eyes opened wide as she digested the possibilities. Just as quickly, though, her shoulders sank, and her eyes filled with tears. "Jake didn't want to sell." She took a shuddering breath. "I let him down. I'm losing everything."

He set the folder on the swing. She could deal with all that later. "No. You may lose the farm, but you're not losing everything."

She sniffled. "After our fight, I thought you might leave."

Charm half smiled and tightened his hold. "Never again."

* * *

Elle felt drained. She should have taken the evening off, but she hadn't expected bad news. Shock and sadness had progressed to anger and resentment during her hours at the restaurant. How dare Bud ignore how hard she had been working — and the potential of her plans. Eventually, the tragedy of the situation had hit her again, and the anger yielded to hopelessness. What would they do now? The farm was the only home Lucas had ever known.

The house was dark except for a light in the hallway left on to guide her up. The green sedan had reappeared in the driveway, so Elle assumed Charm had gone to bed early. Her legs felt heavy as she climbed the stairs. She counted the creaks — stair three, stair four, stair eleven. She knew every creak, every bump, every tiny imperfection.

She paused at the head of the stairs and ran her fingers over a spot in the wall where the paint didn't quite match. Jake had patched that spot after knocking a hole in the wall trying to swing a bed frame around the corner. How could she leave that behind?

"Mom?" Lucas's voice drifted from his bedroom.

She wiped a tear from her face. "You should be asleep," she said, slipping into the room. She sat on the edge of his bed and brushed his hair out of his eyes. Moonlight shone through a space in the curtains and splashed across his pillow.

"We don't have to move," he said.

"I know it's hard, Lucas, but we have to face facts —"

"You're not listening." His voice grew louder. "We just have to win the field trial."

Elle tried to tamp down rising anger. "What do you think will happen if he wins?"

He screwed up his face. "I don't know exactly," he admitted. "Dad said our troubles would be *G-O-N-E*" — he emphasized each letter of the word — "so there's probably gonna be lots of money. And you won't have to worry anymore."

She smiled sadly and stroked his hair. "Honey, that's not what your dad meant. He was expecting Mr. Forbes to pay him for training River. There's no cash prize for winning a field trial."

"You're wrong!" He pushed her hand away and sat up. "You weren't there. You don't know what he said."

His anger shocked her. "I wasn't there, but —"

"You didn't think he could do it. You hated him!"

Her jaw dropped. "Lucas —"

"I heard you! You said you hated him. You said it was all falling apart, and it was his fault."

Like a cold wave, a memory of saying those things in a moment of anger and grief washed over her. "I didn't mean it," she tried to say, but her voice choked. She had meant it. At that moment, her world crumbling around her, she had meant every word.

He glared at her accusingly. "If you believed in him, then you'd help me train River." She didn't respond. He shook his head and lay back down. "That's what I thought." He turned away from her and pulled his blanket up to his ears.

Elle watched him for moment, not trusting her voice, not sure how to defend something so indefensible. River, who had been stretched out on the floor at the foot of his bed, climbed up, circled once, and settled into the back of Lucas's knees with a sigh. She reached across and stroked the dog's head. He shifted his head onto Lucas's hip and gazed at her, his eyes soft.

Her antipathy toward the dog had dissolved over time, not in small part because he had shown Lucas the path through his grief and pain. River never doubted Lucas, and Lucas never doubted River. Did she really owe him any less?

Elle gave his head one more rub and headed into the hall, turning toward Charm's room instead of her own. His door was partially open, but before she could knock or look inside, her brother came up the stairs carrying milk and brownies.

"Hey," he greeted. "I heard you come home."

She brushed past him without returning the greeting and motioned him to follow. "Come talk to me." He followed her back down the stairs to the kitchen and took a seat at the table. She poured herself a glass of milk. "Where are the brownies?"

He pointed to the top of the fridge. "River can get them if they're on the counter," he said with a full mouth.

She grabbed the whole pan and brought it to the table. "Want another?"

The first disappeared into his mouth, and he eagerly took a

second. "Mom didn't bake this much when we were kids," he said after he swallowed.

Elle remembered saying something similar the morning before. "Don't say that to her. It pisses her off." She popped back to the fridge and grabbed a jug of milk.

He drained his glass and refilled it. "I think," he said thoughtfully, "this is a second chance, and she's trying really hard not to blow it."

Elle savored her first bite of the fudgy goodness. It took a moment for her to process what Charm had said. "What do you mean?"

"She made a lot of mistakes when we were kids" — he ignored Elle's snort — "but I think she's trying to make up for it."

Elle focused on her brownie. Mistakes. That was what her mother had told her marrying Jake and having Lucas were, and because of that they'd hardly spoken for most of Elle's adult life. Since the accident, though, her mother had stepped up with no complaints, no snide recriminations, and she had helped more than Elle ever would have asked. And Elle couldn't be more grateful — for her mom or for Charm. The last five months had been a second chance for all of them.

She shook herself out of her reverie and brought herself back to the reason she'd asked him downstairs. "What do you know about Lucas's reasons for training River?"

Charm thought for a moment. "Not much, I guess." He sounded surprised, like it had never occurred to him. "Training River was a project with his dad. I figured that was why it was so important to him."

Elle repeated the conversation she'd had with Lucas a few minutes earlier, her frustration bubbling over. "If we leave before River competes, Lucas will forever wonder *what if*. But what happens if River does compete — and win — and there's no magical do-over?"

Charm sat back and mulled the situation. "Whether there's a magical do-over or not, training River means everything to Lucas. It's a tangible connection to his dad. I'd hate to take that away from him. Especially since…" He let his voice trail off.

*Especially since they were losing his father's farm.* Elle pushed back the tears that had been all too frequent today. Lucas said she didn't believe in Jake, but the words he had overheard were spoken in fear and anger. They weren't true. When Jake was alive, she'd have followed him to the ends of the Earth if he'd say they could do it. She had never doubted him. Not once.

She took a deep breath and sat straight. "I can't save the farm for Jake, but I can help my son fulfill Jake's final wish."

"There's a trial in August."

Two months. Foreclosure was only thirty days away. "Maybe Bud will give me just one more month. Will River be ready?"

"Absolutely," Charm assured her.

- 250 -

# CHAPTER 23

I t's impossible," Dulcie said. She shoved a bucket of dead fish into Charm's arms and stomped outside.

He'd driven to Smokey's place in Louisiana early Wednesday morning, hoping Dulcie would be more accommodating on her home turf. Even before he explained the situation, she had seemed distracted. Maybe it was because, judging by the number of animals in residence, business was picking up. No lion this time, but he'd seen a pair of raccoons, a monkey of some kind, and birds — lots of birds — and he'd had to race behind her to keep up as she'd prepared food for their Noah's Ark.

*What if they're too busy to help out anymore? What if she wants to quit?* He rushed to catch up. "It can't be impossible. Everything that kid has hoped and dreamed for is riding on this." *We need you.*

Dulcie whirled on him. "I knew it! I knew you'd do something like this. Damn dog trainers. Do you remember what you agreed to on day one? River doesn't compete until I say he's ready." She whirled again and continued across the compound to the largest of the enclosures — chain link with high sides and netting on top. Inside a pair of bald eagles stared down at them from a series of high perches at the far end.

Charm followed close on her heels. "This isn't about your reputation, Dulcie. It's about a little boy who's going to lose everything. He deserves to have this one thing to remember."

She jerked the bucket away from him. "Lovely speech, but warm, fuzzy feelings don't win field trials. Training does." She opened a gate and slipped inside the aviary, crooning to the birds.

Charm couldn't see exactly what she did, but moments later, the birds spread their wings and glided the length of the enclosure. His breath caught. The eagles were massive — much larger than he'd realized. No wonder Dulcie didn't want to work with mere dogs when the alternative was working with creatures like this. That said, they couldn't get River ready without her.

"Then train," Charm said when she emerged from the enclosure.

"I can't."

He froze, caught completely off guard. That word…didn't compute when Dulcie said it. Lack of confidence wasn't something she suffered from. "What do you mean?"

She headed back toward the feed room, tapping the now-empty bucket against her leg as she gathered her thoughts. Finally, she blurted, "I don't know enough." After she said it, she sighed, like she'd confessed her deepest secret. "Monday, I watched Layton and his team. There was so much we haven't done. Things they did I didn't know we were supposed to do."

"Like honoring?" Charm said, flashing back to the conversation at the dinner table with Lucas.

She nodded. "Give me a behavior, and I can train it. But I can't train what I don't know I'm *supposed* to train. There's clearly more to this than what's in the rule book." Inside the building, she handed him the bucket again and pointed him toward the sink.

He squirted dish soap in the bottom and turned on the hot water. "So, the problem is you don't know enough about field trials themselves." Thick bubbles began to fill the bucket. "Maybe we should go to one?"

Dulcie pulled a large plastic container from the fridge. "We missed the window. In the South, field trials are held in the spring. The one in Vicksburg in August is one of a kind." Her voice wavered uncharacteristically.

He turned the situation over in his mind. Books and YouTube videos would help but only so much. They needed to see it done right — or talk to people who knew how to do it right. Charm took a deep breath. "I know a solution, but you're not going to like it." She waited. "There's a whole slew of trainers in the area. You can ask them to help you."

Red crept up her cheeks. "Bad choice. They hate me."

Sadly true. Charm remembered that day well — at Brother Jack's after that first training session. "Well, you pretty much called them —"

"Shitty trainers. They said River had no aptitude. Obviously, I was right," she snapped.

"And yet, they're winning field trials."

"We need a different option," she said in a tone that brooked no further discussion.

"Does that mean you're sticking with us?"

Dulcie scowled. "We've put too much into this to quit now. But I can't promise anything. Two months might as well be the blink of an eye."

Not going to worry about that now. "Plan to stick around after training tomorrow. We're having a war meeting at our house at noon."

She rolled her eyes, but Charm flashed her a smile and jogged to his car, relief lightening his steps.

* * *

"Charm, would you get the mayo while you're in there, please?" his mother asked.

"And lemonade," Lucas added.

Charm grabbed both — and the milk he was there for — kicked the refrigerator door shut and delivered it all to the table where a kitchen picnic had begun. His mother and Smokey had their heads together, laughing as they built their sandwiches. In a rare moment of lightness, Dulcie and Lucas warred with forks as each tried to steal bites of potato salad from the other. That was good to see. Dulcie had been distracted at training this morning. Probably still concerned about finding out more about field trials. Ellie hadn't made it home yet, but hearing the squeak of the screen door, he guessed that was soon to be remedied.

"I'm here, I'm here," her voice rang out. She breezed in, paused to get a plate, and joined the throng around the table. "Ooh, that turkey looks good. Toss me a hoagie roll. What did I miss?"

"Nothing except the last of the potato salad." He passed the rolls her way. "We haven't started yet."

"Started what?" Lucas asked. He spread a stomach-turning amount of mayo on a piece of white bread, spread a thick layer of peanut butter on another piece, and then sandwiched several of his grandmother's homemade bread-and-butter pickles between them.

That…wasn't right. Charm shuddered. What was the question? Oh. "Planning. We have two months to get River ready for a field trial. and you and your mom ready to move." A stony look settled on Lucas's face at the word "move." Charm looked at Smokey. "Did Dulcie catch you up on what's happening?"

Smokey nodded and added a second layer of roast beef to his already towering Dagwood sandwich. "She told me River's owner is causing problems, and Elle is having some financial trouble?"

Ellie wrinkled her nose. "That's a nice way to say it. I have some bad news on that front." She put a handful of potato chips on her plate. "That's why I was late. I cornered Bud at the bank and tried to get him to give me an additional month before foreclosing. He shot me down." She sighed. "I don't understand it. He's always been reasonable before. It's only one month."

"Bud Yarber?" asked Smokey as Dulcie said, "Uncle Bud?" at the same time.

Ellie and Charm exchanged surprised glances. "You know him?"

Their mother snapped her fingers. "He was Ava's cousin, wasn't he?"

*Ava. Dulcie's mother and my mom's best friend,* Charm remembered.

Smokey nodded. "One of her few relatives who stayed in touch after she died. He has a couple of kids near Dulcie's age, and she visited with them in the summer a few times. Anyway," he continued, "if that's who you're talking about, I bet he has a buyer for the property."

Ellie froze, sandwich halfway to her mouth. "What?"

"A buyer," Smokey repeated. "Land is valuable around here, especially when it's contiguous to those big commercial farms."

The sandwich returned uneaten to her plate. "I thought he was a nice guy."

"He is! But he's also a banker, and a commercial sale like that would be worth more to him and his bank than your personal mortgage."

She sank into a chair, a myriad of emotions passing over her face as she processed what she'd just learned. Charm squeezed her shoulder.

"That old goat," their mother grumbled. "I'm going to ask around and see what I can find out."

Ellie waved her fingers. "Thank you, but regardless, my job now is to figure out what Lucas and I will do next." Lucas opened his mouth to protest, but she leveled a gaze at him, and he subsided, pink splotches of anger dotting his cheeks. "I see a lot of sorting and packing in my future."

"Our future," Charm corrected. "That's the point. We're all in this together." From a corner of his eye, he saw his mother glance at Smokey and grin.

"I can help with the sorting," Dulcie said, scraping the paltry remains of the potato salad onto her plate. Everyone stared at her. "What? I'm organized. I run a mean garage sale too."

Charm narrowed his eyes. "I don't doubt it. Okay, so River. What do we need to do there?" He picked some turkey off his plate and ate it with his fingers. In the back of his mind, he wished he had a cold beer to wash it down. *Get over it, Freeman,* he admonished himself.

Dulcie swallowed a bite of her sandwich. "River is solid on the basic skills. The next step, then, is a deep dive into field trials. We need to know the details that aren't in the rules."

"I'll help with that," Smokey said.

"Me too," Ellie said. Now it was her turn for stares. "With research or something. I'm good at *that.*" Dulcie grinned at her.

"What about me?" Lucas asked. "What do I do?"

"You're like me," Charm said. "We're the worker bees." He pointed at Ellie and Dulcie. "When they say jump, we say, 'How high?'" Dulcie snorted, and he winked at her.

"That sounds like a sucker job," Lucas said. His frustration from earlier was still evident in his tone.

Charm managed not to laugh. His nephew was wise beyond his years. "Everybody good now? Know what we need to do? Two months is not a lot of time."

"No," Ellie agreed. "But we'll get through it. Together."

Charm smiled at his sister, proud she'd admitted she couldn't do it all herself. Even if it did mean a crap-ton of work for him in the coming weeks. On that note, the meeting broke up. Ellie wrapped her food and headed back to work, and his mother and Smokey took Lucas out to eat at the picnic table. Charm would have joined them, but Dulcie blocked his way.

"Hey, can I talk to you?" she asked, arms crossed over her chest, eyes looking everywhere but at him.

She had the same uncomfortable look on her face she'd had the day before. He frowned. "Yeah, what's up?"

"I need to do something, and I could use backup. Um" — she gritted her teeth as if it was physically painful to say the word — "support."

Considering how she felt about his smile — seriously, what was that about? — he affected a nonchalant shrug. "Sure. What do you need?"

* * *

A slight breeze, barely enough to shift the heavy air, brushed past Charm as he and Dulcie walked to the door of her destination: Brother Jack's. Even that breath of wind was enough to fill his nostrils with the scent of hamburgers, fries, and beer. His whole body shuddered with sudden thirst.

Dulcie stopped short, her eyes scanning his face. "I didn't think. I'm sorry. Maybe you should wait in the car."

Sixty hours since his last drink, each one plucking at the fragile strings of his willpower. *No. Not again.* "I'll be all right," he said with more confidence than he felt. They walked inside, and the hoppy odor hit him full force. He swallowed. "How about I wait here?" he asked, stepping to the right, out of the doorway. He could make a quick exit from here if he needed to.

She nodded and scanned the restaurant, focusing quickly on one of the large tables toward the back. Oscar Strickland waved. Dulcie had asked him to get the professional trainers together, and it looked like he had come through. Tim Layton and three others swiveled their heads to stare at her.

Charm felt her hesitation. "Hey," he said. She glanced his way, and he offered his knuckles. *You can do this.* A ghost of a smile, and she bumped his fist with her own. Then she took a deep breath and crossed the restaurant.

She didn't bother to sit, not that they asked her. "I need help," Charm heard her say, and then the rest of her words were lost in the din of other customers.

"You need anything, Charm?" a waitress asked.

He shook his head and focused on the body language and expressions of the trainers and Dulcie. *It takes guts to do what she's doing,* he thought, wincing sympathetically as she held her ground despite the hard, closed expressions on the trainers' faces. Then something she said landed, and the men shifted a bit, their expressions softening a tiny bit. She caught that too, because she leaned forward and talked more rapidly, her hands moving and emphasizing her words. *Damn. She could be likable and persuasive. Who knew?*

Layton asked her a question. Oscar asked a second. Another a third. She answered each without hesitation. Finally, she stopped talking. She must have asked them a question because they hesitated and looked at each other. One man slowly shook his head, and the others agreed with him. *Oh, no.* She said something else, and at once, the mood at the table shifted. The man who had turned her down a moment before grinned and nodded. The others quickly followed suit.

When Dulcie returned to Charm, the men were still smiling — and so was she. "What did you say to them?" Charm asked.

She glanced back. "I told them it would piss Forbes off if they helped us. They jumped at it."

Charm roared with laughter, and they headed to the car. "I'm impressed," he said. "Really."

Her cheeks reddened. "Thanks for coming out here with me. I might have chickened out if you weren't standing there."

He paused in front of the car. "I was wondering, would you return the favor?"

* * *

Charm and Dulcie walked shoulder to shoulder into the Vicksburg used car dealership. At the door to manager Thibaut Dupre's office, Dulcie paused and held out her fist. "Good luck."

Charm took a deep breath, bumped her fist with his own, and marched to Thibaut's desk. The man looked up and waited.

"I need help," Charm said.

# CHAPTER 24

We're late," Lucas said. Charm was impressed he managed to sound both annoyed and nervous.

Was he worried about a potential Dulcie meltdown or the session with the professional trainers? He hadn't been thrilled to hear his "dad's competition," as he described them, would be helping them. Charm didn't blame him. Lucas had been clear from the beginning that this was his and his dad's project. It hardly looked like that now, but how else would they get it done?

"We're fine," Charm said, his mind too full to worry about Lucas this morning. Though Charm had protested greatly, Thibaut had taken him to not one but two AA meetings last night — one in Vicksburg, one in Collier — and they'd talked for several hours after. Charm had to admit, he'd learned some things, and a tiny part of him acknowledged his mind was more settled today. That part might be larger if it weren't 7:38 in the freaking morning. What the fuck was it with dog trainers and early mornings?

When the field came into view, he slammed on the brakes and stared.

"Are we in the right place?" Lucas asked.

Charm checked the address on his phone. "This is where Dulcie said. And there's her truck." It would have been easy to miss because the edge of the field overflowed with vehicles. Mostly trucks. Some cars. Maybe a dozen in total. Several trucks stood out. Each, except for Dulcie's, sported a brightly colored business logo and had either a silver dog box mounted on the back or pulled a larger trailer designed to transport dogs. These guys didn't leave any guesses about what they did for a living. Charm parked Ellie's truck next to an older Plymouth sedan.

Beyond the vehicles, a small army had split into two groups. Oscar, Tim Layton, and the three other trainers he'd seen at the table were gathered around Dulcie and Smokey. Fifty feet from them another group of eight or nine men chatted among a collection of guns, bumpers and other retrieve objects, duck decoys, and several live birds in cages. One man tossed a bumper for a black Lab, in a routine Charm recognized as getting it jazzed for the work to come and testing its response to obedience commands.

What surprised Charm about the groups was that everyone wore a white jacket. Everyone but Dulcie and Smokey, at least. Who knew field trainers were a gang? Black leather would have been a hell of a lot cooler. He opened his door, and the omnipresent Mississippi heat smacked him in the face. Cooler, but way too hot. Why were they wearing jackets in the summer heat?

Lucas released River from his crate and took a moment to look around. "Why so many people?"

Mindful of the Lab, Charm took River's leash when he jumped to the ground. "These are the trainers I told you about and the guys who help them in the field." *Must be nice to have so much help*, Charm grumped to himself. As he expected, River's ears went up when he saw the Lab. He woofed quietly and pulled toward him.

"Heel." Charm wiggled the leash to get River's attention. To his surprise, though River remained intent on the action in the field, he dropped into position immediately. He and Lucas might not have trained with other dogs before, but River clearly had.

Charm plastered his most welcoming smile on his face as he approached the trainers. He nodded to those he knew and offered his hand to those he didn't. "Hi. I'm Charm Freeman. I really appreciate your help with our project."

"Why are you wearing white coats?" Lucas asked. Charm suppressed a grin. Nice to have a nine-year-old to ask the dumb questions.

"It provides contrast for the dog and aids their visual perception," Layton said.

Lucas frowned and looked at Dulcie. "River will see your signals better when he's out in the field," she translated.

"He's never had any trouble before." He sounded a little sullen.

"We haven't done blinds at full distance before," she said. She knelt in front of him. "You want to win, don't you?" He nodded. "Then we have to do everything the way they do it in real field trials."

He looked at the other trainers. "And they're going to show us what to do?"

"That's right. They're doing us a really big favor."

That made him frown. "Why?"

Charm had to bite his lip to keep from laughing. His nephew was no sucker. Oscar rested his hands on his knees and crouched down a bit so he could look Lucas in the eyes. "They all knew your dad, and they want to help River do the best he can."

"Among other reasons," one of the other trainers said under his breath. Fortunately, Lucas either didn't hear or chose to ignore that remark.

Tim Layton frowned at River. "What kind of distance do you have on this dog?"

"On land? Marks at two-fifty. Blinds at two-hundred," Dulcie said.

The men exchanged glances. "That's…really short for field trials," one said. "Four hundred yards isn't uncommon, and I've seen setups longer than that." The others murmured agreement.

Dulcie waved her hand dismissively. "I understand. We add distance —"

Smokey interrupted her. "We'd really like you to show us some field trial setups and how you train for them."

Dulcie's eyes widened and her mouth dropped open a bit, but she recovered smoothly. "That would be great. I'm glad you brought a dog. One of the things we need to work on is honoring —"

Again, Smokey cut her off. "Why don't we use this session for data gathering? You can show us what we need to know, and River can demonstrate what he's learned so far."

Dulcie's mouth dropped further this time, and Charm could see anger flicker in her eyes. "That sounds like a great idea," she said, her gaze fixed on her father. She pulled out a small notebook. "I'm all set to take notes."

Layton signaled the other group with a piercing whistle. "Let's talk, guys!" He patted Lucas's shoulder. "Want to join us, sport?"

Despite his earlier misgivings, the boy's eyes brightened, and he jogged off with the group of trainers to meet their assistants. Charm smiled, more sincerely this time. He might actually like these guys. He and Smokey started to follow, but Dulcie motioned for them to wait. "Why did you interrupt me?" she asked, frustration evident in her voice.

"These trainers train very differently than we do," Smokey said.

"Obviously." She glanced sideways at the retreating group.

"But they are professionals who get results." His tone reminded Charm that this was no longer the weakened old man shuffling along after his daughter. This was the man who had built a business and run it successfully longer than his daughter had been alive.

"And," Smokey continued, "they're here volunteering their time to help us. We're here to learn from them, not teach our methods."

She opened her mouth to argue, then shut it and nodded. Her cheeks reddened — with embarrassment this time, not anger. "Got it."

Smokey wrapped an arm around her shoulders and gave her a light squeeze. "I know you do."

A bit embarrassed by observing a moment Dulcie probably wouldn't have wanted public, Charm slipped away. He intended to join the other trainers but saw Oscar heading to his truck. He jogged over to meet him.

"Hey," Charm said. Oscar acknowledged him with a grunt but didn't stop what he was doing. He opened a tote in the back of his pickup and dug through it. "I, uh, wanted to say thanks. For helping get this together."

Oscar snorted and pulled out an extra white jacket. He took the time to light a cigarette before replying. "All I did was set up a meeting at Brother Jack's," he said. He took another puff. "I'm glad to do anything that will piss off Forbes, though. Too bad the dog won't win. That would really make old Forbes's head explode."

Charm frowned. "What do you mean he won't win?"

"He's a curly," Oscar said, as if that explained everything.

Charm remembered Jimmy Lee telling him that curlies didn't compete in field trials, but just because they hadn't done it didn't mean they *couldn't* do it. *Right?*

Oscar scoffed in disgust. "Look, the dog will be competing against experienced, linebred Labs trained by professionals."

"Dulcie's a professional," Charm said.

Oscar shook his head. "She may be a professional animal trainer of some kind, but she's not a pro field trainer. She's never even seen the sport, much less competed. A non-Lab who's never been in a trial before trained by a non-pro isn't going to win." He ground the cigarette out under his heel. "No matter how much that kid wants him to." And with that, he tossed the jacket over his shoulder and sauntered back to the group.

Charm followed, a few feet behind, anxiety churning in his gut. *Is he right? Are we wasting everyone's time? Am I setting Lucas up for a huge fall?* The longer they did this, the closer to competition they got, the harder it would be for Lucas if they failed.

Charm expected to be sent into the field, as usual, but since the trainers had brought their own assistants, he was able to stay back and listen to discussion and commentary at the line. They ran a series of *marks* — birds the dog saw fall — and *blinds* — retrieves the handler had to guide the dog to — with their Lab, and then had Dulcie do a series of each with River. A ripple of condescending laughter rolled through the group when Lucas stepped up as handler, but their amusement turned to admiration when River performed each retrieve with little trouble. They were particularly impressed by how well he maintained his line, which meant he needed little handling on the blinds.

"What he knows, he's absolutely solid on," Layton conceded as they wrapped up. "Really impressive for a curly. I'm still concerned about distance, though."

Dulcie ignored the "for a curly" qualifier and held up her notebook. "Noted. It's just one thing on my growing list of things to work on." She read from the list. "Honoring, poison birds, diversion pops, retired gunners, different bird varieties…oh yeah, we've got a lot to do."

Judging by her tone, Dulcie seemed invigorated by the list, not intimidated. Charm wanted to hug her. Screw Oscar.

Dulcie tapped the notebook on her thigh and thought for a moment. "What I'd like to do, I think, is observe each of you training your own dogs next week. Would that be okay? Then we could get together again as a group…" She did some mental math. "Maybe next Saturday?"

Nods and a murmur of agreement rippled through the group. River and Dulcie had won the group over. Charm couldn't help but grin.

"Hey, Freeman," Layton said, as the group broke up for the day.

Charm handed River's leash to Lucas. "Why don't you give him some water and then get him crated," he said. When the boy was gone, he turned to Layton. "What's up?"

"Are you guys set on entering River at Vicksburg?"

Charm stiffened. Was this going to be another conversation like he'd had with Oscar? "Yeah," he said cautiously.

But Layton was focused on something else. "Registration deadline coming up. You entered him yet?"

"Didn't even think about it. How do I do it?"

He snorted. "You don't. Forbes does. He's the registered owner."

Any hope Charm had of keeping the training a secret vanished. "Oh, crap."

"And he's not going to be anxious to do it," Layton added.

Charm frowned. "Why?"

"Because of Goliath. Goliath breaks a record if he wins again this year, and Forbes isn't going to want anything to threaten that or even take some of the attention away from him."

Nausea rose in Charm's gut. *What will we do if Forbes gets pissed and takes River away?* He sighed and rubbed his forehead. "Thanks for letting me know — and for…all this." He stuck out his hand.

Layton shook his hand, gave him a sympathetic grin, and then ambled to his truck. Charm pulled out his phone and found his former boss at the bar in his contacts. "Ping me when Forbes comes in. Thx," he texted, and then headed to his own truck. Before he'd even gotten there, Max sent back a thumbs-up emoji.

Lucas had the doors open, letting the cab cool a bit, and he and River were relaxing on the ground in the patch of shade made by the truck's body. When he saw his uncle, he hopped up and crated the dog for the drive home.

"That was fun," the boy said, climbing into the cab. "They said River did really good." The trainers had included him, and Charm guessed that alone had gone far in improving the boy's opinion of the situation.

"Yep. They know a good dog when they see one."

Lucas grinned. "We're definitely going to win now. Everything is going to be all right — you'll see."

Charm didn't respond, the tight feeling back in his gut. Right now, he couldn't even guarantee River could compete. All he could do was wait until Max texted him. And maybe go to another meeting with Thibaut.

* * *

Charm didn't have to wait long. Forbes spent almost as many hours at Brother Jack's as he himself used to, although in Forbes's case, it was less about the beer and more about basking in the adoration of his sycophants.

When Charm arrived, the hoppy scent of beer enticed him no less than it had the day before, but the stakes of this visit pushed his desire to drink to the back of his mind. He made his way through the Friday post-work crowd to the bar where Forbes chatted with his usual group. Tim Layton made eye contact and nodded a greeting. Charm returned the nod and cleared his throat to get Forbes's attention. Forbes's expression darkened.

*Crap. He knows.*

Charm's anxiety level, already high, spiked. He schooled his features into the most disarming smile he could manage. "Good evening, Mr. Forbes. I was wondering if I could speak with you a minute?"

"What do you need?" Forbes asked. At least those were his words. The subtext flashed "fuck off" like a neon banner.

Charm pushed on. "As you know, my nephew Lucas, was really torn up when his dad died."

"A tragedy," Forbes acknowledged, glancing at the men around them. They murmured their agreement.

"Your generous loan of River meant more to him — to our whole family — than I can say." That was, Charm conceded, one hundred percent true. "I honestly don't know how we'd have gotten through this time without him."

"I was glad I could help," Forbes said, puffing up despite himself. The men around him again murmured approval. Most of them, anyway. Charm caught Layton rolling his eyes, and he and a couple of the others seemed uncomfortable with the show.

*So far, so good.* "You might have heard that we've run into some financial difficulties lately."

"I'd heard rumors. I'm sorry." He straightened. "I'm not sure how I can help."

Charm assumed his most earnest look. "That's why I'm here. Ellie and Lucas are going to have to move. Before they do, we want Lucas to have a shot at fulfilling his father's dream. We want to enter River at Vicksburg."

Forbes burst out laughing. "You want to enter a curly in the biggest trial in this area of the country? Look, why don't you folks put all this foolishness out of your heads and enjoy the time you have with the dog." He focused his gaze on Charm. "Who knows what could happen? By the time they move, I might not even have room in my kennel for *a dog who can't hunt.*"

Charm met his gaze steadily. "That would be amazing, and I'll mention it to Lucas. But would you enter River anyway?" He smiled again. "Just in case. You know nine-year-old boys. They can be stubborn."

Forbes regarded him for a moment. Charm could feel the frustration coming off him in waves as he mulled the possible outcomes.

Charm managed what he hoped sounded like a self-deprecating laugh. "He's a curly. He'll probably fail the first series anyway. But Lucas really has his heart set on competing." His voice was overloud, and other people in the bar looked their way.

Forbes glanced at them, then reluctantly nodded. "Of course. Which stake? Qualifying? Amateur?"

"Open."

Forbes laughed again, but a crack had formed in the facade. Frustration was anger now. Impotent anger as long as others were watching. "Seems like you're throwing away good money, but all right." He waited. After an awkward pause, he said, "It'll be about fifty dollars."

*Shit.* Did he have fifty on him? Charm dug his wallet out of his back pocket. Two twenties. Crap. Before he could say anything, Layton said, "Actually, it's only thirty-six."

Forbes shot him a glare but kept his tone mild. "Thank you, Tim."

Charm smiled and handed him the two twenties. "Great. We're all set then."

Forbes tucked the bills into his own wallet, and then put a companionable hand on Charm's shoulder and walked him toward the door. Charm got the distinct feeling he wasn't welcome anymore.

The hand tightened on his shoulder. "If you insist on seeing this nonsense through, you make certain he has a decent showing. That's my dog, and I don't like being embarrassed." The hand relaxed. "Not too decent, though." There was a warning there. One series, and then out.

"Of course," Charm said through gritted teeth. He started to leave but hesitated when Forbes spoke again.

"By the way," Forbes said casually, "who's going to handle him?

You?" He sounded amused by the prospect.

"Lucas." Charm reached again for the door handle.

"He can't."

Charm turned back, frowning. The insincerity had vanished from Forbes's expression.

"He's a junior," Forbes said. "Juniors have to be related to the dog's owner. He can't handle my dog."

*Shit.* Charm stood for a moment, processing what Forbes had said. This was going to crush his nephew.

* * *

The smell of chicken potpie drifted from the kitchen as Charm jogged up the side steps. "Smells fabulous," he called out, as he came in.

"Your favorite," his mother confirmed. "Dinner is still half an hour out, though." She pulled a head of lettuce and salad vegetables from the fridge and rinsed them in the sink.

He peered around the kitchen. "Not to look a gift horse in the mouth, but doesn't Ellie usually give you a break and cook on Fridays?"

"I volunteered," she said. She dug a peeler from the silverware drawer and went to work on the carrots. "Eleanor talked to a realtor today, and she's on a tear about decluttering and cleaning."

"Ugh." There went his weekend. When was he going to learn not to volunteer to help?

"Yeah, you're stuck," his mom confirmed. At his surprised look, she said, "It's all over your face."

"Great." Like being a teenager again. "Where's Lucas?"

She set the carrots aside and picked up a cucumber. "Well, Eleanor told him to start decluttering his room. So, I expect he's upstairs playing video games."

"Thanks." He kissed his mother on the cheek, snagged a carrot, and headed upstairs. Lucas, he discovered, was in his room but neither cleaning nor playing video games. He was sitting on the floor reading comic books.

Charm flopped on the bed. "Whatcha reading?" He offered Lucas half the carrot.

"*Once and Future*. It was my dad's favorite." He handed Charm one of the comics. "I forgot they were in here." He waved toward his closet and several disparate piles. "Mom says we have to downsize," he said glumly. "Do you think I'll have to get rid of Dad's comic books?"

Charm moved to sit on the floor beside him. "I think there will probably be room for those."

River, who had been stretched out near him, thumped his tail and shifted his head into the boy's lap. Lucas scratched him and managed to look even sadder. "I wish there was room for River."

Charm watched them for a moment, then said, "If you could keep River" — the boy's eyes widened with hope — "would you give up the field trial?" The hope extinguished like a candle flame.

"Winning a field trial is what my dad wanted. He said our problems would be gone when River won. We *have* to do it."

The magic do-over again. Charm was getting mighty tired of hearing about that. "Life isn't that simple. I talked to Mr. Forbes. He said if we don't run River at Vicksburg, he might let you keep him."

The boy's eyes narrowed. "Did he say I *might* get to keep him, or I *would* get to keep him?"

"Might," Charm conceded. "And there's something else. He's going to enter River at Vicksburg, but you can't handle him." Lucas opened his mouth to argue, and Charm held up a hand to stop him. "That's not Forbes. That's a rule. You're too young."

Lucas burst into tears and threw the comic book across the room. "It's not fair!" River jumped to his feet and pushed his nose into Lucas's face. Lucas clung to him and sobbed into his neck.

Charm patted his back awkwardly. "I know. None of this is fair."

"It's all going wrong," the boy cried. "First, Dad died and Mom worked all the time. Now we have to move away, and I can't take River. And Dad's project is all messed up. It was supposed to be him and me. Him and me! Not you. Not Dulcie. Not all those other trainers. Him and me!" He sobbed harder and let Charm pull him into a hug.

"I know," Charm crooned. "I can't fix it. I've tried and tried, but I can't fix it." Tears spilled down his cheeks.

Lucas shifted and hugged his dog again. "River's never going to be mine, is he?"

"I don't know," Charm said honestly. "Do you want to quit? Try to convince Mr. Forbes to let you keep him?"

The boy gazed at the dog and stroked his head. "Do I have to decide right now?"

Charm shook his head. "No. You have time."

Lucas began crying again. "I miss my dad."

Charm pulled him tight and pictured Jake on that rainy night so long ago, giving away every cent he had, swearing to take care of Ellie. Lucas looked so much like him. "So do I," he said softly. "So do I."

# CHAPTER 25

Clipboard in hand, Elle stood in the middle of the barn and did nothing. Where to even begin? The cavernous structure had been a disaster area for months — something about a bucket and Rube Goldberg. She had no idea what Charm had been talking about, and despite his promises to get it organized, it was worse than ever. If they were to put the house on the market, how on earth could they get this presentable enough to show to potential buyers?

She sighed and sat on a hay bale outside the horse stall. Her mother had reached out to a realtor friend who promised to do some digging into any deals Bud might have cooking for their property, and then the realtor had called Elle. "What do you want to do?" the realtor had asked.

"Crawl in bed and bury my head under the covers until all this goes away" apparently wasn't a valid option.

Approaching footsteps pulled her from her thoughts. Charm slumped beside her on her hay bale and gave a heavy sigh. "You look as miserable as I feel," Elle said.

"Your son is killing me," he said. "I just told him he can't handle River in the field trial." He briefly caught her up on his discussion with Forbes and Lucas's meltdown.

"Oh no," she said. She leaned back against the stall wall and racked her brain for any easy solution to this mess. Why did it all have to be so hard on Lucas? *She* could deal with it. Why couldn't the universe leave her son alone? "It's so unfair."

"That's what he said. Everything we try seems to be for naught. I feel like such a failure."

The defeat in his voice woke the stubbornness that had gotten her through after Jake died. "No," she said firmly. "We've lost a battle or two, but we haven't lost the war." He shrugged, and she sat up. "No. Listen to me. My son is healthy. My brother is back in my life." He offered a wan smile. "Lucas has had six good months with River, and he and you have worked miracles with that dog. If he competes in that field trial, it's because neither of you gave up on him."

"What about the house?"

Elle looked around the barn and outside at the fields beyond. "We're not homeless. We have options." She snorted. "I'm not sure what they are, but we have them."

He chuckled. "I've been thinking about it. If you sell the stock, you'll be able to buy yourself some time."

She shook her head. That had occurred to her too. "It would catch me up, but all it would do is reset a ticking clock. If I sell the stock, I'll have zero money coming in down the road."

"True, but it will buy you time to get the house on the market and get it sold," he countered.

She thought about the depressing conversation she'd had with the realtor earlier. "Farms can sit on the market for years here. Selling the stock would buy us a few months if we're really lucky — and really frugal."

"But," he said gently, "it would give us time to get River ready for Vicksburg, and it would give Lucas time to adapt — even if you end up in the same spot later."

She gazed at him, considering his argument. "You're right." She sighed. "I just wish we had a little more cushion. If we sell the stock, we're flat broke if the house doesn't sell."

He screwed up his face, thinking. "Why don't you sell Dad's furniture?"

"It's not mine," she said. "It's Mom's. Jake and I suggested she sell it after Dad died, and she wouldn't hear of it."

"Oh, Eleanor," her mother's voice rang out. She stood in the doorway of the barn, one hand on her hip. "Don't be ridiculous."

Elle's jaw dropped. "That's what you said!"

"Of course, I did. You asked me at Will's wake, for goodness' sake. Selling the things he'd poured his heart and soul into weren't what I wanted to think about at that moment." She wiped the frustration off her face and turned to Charm. "I didn't realize you were out here. Dinner's ready. Could you get Lucas?"

"Sure." Charm gave Elle a companionable bump with his shoulder and hauled himself off the hay bale. Their mother smiled as he passed and then took his place next to Elle.

"You mean I could sell the furniture?" Elle asked.

"Most of it, certainly," her mother said. "There's a piece or two I'd want to hold on to for sentimental reasons. I'll do anything I can to help you and Lucas."

*Not always.* Despite the peace they'd garnered over these past months, unbidden memories of long-ago fights surfaced. "Me and Lucas, but not Jake?"

Her mother gave an aggrieved sigh. "Of course, Jake too. I loved Jake."

Elle crossed her arms over her chest. "You loved him so much you didn't want us to get married. Or have children." As soon as the words left her mouth, she regretted them. Why start a fight — this fight — now?

But her mother didn't get angry or defensive. She looked sad. "I wasn't against your marrying Jake or your having kids" — Elle opened her mouth to argue, but her mother held up a finger to stop her — "I just didn't want you to marry him right out of high school. I wanted you to go to college first. I didn't want you to make the same decisions and mistakes I made."

*Mistakes?* Maybe they *were* going to have this argument now. "So, getting married and having me and Charm were mistakes?" Anger made her voice overloud.

"No." Her mother shook her head vigorously. "That's not what I said. I always wanted you. Both of you. And loved you enough to want you to have — to at least consider — options I didn't have."

*Options.* Isn't that what she was just contemplating? She was too hungry and tired to deal with this right now. But before she could suggest they let it go, her mother grabbed her hand. "Come with me," she said, pulling Elle to her feet.

Elle reluctantly followed as her mother led her up the ladder-stairs into the loft. Her mother wove through stacks of boxes — her things from the old house — pulling boxes down, checking labels, then moving to the next. "It's hot up here," Elle said, pushing at a box with her toe. "Let's do this some other time."

Her mother set a box on the floor and ripped the tape off. "Here. Come look at this."

*Fine.* Elle knelt beside her and looked at the objects within.

"These are from my college days before I dropped out to help your father," her mother said. She thumbed through a yearbook and handed it to her. "This was me playing Mae in *Cat on a Hot Tin Roof.* Ava played Maggie, of course." She pulled out a trophy. "I won the college's Best Supporting Actress award that semester." She chuckled. "There must have been a dearth of candidates."

According to the captions, two of the six photos on the two-page spread were from *Cat on a Hot Tin Roof.* Ava, easily identified by her blonde hair, was in both. Her mother was in one, face to face with her best friend in an obviously tension-filled scene. Elle ran her fingers over the photo, captivated despite herself. She had forgotten that when she was young, her mother's hair had been red like hers.

"I didn't know you acted," she said. She picked up the trophy and read the engraving.

Her mother's eyes took on a distant look, as she remembered happy times past. "Ava and I used to talk about running away to New York City to try our hand on Broadway."

Elle smiled. "Were you any good?"

Her mother sobered and met her gaze. "We won't ever know." She packed the book and the trophy back in the box and interlaced the flaps to seal it. They stood, and she took Elle's hands in her own, her expression intent as she seemed to consider her words. "Every choice means other paths are left unexplored," she said finally. "I made my choices, good and bad. I tried to convince you to *delay* marriage" — she emphasized the word — "because I wanted you to live the life *you* wanted before you made a place in someone else's life. If Jake was the right man at eighteen, he would have been the right man at twenty-two."

The resentment that had gripped her heart for so many years loosened, just a bit. "And Lucas?"

"Options," her mother repeated. "I knew once you had kids, it would be harder to follow your dreams. I never thought you shouldn't be a mom. You're an amazing mom, and I worship the ground that boy walks on. But I wanted you to have the chance to be something else amazing before you got tied down with real life." She looked around the loft. "Will this furniture give you options?"

Elle thought about the conversation she'd just had with Charm. If she sold the stock *and* the furniture… "Yes," she said.

Her mother squeezed her hands. "Then sell it. Do what you want, Elle." She wiped a tear from her daughter's face. "Whether you go or stay, be the person *you* want to be."

* * *

*Go or stay?*

At work on Monday, Elle found herself constantly distracted by that question. She'd thought about it all weekend, even as she had channeled her inner taskmaster and kept Lucas and Charm decluttering, sorting, and cleaning. Charm couldn't make keep-or-save decisions, but he was a champion box packer and mover.

Even Lucas had worked hard once she'd assured him they would keep his video games and his dad's comic books and once she'd agreed to give them time to work with River. Apparently, Dulcie had sent them quite a bit of homework to do between sessions.

Selling the cattle and the furniture would enable her to catch up on her mortgage before the bank foreclosed and leave her a decent cushion. That decision was made and only needed to be implemented. During the extra time, maybe she could figure out a way for them to stay. *Do I want to stay?*

Charm and her mother kept pushing her to follow her dreams. What dreams? What did she want, really? And what about Lucas? Was it fair to uproot him from the only life he'd ever known? What if they risked everything on this grand adventure, and she failed, leaving them worse off than they were now?

Staying looked better and better.

Her cell phone rang, startling her. She glanced at the caller and swiped to answer. "Hi Nadine. You must be psychic. I was just thinking about you."

Nadine White had an unpleasant, high-pitched, nasally voice that made Elle's teeth hurt. It sounded sort of pixie-ish, which didn't fit her at all. She towered at least five foot eleven in her bare feet, and her hobby — when she had time — was powerlifting. To be fair, she didn't have a heck of a lot of time. Nadine sold more houses and properties in Sharkey County than the next two realtors put together.

"Only good things I hope," she said with a giggle. "I wanted to set up a time to sign paperwork and get some photos taken."

Elle sighed. "I'm having second thoughts."

"Many potential sellers do," Nadine said. "Especially in a situation like yours where you're feeling forced out."

Elle made a noncommittal sound in her throat. "We've figured out a way to buy us some time. I think." She sighed a second time. "I just…I don't want to traumatize Lucas any more than I have to. The farm is the only place he's ever known."

"I know. Our homes carry a special place in our hearts. But let me ask you, Elle — as a friend, not as a realtor — what happens when that extra time runs out?"

"I don't know," Elle said. She hated the tears that made it difficult to speak. "I guess I hope I'll have figured out something before that to let us stay."

Nadine took a deep breath. "May I make a recommendation — again, as a friend, not a realtor?"

"Sure."

"You have nothing to lose by listing the house now except some time spent spiffing the place up. The market for farms is so slow, so inconsistent. I would hate for you to miss your chance and not get another one later."

Elle nodded. Nadine was right. Listing didn't mean they would sell anytime soon — heck, they could list and still lose the house to foreclosure down the road. Wanting the best for Lucas meant making the hard choice, even if that wasn't what he wanted. She swallowed back her tears. "Let's get that paperwork signed."

* * *

"Paper plates? Where are the paper plates?"

Elle tried to focus on her mother's question. "What? Oh, um…" She ran through her mental map of the copious items in the trunk and back seat of her mom's sedan. Where did she stash them?

"Found them." Her mother shot her an annoyed look. "Why would you pack the plates with the side dishes instead of with the silverware and cups? Where is your brain today, Eleanor?" Her mother waved off an answer. "Don't answer that. I know where it is."

Yeah, orbiting somewhere past Pluto at the moment, and her body buzzed like it was readying to join it. She wished Charm and Lucas would hurry up and get over here. *Here* was the edge of the field they and the group of trainers were working in.

"Open the tailgate of Charm's truck. We can spread everything out there," her mother said.

"My truck," Elle corrected automatically, but did as she was told. Despite a very long and hectic week trying to get the house ready to go on the market, she had thought it a wonderful idea when her mother suggested bringing lunch to the training group when they got together on Saturday. After two-and-a-half hours frying chicken and making potato salad, her eagerness had waned, especially since —

"You don't have to drop distance," Oscar Strickland said. "Just add the poison bird." The group of trainers swarmed the truck.

"No talk of poison birds around my fried chicken," Elle's mother said, passing out plates.

"This looks fantastic," one of the trainers said, grabbing a leg and a thigh and digging into the potato salad.

"There's bread too." Elle passed him a basket of biscuits. "And honey butter." She looked around for Charm.

"I increase criteria one element at a time." Dulcie reached for the closest piece of chicken. She waved a plastic fork. "If we make everything else easier, River will be able to focus on learning the new thing. Thanks so much for doing this, Elle."

Before Elle could respond, another trainer spoke up. "We don't have time to do that. We have to *increase* distance. All this time spent at a hundred and fifty, two hundred, two hundred and fifty yards is setting that dog up to fail when the distance jumps to four hundred."

Lucas squeezed to the front and held out a plate. "Can I have two pieces?" he asked.

Charm slipped in behind his nephew, smiled a greeting at Elle, and dropped two pieces of chicken on Lucas's plate. "Sure can. Want some potato salad?"

Elle's heart pounded. "Charm, I need to talk to you."

"Sure," he said absently, focusing on his own plate now.

"Why would I jump to four hundred?" Dulcie asked. "What happened to two seventy, three hundred, three twenty?"

"I've seen her do it, guys," Charm said.

"Charm —" Elle said, trying to regain his attention.

"Seriously," he continued. "Dropping the distance lets us get a lot of reps in, and River really gets new concepts quickly."

The trainers spoke at once then, arguing the importance of distance. Elle bit her lip, and then said loudly, "We sold the house."

Everyone fell silent and looked toward her.

"What?" Charm asked.

"We sold the house. Realtor called a little while ago."

Charm looked stunned. "To who?" he asked. "The realtor took pictures yesterday. It wasn't even on the market yet."

"The commercial farm north of us. The same people Bud was going to sell to."

Every person began speaking at once then. They circled her and congratulated her. People patted her back and shook her hand.

"When do you move?" someone asked.

Before answering, Elle searched out her son. He stood nearby, eyes wide, face pale. The pain in his eyes broke her heart. She answered whoever had asked the question, but she spoke to her son. "There still have to be inspections and appraisals and such, but if everything works out, we'll close in the latter half of August."

"What about River?" Lucas asked, one hand reaching automatically for the retriever's head.

She hesitated. "I don't know exactly, but I'll make sure you're here for the field trial."

Charm touched Lucas's shoulder. "It'll be all right, buddy."

Lucas looked at him, then back at his mother. His fingers clenched, and he slammed his plate to the ground. "I hate you!" Two steps back. "I hate you!" He turned and ran, River following close behind. "I hate you!"

Charm started after him, but Elle grabbed his arm. "I'll go," she said. She mouthed a quiet "Excuse me," and jogged in the direction her son had gone. The shock in his eyes broke her heart. Maybe she should have waited and told him privately, not that it would have changed anything. Nothing was going to make this easier on him.

Old broken cornstalks and a faint reminder of plowed rows indicated that the front half of the field had been farmed the previous year. This year it had been left fallow, and various grasses and clovers grew in wild tangles across the uneven ground. The back half of the field was too marshy to plow, and the weeds were taller there. Elle followed bent grass to the edge of a long, narrow pond where she found Lucas sitting on the ground, hugging River and sobbing.

"Go away," he said without looking at her.

She sat next to him. "Honey —"

He shoved her back onto her elbows. "Go away! I hate you! You've messed up everything."

Tears rolled down her face. Was she wrong to sell the house? She hadn't accepted the offer yet. Was there another option? It had all happened so fast. Maybe she was rushing into it.

"I wish Dad was here. Why couldn't you believe in him?" Lucas said.

"I miss him too," she said.

He glared at her. "No, you don't. You hated him." Her breath caught. "I heard you say it!"

He had accused her of that before. She hadn't known what to say then, but she did now. "I think I did hate him for a little while. I was so angry he'd left us alone."

"It wasn't his fault!"

"No. No, of course not. He would never, ever have left us if he'd had a choice." She got quiet, overcome by memories and emotions. "But he didn't have a choice. And neither did I." She rubbed his back. "A lot has changed, hasn't it?"

He nodded. "I hate it."

"I don't," she said, surprised to find it was true. She thought about the long hours at work. "Maybe parts of it. I'm grateful for other stuff, though."

He wiped his nose on the knee of his jeans. "What kind of stuff?"

"Charm. And your grandmother. And River."

Lucas snorted. "No, you aren't."

"I am," she said firmly. "River brought you back to me."

He took a shuddering breath. "I wish it could be like it used to be. I want it to be like it was, so River can live with me forever."

She glanced sideways at him. "Mmm, that's revisionist."

"What does revisionist mean?" He struggled a bit with the unfamiliar word.

"It means you're changing the facts." He frowned, so she asked, "Who owned River when your Dad was training him?"

"Mr. Forbes."

"And what did he ask your dad to do?"

"Train River for a field trial."

"And after the field trial, what would have happened to River?"

Lucas sighed. "He'd have gone back to Mr. Forbes."

Elle nodded. "River never was yours to keep." Lucas looked like he wanted to argue. "Was he?"

His face fell. "No. But I love him."

She wrapped an arm around him and pulled him close. "I know." They sat silent for a couple of minutes, each lost in their thoughts.

"I like that I get to see Grandma a lot now," he said. "If we move, I won't get to see her anymore." Tears made his voice shake.

"Well…we don't know that," Elle said. "We haven't decided where we're going to move. Maybe we'll live here in Collier. Or maybe she'll come with us." She rubbed his head. "I'm pretty sure there's nowhere we could move that would stop her from seeing you every chance she got."

That got a smile, but the smile faded. "I don't want to leave. I like it here."

She nodded. "I like it here too. But I might be able to like other places too."

"Like where?"

"I like the ocean in Biloxi. And I've been to Jackson a bunch of times. And once I went to Atlanta. That's a big city."

"The ocean might be nice, but I don't think I'd like a big city," he said.

"Maybe we could find a place where there's a basketball team."

"Or football?"

"Or football. Or maybe somewhere you could play soccer."

"I'd like to play soccer," he admitted.

She sighed and hugged him close. "I don't know where we're going to go yet, but I promise, we'll be okay."

Lucas stayed there, head on her chest for a long time, letting her stroke his hair and croon to him. She'd have thought he'd fallen asleep if it weren't for the occasional sniffle. Finally, he sat up, his eyes very serious and sad. "I want…" he said. His voice shook, and he stopped and started again. "I want River to compete at Vicksburg."

Charm had told her about the decision Lucas had to make. "Even if it means Mr. Forbes will definitely take him back?"

He nodded. "I'm not giving up on Dad's dream. Plus, River was meant to be a field retriever."

She blinked back tears that threatened again. "You have a very generous heart," she whispered.

He sighed. "I wish it didn't hurt so much."

She half laughed, half sobbed. "Me too."

# Chapter 26

The only thing worse than training for a field trial in Mississippi in August, Charm decided, was moving in Mississippi in August. No. Strike that. Doing both at the same time in Mississippi in August was way worse. But at least the end was in sight.

Charm used his body to hold a box closed and dragged tape across the top, both directions, to seal it. He scrawled the contents on the side and top with a black Sharpie, and then stacked it on top of several other boxes near the door to the hall.

He turned back and scanned the room — the one he'd slept in every night since arriving in January. That wasn't that long, though sometimes it felt like eternity. The room had never been his, really. It was a guest room, but it had become home. Now, except for the bed, it was stripped bare, knickknacks boxed, art off the wall, stuff that had been stored in the dresser and closet either sold or packed. His own clothes and belongings, which had multiplied over the months, were packed and labeled and would be moved into Vlad; only the things he needed for the next few days were still out.

Satisfied with this room, he moved down the hall to check Lucas's room. "How you doing in here, kid?"

"I'm not a kid," Lucas growled without looking at him. His focus remained firmly on his TV screen and the video game he was playing. Half a dozen half-packed boxes littered the room.

"Your mom has told you three times to pack that up."

"So?"

"So pack it up. You've got to get this done today. Or would you rather skip the field trial to do it?"

Lucas glowered at him. "You're not my dad. You can't make me stay home."

"No, but I can refuse to handle River."

"Dulcie would do it."

"Dulcie isn't listed in the catalog." Charm figured there was a way to make a last-minute handler change, but he wasn't going to tell Lucas that.

Lucas threw the game controller. "This is so stupid. Why can't you guys have faith in my dad? He said —"

"I know what he said." Charm paused to get control of his temper. "Lucas, we've been over and over this." And, as the trial date crept closer and closer, the boy had doubled down. Tripled down.

Charm took a deep breath and sat next to him. "You worried about tomorrow?" *First day of the field trial.* Lucas shrugged and didn't answer. "I am."

Lucas looked over, eyes wide. "Don't you think River can do it?"

"I don't know. I think he's ready, but I'm not sure. I'm more worried about me, though. I don't want to make a mistake and let him down. Or let you down."

The boy considered that, and Charm could see the defensive wall around him crumble. "Or let my dad down?" His voice shook.

Charm thought about Jake. It was so easy to see him in the boy in front of him. "Your dad would be so proud of you. You've worked so hard. No matter what happens this weekend, we won't let your dad down — either of us." Charm tugged at one of the boy's curls. "Unless you piss your mom off by playing video games instead of packing."

The boy rolled his eyes and climbed off the bed. "Fine."

Charm hid a smile and left the boy to finish packing. He was proud of Lucas too. Despite knowing River's time with him was limited and despite the disappointment of not handling River in the trial, Lucas had worked with River every free moment he'd had in the past couple of months. And the retriever had responded. Two months wasn't very long, but River had, at least, been introduced to all the concepts, and they were finally increasing distance — *successfully*, he added mentally.

Frankly, learning to handle had been tougher than training River. Well, maybe it wasn't technically tougher, but it was much harder than he had expected. Lucas had made it look easy. Being shown up by a nine-year-old kind of bruised a man's ego. Considering Lucas had wanted to be the handler — should have been the handler — Charm wouldn't have begrudged him a few jabs at his expense. Instead, after one particularly spectacular failure, Lucas gave him a hug and told him if he couldn't handle River himself, he was glad Charm was doing it.

The boy had grown up a lot. So many changes. *I hope you approve, Jake.*

Quick footsteps tapped on the stairs, and Ellie breezed up, clipboard in hand. "How's it looking in here?" she asked, sticking her head into Charm's room.

Charm snapped back to the present. "Good. Everything in here is done except for the bed and what I'll need over the weekend."

She did a quick sweep around the room and made a notation on her clipboard. "Perfect. We can do the last of the laundry on Sunday night and strip the beds on Monday morning before the movers arrive." She blew out a breath of air and sat on the bed. "The movers. Can you believe it? I still can't believe moving day is finally here."

He chuckled and sat next to her. "And the field trial. Win or lose, ready or not. For all of us."

"Are you ready?"

"For the trial, as ready as we can be. It starts tomorrow, so we have to be. And...I'm packed." His gut tightened, as it always did when he thought about what would happen after the trial. When

Ellie moved.

She took his hand. "You can come with us."

He shook his head. "What would I do in a college town?" He smiled then. "That's not my world. That's your world. College girl."

"Not this year," she corrected. "Next year. Maybe. Let me and Lucas get established in Oxford first. Wasn't it cool that Dovye got me a job at the county clerk's office in Oxford?"

"I think it's cooler that Mom's moving with you to take care of Lucas. I even think he's excited about it."

Snort. "He's excited about Ole Miss football. So, have you decided what you're going to do? Go back to St. Louis? I move on Monday, Charm. You've got to make a decision soon unless you plan to sleep in the barn."

He shrugged. "I've still got my job at the used car place. Jimmy Lee says I can crash with him for a while."

Her feelings about that showed clearly on her face. "Maybe Bird would have been a better choice?"

"Pretty sure his wife wouldn't agree." But her point hung in the air. Jimmy Lee, God love him, wasn't good for Charm's sobriety. Sobriety. Two months sober and still the desire for a drink would wake him in the night.

A sudden craving clawed at his throat. A beer or two would go a long way toward easing his nerves right now.

"Do you need to call Thibaut?" Ellie asked.

He startled — he'd forgotten she was there. "No. Maybe. No. I'm fine."

She didn't look entirely convinced but shrugged and refocused on her clipboard. "If you're done in here, Mom could use your help in the kitchen. I want to get as much done tonight as we can. I expect we'll be too exhausted this weekend."

He saluted. "Aye, aye, Cap'n." But he hung back on the way downstairs, his thoughts slowing him down. Everyone had a plan but him. The world had turned upside down and sideways, but somehow Charm was right back where he started.

* * *

Charm and Lucas rolled into the location for the first day of the Vicksburg field trial at five thirty for a seven o'clock start. Already some of the professional trainers with their big rigs had arrived and set up in locations that would be shadiest through the hottest part of the day. Dulcie had snagged a particularly excellent location under an expansive oak. Other trainers had crowded close on either side of her, leaving no space for Charm. Before Charm could grouse, she signaled for him to wait, and then backed her truck out, leaving him to take one of the best spots available.

"I've got a reflective tent for the bed of the truck," she said, when she returned carrying something large and silver. "We should be able to keep River comfy all day. If he does get too warm, we can put him in the cab and run the air conditioner."

"Good morning to you too," Charm said.

"Hi, Dulcie! Hi, Smokey," Lucas said brightly. He jumped into the bed of the truck to help erect the tent.

"Good morning, young man," Smokey said.

Dulcie had her work face on and no time for social niceties. "Lucas, can you handle River? Dad, help him. Give River a chance to see what's going on and to pee if he needs to. Keep him away from the other dogs, and try to get him to relax. Charm, let's walk and get the lay of the land."

*Fine, Miss Bossy.* But he followed her anyway. Instead of heading directly to the field, she walked through the rapidly filling parking area, noting where people they knew were setting up. Layton's rig was set up next to a fancy RV. Forbes's, no doubt. Charm kind of hoped he ran out of gas on the field.

"Are your mom and Elle coming?" Dulcie asked.

"Yeah. They're making sure we have enough food and drinks for the day." They would probably pack enough to feed every trainer here. "They'll be here before seven."

Dulcie pointed to an area between the parking area and the field where some people were already setting out chairs. "Over there will be a good place for them to set up. Damn." She snapped her fingers. "I brought another tent to keep the sun off, but I forgot chairs."

"No worries. Mom will bring extras."

"Good. Thanks." She pointed toward a tent with a table set up beneath it. "That must be the marshal's table. You'll check in there." She pulled her phone from her pocket and checked the time. "Maybe give them another half an hour."

He nodded. "Big field," he said, looking beyond the table. Rough mowed on a diagonal with areas of heavier cover. A couple hundred yards out, a dirt road with drainage ditches on each side bisected the field.

"That road will be a challenge," Dulcie said, squinting at it. "Dogs could perceive it as a boundary and not want to go past. The diagonal mow might pull them off their line too."

"What's with the hay bales?" Charm asked. Large round bales and occasionally stacks of square bales had been placed in several locations in the field.

"They'll hide the gunners."

"Oh. Yeah." Stupid question.

She shrugged. "Don't worry about it. We're all overwhelmed."

They walked back then and found his mother and Elle had joined Lucas and Smokey at the truck. "We found a place for you to sit and watch," Charm said. "I think River will have to stay here, though."

"Why?" Lucas asked, sounding offended.

"He can't watch other dogs run before his run," Dulcie said.

"Good morning, all."

The group looked over to find Oscar Strickland beaming at them. Well, mainly at Ellie. She offered a friendly smile and asked, "You running a dog today?"

"Nope," he said. "Thought I'd come support Team River."

Charm managed not to roll his eyes. "Good. There's a crap-ton of stuff in the car. You can be the designated packhorse."

Oscar shot him a glare but managed to keep his smile intact for Ellie. "Happy to. Just point me in the right direction."

She wrinkled her nose. "Plenty of time, I think. How many dogs are going to be here? It seemed like every other vehicle on the way down had a dog box."

"Sixty-two," Oscar said, "which is a good size stake, but this isn't the only stake at the trial."

Ellie looked blank.

"This is Open," Oscar explained. "There's also Derby, Qualifying, and Amateur."

"Different classes," Charm translated. "Called stakes."

"Oh." Ellie looked around. "Where are they?"

"Different fields around the area. Amateur starts at the same time as Open. I think Derby is this afternoon, and Qualifying is tomorrow."

"Oh," she said again. "So how does this work?"

Lucas facepalmed. "Mom!" He drew the word out in an aggrieved whine. Charm barely hid his smile. Lucas had explained the workings of a field trial on no fewer than four occasions. For all Ellie had tried to support Lucas these past couple of months, she remained profoundly disinterested in the details.

"This is Open," Oscar repeated. "There will be four separate series — different tests. The first series is land marks."

"Marks?"

"Birds the dog sees fall. It's a memory test. This series will probably take all day today. The dogs who pass will come back for the second series tomorrow."

"So not all the dogs will pass?" Ellie looked at River and frowned.

Oscar shook his head. "Probably only about half will pass."

She absently stroked River's head. "If he passes, what happens tomorrow?"

Dulcie spoke up. "Second series. Land blind."

Oscar nodded. "Those are birds the dog didn't see, so the handler has to guide him with whistles and hand signals."

"I've seen you do that," Elle said to Lucas. He nodded.

"Third series is water blind — that will probably happen tomorrow too — and final series is water marks on Sunday. Probably only a dozen or so dogs will make it all the way to the fourth series."

"River will do it," Lucas said. Charm wished he felt as confident as Lucas sounded.

Oscar bent down and looked him in the eye. "I know he's going to try his hardest. But sometimes really good dogs don't make it through. That's okay, though. That doesn't mean they don't have talent."

Lucas's jaw tightened. "River's going to win. You wait and see."

"Will they retrieve those plastic bumpers?" Ellie asked.

Charm could see Oscar's eyes widen. "Um, no," he said slowly. "This is a hunting competition. They retrieve real birds. Most of the time the birds will already be dead — the gunners will place or throw them. There's often one live flyer that will be shot, though."

"What if they miss?"

"They'll call 'No bird' and do it again."

Dulcie tapped Charm's arm. "It's time to sign in."

Charm nodded. As he started to leave, Oscar said, "Hang around down there after you do. They'll run a test dog, and you'll get a chance to see the marks and ask questions."

"Thanks," Charm said sincerely. To his surprise, he was glad Oscar was there to share his knowledge.

A queue had formed in front of the marshal's table. By the time Charm got signed in, it was approaching start time. He checked in and got a catalog, a number — twenty-seven — and a list of running order, and then he joined other handlers to watch the test dog run the course.

This, someone — one of the judges, maybe — explained, was to be a land triple with an honor. *Triple* meant the dog would see three birds before being sent and would have to remember where each was. *Honor* meant that after retrieving his three birds, River would sit — off leash — next to the mat while the next dog did his retrieves.

The first bird would be thrown from a station toward the south end of the field — the end closest to them — about two hundred yards out. The station was this side of the dirt road that bisected the field. The bird would be thrown into the dense cover of the drainage ditch on the far side of the road.

The second station was more to the middle of the field. A dry creek bed wound its way between the area around the first station and that of the second station. The bird would be thrown into the weeds and chaff in that dry creek bed.

The third station was closer to the northern edge of the field, and the bird would be a live flyer. That one was the longest run, by far. *Too far for River?* Looking at the field now, it seemed farther than anything they had ever done.

"For a dog solid on distance, that's the easiest mark," said a voice to his right. Charm looked over to see Tim Layton squinting at the third station. "Long, but not a lot to confuse the dog. If he's solid on distance." Layton let the statement sink in, then continued, "Watch the test dog. He'll get the live flyer first. Then the shortest one in the middle. Then the first one straight ahead of us."

And that, as Layton predicted, was exactly what the test dog did. Sort of. He found the live flyer easily enough, but he had trouble with both the middle and left birds. He ran through the area of fall for the middle bird and went instead beyond it, even beyond the road and the fall area of the first bird thrown. Eventually the gunners had to call him back to the right area. When he went for the final bird — the first one thrown — he again went past it and hunted well into the field beyond the road, but he eventually found his way back to the area of fall and picked up the bird.

As soon as the test dog finished, Charm headed back to find his family. *If the test dog couldn't do it, how does River have a chance?* His stomach roiled and threatened complete rebellion. Maybe Dulcie wanted to handle River. Charm was trying to figure out how to lower Lucas's expectations when he happened to catch a glimpse of Ray Forbes, standing with an even larger group of people than usual.

Forbes saw him as well, and in an instant the joviality slipped from his face, replaced by a glare so cold it made Charm shudder. In a blink the look was gone, and he turned deliberately away.

Charm hurried away and found his family had set up an oasis in the viewing area with shade tent, chairs, and a rather extreme number of coolers with drinks, ice, and food. "We're number twenty-seven," he said, kneeling between Ellie and Dulcie.

"That's a good draw," Oscar said. "You've got time to see the early dogs run, but it's not so late that River will be too hot to run."

Charm counted heads. "Smokey watching River?"

Dulcie nodded. "Making sure he doesn't get too hot or too hyped up."

"This will be the only series today," Oscar said, helping himself to a cold bottle of water. "Once you've completed your run and honor, you don't have to stick around. All you'll need is somebody to see if he made the cut for tomorrow. That info should be posted on the website."

"Good to know," Dulcie said. "I'll probably stick it out, but maybe y'all could take River home so he doesn't overheat."

Lucas grabbed her arm. "It's starting."

Conversation died then, as they focused on the activity in the field. Some of the dogs did well; some didn't. All had some manner of trouble. Dulcie was right — the road did cause problems for some of the dogs. Forbes's best dog, Goliath, ran twelfth. Every pickup was clean with minimal hunting needed. Charm whistled long and low. Forbes might actually deserve to be a little cocky about a fifth win.

Even with their shade tent, the heat grew oppressive as the sun rose higher and higher. No wonder this was the only field trial in the Southern states during the summer. Charm and River were in the cab of Ellie's truck blasting the air conditioning when Lucas came to tell him it was time to get ready.

*Breathe. Breathe. It's going to be fine,* Charm told himself. His hands shook when he pulled on his white jacket and then slipped a loop collar over River's head. River, who had settled well earlier, was cool enough now to feel Charm's nervousness. That charged up his own nerves, and he lunged ahead. "River, heel!" Charm snapped.

"Take your time," Dulcie said, falling in beside him. "You're not in a rush. There's still one more person to go before you have to be ready."

Her tone calmed him more than her words. He blew out some of the tension that had grabbed hold of his middle and nodded. As Charm made his way toward the line, a murmur rolled through the crowd. He heard the word *curly* several times. There were chuckles, too, and Charm frowned. "Go get 'em, River!" he heard someone say, and some of the irritation drained away.

Then they were at the line. The dog that had run before them was sitting just beyond the mat, ready to perform his honor. Charm gave the dog's handler a nervous smile. Thank goodness Dulcie and the trainers had drilled River on honoring, so he was accustomed both to working with other dogs close and honoring for others.

"Are you ready?" asked a judge.

Charm took a deep breath. "River, heel." He made sure the dog was positioned well and focused. *As ready as I'll ever be.* He signaled the judge.

A shotgun blast sounded out in the field to the left. Someone in a white jacket threw the first bird. A second blast, and the second bird was thrown. Then — there! — the live bird was released. It broke high, very visible, and the third blast brought it down. River stood trembling, staring where the live flyer had gone down. *Can he handle the distance?* Charm lined him and let him go.

River was off at a gallop on a dead straight line. One hundred yards. Two hundred. As he approached three hundred yards, he began to slow. *You're not there yet. Keep going.* Charm saw him falter and put his nose down.

*No, you're not there yet. Keep going.* River paused, raised his head, and then kept going, still on his line — so straight, he practically tripped over the bird. He grabbed it, and Charm tweeted his whistle three times. River returned as fast as he'd left. Charm heard the murmur behind him and felt a glimmer of satisfaction. *Take that.*

River delivered the bird to Charm and swung into place for the next retrieve. Charm lined him up for the second bird, the short bird in the middle. River ran to the area of fall, but he did a couple of loops before he came up with it. Okay. Was that too much? Would it get him cut? Charm had no idea.

The third bird was much like the second one. River lined directly to the area of the fall. He wasn't fooled by the road, and he didn't hunt way beyond the area of the fall like the test dog had. But it seemed to take forever for him to find the bird in the ditch. He almost looked like he was doing it on purpose, enjoying being free in the field. *Oh Christ, just get the bird.* And he did.

Charm was surprised by a round of applause when River handed off the third bird. They weren't done yet, of course. They took their place beside the mat for their honor. "Sit," Charm said. "No bird." River wouldn't get to retrieve these.

Several people congratulated him on the way back to the truck. His family met him there, excited and full of compliments. "It wasn't perfect," he said.

"Competing in Open with a curly? You expect a lot," Dulcie said, giving River a well-deserved bowl of water.

"Was it good enough to come back tomorrow?" Lucas asked. They all looked at Oscar, who shrugged.

"I honestly don't know," he said. "Why don't you guys pack up and head home? I'll call and let you know if he made it."

Charm blew out a deep breath. "I think I'll stay," he said. Dulcie and Lucas decided to stay with him, so they sent River home with Ellie and then traipsed back to the viewing area to watch. Charm made himself a sandwich. Then ate a bag of chips. Then some cookies. He pulled a Coke from the cooler and wished it was beer — anything to calm his nerves, which were somehow worse now that all he could do was wait. He was going to have to go to a whole series of meetings tonight.

He dug into the cooler and found some string cheese. If he kept eating like this, he was going to have to make time for an Overeaters Anonymous meeting too. He sighed.

After the last dog ran, Dulcie went to the marshal's table to wait for them to post the list of dogs called back for the second series tomorrow. After several hours — or twenty minutes — she reappeared, looking serious. "Only thirty-six dogs were called back." She smiled. "River made the cut."

Lucas erupted into cheers, and Charm allowed himself to relax. They'd done it. Forbes was going to be pissed, but right now Charm didn't care.

"One down," Dulcie said.

"Three to go." He grinned. They were going to kick some field-trial ass.

# CHAPTER 27

Despite the high note that ended day one, Charm was pretty sure everyone, including Lucas, would have been glad to skip day two if it had meant sleeping past four thirty. They dragged, they grumbled — when they spoke at all — and they approached their tasks like they were on their way to the death chamber. But they managed to get on the road by five thirty and arrived at the location for day two by six twenty.

All the good spaces were taken, of course, and Dulcie hadn't saved him a spot in the shade today. They didn't really need it — Dulcie's reflective cover worked great — but it gave Charm something to complain about.

Dulcie was, as usual, unsympathetic, but she shoved her coffee mug into his hands. "You need this more than I do," she said. "Go sign in, and we'll get the tents set up."

Ugh. Too much sugar. But at least it was caffeine. Charm signed in and checked the running order. River was running sixth, Goliath next to last.

"They rotate the running order," someone said. Charm didn't recognize the man but nodded politely. "That way the same dogs don't go first or last every time. You'll keep your original number"

— the man tapped the numbered armband Charm had been given the day before — "but your actual running number will vary."

Oh. That made sense.

Before Charm could thank him, the man stuck out his hand. "I'm Rob. I handle Blue."

Charm had no clue which dog was Blue, but he didn't suppose it mattered. He shook his hand. "I'm Charm. I'm handling —"

"The curly, right? Everybody was real impressed with him yesterday. Don't really see curlies in field trials. A few have gotten their Master Hunter title, though."

"So I've heard. You're running this series?" Stupid question. Why else would he be here at this ungodly hour?

"Yeah, we're number twenty-six. Running fifth today."

Charm shook his hand again and managed a genuine smile. "Good luck."

The man glanced at the field. "Thanks. I think we'll need it."

The judges were ready to start. The group gathered around this morning was significantly smaller than the one the day before. The marshal's table was on a levee that divided the grounds into two halves. A lake dominated the left half. The right half was fields. The test dog and his handler walked to the mat, which was positioned out in the middle of the levee, facing right, toward the fields.

The blind was planted far to the handler's left in a roughly mowed field similar to the one they'd hunted in yesterday. Directly in front and to the right of the handler was a fallow field of tall weeds and areas of dark shattercane — an ugly field that would confuse a dog's line and could swallow a bird and never give it back.

*Thank goodness the blind is in the mowed field, and the dogs won't have to hunt in that mess.* Except they would. Before the dog was sent for the blind, a mark would be thrown deep in the shattercane to the right of the center line. The dog had to ignore the mark he had seen and first perform the blind. Then he had to find the thrown bird in all that brush.

Charm began to shake. They hadn't trained for that. They'd trained diversion birds and poison birds, but they hadn't had to ignore a clear mark in favor of a blind. *Shit.* He didn't know how to do this.

The test dog's handler indicated he was ready. A shotgun blasted, and in front of them, a gunner tossed a bird. The dog wiggled with excitement, his eyes focused on the spot the bird fell. His handler turned almost a full ninety degrees to the left and tapped his thigh. The dog hesitated, then swung his butt and positioned himself in heel position. Clearly, he had done this before, even if River hadn't.

The handler sent the dog. After fifty yards, he whistle-sat the dog, and sent again, correcting the dog's line. That sequence repeated five times before the dog reached the spot marked as the location of the blind. The handler tweeted several times, cueing the dog to return, which he did, wagging happily. The handler then set him up for the mark. Despite the weeds, the test dog found the mark after a short hunt and returned successfully.

Easy peasy.

Charm was fairly certain he was going to lose his breakfast. Not that he'd had any.

By the time he found his family, everyone had arrived, including Oscar. "Interesting set up," Dulcie commented.

"Yeah, they're being tough this year," Oscar agreed.

*He sounds worried. How bad does it have to be for Oscar to sound worried?* Charm's anxiety ratcheted up. "I don't know how to do this," he said.

"River does," Lucas said, sounding not at all concerned. "He can do anything."

"What's the running order?" Dulcie asked.

Charm double-checked. "I'm sixth."

"That's not a lot of time to watch." She touched Lucas's shirt. "Go find my father and tell him Charm is sixth. You can help him get River ready." She pointed to Charm. "You. Sit. Breathe. Watch."

And they watched. Like the day before, no one was perfect. The mark tended to pull the dogs back toward the center — that was why it took so many casts to get them to the blind. Some took a lot of casts. None took fewer than four. All were excited to pick up the mark, and most had less trouble than Charm had expected. The mark wasn't intended to *be* difficult; it was intended to make the *blind* difficult.

His turn came quickly. As they walked to the mat, River felt more focused than he had the day before, which was good since Charm felt like he might blow apart in a stiff wind.

"Are you ready?"

Charm faced the visible gunners and ensured River was in heel position, then signaled the judge. Moments later, a shotgun popped, and someone tossed the bird.

*Now the hard part.* Charm turned to his left and patted his leg. "Heel, River." The dog glanced at him and then back to the field. This wasn't the right order. He patted his leg again, and after what seemed an eternity, River swung into position. *Just line up like you usually do.* Charm could almost hear Dulcie scolding him for making this a big deal.

Deep breath. *Get a grip.*

He lined River toward the blind. A hay bale had been positioned between them and the bird, so no matter how perfect River's line, Charm would have to handle. Fine. He could do that.

"Back," he said, giving the cue for a blind, not a mark. Did River get the difference? No clue, but he was off like a shot — and he held the line. Two-thirds of the way to the hay bale, Charm blew his whistle. River spun around and dropped into a sit.

The other handlers had handled their dogs around the right side of the hay bale, because that was the side closest to the mark, and that was the side the dogs had naturally pulled to. Charm didn't. He didn't want River thinking about the mark if he could prevent it. He cast River on a diagonal that would take him to the left. When he thought the line would be correct, he whistle-sat River once more and cast him toward the planted bird.

Two casts, and River had the bird. That was two fewer than any dog before him. Charm tweeted several times to call the dog in. Adrenaline made his hands shake as he took the bird and lined up for the mark. None of the big loops today. River was focused and ready. He ran straight to the mark and brought it back without hesitation.

As soon as Charm stepped off the mat, the gallery of watchers erupted into applause. He couldn't stop grinning, as he made his way back toward his family.

"Good dog that," someone said, as he passed.

"Thanks," he replied — and pulled up short. Mr. Forbes smiled and offered his hand.

"Very impressive," he said in a booming voice. "I always knew this dog was special." People around them murmured their agreement. "Gave us some trouble early on, but we never gave up. Never gave up." He put his arm around Charm's shoulder and led him away from the crowd.

"You've done a marvelous job." He was still smiling, but his eyes held nothing but fury. "I wouldn't have thought he had it in him. First curly to run in Open, I believe. Maybe next year he'll win a trial."

Charm stopped and faced him. "Who says he won't win this one?"

As soon as Charm said the words, he knew he shouldn't have. The smile didn't leave Forbes's face, but his tone turned to a hiss.

"This is Goliath's year — do you hear me? Goliath's year. I think I saw River limping. I bet if you run him by a vet, he'll recommend you take him home and rest him for the weekend. It's what's best for…the dog."

Charm backed away. *Is Forbes threatening River?*

"Uncle Charm, Uncle Charm!" Lucas bounded up and threw his arms around his uncle. Charm glanced down at him, and when he looked up again, Forbes was walking away. "You did so good," Lucas said. He took River's leash. "River is the best dog ever!"

"Yeah, he is," Charm said. He watched Forbes until he was out of sight. "Let's take River back to the truck."

Dulcie met him at the truck, all smiles until she saw Charm's face. She took River's leash and sent Lucas to watch with his mother and grandmother. "What happened?" she asked.

When Charm had caught her up, she swore some rather colorful epithets. "Do you think he'll do anything if we don't pull him?"

"I have no idea." Charm shrugged. "He's the owner. If he really wants to, he can take him away and physically stop me from running him."

Dulcie thought for a minute. "Okay, then you and River aren't going to be anywhere he can find you. Get in the truck and go somewhere away from here. I'll catch the others up. Do you have your cell phone?" He nodded, and she pulled hers out. "Thank God, I've got signal. Go. I'll let you know when you need to come back."

He was so accustomed to following her orders, he didn't even hesitate. River was locked in his crate and they were off the trial grounds before it even occurred to him that he had no idea where to go. *Where can I go that Forbes can't find me?* Not home. Certainly not Brother Jack's. Thibaut's. To Charm's knowledge, Forbes didn't know he was working in Vicksburg, and he was pretty sure Layton wouldn't tell him.

Fortunately, Thibaut loved adventure. "We may be here until late afternoon," Charm warned, but Thibaut was unfazed.

"Put your truck in the far service bay — tell Tony I said to let you in. The lift is broken, so we're keeping it closed up. You and the dog stay out of sight in the back and play Candy Crush or something."

Charm snorted. "Unless I explicitly tell you someone is coming for me, don't tell anyone I'm here."

"Not a soul," Thibaut promised. He grinned at River. "He's doing good at the trial?"

"He's kicking ass."

"Good!"

When Charm called Dulcie, she said, "Forbes came looking for you, and he's pretty pissed that you're not here. Don't sweat it. We have a plan. I'll call when this series is over and let you know if you made the cut."

"We totally made the cut."

"I know." He could hear the grin in her voice. "They'll rotate starting numbers again, and you'll run close to the end in the next series. I'll call you back in plenty of time to get River warmed up."

"But what about watching the test dog?" Without that intro, he would have no way of knowing what to do.

"Like I said, don't sweat it. We'll get you back in plenty of time to see a couple of dogs ahead of you run."

"But Forbes…"

"Stop worrying. We have a plan." And with that, she hung up.

*Great, they have a plan.* He wished someone would tell *him* the plan.

* * *

It turned out that playing Candy Crush and watching cable news over and over weren't exciting ways to pass the day. Dulcie called at one to let him know, officially, River was one of twenty-eight dogs who had made it through. She said Forbes had been back a couple more times, but they could honestly say they hadn't seen him.

"How did Goliath do," he asked before she hung up.

"Textbook. Took a couple more casts to find the blind than River did, though." Satisfaction shone in her voice.

Oscar called him half an hour later to let him know River was running twenty-sixth, but this series was going fast. "Get back here," he said. "Park as close to the marshal's table as you can, and head right to it. Stay near it."

That seemed like an obvious place for Forbes to look for him, but Charm didn't argue. Oscar might not be a fan of *his*, but he hated Forbes, and he adored Ellie. Charm could trust him. He thanked Thibaut, who wished him luck, and headed back. Handlers whose dogs hadn't been called back had left, so finding parking wasn't that hard.

Charm had barely gotten River out of his crate before Oscar grabbed his arm, pulling him toward the marshal's table. Lucas grabbed River's leash. "I'll hold on to River, Uncle Charm," Lucas said, heading in the opposite direction.

"Wait. Where's he going?" Charm asked.

"Don't worry about it," Oscar said. "Do what I told you," he yelled to Lucas.

Charm stopped moving and jerked his arm free. "Tell me what's going on."

Oscar glowered. "Lucas is taking River over there" — he pointed to a truck Charm didn't recognize — "and you and I are going to watch a dog or two before your turn." He tried to pull Charm forward, but Charm stubbornly dug his heels in.

"Why is Lucas taking River over there? Where is Forbes?"

"That's a buddy's rig. No connection to you or Forbes. No one will look for River there. And Forbes is…occupied."

"What does that mean?"

"It means you're wasting your opportunity to see what you have to do." Oscar walked off then, and Charm had no option but to follow. Oscar led him to where they could see the action on the field. The mat was in the same location on the levee, but instead of facing the field, the handlers were facing the large area with the lake.

Charm watched a dog and handler take their spot on the mat. Oscar narrated. "This is a simple water blind. No diversion, no poison bird, no mark. Just the single blind, and the bird isn't even that far away on the other side."

"What's the challenge?"

"Swim length, and the in and out. Wind isn't helping either."

The handler on the mat sent his dog. The lake, Charm guessed, was created specifically for retriever field trials. It had an extremely irregular edge with several fingers jutting in. Some were thin, some were wide, some were curved. The line to this blind required the dog to enter the water on a curve — without cheating and running the bank — then to cross a finger and go in again, this time for a long swim through cattails and decoys to the far bank. The marker for the bird was barely twenty-five yards from the exit point *if* the dog held his line.

"Most of the dogs are doing all right with the initial line," Oscar said, as they watched the dog run. "But the wind is creating a bit of a current that's pushing dogs into the worst of the cattails. Initially the handlers were doing a fair amount of recasting to keep the dogs on their line across the wide bit. Now they're trying to avoid so much correcting in the water by whistle-sitting on that jut of land and making an initial cast left of the bird, so the dogs will fade onto the correct line. Seems to be working better."

"Goliath?"

"Took the left line. Nailed it."

Charm nodded. Seemed straightforward. He hoped.

"You ready?" Oscar asked. He turned back and waved to someone. "Lucas is bringing River. Let's go."

The moment felt surreal. Where was Forbes? Where was the rest of his family? Who had helped Lucas hide River — and was that really necessary?

Lucas tucked the leash into Charm's hand. "Good luck, Uncle Charm!" he said, and disappeared into the crowd.

*This is so fucking weird.*

Nothing he could do about it. It was his turn. He walked onto the levee for the second time that day and took a moment to get his bearings. There was the marker for the bird. The direct line was clear. A strong gust of wind buffeted him a step sideways, and he saw the ripples on the water. Yep, that would blow any dog off his line.

What should he do? Stick to his line like the early handlers did? Or follow the strategy the more recent handlers used. Dulcie would kill him for not trusting the direct line, but these seemed like extreme circumstances. Still…

"Are you ready?"

Charm patted his leg and called River into heel position. He signaled to the judge, lined the dog, and sent him.

River burst forward on a dead perfect line. The dog Charm met back in January would have run the bank, but now he plunged into the water with no hesitation. Charm took a deep breath. Dulcie wasn't here; he was. When River emerged onto the finger of land, Charm whistle-sat him and cast him on a line somewhat left of the marker.

River hit the water again and swam hard. Maybe the wind died down; maybe the dog understood to hold his line no matter what. His line took him too far left. Way too far left. Charm had to recast twice to get him back on line. Once he did, River found the bird easily and began his trip back.

Charm felt sick. He'd taken a risk, done exactly what Dulcie would have told him *not* to do, and guessed wrong. Had he ruined

River's chances? He hadn't seen the other dogs run, so he had no way to judge.

When they walked off the mat, there was polite applause, but nothing like there had been in the first two series. Oh God, he'd screwed up. He was sure of it.

Oscar met him at the end of the levee and pointed him toward the truck. "You and Lucas take River and go to Dulcie's house. Now."

"Dulcie's? Why?" Charm asked, but Oscar was already jogging off.

Lucas met him at the truck, gave River a hug, and put him in his crate. "No one will look for River at Dulcie's," he explained. "Oscar says it's just in case."

"Whatever." He was suddenly sick of subterfuge and field trials and any other sort of drama. What he really wanted was a trip to Brother Jack's to see Jimmy Lee and Bird and Max and all his friends. But not with Lucas and River in the truck. He headed out and hopped on the I-20 toward Tallulah.

Smokey seemed the sort to have a liquor cabinet. Maybe he could snag a drink there. He was so damn tired.

* * *

Dulcie and Smokey pulled into their driveway right behind Charm and Lucas. Charm didn't want to think about how fast she must drive. Maybe that was why she didn't complain about the frequent drives to Collier.

"You guys are sleeping here tonight," she announced.

This was unbelievable. River was a field trial dog, not the Maltese Falcon. "Why are we taking this so far? Did Forbes really want to take River away?" Charm asked.

She glanced at Smokey, who looked vindicated. "Well, we don't know for sure." Defensiveness laced her words. "We do know he came looking for you several times and had other people looking for you."

"Maybe he wanted to make a deal. Maybe he wanted to

apologize for being an ass."

She tilted her head and gazed at him.

"Okay, he didn't want to apologize. But it irks me that I might have blown the third series because of made-up drama. Speaking of, do we know if River made the cut?"

Dulcie shook her head. "Elle will call later." She unlocked the door and let them into the blessedly air-conditioned house. "You were the one who suggested he might try to take River away."

"I said he could. He's the owner."

"I thought it was fun," Lucas declared plopping onto the sofa. "I hate Mr. Forbes."

Charm and Dulcie glanced at each other. "Your mom doesn't like you saying that word," Charm said.

Lucas's face grew stony. "I do hate him," he said. "His job took my dad away, and tomorrow he's taking River."

Ellie would want him to argue and explain why hate was bad, but frankly, the kid had a point. Win or lose, tomorrow Forbes was taking River out of their lives. Charm hated him too.

"Anybody hungry?" Smokey asked. "How about we grill some hamburgers?"

For all that Smokey and Dulcie were excellent hosts, the mood remained somber through the evening. Charm's mother dropped off clean clothes and toothbrushes shortly after dinner and let them know River had made the cut for series four. But despite the celebratory mood her news inspired, she was too tired to stay for more than a few minutes. Smokey excused himself to go to bed early, and even Lucas was ready for bed by eight thirty. Dulcie made a bed for him on the couch and tucked him and River in with a kiss.

The desire for a drink beat like a drum in the back of Charm's head. Too frustrated for a meeting or even to call Thibaut. Too anxious to do any of the redirection rituals he had learned. He was sick of the charade.

"I'm not a very good houseguest tonight," he said when she came back in. She made a noncommittal noise and motioned him to follow her. "I thought I might go out for a while. To clear my head."

"You mean to get a drink?" She opened a hall closet and dug

through it.

"Look, Dulcie —"

"Doesn't take a brain surgeon to see you're struggling." She emerged with two boxes. "Clue or Monopoly?"

Charm stared, his mind churning. Half of him wanted to throw a fit that she called him out about drinking. The other half was, irritatingly, relieved. A third half was bemused that she thought board games were a good distraction. "Clue," he said grudgingly.

They set the game up in the kitchen. Two games later — Dulcie won both handily — they, too, were ready to crash. Tomorrow was another early morning. "Where am I sleeping?" Charm asked.

"We turned the guest room into an office, so you're bunking with me."

He followed her down the hall. "Are we having sex?"

"Not in this lifetime."

Good to know.

Dulcie grabbed her sleepwear and disappeared into the bathroom. Charm stripped to his boxers and sat on the edge of the bed to wait for her. It occurred to him that this was the only way she could be sure he didn't slip out during the night. The board game, sharing her room — this was all to ensure he didn't fall off the wagon.

She came back wearing a long T-shirt and climbed into bed. "Bathroom is yours," she said through a yawn. He didn't get up. After a minute, she rolled over to look at him. "What?"

"Thank you," he said.

She turned back over. "You're welcome. Go to bed."

Charm grinned and went to brush his teeth. On the way back, he paused and listened. What had he heard? There. He heard it again. He followed the sound down the dark hall to the living room. As his eyes adjusted, he could see Lucas holding River — and crying.

"Hey, buddy, what's wrong? Have a bad dream?"

Lucas shook his head. "I don't want him to take River."

Charm sat on the couch, and Lucas buried himself in his arms and sobbed. Charm tightened his arms around him. "It's okay," he murmured.

The boy looked up. "It's not okay! I'll never see him again. I'm moving away, and I'll never see him again." His tears splashed onto Charm's chest.

"You don't know that," Charm said, pulling him close again and rocking him. But even he felt the emptiness of the words. Once Mr. Forbes took River back, it was likely Lucas wouldn't see him again.

*I should have stopped this months ago. I shouldn't have encouraged him to train River in the first place.* Self-recriminations filled Charm's head. He'd known this would end badly. He had known the first time he saw Forbes that he wasn't the sort to give anything away for free. How could this have ended any way *but* badly? This was his fault, and now the kid was going to pay.

Lucas took a deep, shuddering breath. "Even if we win tomorrow, nothing is going to change, is it?"

Charm hesitated, then told him the truth. "No."

A shudder ran through the boy, but he didn't erupt into sobs again. "At least River gets to be a hunting dog. That's what makes him happiest."

Jesus, this kid was killing him.

"And," Lucas continued, "I'm glad I did this for my dad. Since I'm leaving."

"You've done an amazing job." Charm swiped away tears. "I'm sorry it didn't work out the way you thought it would."

"Me too." The boy relaxed against him, still crying, but not as strongly. "There probably wouldn't be room for River at the new place anyway."

Charm held him until the boy's breathing became deep and easy. Poor kid. Damn Forbes for doing this. After all the kid had been through...

He shifted carefully and lowered Lucas onto the couch, pillow under his head. He tucked the blanket around his legs, then patted the edge and directed River to stretch out next to him. He rubbed the dog's ears. "Take care of him," he whispered.

When he stood to leave, he was surprised to find Dulcie standing in the doorway, watching him. "How long were you standing there?" he asked.

"Long enough." She held out her hand and led him toward her room.

"Are we going to have sex this time?"

"Maybe."

# Chapter 28

Scratched? What do you mean scratched?" Dulcie demanded. Charm showed her the running order he had picked up at the marshal's table when he went to check in for the fourth series. Only he hadn't been allowed to check in, and River's name had a line drawn through it. "Forbes pulled him."

Lucas pulled at his arm trying to see. "What does that mean?"

"It means I've had enough of this shit," Charm said and stalked away.

"Charm, don't!"

But he was done. Completely done. He stomped through the parking area, weaving among trucks and dog pens and crates until he reached the flashy RV Forbes used. He yanked the door open without knocking and stormed inside.

Emerson Forbes gasped and clutched at her throat. Ray Forbes jumped to his feet. "What the hell do you think you're doing, Freeman?"

Charm held up the day's running order. "Why did you scratch River?"

"Where were you yesterday?"

"Vicksburg. With a friend." That was technically true. "You're the one who told me to take him to a vet. No sign of a limp, by the way. Why'd you pull him?"

Forbes stepped into Charm's space. "You know why."

"I know you're scared River is going to beat your precious champion."

Forbes laughed. "He doesn't have a chance of beating Goliath."

"Prove it. Get him back in the trial."

"It's too late. River's out."

"You want to win so badly, you're willing to destroy a little boy —"

"This is Goliath's year! I've put a lot of money into that dog, and he is going to break that record."

"Yeah. You're so sure of that, you're afraid to let him go head to head with a curly."

"That ship has sailed, Mr. Freeman. River is done. Get out of my trailer!"

Charm gritted his teeth and turned to the door. "I'm going to destroy you, Forbes."

Ray Forbes gave a short bark of laughter. "You're an unemployed bartender. How the hell could a nobody like you, destroy me — a pillar of the community?"

Charm relaxed, almost smiled. "You see, that's where you're wrong. The *community* doesn't love you, Mr. Forbes. It loves your money." He saw the truth of the statement stab like an arrow. "The community loves Ellie, and it loves Lucas. I am going to make it my mission in life to make sure everyone knows what you did to that little boy who was simply trying to make his dead father proud." The sneer stayed on Forbes's face, but he paled.

"Everywhere you go, people are going to whisper and point. There won't be any more signs congratulating you on your petty wins. There won't be any more lackeys hanging on your words at the bar. I am going to make you a pariah."

"I'll sue you for slander," he said. The threat was empty, and it showed in his eyes.

"Go ahead. Truth isn't slander. Won't the details of the case look great in the newspaper?" Charm opened the door.

"Stop."

Charm kept going.

"Stop!" Forbes followed him outside. "I'll get River reinstated. But Freeman — if that dog even appears to beat Goliath, I'll make sure that boy never sees him again."

* * *


The area for the final series was an expansive space with fields and a pond fed by a winding stream. Charm caught up with the small group waiting to watch the test dog just as the dog and its handler walked to the mat. "What did I miss?" he asked Tim Layton.

"It's a triple." He pointed. "First bird thrown is to the left, way back there. More than four-hundred yards, easy." Charm squinted. He could barely see the gunners in their white coats. *How will River see them throw a bird?*

Layton continued, "Second bird thrown" — he pointed to the right side of the field — "is over there. Two hundred plus yards. And the live flyer is there in the center at about a hundred-and-seventy-five yards."

Charm nodded and analyzed the terrain. Each line would take the dogs into either the stream or the pond. The mat was at the top of a long slope — a hill in western Mississippi terms — with a row of shattercane at the bottom. Past that, the field was mowed and dotted with the occasional hay bale. Coarser grasses grew along the edges of the stream, and trees grew in spots around the large pond.

The test dog picked up the live flyer easily. The second bird thrown — the one on the handler's right — lay in a cluster of trees at the top of a steep bank after an oddly shaped in-and-out through the edges of the pond. The dog angled slightly when he hit the water and ended up coming out of the water past the bird. He found it after a short hunt. The longest one gave him the most trouble, requiring a significant hunt. Charm doubted he'd be the only one to do so.

Forbes intercepted him on his way to find his family after the test dog finished and handed him an updated running list. "River is back in," he said gruffly. "I told them it was a miscommunication between me and my handler."

Charm nodded and started past him.

Forbes grabbed his arm. "Remember what I said."

Charm jerked loose. "I remember." He stalked away. *Where's Ellie?* He scanned the viewing area and didn't see their sun canopy.

"Hey, there he is. Charm!"

He turned to see Dulcie waving at him from the parking area. *What's she doing out there?* He altered his course to meet her and saw she wasn't alone. It wasn't even just their families and Oscar. Jimmy Lee and Bird were there. And Max. And Thibaut, with a grin as wide as the Mississippi. A lump formed in his throat.

"What are you guys doing here?" he asked, unable to suppress a smile as bright as Thibaut's.

"What do you think?" Jimmy Lee asked.

Dulcie wasn't smiling. "What happened?" she asked in a low voice.

Charm gave her what he hoped was a reassuring smile and spoke loud enough for the whole group to hear. "Had a bit of a…miscommunication, but we're fine now." He handed Dulcie the list. "Twelve dogs total. River was moved to the end of the running order. Goliath runs sixth."

"Hey, I could use some help getting set up," Ellie called out.

Thibaut hung back as most of the group followed Ellie down the row to her truck. Charm stuck out his hand. "Thanks for coming," he said.

"Glad to. You looked pretty stressed yesterday. How you doin'?"

Charm grimaced. "Tough night, but I got through with help from a friend. Speaking of, how'd you hook up with everybody? I didn't think you knew my family."

He chuckled. "I don't. But there's only one curly running. I take it he's still kicking ass?"

They walked toward the edge of the field where the spectators had gathered. "So far." He thought about Forbes's threat. "We'll see what happens today."

As buoyed as he was by the appearance of his friends, the run ahead weighed on him. Should he tell Lucas about Forbes's threat? Should he mishandle River to be certain he didn't win?

"Uncle Charm, Uncle Charm!" Lucas's voice pierced his thoughts. The boy pointed to the mat. "It's Goliath's turn."

Indeed, the chocolate Lab and Tim Layton were preparing to run. Charm watched the field as the three marks were set, then as Layton sent Goliath to do what he did best. Like the test dog, Goliath breezed the live flyer. He kept his line on the second bird, retrieving it faster and more cleanly than the test dog had. Then came bird number three, the first bird thrown, the one so far away. Goliath took a clean line and swam true. He faded a bit in the water but his line through the final field got him pretty damn close to the fall.

And he couldn't find it. Not straight away anyway. The crowd held its collective breath as he looped and circled and serpentined through the area. Then he paused and — there! — he had it. Layton's tweets rang across the field, and the dog returned at full speed. The moment Layton slipped the dog's collar over his head, the crowd erupted into thunderous applause. Charm joined them, cheering enthusiastically.

When he sat down, though, his mind churned. Goliath had been good, but not perfect. Was it enough for him to win, or did he leave the door open for someone else?

"Are you okay, Uncle Charm?"

Charm looked up to find the boy standing next to him, gazing down with concerned eyes. "I'm fine, kiddo. Thinking about my strategy."

Lucas looked out at the field, his eyes distant. "I'm going to get River ready. Want to come with me?"

He followed the boy away from the crowd. With fewer people in attendance, it wasn't a long walk to the truck anymore. There were only a few dogs left to run, and the trial would be over. Lucas's time with River was almost gone.

Smokey had River on leash, out of his crate chasing a bumper. "Hey there," the older man said with a smile. "How did Goliath do? I heard the applause."

Charm watched Lucas take River's leash and sit beside him in the grass. He shot Smokey a significant look. "He did well."

Message received. Smokey knelt beside Lucas and tousled his hair. "Win or lose today, that dog there is here because of you."

"My dad knew he could do it," the boy said in a quivering voice.

"But River did it for you. He loves you."

A tear spilled down the boy's cheek, and he swiped it away. "I love him too."

Smokey rose and patted Charm's shoulder on the way past. Charm eased down beside the boy, scooting a bit to be in the shade.

"Do you think River could win?" Lucas asked.

"I think he has a good shot."

The boy nodded and fell quiet for a minute. Then suddenly he said, "It's okay if he doesn't win. You won't have to feel bad. I'll know you did your best."

"Thank you for that," Charm said, his voice thick.

"I know we're supposed to walk around and get him focused, but…can we just sit here for a while?"

Charm nodded and put an arm around his shoulders. "I won't tell if you won't."

They sat without talking. Lucas stroked the dog and teased him with the bumper and played with his feet. River stretched his back feet out behind him, rolled over to get belly rubs, and snorfled Lucas's ears until the boy laughed despite himself.

And then it was time.

Lucas called River, and the three of them walked the path to the marshal's table. There Lucas stroked River's head and handed Charm his leash. "Uncle Charm?" he said. Charm paused. "Kick Goliath's ass."

Charm nodded and walked to the mat.

This was it. River's last shot. Win or lose, he'd always be the first curly to compete in Open.

"Are you ready?"

Charm sighed and looked down at the eager, focused dog beside him. This was what he was meant to do. Yes, they were ready. He signaled to the judge.

To his left, far into the field, a shotgun popped. He wasn't sure he even saw the bird, though he saw the movement of the white-coated men in the field. No time to wonder if River had seen it. To his right, the second shotgun blasted. The gunners flung the bird end over end into the tree line at the top of the steep bank. Finally, the live flyer, so close it was almost a gimme.

Charm lined River up for the live flyer and sent him. Down the hill, across the shattercane, into the mowed pasture. He hit the stream at the perfect angle, plunged in, crossed, and popped up on the other side on the same line. Beauty in motion. Charm swore River laughed when he picked up the bird. Too easy.

The second bird had caused problems with some early dogs. Not River. When he reached the top of the steep bank, the bird practically fell into his mouth. Exquisite.

Charm watched him return, Forbes's words echoing in his mind. *"If that dog even appears to beat Goliath, I'll make sure that boy never sees him again."* And Lucas, almost as if giving him permission: *"It's okay if he doesn't win. You won't have to feel bad. I'll know you did your best."*

River swung into heel position and released his prize into Charm's hands. Charm squinted at the faraway mark. So far. Even he hadn't really seen the bird fall. No one would fault him if River's line was off a bit. No one would know.

No one but him and Jake.

He patted his leg and lined River toward the field. River deserved his chance. *This is for you, Jake.* He sent the dog.

Down the hill. Through the shattercane. Across the wide expanse of pasture. He leaped into the pond and swam hard toward the other side. This was the widest spot to cross, but his speed didn't slow. When he emerged on the other side, he sprinted off again.

Directly to the bird.

Charm didn't even get a chance to tweet his return signal before River had a solid grip on the bird and was on his way back. When Charm handed the bird to the judge and slipped River's collar over his head, the gallery went wild.

His family and friends met him by the marshal's table, their somber faces a marked contrast to the excitement around them.

Lucas knelt and wrapped his arms around River's neck. "You did really good, Uncle Charm."

It didn't feel so good.

"What happens now?" Thibaut asked.

Oscar answered. "We wait while the judges decide. It's not just this series that determines the winner. They'll compare the performance of each dog through the whole trial and determine the top four placements."

The group trudged back to the viewing area. Charm tried to smile at the people he passed, people who looked confused because the group looked more like funeral mourners than people who had accomplished something no one else had.

To pass the time, they, like others around them, broke down their "camp" and packed their trucks. Thibaut stayed close to Charm. Charm appreciated it, but drinking wasn't even on his list right now. The only thing he wanted in the entire world was to make Lucas smile again.

Half an hour passed. Forty-five minutes. As the clock approached an hour, Thibaut asked, "Is it supposed to take this long?" As a group, they looked at the marshal's table, where a group of judges had their heads down in deep discussion. Oscar shook his head. "Nope."

After another fifteen minutes, a flurry of action at the marshal's table caught their attention. Trophies and ribbons were arranged for presentation. The marshal called out to get everyone's attention and motioned them over. Charm exchanged a glance with Ellie, then took River's leash from Lucas and walked over.

The twelve who had run the final series arranged themselves informally in a semicircle in front of the marshal. Dog, handler, and owner stood together. Goliath, Layton, and Forbes stood near the far end. *River is Forbes's dog; I should join them.* He stayed where he was.

The marshal, a craggy older man who reminded Charm of Clint Eastwood, came to the front and after a smattering of applause thanked everyone for an exciting, successful trial. He thanked their sponsors and presented several special awards. Finally, he was ready to reveal the top four placements.

"The judges had quite a time coming to an agreement on these winners," the marshal said. "I think you'll agree that these dogs are the best of the best." Applause.

"In fourth place is Mama Watch Me Now, owned by Tucker Green and handled by Russ Evans." Charm clapped enthusiastically. Russ was one of the professional trainers who had helped them get River ready. Russ accepted the ribbon and trophy with a humble smile.

"In third place" — Charm bit his lip in anticipation — "Field Champion Life Ain't Fair for Ruth, owned by Nate Davenport and also handled by Russ Evans." Charm blew out his breath and clapped again. Was River one of the top two? Or did he fail to place at all?

"These final two placements are special, because both dogs are owned by the same man." The entire crowd reacted. Goliath and River were the only two dogs in the final twelve owned by the same person. "One dog," the marshal continued, "is a curly-coated retriever — the first to ever compete, much less place, in Open at an AKC field trial. The other has won this trial for the past four years and could possibly win for a record-breaking fifth time."

The crowd loved it. Forbes studiously avoided Charm's glances and magnanimously accepted the pats and congratulations from the people around him. *Puffed up like a damn peacock,* Charm groused inwardly.

The marshal waited for the crowd to grow quiet. "Ladies and gentlemen, this year's winner is…" He paused to let the anticipation build. Then: "Field Champion Goliath for the Win, owned by Ray Forbes and handled by Tim Layton."

The crowd exploded with cheers and congratulations. *Second. We took second.* Charm was so swamped by people thronging around him, he couldn't even get his own ribbon and trophy. They had to be handed through the crowd to him. Another group surrounded Forbes, who accepted all the praise as if it were his due. He posed for photos and spoke loudly about Goliath's talent. No mention of River at all.

And then Forbes looked toward Charm, and their eyes met.

Forbes's smile stayed in place, but his eyes were cold.

It was time. Charm's fingers tightened on River's leash. "Let's go, buddy."

A hand on his stayed him. He looked down into Lucas's earnest face. "I'll take him," the boy said. Charm let him take the leash. Lucas paused and rubbed the dog's ears once, then walked to Forbes.

The crowd parted for the little boy.

Lucas gazed at the man for a moment, then extended his hand. "Congratulations, sir. Goliath is a really good dog." Forbes shook his hand, shocked into silence. Lucas looked down at River, and then handed Forbes the leash. "River is a good dog too. Thank you for letting me work with him." His voice shook, and his cheeks were pink with emotion, but he didn't shed a tear.

Forbes had the grace to look abashed. "Thank you, son."

Pride, love, and fury whirled within Charm. This wasn't how this was going to end. *I didn't spend years as a carnival barker for nothing!* He jumped through the crowd and put an arm around Forbes's shoulder.

"Let's have another round of applause for Mr. Forbes." He led the ovation, ignoring the warning glare from the man beside him. "I want to be sure y'all really understand what Mr. Forbes did here today.

"Mr. Forbes had faith in River when no one else did. He believed in him enough to import him from New Zealand, and then when the dog didn't seem to be suited for field trials, he refused to wash him out. In fact, I think every professional trainer in the area had a chance to work with this dog." The crowd laughed.

"That's when he found Jake Gibson and his son, Lucas." Murmurs about Jake floated through the crowd, and a few people reached out and patted Lucas. Charm smiled down at him. "When Jake died, Mr. Forbes knew how important River was to my nephew, and he took the risk of putting his valuable dog in a little boy's care. I tell you, we had to use some pretty unconventional methods to get this dog ready for this trial." The crowd laughed, and the trainers who had been involved nodded. Forbes glanced at Layton, who shrugged and confirmed it.

"And that's where Mr. Forbes came through yet again. You see, Lucas and his mother have to move, and Vicksburg was the only trial they could possibly enter before they left. That put Mr. Forbes in a pickle. This was Goliath's record-breaking year. How could he put that at risk?"

Forbes had hardly moved since Charm started speaking. Every word that built him up would make a more devastating fall if Charm kicked out the supports. Charm saw the anxiety in his face and paused, letting it build. Then Charm turned away.

"But he's a great man. A generous man. And he took that risk. And I'd say it paid off!" Everyone laughed. "Congratulations, Mr. Forbes. You have both your record-breaking champion and the first curly to not only compete, but place, in Open. Who knows — he might be the first curly to ever become a Field Champion." He saw Forbes's eyes widen at the thought. *Got him.*

Forbes visibly relaxed as the crowd once again cheered and congratulated them. Charm waited for the excitement to die down, then put a hand on his shoulder. In a low voice, he said, "Mr. Forbes, if you want that curly to get that field championship, you and I need to talk."

# CHAPTER 29

Moving day. Charm and Dulcie pulled into Ellie's driveway and stopped. A large yellow moving van was backed up to the house, the front door was open, and men were moving in and out carrying furniture and boxes. But other than that flurry of activity, the farm looked…empty. No animals of any kind. No farm implements stacked around the barn. Not even a hose stretched across the drive.

This wasn't their place any longer.

Charm pulled in and parked near the kitchen, out of the movers' way. "Wait here for a minute," he said. He left the truck running and jogged inside.

"Where the hell have you been?" Ellie waved her clipboard at him. "This is not the day for you to be missing in action. The movers will be out of here within the hour, and then we have a whole house to clean." Just like Ellie to scrub clean a place she'd never see again.

"Sorry. I had some business with Dulcie."

Ellie frowned. "Business?"

He looked down and kicked at the (immaculate) floor. "Yeah. They have some new clients. I'm, uh, her new training assistant. A kind of trainer-in-training."

Ellie's frown slowly slid into a smile, and she threw her arms around him. "That's fantastic. Congratulations!" She stepped back. "I admit, though, I'd kind of hoped you were going to travel."

"I am." He smiled then. "Smokey's mentor recommended them for a job with the Swedish Royal Navy. I'll be going to Sweden with Dulcie to check it out. Maybe to help too."

They hugged again, but when Ellie stepped back, her eyes were filled with tears. "It just hit me that we won't be seeing each other anymore."

He shook his head. "Don't believe it. You can't get rid of me that easy. Smokey is going to be close to wherever Mom is. I'll be around if you need me."

"I know," she said seriously. "Thank you, Charm. For everything."

He folded his sister into his arms and squeezed her tight. "I'm proud of you, Elle." He stepped back. "You're going to make me cry. Where's Lucas?"

She pointed at the ceiling. "Cleaning his room. Not doing so well."

Charm nodded and gave her hand one last squeeze, then headed upstairs.

The movers were done up here. His footsteps echoed in the empty space. Like the farm, the house had yielded its claim of "home." This wasn't their place anymore. Lucas was in his bedroom sweeping up the dust and miscellaneous trash left behind. Well, sort of sweeping. Mostly he was standing in the middle of the room rearranging the dirt.

Charm leaned on the doorframe. "Hey."

Lucas looked up, surprised for a moment, then his eyes grew accusing, and he looked back down. "I thought you were gone." The broom swished violently from side to side stirring a cloud of dust.

"You can't get rid of me that easy."

Lucas swept harder.

Charm stilled the broom and laid a hand on the boy's shoulder. "Hey." Lucas didn't look up. "Hey. Come talk to me."

Grudgingly, Lucas released the broom and followed him to the edge of the room where they sat next to each other on the floor. They sat in silence for a long moment.

"Are you mad because I didn't win yesterday?" Charm asked finally.

"No." The boy's hand went automatically to the pocket of his jeans where Charm could see a red ribbon sticking out.

"It was nice of Mr. Forbes to let you keep that." Forbes had kept the trophy. Of course.

Lucas pulled it out and gazed at it for a moment, then tossed it in the pile of trash in the middle of the room. "I don't want it."

"Why?"

"Because he lied!" The boy's voice quivered with a mix of anger and sadness.

"Who lied?"

"My dad. He said our problems would be gone, but he lied. Nothing is ever going to be right again."

Charm thought about that for a minute. "I don't think he lied," he said thoughtfully. "I think 'right' looks different than you thought it would."

Lucas frowned. "What do you mean?"

"Well…" Charm rubbed his chin. "River has proven he can run field trials. That's what you wanted, right? And your mom, she's moving, but she's going somewhere she can pursue a dream she's had for a long, long time so she can make a really great life for you."

"What about you?"

*Not fully convinced, but listening.* Charm tickled his ribs. "I got my family back — and a new friend and a future. Your grandma got her family back, too, and she's moving all the way to Oxford with you so she can see you every single day. And after River retires, he'll come live with you too."

The last sentence penetrated Lucas's brain and he looked up, eyes wide. "What?"

Charm snapped his fingers. "I knew I forgot to tell you something." He grinned at his nephew. "Mr. Forbes hired Dulcie to train River for next year's field trials. He's going to live with her and Smokey, and you can see him whenever you want and even help train him. School permitting."

The boy jumped to his feet, mouth open.

But Charm wasn't done. "After he earns his Field Champion designation, he's going to be retired to stud. Forbes said he can live with you then."

Lucas stared at him. "I can see him again?"

Charm climbed to his feet and looked through the window. "Look outside."

Lucas ran over and peered outside. Dulcie and River stood on the lawn. "River!"

Charm caught his arm before he could run downstairs. "Your dad would be really proud of you, Lucas."

A smile bright enough to shadow the sun spread across the boy's face. He ran to the door and paused. "He would be proud of you, too, Uncle Charm." Another grin, and he was off, thundering down the stairs, calling for his dog.

Charm watched the reunion from the window and waited for the lump in his throat to subside. Jake *had* been right, and Charm was so, so grateful. *Thank you, Jake,* he sent into the ether. And then he strode downstairs to help his sister move.

THE END

# Acknowledgments

It takes a village. That's not original, but it's accurate. This novel wouldn't exist without the help and support of so many people.

First, my critique partners, who read the first draft chapter by chapter — William Vaughn, Margot Ayer, Veronica Richards, and Laura Cameron. Your advice and feedback were oooh, so necessary, but your ongoing support was even more invaluable. You gave me the confidence that I had a good story, and knowing you were waiting to read kept me going.

Second, my editors, Alison Imbriaco and Amanda Sumner. I'm not a bad editor, but your skills blow me away. Nothing is so humbling as a good edit — and you two are the best.

Next, my beta readers — Linda B. Myers, Kay Alexander, Betty Watkins, Stephanie Watkins, Sarah Shull, Karrie Dollar, and LaDonna Blanchard. You're a motley mix of authors, readers, and subject matter experts, each with a unique point of view that gave me great insights and made my story better.

I also need to include some people who were both subject matter experts and inspiration. Sarah Shull is a triple threat — curly owner, field trial participant and judge, and veterinarian. Thank you so much for answering my questions. Also special thanks to the people who provided the curlies who share my life — Karleen Swarztrauber, Dawn Fleming, Cathy Lewandowski, and Iryna Dergunova. Your beasties make up the best part of who I am.

Of course, I can't forget three very special people — Jason Alexander, Christie Frachioni, and Sharon L. Fisher. You don't just support my writing; you support *me*. I couldn't do it without you. Love you all so much!

Finally, I would be remiss to leave out the man who is, in many ways, the inspiration for this book — Bob Bailey. Bob taught me everything I know about training, including how to think out of the box. He's not mentioned explicitly in the novel, but I managed to sneak in some subtle references. IYKYK.

Thank you all. Truly. From the bottom of my heart. This book — and my life — is better because of you all.

I hope you've had a wonderful time reading about Charm and River. If you did, please help other people enjoy the story, too. A review on Amazon or Goodreads or, really, anywhere would be fantastic. But you know what else would be fantastic? Tell a friend. If you know a dog lover, tell them about this story. Maybe share it with your book club! Help others fall in love with River, too.

I would love to hear from you! I'm not on social media, but I'm on email. Feel free to drop me a note at doubtingriver@gmail.com.